MICHAEL

LAST DAYS LIGHTNING

REVELATIONS
BOOK TWO

TERRY JAMES

Michael
Terry James

CKN Christian Publishing
An Imprint of Wolfpack Publishing
9850 S. Maryland Parkway, Suite A-5 #323
Las Vegas, Nevada 89183

cknchristianpublishing.com

Paperback ISBN: 978-1-64734-526-6
eBook ISBN: 978-1-64734-341-5
Library of Congress Control Number: 2021935477

MICHAEL

PROLOGUE

Babylon, Iraq – April, 2003, 1710 hours

Lance Corporal Rodney Glass stood with Private First-Class Reginald Johnson overlooking the swampy sand bog. A number of American troops went about the business of setting up barriers to the archeological dig.

Their day's work was finished, having secured the periphery of the long depression suspected to have once been a part of a channel carved by the Euphrates.

Both Glass and Johnson waited for the half-track troop carrier to noisily pull the heavier truck from the bog it had become stuck in a half-hour earlier. When the racket subsided, Corporal Glass spoke.

"We need four men around the immediate perimeter tonight" he said. "You will be relieved at 0100 hours."

"What's this all about?" Johnson asked, scanning the trench-like depression that ran several hundred yards more or less from north to south.

"Something about those archeologist guys thinking

there's something important buried in that trench," Glass answered.

"Must be important. Having us guard an old riverbed, when there ain't any enemy left," the black soldier said with a smirk.

"Yeah…well…the looters are already out there where we haven't secured the areas. They want this one guarded for some reasons way above your and my need to know. That's all I know," Glass said, turning to an approaching soldier, who walked up the slight grade from somewhere near the trench to be guarded.

"Lance Corporal Glass, there's some reporters or something who've been given permission to have a look. Here's the paperwork."

The private handed Glass the official form and he examined it, leafing through the several pages.

"Looks like you'll have company tonight, Johnson. Says here that some news guys have permission to look around. They'll be here around 2000 hours."

"Maybe they'll let us know what it's about," Johnson said, squinting into the bright, Iraqi distance at the rolling, oily, swamp-like terrain.

"Yeah. Why don't you try to find out from them," Glass said with a half chuckle, folding the papers and handing them to Private Johnson.

2018 hours

THREE SMALL, open army vehicles approached from the southwest and rolled to a stop, one behind the other. Private Johnson moved to near the lead carrier to greet the party of eight men and five women. All were in civilian attire except the drivers.

A lieutenant colonel who had driven the lead carrier strode quickly to Johnson, who saluted.

"Johnson," the officer said, returning the salute and looking at the name above the right breast pocket of the soldier's fatigue shirt. "These are reporters. We will be looking over this site for about half an hour."

"Yes sir," Johnson replied, glancing quickly at the men and women as they walked to near the depression in the sand some twenty feet away.

Lights strung by the Army Corps of Engineers days before illuminated the ancient riverbed. Another military vehicle rolled to a stop behind the other three.

"That will be the archeologists to brief the reporters," the officer said, turning from Johnson to walk quickly in the direction of the two men who shuffled toward him.

The three men moved to join the reporters strung out along the west bank of the depression. Several of the journalists snapped photos, chatting with each other as they moved to different positions to get better views.

"Is this the area of the find?" A female journalist with a British accent pointed to an area that was a darker orange-brown color and stood out against the lighter-hued surrounding sand.

"Yes," one of the archeologists nodded affirmatively. "We've done a number of magnetometer scans, and there appears to be a difference in the various striations of soil that are significant in roughly the area you've pointed out."

"What does that mean, exactly?" The woman moved closer to the roped-off edge of the bank while she asked the question.

"We surmise these are indications of a mud-brick

structure that lies just beneath the surface. It might indicate a building that was constructed as a burial chamber...likely for a royal figure."

"Whose?" she asked with increased curiosity in her voice. "Have any idea?"

"Not at this point," the khaki-clad scientist said.

"Any guesses?"

"No. We can't get into speculation at this point. It might be nothing more than an anomaly...a geological formation that's no more than an oddity."

The journalist pressed her questioning, following behind the man, who began walking to join his colleagues. The archeologist, without turning to talk to her while he walked, put up his right hand in a gesture that signaled for the questions to stop. "We begin the excavation tomorrow," he said. "We'll let you see some of that activity then. You'll have your questions answered, and we'll have ours answered, perhaps as early as tomorrow."

∾

2331 hours

PRIVATE JOE SUTTER leaned his M16 against the right door of the Jeep after placing the weapon's butt on the floor below the front passenger side. He unsnapped the side pocket of the right leg of his desert-camouflaged fatigue pants.

He pulled out a Zagnut bar, his favorite, unwrapped it, then took a bite.

Private Reginald Johnson walked toward the Jeep, his mind on home and the fact that if he were in Chicago this Friday night, he would just be getting started on one of the all-night parties his friends were no doubt even now beginning.

No. He caught his mind wandering. He was now half a world away, and it would be the middle of the day in Chicago.

Something was wrong. His young, sure legs suddenly felt as if they were made of rubber. He had to fight to regain his equilibrium, a low, rumbling, sound accompanying the shaking.

Johnson watched the Jeep less than ten yards from him rock side to side, then bounce up and down as if hopping across the sand. The soldier sitting in the driver's seat held tightly to the steering wheel, yelling while the vehicle seemed as if it would bound into the depression being guarded. Flashes from exploding lights while several of the light poles crashed to earth burst in a dazzling display of the quake's power.

The earth ceased to shake after forty seconds, and Johnson surveyed the area. Several of the temporary lampposts the engineers had erected had fallen. The other lights continued to burn, but enough of the lamps were out to cause the dimmed illumination to cast an eerie glow across the small dunes and the shadowy banks of the ancient riverbed.

"Earthquake!" Johnson yelled, swearing while reaching for the side of the Jeep.

"You okay?" he asked Sutter, who reached to take the M16 then exit the vehicle.

"Hey! Look at this!" a soldier shouted from near the rope cordoning off the archeological anomaly. Johnson, Sutter, and the other soldier trotted over to see the cause of his excitement.

The earth shook again, once more accompanied by the low, rumbling sound. It lasted only several seconds.

"Look!" The young man pointed at the floor of the depression with the M16 he held in his right hand.

The brownish-orange sand mound that appeared different from its surroundings had collapsed at its southern end.

"There's something metal in that hole," the soldier said.

The light was insufficient to give the men a clear view of what the quake had uncovered.

"Get a couple of flashlights," Johnson ordered. One of the troop members ran to the Jeep to retrieve the army-issue, rubberized flashlights.

Johnson took one and shined it on the object that was barely exposed. Another of the men pointed the other light into the breach of the anomaly.

"Looks like it's gold-colored," Sutter said.

"Man! We've got something here," another of the soldiers said.

"Should we try to knock off some of that sand?" he asked.

"No," Johnson replied. "That whole thing might collapse if there's another quake." He pulled the walkie-talkie from his belt. "Sergeant-Major," he said into the device, "that quake we just had has opened up that riverbed thing. There's something shiny and gold-colored partly showing through. You better send somebody over here."

~

Next morning, 0800 hours

A CROWD of irate journalists milled about in front of the wooden barriers erected by army troops before daybreak. They shouted in the direction of Lieutenant Colonel Brad Dixon, who turned one ear toward a first lieutenant who tried to talk above the uproar.

"They're ticked off, sir," the officer was saying. "They're not happy about the order to keep them from the dig while we're removing that artifact."

Dixon nodded that he understood.

"No one is allowed beyond that point, I don't care how unhappy they are," he said. "Let me know when they're ready to move the thing."

"Yes, sir," the young officer replied then strode toward the big army truck that blocked view of the site from the reporters' perspective.

Dixon, accompanied by two other officers, walked to the barrier opposite where the journalists shouted questions.

"What's up with keeping us from the site, Colonel?" one reporter's angry inflection echoed the mood of his colleagues in the gathered press assembly.

"You will all be given a briefing on the whole matter," Dixon said. His words only brought more intensive questioning.

"Sir, one reason we're all here is to assure the rest of the world that America isn't damaging or destroying Iraqi antiquities," said the reporter. "There's already a lot of speculation about the Bush administration's disregard for these artifacts." The reporter's spoken thoughts were obviously the sentiment of the others, who nodded in agreement while mumbling their own displeasure with the army's decision to keep the removal of the artifacts secretive.

"I understand your need to find out all you can, but for now the site is off limits," Dixon said. "We'll have a release of information on much of what's going on later today. You'll be informed as to the time the release will be available."

With that, the lieutenant colonel and his entourage, amidst shouts of protest by the journalists, turned and walked back toward the huge vehicle that would transport the excavated artifacts from the ancient Euphrates riverbed.

More than a decade later

SOMETHING GLINTED IN THE HIGH, afternoon sun. A man shielded his eyes with his fingers in salute fashion. The object was a curiosity, a shining object seemingly embedded in the multicolored desert promontory.

This wasn't a natural outcropping from the reddish-browns and tans of this Mesopotamian landscape. He must get up the earthen slant of the promontory, must examine this strange anomaly.

When he tried to step up on a small boulder to get to the place that would be a clear path up the mound, his leg wouldn't move. It was as if gravity held him glued to the sandy surface on which he stood. He struggled again and again to lift one foot, then the other. Still, he remained affixed to the crusty surface just beneath the steppingstone.

"Dr. Faust!"

Hearing his name shouted from somewhere behind, he turned to see where the voice was coming from.

"Randolph Faust!" the voice shouted again, and he squinted in the brightness to see who beckoned.

He saw no human figure when he scanned the desert horizon. He turned and noticed his booted feet were now free to move. He could now again start up the promontory with the first step on the rock platform.

But, when he turned to do so, the small, rounded rock was no longer there. The entire promontory was no longer there. The glinting object at its crest was no longer there.

He again shielded his eyes from the sun's painful glare and looked into the distance. The landscape had changed to that of the familiar Washington, DC, National Mall. The Washington Monument obelisk pointed skyward, and upon its tip rested the glinting object that had moments before been protruding from the Iraqi hill's crest.

"Dr. Faust."

The voice again startled him, and he turned to face the opposite direction.

"Tyce? Tyce Greyson?" he questioned, seeing it was the journalist friend he had known since the younger man's childhood. Greyson smiled, his eyes portraying amusement, apparently over the older man's inability to understand his circumstance.

"My old friend, Randolph," the figure said, moving forward to reach for Faust's hand. But now, the man had transmorphed, changed from the younger man to an officer in an Israeli uniform. It was a familiar face.

"It is I, Randy. Morticai Kant." The broad, age-creased face of Faust's long-time friend displayed an expansive grin.

"What is this about, Morticai—?"

Faust's mind reeled with confusion. He struggled to comprehend his situation, moving to take the Israeli's extended hand. But the hand wasn't there in the next instant.

A loud, fluttering sound, like that made by a flock of

large birds taking flight, made him swing quickly around.

In place of the Washington Monument now stood a gigantic Star of David, as white as the former obelisk that had stood there previously. Resting atop the cross bar beneath the star's center point was the golden object.

"Dr. Faust?" the voice seemed to shout at him from directly overhead. His body began to shake violently.

"Dr. Faust?"

His eyes fluttered and looked into the worried eyes that soon became surrounded by the familiar face. "Ramon?"

"Yes, sir. It is Ramon."

Randolph Faust raised to his elbows on the bed, then swung his legs slowly over the side.

"You were moaning and talking, sir. You really should lie back down."

"No...no, Ramon. I'll be okay," Faust said, rubbing his temples with fingertips.

"The doctor says you need complete bed rest for at least two days, Dr. Faust," Ramon Gutierrez said, putting a hand on the older man's shoulder.

"Yes. Yes. I'll rest," Faust said, staring at the floor, trying to get his bearings while coming to full consciousness.

"That was a dream unlike any other," he said, looking up into the dark eyes of his domestic helper, who was also his much-loved friend. "It has meaning that I must understand."

"First, you must get well, sir," Ramon said, nudging him back against the pillow.

~

At the same moment in Maryland

TYCE GREYSON SQUINTED to see between the flashes, concentrating on the taillights of the tractor-trailer rig through the sheets of rain the wipers could only partially sweep from the windshield. Lightning whited out the massive trailer's rearmost parts, causing him to lose sight of the red brake lights for critical seconds between the brilliant bursts.

The car slowed, then sped forward again when hitting each overflow pocket created on the interstate by the wind-driven torrent. Each succeeding gush smashed violently against the BMW's underside.

Tyce wanted to brake—to slow enough to back away from the trailer's rear. He needed to pull over, get onto the side of the interstate and to safety away from the traffic until the storm let up.

The headlights looked to be almost against his rear bumper. Braking would cause the trailing vehicle to slam into the BMW, initiating a chain-reaction series of rear-end crashes.

He let up on the accelerator, hoping to put some distance between his car and the semi's trailer without using the brakes. He glanced at the rearview mirror, then his eyes again focused on the rain-obscured brake lights of the tractor-trailer rig.

In a millisecond, the rig's brake lights flashed their warning, but it was too late.

Tyce instinctively whipped the steering wheel to the right toward the only possible opening his past minutes of concentration had convinced him might afford safety from the raging traffic. He sensed the BMW leave the earth as if it had leaped of its own will into the black night, into the darkness suddenly devoid of vehicle lights left somewhere behind.

The sensation was of weightless flight that seemed interminable. Only seconds left of life. *No time to think... to glory in good deeds performed...to repent of sins...*

The car's glass vista seemed an expansive screen of the ebony, starless cosmos while he flew toward his destiny. A flash of near-blinding lightning lit the heavens. In an instant of brilliance beyond any he had known, the effulgence appeared to take on superhuman shape and form—a massive manifestation of illumination, with great, expansive wings that stretched across the BMW's windshield horizon.

The light-creature's fearsome gaze, looking directly into Tyce's own eyes in that terrifying moment, discharged golden, electrical shards that seemed to pierce the core of his brain, engendering a euphoric sensation of immortality.

COLD, abrasive rain pelted his face and neck while he heard voices that seemed far away yet drawing near.

"He's coming to," one of the voices said.

Tyce Greyson felt a warm hand against the left side of his neck just below his chin.

"You'll be okay, friend. Just stay still for us."

With his vision returning, Greyson saw flashing red and blue lights through the water cascading down the BMW's windshield.

"I'm okay," he said, trying to brush away the man's fingers against his neck.

"We have to check things out, my friend," the man said. "I'm with EMT. You've had a really bumpy ride."

"Oh, yeah...I remember. Did you see that—that thing?"

"What thing?" the man asked disinterestedly, beckoning with his free hand to his associate, urging her to bring him the medical kit she was holding.

"It was some kind of light creature," Tyce said. "The car almost hit it, I think."

"No. We haven't seen a...light creature," the medic said. "Probably just lightning you saw." He began feeling Tyce's neck more thoroughly before removing the stethoscope from the medical bag.

"No...no—it was some kind of winged creature, like it was made of pure energy or something." Tyce tried to straighten up from behind the steering wheel. "Oh, never mind," he said with irritation. "I need to get out of here."

"I don't recommend it," the man said. "There's a good chance you might have internal injuries."

"I'll take the chance," Tyce said, brushing aside the medic's continued efforts to listen to his heart and lungs. "Thanks, though. I appreciate your wanting to help."

The EMT backed away. If an injured person refused advice and hurt himself, the patient would have to do so on his own—a matter of liability. He allowed Tyce to try to extricate himself on his own.

Another man standing by reached to give Tyce his hand.

"You know, it's amazing that you landed this far off the road without getting really messed up," the stocky man in a yellow rain-slicker said. "Steady now," he said, steadying the man he had helped from the car. "Your car doesn't even look much bunged up. Just a little muddy."

"Well, I feel a little more than *bunged* up myself," Tyce responded, "but, overall, I seem okay."

"You must have flown fifty feet off that embankment," the Good Samaritan said.

"Probably broke an axel or something," Tyce said, looking over the BMW as well as he could in the flashing police and rescue vehicle lights coming from the interstate at least ten feet above where he and the car had landed.

"Thanks," he said, pulling on the offered hand while the man tried to help tug him from behind the wheel. "Thank you for helping," he said again, shaking the hand that had extracted him.

"Gerald Anthony," the man offered his name, pumping Tyce's hand a little too vigorously. He winced.

"Sorry," Anthony said. "Look, you might ought to listen to those emergency people and let them check you out."

"I'll be okay," Tyce said, bending, then kneeling, to try to see if there was damage beneath the car.

"I'm the driver of that semi that caused all this," Anthony said. "That's my rig over there." He gestured toward the tractor-trailer that was buried to the top of its tires in mud.

"Oh. I'm sorry... Did you get hurt?"

"Naw. I'm like you. I seem to have landed right," the driver said. "I'm waiting for some guys to get here. I don't even know what I'm carrying."

"How long was I out?"

"Must have been about fifteen, twenty minutes," Anthony said. "That's some odd cargo, I can tell you. I shined a light in there. The doors popped open when I hit bottom—"

"—Oh? What kind of cargo?"

"Like I said, I don't know what I'm carrying, but I ain't never seen anything like it in my years of transport."

Anthony started toward his truck thirty feet ahead of Tyce's car. "Wanna have a look?"

"Sure," said Tyce. "I'm soaked already. Why not?" They started toward the rear of the trailer.

"Mr. Greyson," the female EMT walked quickly toward them and held out her hand. "Here's your wallet, sir. Please check it to make sure everything is in order."

"Why do you have my wallet?"

"You might have been hurt really seriously," she said, "and we needed to know if you might have any personal medical information we would have needed to know."

Tyce checked the contents. "It all seems to be here."

"I need to get you to sign this, please," she said, holding out a clipboard covered against the rain. "It's just a release saying we offered assistance…to transport you to a medical facility. We need your release against liability. You know, you still need to get checked out."

"No, thank you," he said, after quickly looking at then signing the form while she held a flashlight over it.

Moments later, the two men stood behind the huge trailer. The door was opened enough that he and the driver could stand side by side while the driver aimed the powerful flashlight beam into the trailer's interior.

"That crate broke open. Ever seen anything like that?"

A massive sarcophagus rested among the thick, broken pieces of plywood. Its golden contours glinted in the flashlight's beam.

"Where are you taking it?" Tyce Greyson asked, as he started to climb through the opening in the doors.

"That's off-limits," a voice said from somewhere behind them.

Greyson and Anthony turned to see three men approaching.

"Just forget about what you saw," one of the men said.

"It's just part of a prop for an Egyptian display that's going to be set up in DC."

"Then why is it off-limits?" Tyce's reporter's hot spot was touched by the hostile manner of the directive.

"Because this says so," the man who had issued the order said, pulling from his coat pocket a wallet with a badge affixed to its interior flap. "We're with TSA. It's off limits—that's all you need to know."

"We need you up front," the man, who seemed to be in charge, said to Anthony.

"Nice meeting you, Mr. Greyson," he said, surrounded by the TSA agents, while walking in the direction of the red flashing lights near the truck cab.

CHAPTER 1

Lightning and thunder simultaneously burst the blackness asunder. Immense, winged creatures swung white-hot, glowing swords at each other, each blow cutting deeply into the glistening, golden skin covering their bodies that bulged with massive supernatural, muscular sinew.

The wounds gaped, spurted white, slag-like plasma, then closed, bubbled, and healed instantaneously.

They clashed somewhere above earth in an unidentifiable dimensional sphere. Yet, the Dome of the Rock somehow seemed to be affixed atop Moriah within the translucent field of battle while the gigantic, winged beings, brilliant in their effulgence, slashed mightily at each other.

The environment about the battling creatures suddenly spewed with pyrotechnics that all but caused the scene to fade within its radiance. Another being, larger than the two swinging their weapons, appeared from the profusion. One of the creatures that had been engaged in the fight spread its wings and, within a microsecond, vanished with a hissing sound.

"Tyce!"

The female voice pierced to the center of Tyce's brain. His surroundings took on a shape and form that were familiar. His legs and arms shook spasmodically while he struggled to regain full consciousness.

"Tyce! Are you okay?"

He examined his hands, then, blinking, glanced at his surroundings.

"You were just staring off into space, your mouth wide open, like you were seeing something that frightened you," Michelle Martin said, gripping his arms to steady him.

"These…these…things were fighting," Tyce said. "They had wings, and swords. They slashed each other, then their wounds instantly healed, as if they were immortal—"

"—you had better sit down," Michelle said, guiding Tyce toward a chair near one wall. "That was some nightmare you had."

She looked into his eyes, seeing the still-dazed expression. "You're still having flashbacks from the accident and the winged thing you said you saw." She cupped his chin with her index finger and thumb pinched together, still looking into his eyes. "You really need to get examined."

"No," Tyce said. "It was real. It was some kind of cosmic battle scene…over Israel. These…creatures… were fighting above Jerusalem."

He stood and nearly collapsed, the hypotension that was more pronounced as of late making everything go dark for a fleeting second. Michelle again held him and urged him to be seated.

"I'll be okay." He walked a few steps, and the action returned full balance and his ability to think clearly.

"You have your mind on that Israeli—what's his name?" Michelle asked.

"Morticai Kant."

"It makes sense," she said soothingly. "The winged creature you thought you saw during the wreck...the meeting scheduled with this IDF guy. That, and you probably had a concussion in that bounce you took."

Tyce sat in silence, the scene he had just witnessed running through his mind. It was no dream. He hadn't been asleep, but standing, moving toward a window to view the great, white obelisk that was the Washington Monument in the distance.

He stood slowly to prevent the recurrence of the low blood pressure. He moved to the window to complete his intention—to view the mall that sat a half mile from the hotel suite.

Michelle handed him a squat glass containing bourbon and Coke with ice. "Sounds like something from a Spielberg flick," she said, trying to lighten her journalist-partner's somber mood. "Maybe it's just too many *Star Wars* movies."

Reagan National Airport – Sunday, 5:30 p.m.

Tyce went over the interview elements in his mind. He silently mouthed his self-assigned agenda for the few brief minutes he had been granted by the Israeli government.

One: Find out what Morticai Kant is here to discuss with people at the White House and at the State Department. Two: Find out why the Israeli prime minister had, according to the chief editor of *Western World Union* magazine, asked, personally, that he—Tyce Greyson, a freelance journalist—be on hand to talk with Kant upon his arrival in DC.

Tyce rummaged through the cloth briefcase and retrieved a microcassette recorder. He thumbed the forward button, then the reverse, to make sure the battery was good.

He stuck with the old reel-to-reel microcassette rather than changing to the digital. There were just too many commands to remember. He needed the time to concern himself with the questions that needed asking, not to be fiddling with digital recorders.

He held the "record" button and spoke into the mic at the top of the device: "First session, Morticai Kant, Reagan…"

He rewound and listened, satisfied, then, that the instrument was doing its job.

He stood from the chair of the small lounge and walked to the huge window that looked out on the concourse. The Washington Monument stood miles in the distance, a small, white, erect sliver against the gray afternoon sky.

The security checks he had gone through to get clearance for waiting in this lounge for private jet arrivals were excruciatingly detailed. Somebody at State had been sent to search through his several computers. Why, he didn't know. Technology made it almost assured that everything he had done over the Internet had been captured by somebody, somewhere in the ever-tightening security web this government and others cast constantly in their snooping efforts.

The questions seemed as if they would never end.

Every detail of his days at the J schools, at his jobs, had been painstakingly explored. What might it have been like when journalists could just meet a subject—with no preauthorization—and simply ask questions?

Now, since 9/11, everything had changed—had to be tightly controlled. Nazi Germany had nothing on 2015 Washington, DC, when it came to having to "show someone's papers". But here he was, recorder in hand, peering into the darkening skies of the late-DC afternoon. He would have, Eldridge Stanton had told him, at least forty-five minutes to interview Morticai Kant—just the two of them.

Sure enough…to this point, at least…he was the only person in this private lounge who was to receive the envoy from Israel's prime minister. When he had tried to learn more about why the special treatment, Stanton had said only, "It will all be made clear to you in time, Tyce. It's an opportunity of a lifetime."

All he knew about the Israeli's flight was that it had been diverted from landing at Dulles. Such flights, he knew from experience in covering the diplomats shuffling around the world, required powerful influences to secure such diversions from, for example, Dulles, a secure airport, to Reagan, which handled less security-essential incoming flights. Morticai Kant was apparently one important *blip*—as DC reporters referred among themselves to important people they targeted for interviews.

Tyce moved away from the observation window, returning to the small sofa near the center of the room. He fidgeted through the fabric of the soft business case to retrieve several folded pages of typed notes he had worked on following his meeting with Stanton.

His thoughts returned to the night of the accident,

then forward to his brain glitch—or whatever it was—while standing, looking out the window at the DC hotel earlier that day. The winged creature that filled his windshield against the black, stormy skies while his BMW launched from the freeway haunted his every waking moment. The piercing, mesmerizing eyes he had seen burned into his remembrance almost hourly while moving through his daily life. The beings in each case had to have some relevance to each other. They weren't figments of his imagination. Both encounters had been starkly real...were not the stuff of dreams...

"Mr. Greyson."

Tyce was startled and jerked slightly, looking to the man he hadn't heard entering the small lounge. He stood after pushing the papers back in the case. "Yes. I'm Tyce Greyson," he said, his eyes meeting those of a tall, young man wearing a navy-blue business suit.

"I'm Michael," the man, who looked to be in his early thirties, said, thrusting his right hand toward Tyce with a smile.

His handshake was firm, but not like so many he encountered—not one that seemed intended to exert power over the one receiving the handshake but rather expressed genuine friendliness. "I've been sent to tell you the plane from Tel Aviv is on schedule," he said. "Mr. Kant and his party will arrive at six fifteen."

"Thanks," Tyce said, assessing Michael's facial expression and demeanor.

The man said nothing for a few seconds, seeming to assess Tyce in return; then he spoke. "I am sent to express appreciation on behalf of Israel for your agreeing to assist in a very necessary mission." The man's intense gaze gave Tyce a moment of discomfort so that he had to break eye contact. He turned and bent to pick the case from the sofa.

"I know nothing of a…mission, Michael."

"You will be given a briefing when Mr. Kant and his party arrives," Michael returned. "I've been sent to say that your help is most needed and appreciated. It will prove to be, I assure, the most exhilarating experience."

What mission? This was just an interview with them. And, who talks like that? The thoughts traversed Tyce's swiftly flowing analytical cognitive process. He considered silently that the man might have English as a second language. An Israeli, maybe, whose training and youngish age caused him to present a more formal demeanor. His words and posture seemed, however, neither unsure nor irritatingly overconfident. Tyce decided he liked this…Michael.

"Mr. Kant's plane is arriving now," Michael said.

Tyce looked at his watch. It read exactly 6:15. He walked to the observation window and looked eastward. A gleaming Gulfstream 650ER taxied toward the parking ramp, its landing/taxi and position lights brightly disrupting the now-black, late-fall sky.

A flight line worker motioned with lighted, yellow-coned flashlights, directing the aircraft's pilot as he steered the G-650 to the designated round, yellow spot painted on the parking ramp.

"Exactly on time, as you said, Michael," Tyce said, looking back to the young man who had given the ETA.

Tyce scanned the small lounge with a quick sweep of his eyes, then looked back to see that Michael was no longer there, having apparently slipped out as stealthily as he had come into the room earlier.

Morticai Kant, a short, stocky man, extended his right hand to Tyce a few minutes later. The gray-blue eyes glinted with good humor, matching the lilt in his accented voice.

"Good evening, Mr. Greyson," the balding Israeli with the neatly cropped beard said, shaking the American's hand vigorously. "Thank you for meeting us. I hope we don't interfere with your evening plans."

"No, sir," Tyce said. "Meeting you is at the center of my plans."

"Ahhh! That is good. Then, we shall proceed," Kant said with subdued laughter in his tone.

"Your man, Michael, got your ETA exactly on the mark," Tyce said.

"Michael?" Kant's expression changed to that of not understanding. "I have no staff member named Michael."

Tyce was equally confused, his eyes darting from those of Morticai Kant to those of the four men and the woman who had accompanied the Israeli envoy from Tel Aviv.

"I guess, then, he was from the State Department or another agency," Tyce said, almost as if speaking to himself.

The Israeli's countenance was changed. His tone became serious.

"This Michael," he said. "Tell me more about him."

"He was a young guy," Tyce began. "Early thirties, I'd guess. He was tall, about six-three, medium build, light blond hair, I'd say—"

"—What did you discuss with him?" the Israeli said, almost rudely interrupting Tyce's verbal recollection.

"He just alerted me to your soon arrival. Said he was sent to thank me for my help in an important 'mission', he called it."

Kant's expression was one of concern even more pronounced than his already-perplexed countenance conveyed. The Israeli said nothing, letting his gaze linger for several seconds into Tyce's eyes before turning to say something quietly into the left ear of the young woman who stood just behind him.

She nodded, looking downward, obviously concentrating to catch all his instructions. Then she turned and walked from the lounge when he had finished.

Morticai Kant again turned to face Tyce before speaking. "Yes. the person you talked with was probably from your State Department," he said.

Tyce didn't think for a second that the Israeli meant a word of it.

~

Monday, 8:30 a.m.

TYCE SIPPED LONG from the mug of coffee, watching the *NBC Morning News* anchor read the headlines. The Israeli prime minister spoke in front of a cluster of microphones when the scene on screen cut from the female broadcaster to the news conference recorded within a government building somewhere in Jerusalem.

"I will repeat here what was being said long before the start of this building crisis, and let the chips fall where they may," he was saying. "In our time, the biblical prophecies are being realized. As the prophet Amos said, 'They shall rebuild ruined cities and inhabit them. They shall plant vineyards and drink their wine. They shall till gardens and eat their fruit. And I will plant them upon their soil never to be uprooted again.' Ladies and gentlemen, the people of Israel have come home never to be uprooted again."

The anchor picked up the report while the video in Jerusalem continued.

"Israel's prime minister has rarely used Bible references in such a news conference before an international audience," she said. "His remarks, using prophetic portions of the Old Testament, have, until recently, been reserved for mostly Christian evangelical audiences that see Israel as God's chosen nation. One expert on the Middle East had this to say about the apparent change in attitude about bringing Bible prophecy into the rhetoric while the crisis seems to be accelerating."

The screen changed to present a well-known Palestinian Authority pundit, who spoke in accented English.

"The prime minister seems to be attempting to deliberately antagonize the leadership of all of Israel's surrounding neighbors with his elevated, inciting taunts," the commenter said. "He claims that God is on Israel's side in the conflict, and that any force that tries to go counter to that Jewish state will suffer the wrath of the Almighty. It's as if the Israeli leadership has lost its collective mind. It is a very dangerous road the prime minister is treading."

Tyce concentrated on watching the collection of journalists and others surrounding the Israeli leader while he answered reporters' questions. He leaned forward, almost spilling hot coffee down the front of his shirt when he saw in the crowd of milling men and women a striking, male figure in a dark suit, standing almost stiffly at attention. The young, blond man seemed to be looking directly into the camera's lens.

"It's him!" Tyce's eyes widened as he sat upright, staring at the man in the recorded video—the man who seemed to be looking back at him.

"Michael!"

The ringing phone to his right broke Tyce's concentration. He picked it up and looked back to the screen. The man he knew as Michael was no longer among the throng.

"Hello?"

The female voice on the other end of the call drew his reeling thoughts to the matter at hand. "Hello? Mr. Greyson?"

"Yes, yes…I'm Tyce Greyson."

"I'm Essie Jorba," the woman said. "I am an assistant to Morticai Kant. We weren't introduced last evening because I had to leave before we could meet." The soft, slightly accented voice pulled Tyce's thoughts the rest of the way from the astonishing scene he had just witnessed.

"Yes. I remember. I'm sorry we weren't introduced," Tyce said, not knowing what else to say.

"Me, too. But I hope you will agree to meet with me at your convenience—perhaps later today—and we will have our introductions then."

5:00 p.m.

TYCE FIDGETED WITH THE INSTRUMENT, trying to make it respond. The iPhone had gone haywire and would respond to commands only sporadically. He admitted it to himself—he was addicted to text messaging, and any disruption of sending and receiving the instant communications brought him anxieties akin to detoxing from chemical dependency.

What did this young woman—Essie Jorba—have in mind for the meeting she requested? It had something to do with the interview with Morticai Kant—the interview that never took place. Everything changed when Tyce had mentioned the encounter with Michael. Kant had apologized, saying something had come up requiring his immediate attention. The envoy had then quickly left with his entourage.

This must be a meeting that has something to do with the interview the Israeli had assured him would be arranged.

Tyce tossed aside the phone, disgusted that it had apparently come to its end.

He was to meet the girl at seven o'clock in the lobby of the St. Gregory Hotel. She had said she would buy dinner. It would be, she said, on the Israeli government's tab.

He was always up for a free meal. Where better to get such a meal than downtown DC, where free meals were doled out by the millions from the federal coffers? As long as the printing presses could stamp out the currency, all was well with the welfare state. The deficits kept building, and nobody seemed concerned—although, there were those who said the crash was coming, and great would be the fall...

Tyce's thoughts kept flipping back to the scene on the television screen from Jerusalem. Had he really seen the man who had given his name as Michael? No...couldn't be. The Israeli prime minister's presser was the day before. Not even a Concorde—no longer in service—could get someone from Jerusalem to Washington in that short time span. Maybe the Blackbird—the SR-71— could do it. But, that bird, too, was now a museum piece. It couldn't possibly be the same guy...

Twenty-three minutes later, Tyce stood in the waiting area of the restaurant. The girl had said she would meet him, but she didn't. He checked his watch. Five minutes late, he considered with irritation.

"Mr. Greyson!"

He turned to see the shapely figure of Essie Jorba approaching at a near jog. "I'm so sorry," the girl said, breathlessly approaching and holding out her hand.

Tyce took the hand, looking into her eyes of dark green. She was a really beautiful woman, he considered, seeing her lovely face expressing genuine regret for her tardiness.

"No problem. I just got here," he lied, forgetting his earlier impatience.

"I made a reservation, so we should get in quickly," Essie said, looking around the area for the host or hostess. Once they were seated, she looked at him, her hands clasped on the table, her head tilted slightly when she spoke.

"May I call you Tyce?"

"If I can call you Essie."

"Done. See, we're already on mutually acceptable negotiating terms," she said, her pretty eyes brightly reflecting light from the flaming candle wick at the center of the table.

"Oh? Are we in negotiations? What are we…negotiating?"

Essie again tilted her head, her pretty face forming an expression that told him the matter on her mind was a serious one. "Morticai wants you to consider taking on a…special assignment…for the state of Israel."

She shifted forward, her elbows on the edge of the table. She gesticulated, making her case with a slender index finger upon the white tablecloth. "You have been… selected…because of an association with a close, trusted friend Morticai has known for many years."

"Who?"

"Dr. Randolph Faust is the man who has been Papa's —Morticai's—confidant for more than thirty years."

"Dr. Faust? Yes, he's a long-time family friend."

"And that is apparently why he recommended you in this…this most important matter."

"Wait a minute," Tyce said. "Papa? You called Mr. Kant *Papa.*"

"He is my father," Essie said, her expression projecting her desire to get past the fact and on to the project she had been assigned: to enlist Tyce Greyson.

Tyce obliged her wishes to get on with it and said in businesslike fashion, "Why did Mr. Kant not do this himself?"

"Because I'm so much sexier and seductive, of course," she said. "How could you say no?"

Tyce laughed, seeing the deadpan look on Essie's face.

"See, I've already got you on our team," she said, then broke into a giggle.

"Okay, we'll see. What's it about?"

"Oh, no. That part will have to come from Morticai's own lips," she said, looking around at the other diners. "Too many ears around here. And, besides, I haven't got the details. Only Morticai can fully divulge what's needed of you."

"Okay, then." Tyce sat back in the chair and looked sternly at his dining companion. "I guess all that's left to do is to enjoy dinner and be sexily seduced by surely one of the prettiest women I've ever met."

Their mutual laughter ended when Tyce's expression suddenly grew somber when he spotted a tall, blond man near the main entrance to the restaurant. It was Michael! He stood as if at attention, his gaze riveting Tyce's.

"Excuse me," Tyce said rising from the chair and quickly making his way toward the large entryway. Essie watched him weave between the tables in his hurry.

Tyce's glances from side to side to avoid bumping into diners momentarily took his eyes off his destination. When he arrived at the entrance, the man wasn't in sight.

Tyce rushed through the doorway into the huge foyer. The waiting area was empty except for the object of his attention, the man who stood near a floor-to-ceiling window, peering into the evening.

"Michael!" Tyce's call blurted louder than he intended.

Michael turned and smiled. He didn't offer his hand, and Tyce didn't feel the gesture was necessary, either.

"Tyce," Michael said as the journalist approached. "How is your evening with Miss Kant?"

"You mean Jorba—Miss Jorba," Tyce responded. He didn't know why he offered the correction.

"Miss Kant is most effective," Michael said, his countenance seeming to indicate that he harbored knowledge beyond his young years.

"Who are you, Michael?" Tyce asked, his patience finished with the intrigues of the last couple of days. "Morticai Kant doesn't know who you are or who you represent."

"The important thing, Tyce, is that we are all on the same team. It is teamwork that will win the day."

Tyce started to retort that he was tired of the esoteric dealings he'd been subjected to. Somehow, he was unable to verbalize the frustration. Instead, he remained silent, and listened to the man's words.

"I've been sent to encourage you to have no fear in

your—dealings—as you call them…with the enemies of Israel," Michael said. "All is well, my friend."

"What is this about, Michael?" asked, taking a step closer to him.

"Tyce!" Essie shouted from across the expansive foyer. He turned to watch her while she moved quickly toward him.

"I'm sorry, Essie. I had to talk with Michael, here—" He turned back toward the big window.

"Who?" Essie looked past him but saw only the window.

Tyce looked at the window, then at Essie. His partner in conversation of a moment before was gone.

CHAPTER 2

Next morning – 12:18 a.m.

Tyce's thoughts vacillated wildly between the strange events that had taken place in his life lately.

The unbelievably strange visions—or whatever they were—of the winged creatures. This stranger, Michael, even more weird in some respects. Yet neither was a figment of his imagination. They were real—more real than the glass of water he held in his hand now as he downed a sleep aid. His being solicited to help Israel. Him, a journalist with no diplomatic experience whatsoever. What could he possibly contribute?

One thing sure, Essie's father had sent the right person to twist his arm in the solicitation. Her loveliness caromed about in his thoughts. She was a beautiful girl—sexy and seductive—just as she had teasingly suggested.

But what was this girl really like? How could she be the soft, feminine woman of such beauty she appeared to be if she worked as an Israeli clandestine services operative?

But she was her father's daughter... Morticai Kant surely would not expose her to the dangers often faced by clandestine services operatives. Maybe she knew only the sorts of things most personal assistants within the Department of Defense knew—the kind of information personal secretaries would know. Maybe just administrative things were stored in that pretty head...

Something told him *no.* Her persona sparked with brilliance, with intelligence that manifested supreme, though unpretentious, confidence in the knowledge with which she was entrusted.

The twinge of guilt returned. The nagging sense of being unfaithful to Marial... He was having thoughts he shouldn't have about this beautiful Israeli woman.

Her name—Jorba, not Kant—meant she was married, most likely, despite her flirtatious appeal.

Everyone told him that he must get on with life, that Marial would want him to find happiness. It had been two years. But it was like yesterday in the burning core of his ever-present memory of the girl he loved and lost so soon...so very soon.

The tug of sleep ate at his cognitive process, made his body ache. He probably shouldn't have taken the sleeping pills...should have been patient to let the sleep come naturally. Six o'clock a.m. would come around quickly. He had to get some sleep to be alert for the nine-a.m. meeting with Morticai Kant that Essie said she would arrange.

Tyce awakened suddenly, his eyes sweeping the darkness of the bedroom, trying to see what made the sound that caused him to wake up so abruptly. He rubbed his eyes, trying to come to full consciousness. Maybe he didn't hear anything. Maybe it was just a sleep glitch of some sort.

He sat on the edge of the bed, deciding to check if all was well in the apartment's small living room. Had something fallen?

Only the ambient, DC-area light illuminated the apartment while he moved through the bedroom door. He flipped on the living room's light and looked for anything out of place.

Everything was in place… He snapped the light off and started to return to the bedroom but decided instead to moved to the double French doors that led to the apartment's patio. After drawing the cord that pulled back the drapery covering the doors, he stepped onto the balcony suspended ten stories above the streets.

The city glowed with its early-morning lumines-cence; its tranquility disrupted by faint sounds of sirens somewhere in the far distance.

When Tyce moved away from the balcony's high rail-ing, he found himself in total darkness. He looked back to the city, but it wasn't there. He could see nothing. It was if he was engulfed by a fog of unprecedented density. The balcony's familiar objects were nowhere in sight. There was nothing familiar.

Was he dreaming?

No. This wasn't a dream. He felt his arm, ran his hands over his body.

This was no dream.

His surroundings suddenly erupted with blinding flashes of light, thunderous noise crashing as the light-ning burst around him. A spectacular bolt blinded him, thrusting his entire body through with paralyzing effect, knocking him to his knees. He lay in the fetal position, every nerve seeming as if it were blazing with fire that, strangely, did not burn—rather heightened, somehow, his every bodily fiber and every cerebral synapse.

He was able to turn his face upward slightly, his eyes wide with astonishment.

Brilliantly white beings of light clashed in battle. Winged creatures of immense size and power, their incredibly muscular bodies rippling, swung enormous, glowing-red swords, each trying to destroy the other.

Tyce tried to move but could manage only to straighten his limbs from the curled position into which the lightning had forced him. Yet, he felt no pain. He actually felt energized and aware on a level he hadn't known before.

Like before when he watched the creatures battle, another being of stupendous size and radiance intervened. One of the creatures spread its massive wings, then disappeared with a hissing sound.

His surroundings darkened and faded from his conscious thought to blackness. He awakened, sprawled on the balcony floor, shivering in the forty-degree, early-DC morning.

Fifteen minutes later, Tyce stuffed the tools of his trade—the microcassette and several journals full of notes—into the soft brief bag. He retrieved one of the small books from it and thumbed through its pages.

He had searched his phone for the number, but couldn't find it, because he hadn't yet put many numbers into the new device. Then he remembered jotting it down in one of his many notebooks.

Yes! *There*!

He pressed the phone's number pad, hoping it wasn't too early. Not everyone in Texas would be awake at this early hour. It was 7:02 a.m. in Washington—6:02 a.m. in San Marcos.

Regardless, he had to make the call…had to learn more before meeting with Morticai Kant.

Events of the recent hours tortured his reeling brain. The positive side of the torture was that the vivid scenes that still played cerebrally drove away all early-morning drowsiness.

He listened to the message when the voice on the other end picked up. The announcement issued in a Spanish-accented, female voice: "This is the residence of Dr. Randolph Faust. Please leave the number where you can be reached, and Dr. Faust will return the call."

It was the voice of the old biblical archeologist's long-time housekeeper, Felecia Cortez.

"This is Tyce Greyson," Tyce said after hearing the beep prompting him to record his message. "Dr. Faust has my cell number. Please have him call me as soon as possible. It is quite urgent." He was disappointed that Faust hadn't picked up so he could ask the questions that he very much needed answered before meeting with the Israeli.

9:02 a.m.

"Good morning," Essie said cheerily, reaching to Tyce and putting her arm through his arm, which she had caused him to bend at the elbow. She escorted him into the hotel suite's large living room, holding her free hand against his arm and patting it gently while she spoke.

"Morticai is on the phone to Tel Aviv. He's speaking to Bibi—about you, I think…"

"About me? How do I rate that level of—"

"—You are quite important to us," she interrupted, pressing the palm of her hand against his arm. "That includes to the prime minister."

Essie changed tone to that which was quizzical. "How was your sleep?" she asked. "It was rather late when we parted last evening."

"To be honest, I had a hell of a night."

"Oh? No trouble, I hope."

The words were issued in a way that piqued Tyce's reporter's suspicion button. That she was expecting possible trouble to be coming his way was the impression engendered.

"Just had a nightmare or two," he said.

"Perhaps it was dinner that didn't set well?"

"Probably."

Tyce's phone-jingling prompt summoned him to a text message: "Sorry I missed your call. Let me know when you are free to talk. –R. Faust."

"How long do you think your father will be on the phone?" Tyce asked. He knew it was a stupid question, and Essie's glassy-eyed glance without answering affirmed that it was indeed a stupid question.

"I need to make a call," he finally said, after a few uncomfortable seconds.

"Why don't you make your call?" Essie said. "I have a couple of things I need to do."

Tyce fingered the number pad while he watched her walk from the room. Moments later, he heard the familiar voice.

"Randolph Faust."

The essential greetings out of the way, the journalist said, "There's something going on with me. I need answers. At least, I need information that will keep me from going nuts."

"Oh? You think I have the answers?" his old friend asked, slightly amused at the inflection and words Tyce had chosen.

"I'm here in DC with your friend, Morticai Kant. They've told me I'm being recruited for something. Don't know what, yet...something to do with the Israeli government."

"Yes," Faust said. "I suggested they interview you for a...project...of some sort they have in mind. I don't know exactly what that entails, either."

"Well, I guess I'm about to find out. Mr. Kant is in another room. I'm in their hotel suite. He's on the line to the Israeli prime minister, I'm told."

"Sound's like things are cooking!"

Faust's words were positive in tone—upbeat.

"I just don't want it to be yours truly who's cooking," the younger man said.

"Oh? Is there a problem?"

"Dr. Faust, you remember all of that strange stuff going on with me during and following my visit to Patmos?"

"How could I not remember?"

"Well, I'm having...some very strange sorts of things going on in my life. I'm having—I don't know what else to call them—I'm having visions. Visions of huge, winged creatures of light. They are fighting but are indestructible."

"These are not...dreams?" Faust asked.

"No," Tyce said. "I'm wide awake when they happen. They started when I had a car accident. I was behind this semi rig, and I swerved out of the lane to keep from running up under the trailer when the truck driver jammed on the brakes. I left the interstate. While I was flying through the air—the highway was probably fifteen feet above the roadside ditches... When I left the highway, I saw the huge, winged being. It was looking at me through the windshield. That was the last thing I saw before waking up after the car had landed. Somehow it landed so as to not roll or flip or whatever."

"Thank God," Faust said. "You experienced a miracle, I think."

"Yeah, I wouldn't argue with that."

"Have you told your folks?"

"No. I'm a big boy. Don't want to worry them with my goings-on."

"Are you okay, Tyce?"

"Yeah. Except for the fact that I'm having these winged creatures suddenly invade my life, as I said. I've had two other incidents. First, I was looking out a hotel window and it happened. The second time, I was on the balcony of my apartment when it happened. Everything just turned totally foggy around me. Then, there was a terrible electrical storm and I seemed to have been struck by the lightning. I was paralyzed and saw all of this fighting. These things had huge, glowing swords, and every time one would strike the other, a gaping cut —a wound—would appear, but some white, liquid-like stuff would gush out, and in the next instant the wounds were healed, as if the cut had never been there. Next, the other winged creature—the same one I think I saw when leaving the interstate during the wreck—he showed up and caused one of the beings to spread its wings, make a hissing sound...it then just...*poof!* It just disappeared, and the visions ended."

There was silence on the line for several seconds. Tyce spoke again before the archeologist could get his words out.

"Oh, yeah, a couple of other things. During the first of those visions, or whatever they were, the battle between these things was being fought above Jerusalem."

"Jerusalem?!"

"Yes. It looked to be above the Dome of the Rock on the Temple Mount."

"I need to talk with you in-depth about all of this, Tyce. We are in strange days. I need to tell you some things about...how I came to recommend you to the Israelis. I had planned to do just that within a day or two—"

"—Oh? What about that? That was the reason for my call. This all seemed to start around the same time these Israelis began soliciting my cooperation. I need to know. And there's this other thing. This weird young guy, says his name's Michael... It's just crazy. He has suddenly appeared, then vanished—or seemed to—a number of times. Says he's been sent to reassure me that all is well, and to thank me for wanting to help the Israelis. Mordicai Kant says he has no idea who this guy is."

"My Lord!"

Again, there was silence on the other end of the line, as if the old man had lost the ability to speak.

"Dr. Faust? You there?"

"Yes...yes. I'm here. This...Michael. Tell me. How did he look? What were the circumstances?"

"Mr. Greyson! Tyce!" Morticai Kant entered the room.

"Dr. Faust, I have to go," Tyce said quickly. "Mr. Kant just got off the phone."

"We have to talk, Tyce. Call me when you are free," Faust said to end their conversation.

Morticai Kant thrust his hand toward Tyce. "Good

morning, I hope I didn't interrupt your phone conversation."

"No. No," Tyce said, returning the handshake. "I was on the phone to our mutual friend, Dr. Faust."

"Oh?! And how is Randy?"

"He seems to be fine for being eighty-seven."

"He is a remarkable man. Still in good health and actively interested in his archeological projects."

"Yes. He's quite a specimen," Tyce agreed.

"I see that Essie told you about our finding you through...our mutual friend."

"Yes."

"We researched your background thoroughly, as I'm sure you would expect. Dr. Faust directed us to the right man, we're convinced."

Tyce said nothing; each man seemed to expect the other to say something next. The Israeli finally spoke.

"The Israeli government needs an operative that will most likely never be suspected as being such," Kant said, gesturing with his right hand for Tyce to be seated in a chair across from the one in which he had seated himself.

"You have made a reputation as a reporter—a well-known international journalist. You particularly are known to be a journalist who specializes in—shall I say —*anomalous* subjects."

"Weird stuff, you mean?" Tyce said in a somber tone.

"Have I offended?" Kant was genuinely taken aback at the idea that he might have said something amiss.

"No," Tyce said, laughingly. "You describe the crazy work I do quite accurately, I think. Some wouldn't be so kind. Some would call what I do 'kooky'."

"Oh, we are quite impressed with your work and with the subjects of your work history," the Israeli said, obviously pleased he hadn't offended the journalist. "It is your acumen in covering the subjects upon which you report that most interest us, Mr. Greyson. May I call you Tyce?"

"Your daughter and I are on first-name terms," Tyce said.

"Oh, yes. Essie is my little sweetheart. She always breaks ground in paving the way for her Abba."

Tyce noted the Israeli's use of metaphor, the rendering in the accented English somehow amusing him and relieving his otherwise tense anticipation of what this was all about.

"Tyce, the matter at hand involves the Iranian movement into Iraq, and much more. Their nuclear ambitions, their involvement with the Russians, and I'm sad to say, with this current United States' corrupt, deep-state establishment."

The journalist straightened in the chair, the mental cogs turning.

"That's a geopolitical matter. What do I know about the ins and outs at that level?" It was all Tyce could think to say.

"Ah...But, you are a quick study, and will, we believe, rapidly become expert." Kant sat forward in the chair.

"Your entrée—your segue—into the things we need our operative to accomplish involves something that fits the model of your reporting history."

Both men eyed each other, neither speaking. Kant spoke after seeing that the reporter was waiting on his further explanation.

"It involves an archeological dig in Iraq—in Baghdad," Kant said. "There has been discovered an ancient relic. All of the players I mentioned—the Iranians,

Russians, and American deep-state globalists—are in the mix in matters surrounding this strange find."

"What is it?"

"All I can tell you at this point is that it is a very, very old sarcophagus, apparently made almost entirely of gold."

CHAPTER 3

"Sorry to keep you waiting, Tyce."

The lanky executive shook Tyce's hand, then walked around his desk and pushed a button on the intercom atop the credenza behind his desk chair.

"Sheila, bring us some coffee, please," Eldridge Stanton said, then turned to look at Tyce.

"Is coffee okay?"

"Fine," Tyce said, sitting on one of two small sofas in Stanton's spacious office.

"Anything in it?"

"What? No, just black."

"Bring us two coffees—black," the magazine CEO said, then returned to sit in the sofa across from his recently hired freelancer. "Now, what's this all about? What's going on with all this intrigue?" He crossed one leg within the expensively tailored suit over the knee of the other and smoothed the gray, pin-striped material.

"I thought you knew what it's all about," Tyce said. "You're the guy who told me it was the opportunity of a lifetime." His words spilled out with half-joking inflection.

"I knew only that it will pay you very well. That, and it will get you introduced to some important people—"

"—and will guarantee *Western World Union* magazine an exclusive on what they're calling one of the most important archeological finds thus far in history," Tyce continued with the teasing tone.

"Yes, well, that, too," Stanton said in an agreeable tone.

"It has something to do with an ancient sarcophagus they found in Iraq, near Babylon," Tyce said.

"Who found it?"

"I take it that a group of international archeologists— a European-based consortium of some sort—has the rights to the dig. They want me to cover the discovery from the standpoint of the esoteric things involved for their magazine, *Archeology/Europe Today*. You ever hear of it?"

Stanton shook his head negatively after sipping from the coffee that had just been delivered.

"'Esoteric things'? What kind of things are they talking about?"

"I can't say until I've been given access to the things involved," Tyce said, reaching to take the steaming cup of coffee from the saucer on his side of the low table between the sofas.

"I was told by Morticai Kant that the magazine principals are friends of Israel. He wasn't very forthcoming, only saying that this sarcophagus and what it contains is staggering in its likely implications for the world. I won't be given any more until I agree to take the gig and am in Israel."

"You will take the...gig...of course."

"Is that an order?"

"Well—you are under contract."

"To write for *Western World Union*," Tyce continued with the banter.

"Part 2, subsection 4, paragraph B: 'The party of the second part will act as reporter as directed by *Western World Union* magazine, not limited to assignments within *Western World Union* magazine's in-house needs…'"

Tyce put the cup to his lips, eyeing the CEO over its rim while Stanton quoted the contract stipulation. He then said, calmly staring into Stanton's smug expression, "'Party of the second part reserves the right to resign upon one week's notice, upon return of any advances for work anticipated…'"

"Aha!" Stanton roared with laughter. "You really do read your contracts carefully!"

"Read them? I help write them—meticulously," Tyce said without breaking his calm façade.

"You *will* take the assignment?" There was a slight plea in the CEO's questioning tone.

The journalist sat forward, placing the cup on the saucer. "This sarcophagus thing," he paused, his thoughts reeling with implications for himself, never mind for the world. "There are things about this sarcophagus and other things going on in my life these days that, if I told you, you would think I was a candidate for a psychiatric ward. You certainly wouldn't want me working for you. I'm not sure I shouldn't commit myself.

THOUGHTS OF THE HUGE, golden object he saw within the tractor-trailer rig the night of the accident continued to carom in his brain while sitting at a light in the DC afternoon traffic.

His learning about the Israelis wanting to talk to him about a writing assignment...before the accident...before looking into the truck's trailer. The consortium seeking him for the assignment—whatever it might entail—must have involved the sarcophagus, even before the accident and the whole, strange experience of the massive, winged creature of light just before he blacked out.

The stranger in the business suit—Michael. The visions, or brain glitches, or whatever. The supernatural, winged beings of blinding light clashing, not once but twice.

A horn sounding in several long blasts rudely brought him back to the business at hand. He gunned the BMW, cursing beneath his breath at the impatient driver who had honked.

Another two blocks and he would pull into his parking garage. He looked forward to at least four hours alone with the desktop PC. There were several short articles and a column he had to finish within two days. Most of the work was done. He just needed to smooth it out—do final revisions on his end before handing it to Michelle Martin for her expert, ready-to-print edit.

One more stoplight and he would be home.

The dark-gray car that carried the driver who had blasted the horn at the previous stoplight pulled up beside him. Its windows were dark, and Tyce's attempt to see the passengers were fruitless.

He glanced at the red light then back at the window on the car's passenger side.

The dark window glass began its descent. Suddenly, Tyce was staring at the end of a machine pistol barrel.

He could see a man's finger jerking on the trigger,

trying to fire the weapon. After several seconds of effort, with Tyce frozen in place, paralyzed with the knowledge that he was about to be murdered, the sedan roared away. The gun had never fired.

The car turned sharply left onto the street crossing the one on which Tyce's BMW sat, tires screaming as the fleeing car fishtailed before straightening and disappearing in the distance.

Tyce, still unable to move, looked down, checking himself. Had he been hit? No. The gun had never fired.

He looked up, his mind clearing. Several pedestrians stared at him, gawking over the attempted murder they thought they had witnessed.

His eyes met those that were familiar. Standing among the gawkers was...was Michael! When Tyce blinked, not believing his eyes, the man was gone!

Tyce was still shaky fifteen minutes later while he looked up Morticai Kant's phone number on his cellphone.

Would they try to follow him to the apartment? Should he not have come here? Rather, should he have driven straight to a precinct police station?

He picked up the nine-millimeter semi-automatic pistol and looked to make sure the clip was in the handle. Yes. And the gun was heavy. The clip was fully loaded.

"Tyce?"

The familiar voice was welcome, soothing.

"Yes, Essie. It's me."

"Are you okay? You sound...anxious."

"No. I'm not okay. Somebody just tried to shoot me while I sat in my car."

There was silence on the line for a few seconds.

Morticai Kant was next on the line, his accented voice full of concern. "Tyce? What happened, please?"

"I was sitting at a red light just down the block from my building. A car pulled up beside me, the window rolled down, and I had an Uzi or something stuck in my face."

"But you weren't hurt?"

"No. I could see he was trying everything to make the gun shoot, but it wouldn't fire. They then took off."

"Thank God," the Israeli said. "Are you okay? Have you called the police?"

"No, I haven't been able to think about anything much. It shook me up, I can tell you that."

"I am pleased that you thought to call us, Tyce," Kant said. "It very well might have something to do with your contact with us."

"Gee, you think?" Tyce's words, he considered after saying them, were rude, unthinking.

"I'm sorry, Mr. Kant—Morticai. I've never had an Uzi pointed between my eyes. It might be standard activity with the Mossad, but for me, a small-time writer, it's not standard operating procedure."

"Yes…yes. I understand," Kant said, his tone serious. "We must do something about this…situation. I'm sending one of our agents to oversee your safety. Once we are on the plane to Tel Aviv, there will be no reason for concern."

"I haven't said I will take the job," Tyce said, picking up the pistol and sticking it in his pants pocket.

"Oh? Essie told me you would accept the assignment."

"She did?"

"Here she is. I'll let you and her get the story straight. I'll send my personal security man. He will be there within a half hour. Do you have a weapon?"

"Yes. A nine-millimeter pistol."

"Well, don't use it on my man. His name is Ehud Begin." Before Tyce could reply, the phone at the other end had changed hands.

"Tyce? Morticai said you are still uncertain about joining us?"

"Well, not really," he said with a slight chuckle. "Actually, I haven't had this much fun since the snake bite while I was in Patmos."

"Oh? Then this means you will be coming to Israel with me." She hesitated and corrected herself. "With us?"

Her completely ignoring the snake-bite remark that should have, in his opinion, made her question what he meant, Essie's Freudian slip—at least that was how he interpreted her slip—meant more to him than she could imagine.

"That's what it means," he said, after a momentary pause to think on her words.

The line was silent for another several seconds before she spoke, "Ehud will deliver you, then, to the building and to the introduction to the artifact, to some of the facts surrounding it."

"Somehow, I feel like the...artifact...and I have already been introduced," Tyce said.

She ignored his quip, her voice taking on soft intimacy. "Tyce...I am very pleased that you will be coming with us."

Bethesda, Maryland – next day, 9:15 a.m.

EHUD BEGIN CONTINUALLY GLANCED into the rearview mirror and side mirrors, then back to the roadway ahead. Tyce found himself also scanning the traffic surrounding the US government sedan that had been provided to the representative of the Israeli government.

The Israeli security agent had spent the night at Tyce's apartment, having put him at ease with the protection provided. Tyce already had developed a high degree of respect for both Israel's security and for the individual.

The evening had been spent with the Israeli agent instructing him on the next day's meeting. Greyson was not to mention anything about Israel's *true* interest in his services—to get inside the things going on with Russia and Iran moving into Iraq. Those nations were attempting to get a foothold in the region through the innocuous area of archeological antiquities.

Tyce Greyson's true mission was to investigate other arenas those diabolist states were actually interested in cracking. It was thought by the Mossad that the journalist could, under cover of writing about the strange history of the artifact for *European Archeology* magazine, not raise Russian and Iranian eyebrows. Not having a history of clandestine activity for governmental entities, rather only a well-known history of investigating strange matters, Tyce, it was reasoned, would be under little suspicion by the super-suspicious Russians and Iranians. Israel's security was Tyce's actual priority.

The consortium's only knowledge about the reporter was that he was there to write a world-class piece for their magazine, for publicity/propaganda reasons. This would divert too much attention from concentrating on the project involving the sarcophagus and its contents.

The fact that the sarcophagus haunted his personal life—its intervention as part of the accident that stormy night and the harbored secrets they wished to obfuscate provided him more incentive for taking on the job than he could have resisted even if he wished to do so.

"Your name—Begin—any relation to the former prime minister?" Tyce asked.

"Menachem Begin was my uncle, my great uncle," the agent said, never taking his eyes from the task of scanning the traffic.

The journalist's phone chimed, breaking his own observation of the traffic around them and the surprise of learning the agent's relationship to one of Israel's top historical leaders.

"Dr. Faust," Tycc said, having read the name of the caller.

"Are you where you can talk, Tyce?"

"There's just me and Ehud, the security agent Morticai sent to babysit me."

"Have you had trouble?"

"Somebody stuck an Uzi between my eyes. Other than that, all is cool."

After Tyce relayed the details of the incident, Faust spoke. His tone conveyed that he didn't find the younger man's words and intonation necessarily amusing. "Have any idea of who they were?"

"Not the slightest. But there's something else. The guy—Michael. I looked at the crowd of pedestrians nearby; he was among them."

"What happened? Did he say anything?"

"Like before. When I took my eyes off him for a couple of seconds, I looked back, and he wasn't there."

The old archeologist was silent on the other end for a few seconds.

"I have a feeling you suspect you know who this Michael is," Tyce said, breaking the silence.

"No. I don't. But, I wonder—"

"—You wonder what?"

"Like I said, Tyce. These are very strange times. There are prophetic considerations."

"Prophecy? You think it's like the Patmos vision? This involves Bible prophecy? Is that your take on this?"

"The fact that your question references Bible prophecy makes me think you must think the same. There are prophecies for the last days—the very end of this dispensation, the Age of Grace—that...that seem to be astonishingly close to fulfillment."

"What prophecies?"

"The way things have come together just recently," Faust said. "The Ezekiel, Gog and Magog forces—Russia, Iran, and now even Turkey and others beginning to form a coalition. Israel being more and more isolated, with all but a few United Nations' countries against the Jews. Even the US and other allies—or supposed allies—of Israel seeming to betray her at every opportunity. Then there's this 'Roadmap to Peace' process, or whatever they're terming it now. A constant effort to make Israel give up land for peace."

The archeologist fell silent, then continued when Tyce said nothing.

"I'm just wondering what other, less geopolitical—" Faust searched his thoughts for the proper designation "—what other matters might be shaping up for fulfillment."

"You mean things like these sword-wielding, winged beings I've been invaded by—this weird, blond guy that keeps popping in and out of my life?"

Tyce turned his head to glance at the driver, who looked back, his expression one of interest.

"I have an idea of what it's about, but I'm not prepared to say until—"

"—Until what?" Tyce sounded frustrated.

"Until I understand a little bit more about this…this archeological find you are about to see. Until some people within the Israeli government have had a chance to brief you on all that might be involved."

"Well, I hope meanwhile that I don't get whacked, as Tony Soprano in that old mob TV series might put it."

"I guess you wonder about all of that you just heard," Tyce said after ending the conversation with Faust, looking at Begin, who glimpsed quickly at him then continued to scan the surrounding traffic for possible threats.

"I've heard stranger things," Begin said.

"This is craziness. I sometimes think I'm going nuts," Tyce said, joining the driver in checking the traffic.

Begin said nothing, looking briefly in the direction of his passenger, then resuming his vigilant assessment of their surroundings.

"This artifact that you're taking me to look at," Tyce said. "What do you know about it?"

"I'm security. I know little about the artifact. I'm here to see that there are no security breaches," Begin said, matter of factly.

"Well, let me tell you, Ehud. I feel that my security has definitely been breached," Tyce quipped while they approached a looming building, the Israeli then turning into the dark basement-parking entrance.

Less than two minutes later, the men rode the small elevator into the bowels of the building, coming to a stop that seemed to Tyce to be several stories below ground level.

The doors slid open, revealing a long corridor leading directly ahead, the hallway lit dimly by sparse lighting inset near the ceiling. The sense was of dungeon-like surroundings, the odor emitting the dankness of mildew while they walked.

"Nice place," the journalist said lightheartedly.

Begin said nothing, while fiddling with a hand inside his suit-coat pocket for a half-metal/plastic card key.

They turned right into a hallway that bisected the corridor. Moments later, Begin stopped in front of a large door. The Israeli pushed a button located above the door's opening device. The light within the button illuminated and Begin inserted the card key in the slot below the button, permitting entrance.

The smells of antiquity were more pronounced while they walked through several small corridors and rooms. There was scant light; Tyce was barely able to make out the walls.

"Why is it so dark and damp?" he asked. "It's like being in a tomb somewhere in Egypt."

"It is that exact environment we must maintain to ensure the preservation of the artifact."

The accented voice startled Tyce. A man had suddenly stepped from a door along the wall. "We must keep the light to a minimum," he said. "Light, by its very presence, can cause deterioration."

The small, thin man offered his hand to the journalist.

"I am Harnak al Mufi," he said. "I am charged with coordinating the carrying-out of the project."

They continued to walk while the Egyptian talked. "We have a number of artifacts in these chambers, thus must maintain certain environments," he said. "Here, let us go into an area perhaps more comfortable."

Al Mufi inserted a card into a door along the darkened wall and they stepped into a brightly lit area, where lab-coated men and women attended to various objects on laboratory worktables.

"These are project scientists assigned to the various artifacts," al Mufi said. "Let us go to the heart of our little project center."

Momentarily, the Egyptian stepped aside, allowing Greyson and Begin to precede him into another room.

"Tyce!" Morticai Kant moved from a conference table to take Tyce's hand. He introduced him to the several men in the room who, unlike the people dressed in lab coats, all wore business suits.

"These gentlemen represent the consortium that oversees the Mesopotamia archeological dig we've discussed," Kant said. "We want to give you a full explanation of what we believe we've found in the ancient Euphrates River channel. It is most profound, according to the experts."

"Where is the sarcophagus?" Tyce asked, his brashness domineering his journalistic curiosity, forcing the question to come almost involuntarily.

"In due course," one of the men—a short, stout-physiqued Englishman said. "We want to first orient you to what we believe we have."

"You will be shown the artifact, Tyce, as soon as we've finished here," Kant said, hoping to take the hard edge from the man's matter-of-factness.

"I have a question before we get started," Tyce said, choosing to be oblivious to the Englishman's brusqueness. "Why is an Iraqi artifact here in the basement of a Washington DC building, and being handled by a European consortium?"

The men looked at each other with raised eyebrows, expressing without words their uncomfortable puzzlement.

"Ah, gentlemen. I warned you that we have a first-rate journalist in Mr. Greyson," Kant said with a laugh. "I'm afraid we are in for several probing questions. But that's what we agreed to when we invited a reporter his acumen into the project."

"It really boils down to," a man representing Belgium said, "the fact that the United States controlled the dig at the time it was extracted from Babylon in 2003. The American military removed it and kept it under carefully controlled circumstances until recently, then the consortium secured the rights to...proceed with the project."

Tyce studied the Belgian's face for a moment. "The US Army just took the artifact from the country it was occupying?" he asked. "This was a charge made at the time, as I recall. That the United States was raping Iraq—taking its antiquities, its artifacts."

"Mr. Greyson," the man returned, "it is my understanding that this particular artifact was sent to America for purposes of preserving it. It is one of the few locations that has the...facilities...to control the environment essential to its preservation. Once exposed to the elements, deterioration began to take effect—entropy, you know?"

The German representative within the consortium spoke in near-perfect English, and with authority. "We of the European consortium have provided the private funding as part of an agreement that no US taxpayer funds be used to carry out certain...experimentations... with the contents of the sarcophagus."

"What does it contain?" Tyce's words again prompted the men to exchange sheepish glances with each other. "What's all the lab coats about out there?" He motioned toward the rooms he and Begin had walked through on their way to this conference room.

"For now, let's just say we are dealing with a…genetic engineering project," the German said. Unlike the others, he wasn't intimidated by the reporter's audacity.

"Okay. Let's say that… So, what am I doing here? I know nothing about…genetic engineering—or very little about it," Tyce said, looking into the German's eyes for any signal of dissolving the man's demeanor that gave an impression of self-assigned superiority. He saw no such dissolving.

"Why the interest now, after all these years? Why are you just now using this artifact—whatever it is—to carry out experiments? Or, have there been experiments already?"

The German, a tall, physically well-conditioned man of about fifty years, spoke again.

"The advancement of knowledge and the technology involved in what the geneticists need to do have just recently reached the point—the state—that makes it possible to achieve their goals."

Tyce studied the faces of the men, his eyes finally fixing on those of Morticai Kant.

"You said you wanted to give me a full explanation—I think you said—of the sarcophagus."

"Then, let us be seated and begin doing just that," the Israeli said, motioning for everyone to take a seat.

The German sat down behind a control panel atop the big conference table. When he manipulated the panel's buttons, the large wall across from the tabletop from where Tyce sat parted at its center. Each half of the wall slid to the sides, exposing a huge screen.

The screen activated when the German pushed other buttons, revealing the object that Tyce knew in his gut would be the sarcophagus he had seen in the trailer the night of the accident. The façade of the sarcophagus had been polished to perfection so that it glinted brightly while the camera did its work.

As he manipulated the controls, the camera view changed from presenting the full-length side view of the huge vault to a perspective from above.

"This burial chamber is the greatest archeological find since the tomb of Tutankhamen was discovered early in the twentieth century," the German said, while continuing to work the controls. "The gold value of the sarcophagus is beyond imagination. But the contents are priceless."

After less than one minute, the German man pressed a button and the screen snapped to black, the doors that comprised the wall sliding together.

"What about those contents?" Tyce said, frustration tinging his question. "When do I get to see what's in the sarcophagus?"

"In due course," the German answered, unaffected by the irritation in the reporter's voice. "The important matter to address at present is your education on what needs be done in your work for the project."

Tyce sat back from his elbows on the conference table position and relaxed in the big, leather conference chair. "Okay. Educate me," he said with feigned resignation in his voice.

"We of the consortium desire that the artifact be presented as a discovery that portends great understanding about the origin of our species...the human race."

Tyce concentrated on the German's words: "Evidence obtained from within the sarcophagus indicates that we, ourselves, are not of this sphere, but are extraterrestrials."

CHAPTER 4

The educational session was totally unsatisfactory. Tyce fumed in sullen silence while looking at the Washington Monument and other Mall structures while Ehud Begin drove him toward his apartment. His questions hadn't been answered; he had not gotten to look at the contents of the sarcophagus.

He wanted to tell them he wasn't interested in the job because of their dishonesty and obfuscation. He was promised a full disclosure.

The astonishing claim of what they had found in that coffin was what kept him committed to the project—at least until he could get a look at the contents and determine for himself what it was really all about. All he got was a closed-circuit TV view of a closed casket.

What did Israel and the trip to Tel Aviv have to do with his writing about the sarcophagus—and the stunning information it contained—that they *claimed* it contained? All of these were questions that Kant promised to answer on the way to Israel.

"What do you think is in the sarcophagus?" Begin,

who had sat in on the meeting, asked, all the while continuing his constant looks into the mirrors and around their vehicle at the traffic.

"I thought you were just here to provide security," Tyce said, his thoughts disrupted, poking at the agent who had become his friend over the past hours.

"It's all quite interesting, with the sarcophagus being so important in some genetics project," Begin said, ignoring Tyce's jab.

"Yeah, I suppose it is."

Tyce looked out the window while the Washington Mall whisked by on his right, his thoughts on the driver's words.

The members of the consortium were tight-lipped on what was in the burial chamber. It was as if they wanted him to write a propaganda piece for their magazine's readership without his knowing the full story.

They promised he would be given all he needed to do the story, but he had been around long enough to sense when to know that the real story would remain behind proverbial closed doors. He sensed in the deepest reaches of his core that full disclosure wouldn't be given up to public consumption in this case. Just how much each of the consortium members themselves knew was a question equal to the mystery about what was really going on with the artifact. Only the German gave the impression that he had a full grasp of the strange project.

Tyce was expected to write an in-depth story on the find, a piece that would make the Israeli investors believe so strongly in the project that the funds would flow like the falls of Niagara. But, if the first session to... *educate*...him was any indicator of their giving him what was needed to produce such a brilliant piece of propaganda, the mission would be impossible. He knew little more now than before he sat down at the conference table to view the artifact. It was the *real* artifact he needed to know about—whatever lay within the golden coffin.

Then, there was the matter of what this whole thing was really about. Why did Israel choose him, and what was the actual thing they wanted to accomplish within all these intrigues?

"That's the largest sarcophagus I've ever seen," Begin said. "I've seen many of the Egyptian antiquities, and none of them is anywhere near the size of this thing."

"What do you think?" the journalist asked, glancing at Begin before turning to again look at the passing DC landscape.

"Must be some large animal they used in their Babylonian worship system or something," Ehud said. "Maybe a water buffalo...something they believed was a god. I remember the story of Nebuchadnezzar...his grazing like a herd animal when he went mad for a time."

"Could be something like that, I guess," Tyce said. "I don't know why they would be interested in the genetics of some three-thousand-year-old water buffalo, though. That doesn't make sense."

Both men were silent for several seconds before Tyce spoke. "It doesn't make sense, because he said the contents of the sarcophagus proved that the origin of humankind is extraterrestrial. What? Do we come from bovines?"

"Do you believe they really have proof of that claim?" Begin's question was laced with incredulity.

"I'm sure not going to take their word on it," Tyce said. "They will have to show me. The scientists, the geneticists will have to...educate me, if I'm to put out that kind of information."

He fumbled through the briefcase for his chiming iPhone. He saw the name Essie Jorba on the display.

"Essie!" His greeting betrayed his enthusiasm in seeing that she was the caller.

"Tyce!" Her enthusiasm matched his.

"Do you have plans? For this evening, I mean?" Her tone was one of hope.

"What you have in mind?"

"I just would like to see you," she said, her voice trailing off.

"I would like to see you, too," Tyce answered.

There was hesitation before she spoke. "I thought I might make a special Mediterranean something for us. Can we use your apartment?"

The dinner date made, Tyce turned to Ehud Begin. "You are hereby off duty this evening," he said with a huge smile.

TYCE SURVEYED the small table Essie had set following the past hour and ten minutes of food preparation. She looked at him with wide, inquisitive eyes after he had taken a couple of bites from the plate of Israeli cuisine.

"What is this?" he asked, moving the food within his palate. His lack of expression frustrated her, and she pressed him.

"Do you like it?"

"What is it?"

"It's *shishlik*...made with chicken."

"And what's this?" He held up the food between his fingers, then took a bite.

"Fresh-made braided *challah* bread. Do you like it?"

"And what's this stuff?" He pointed with his fork at small bowls surrounding his plate.

"It's for the *challah* bread. It's *hummus* and *baba ganouj*." Her answer was quick, with frustration in her voice.

"What's it made of?"

"Chickpeas and eggplant."

"And what's this?" He again pointed to the food to the right of his plate.

"It's *horiatiki salata*—a tomato, cucumber, and olive salad. Do you like it?"

Tyce had watched her from the apartment's small living room while she prepared the meal. She had no doubt thought he was too busy with his nose in the computer that sat atop a coffee table while he leaned over the keyboard to notice her move about the kitchen working on the meal.

But he had noticed: her graceful, feminine form moving beneath the silky material of the lavender-blue dress she had chosen. Her auburn hair, perfectly contoured to her lovely, oval-shaped face, its highlights reflecting the scant light even now that flickered from the large candle she had placed between them on the table. The beautiful eyes of a color he couldn't quite determine. Essie was a work of art...and a very good cook.

She had tried very hard to please him. She had done so, so much—much more than she could imagine.

Tyce looked at the woman who said she awaited his verdict. He said nothing but dabbed his mouth with the cloth napkins she had brought to the meal, stood from his chair, and came to her side, holding out his hand and bidding her to stand.

"The meal is perfect, Essie. Just like you." He kissed

her and felt her submit with a soft, warm kiss in return in the senses-heightening of the special moment.

"You *are* just about perfect, you know."

His words brought a momentary shyness from the eyes, he now determined, were of the most beautiful green he had ever beheld.

Essie glanced at him, then turned back to the meal, obviously wanting to break away from the intimacy of the moment. "I'm glad you like it," she said. "I have special wine." She went to a counter and took a bottle from a metallic bowl, then poured them each a glass when she returned to the table.

"I think you will like it," she said, still not making eye contact.

Tyce's imagination rumbled with the thought that had been haunting him. The name...Jorba. Essie Jorba, not Kant, the last name of her father, Morticai Kant. Was she married? Was Jorba her married name?

"Yeah, I'm sure the wine will be great—like everything else," he said, taking his seat across the small table from her.

"Essie...I have a question. I'm a reporter. I'm not too good at nuance..."

She said nothing, but her raised eyebrows said, "What do you want to ask?"

"Are you married?"

"What makes you think I'm married?" she asked in a flat tone.

"The last name—Jorba. Not Kant."

"That's my father's idea...and that of his paranoid friends. Jorba is my mother's maiden name...Vivah Jorba. Mordicai hopes the last name will prevent my... abduction...for purposes of using me as leverage...by Israel's enemies. He's a close associate of the prime minister. Using Jorba rather than Kant is just a security matter."

"Thank God," Tyce said in a relieved whisper.

"What?"

"Nothing. Thanks for telling me. I was afraid I was out of line with the...never mind."

"And, what about you?"

"What about me?" Tyce sipped from the long-stemmed wine glass Essie provided.

"Morticai said you were married," she said, looking at him over her own glass.

"'Was' is the operative word. I *was* married. My wife, Marial, died almost three years ago..." Tyce's voice trailed off, his eyes diverting from hers to wander into memory of Marial's loss.

"Oh, I'm very sorry," Essie said, not knowing what else to say.

"She was very sick, so it was best for her. They couldn't help her."

Essie said nothing, but studied Tyce's face carefully, then she abruptly switched subjects.

"And now—the dessert!" she said brightly, getting up and going into the kitchen. She returned momentarily with two large plates.

"We have *baklava*, a rolled sweet pastry with nuts, *hamantaschen*—the triangle-shaped fruit- and cheese-filled pastry you see there—and *rugelach*, cream-cheese cookies."

"What goes best with wine?" he teased.

"Everything is good with wine," she said with equal banter in her tone.

Both, without taking time to reflect on it, realized in that upbeat moment that life was meant to go on, and that their relationship bore bright promise.

~

"MY FATHER WISHES to speak with you," Essie Jorba said after a minute of talking with Morticai Kant.

Tyce took the cell phone from her while they sat in the back seat of the government sedan driven by Ehud Begin's relief bodyguard, the agent of the service Kant insisted on continuing.

"If you don't mind, will you please step into the hotel for a few minutes when you arrive with my daughter?" the Israeli's voice said in the phone's earpiece. "There's a matter we should discuss."

"Oh? What's up?" Tyce glanced over at Essie, whose expression was also one of curiosity.

Less than ten minutes later, the agent drove the car into the basement parking garage, and five minutes more brought them to the eleventh-floor hotel suite.

Morticai Kant bore the familiar, worried expression etched permanently into his sixty-two-year-old face by years of clandestine security work for Israel's Mossad. "It involves the attempted...assault that was made on you earlier," Kant said. It was obvious that he wanted to get directly to the point. "We think we have determined the source of the attempted assault," he said, after being seated across from Tyce and Essie, who sat on the sofa, a coffee table between themselves and the Israeli.

"We believe this is a group—a very small group—that operates outside of boundaries set by the CIA. We don't know if this group is a part of the CIA or is separate altogether. If so, they would likely be some organization that also operates within internationalist circles. That is, they are likely devoted to internationalist or global-order initiatives, rather than to national or sovereign autonomy among national governments."

"The *deep state?*" Tyce asked. "They want to bring in the so-called new world order, you mean?"

"Yes. That is your American term—the 'deep state'. These who tried to eliminate you are secretive operatives, we believe. They are likely commissioned by some within the American government, and by others within other governments. These want to establish a new, global *economic* system, for which they, of course, would be head governing authority."

"Why kill me? What would that accomplish?"

Kant considered the question, seeming to search out an answer to the matter he had wondered about himself without satisfactory resolution.

"Probably it was aimed at intimidating others in the project…to frighten some."

"How do you know all this?" Tyce asked, finding it hard to imagine his own importance in such James Bond-like intrigues.

"There are ways to get such information," Kant said, wanting to get past the American's question. "They won't be a significant threat to you, or to the project, once we are in Israel," he said, glancing at Essie, then back at Tyce.

"What about while we are still here?" Essie's tone was hard-edged, her own eyes locked onto her father's.

"I would like you to stay here, with us, once you have gathered your personal items," Kant said, disengaging from his daughter's intensive gaze.

"We need to trust only in our immediate circle of people, while in Washington," he said.

"Well, having had a machine gun pointed at my face, I certainly won't argue with you." Tyce's tone was jocular; Essie's wasn't.

"Abba, you must make sure he is protected," she demanded

~

Morticai Kant bid goodnight, saying tomorrow would be a "most difficult day". He was to meet directly with the president of the United States in the Oval Office. Although the Israeli was the prime minister's envoy, with full diplomatic authority to represent the Israeli government, the cavalier, even dismissive attitude with which the White House interacted with Israel's officials since the president took office meant that Kant faced an adversarial atmosphere, which such meetings inevitably produced.

Tyce Greyson had been credentialed as an independent White House reporter during the early part of the first administration. He had heard from friends within the White House staff of the president's condescending manner in talking with the prime minister. Even the president's own people, in several cases, were appalled at the treatment given the Israeli head of state upon his first visit to the White House under this administration.

Kant hadn't said what tomorrow's meeting was about, but it almost certainly involved, in part at least, the president demanding that Israel's government give in to administration demands of whatever sorts as part of the ever-present Middle East peace process.

"Morticai has much on his mind," Essie said when her father left for one of the suite's four bedrooms. "They were rather abrasive in their summoning the prime minister. He was equally unyielding, telling the president he was too busy trying to keep Israel safe from enemies on all sides except the Mediterranean to personally fly over to meet with him in the White House. So, he sent Morticai. It's well he did so. Papa is one tough old bird."

Tyce's broad grin brought a puzzled look from the pretty face.

"Did I say something amusing?" she asked.

"No, no… It's just funny when you use American slang like 'He's a tough old bird'."

"It is true, nonetheless. He has faced down the likes of Vladimir Putin."

"Oh? What was that about?"

"It involved a time in Moscow only a few months ago when Putin wanted to know about our natural-gas deposits within our territorial waters. Putin wanted to know how far Israel had progressed in developing technologies that could extract the gas for transport to other nations."

Essie began to relay the story of her father's toughness. "Abba told Putin—who is one of the last of the KGB monsters, you know—that Russia would know when the technology had come to fruition. There would then be competition regarding energy availability that would change the dynamics of the region."

Essie laughed, putting two long, perfectly manicured fingertips to her lips to stifle her own amusement at recounting the remembered moment.

"Putin's face turned crimson! He wasn't used to being talked to in such a way! Eli Hamuch, Morticai's top aid on the trip, said later that he was afraid ol' Vlad was going to have us all shot."

"You were there, huh?"

"Oh, yes. I wouldn't have missed it."

Tyce stood from the sofa and reached to take her hand, gently tugging her to her feet. "You are amazing, Essie Jorba," he said softly, looking down at her, holding her with a gentle grip on her arms. She responded by putting her hands beneath his arms, against his sides, and moving closer.

"Not really—" she started to say. Before she could finish, his lips were against hers. Essie looked into his eyes when their lips parted. Her expression was one of innocence that begged explanation.

"Thanks for paying attention to me," Tyce said. "I don't deserve it. But thanks. It means more to me than you can know."

She said nothing, but, almost shyly, looked away.

"I'm beat, Essie. See you bright and early in the morning?"

"Yes. I am always up early," she said.

TYCE HADN'T THOUGHT the feeling would return—at least, not anytime soon. Essie Jorba had rekindled thoughts—emotions—not of sadness because of Marial's passing from his life, but deep feelings of growing intimacy, like those when he and Marial had first met.

Holding Essie close didn't make him sense the guilt he had felt to this point on those few occasions he had gotten close to women. Each of those times he had felt uncomfortable, as if Marial's voice was hauntingly reminding him of their love for each other.

With Essie, the voice wasn't there. Yet Marial's beautiful, loving countenance was in his mind's eye—even now, while he unpacked the few belongings he had brought with him from the apartment, to stay for now under the protection of Morticai Kant's security people. He wondered if it was some sort of release given him by

Marial from the other side—an approval to move on with life…and love.

The Israeli security contingent surrounded the suite. Kant had ordered a stepped-up vigilance since the attempted assault at the stoplight. He had even called in Israeli security people from the Washington embassy pool. It was likely, however, Tyce thought, while stuffing underwear into a drawer, that it was Morticai's concern for his daughter more than his concern for the safety of Tyce Greyson.

That was as it should be. Essie. Her beauty, her fragrance, even now lingered, while he finished unpacking the small suitcase then slid the drawer shut.

What was this strangeness in his life? His own importance as a mere journalist couldn't possibly cause such a stir among those who concocted such grandiose plans as those of bringing in a new world order. His joining the project—whatever it was all about—didn't pose a threat of any sort that he could figure.

The battling, winged creatures—gigantic, almost human forms of light that weren't dreams, but were as real as his surroundings now.

Michael—the tall, young, blond man that apparently no one but he, himself, could see.

The massive, golden sarcophagus—at the center of the intrigues that agitated and pulsed within his thought process constantly.

Randolph Faust—who had landed him in the middle of the project, and their interaction with the still inexplicable goings-on in times following those years after the visions, the prophetic episodes.

Tyce had moved into the bathroom, where he flipped the light switch upward and the room lit brightly. He went to the lavatory and sat his shave kit on the counter.

He started the water in the basin running and touched the stream every few seconds to determine the warmth he wanted, opened a new package of hotel soap, and washed his hands, then his face.

Looking back at him in the mirror was an older man than he wanted to see. The tough years of travel around the world reporting in places like Afghanistan, Pakistan —even Syria and Africa—had taken their toll. The eyes no longer sparked with the same youthfulness. But, he thought, the overall appearance was one of a mature, accomplished man of worldly acumen. He mopped his face with the towel, satisfied with the new, more upbeat assessment than when the image first greeted him.

As Tyce continued looking into the large mirror, the reflection began to get ever darker, as if it was being turned to a lower rheostat setting. The ambient light, too, darkened until he stood, frozen in total blackness.

Unable to move an inch in any direction, he was forced to peer directly ahead, where moments before the mirror had been alive with his own image toweling his face dry.

From the center of where the mirror had been, a pinpoint of light pierced the blackened surface, then spread until a scene appeared before his mesmerized gaze.

Several men—some in khaki uniforms, a few in casual, civilian dress, and several more in Middle Eastern clothes and headdress—stood around a table. The men in civilian dress spoke in Russian to the khaki-clad members of the cabal.

The scene was at the same time surreal and laser-focused in its image. Tyce was fully aware of every word spoken, and he both heard and understood what was being said, although he knew nothing about the Russian language.

One man had the attention of the Russians in the civilian attire and those in the khaki.

"Are you certain these can be trusted to carry out this mission?" the man asked.

"Yes, sir, Comrad Kaskakov," one of the uniformed men replied.

"This will destroy their most sacred site," Kaskakov said, with questioning still in his tone.

"These hold that Mecca is a false place of worship," the same man answered. "They see Medina and others as the legitimate centers of worship."

The others gathered closer around the table as the Russian, apparently in charge, bid them to do.

"Tell them exactly what is planned for this false place of Islamist worship," he said, looking at the Russian army colonel, who held a pointer in his hand.

The soldier began pointing and touching various areas on the map that lay before the group on the big table's top. He spoke to the robed Middle Eastern men in Arabic—a language that Tyce neither understood nor spoke, but somehow understood perfectly now.

"This is where the stone of worship resides, as you know." He tapped the tip of the pointer on the location on the map representing Mecca. "This will completely remove this satanic place of false worship forever from the earth," he said, looking at each of the Arabs.

They mumbled gleefully among themselves, laughter and hand gestures thrusting above their heads as they chattered approval.

"You will be expected to fire the missile from here." The colonel tapped a point on the map. "This is a nuclear-tipped missile—very similar to the sort the Israelis have in their arsenals."

The Arabs nodded and glanced at each other.

"Israel—the Jews—will receive blame for having launched the strike against Islam."

Again, the Arab contingent erupted in gleeful approval. "Allah be praised," several shouted.

The vision before Tyce's eyes began to transmorph into a scene within an ornately decorated room of dark, wooden walls and scant light coming from small windows spaced ten feet apart near the high ceiling. Three men in business suits stood in conversation near the center of the room. When one of the men spoke, it was in Russian.

"The Western world already is turned against the Jew. This will complete the process of assuring our control in the matter of energy," the man said.

"They will be too busy trying to stave off the hyenas of world opinion to think on competing in energy development for Europe and beyond," another man said.

"We will be the lone provider of natural gas, once their potential for gas production and export are no longer a factor," the man who commented first concluded.

Suddenly the lights were again illuminating the bathroom. Tyce blinked, looking at his own image in the mirror, trying to reorient himself to his surroundings.

He stumbled into the bedroom, finding the edge of the bed to sit on. He kneaded his eyes and tried to shake off the impact of what he had witnessed in the past moments. Was he going nuts? Was it a dream—a dream in which he still found himself?

No. It was a vision. And it was a true vision, not a dream…

What did it mean? Who was he to tell? Who would believe him?

The Russians! Essie said her father had faced off against the Russian leader over the natural-gas production potential in Israel...just under the nation's territorial waters. Did Putin want Israel's ability to produce gas and oil for Europe and others so badly that he was willing to unleash a nuclear weapon against Islam? To get Israel blamed, thus, to cause the world's anger to turn upon the Jewish state?

He searched his memory for things he had once heard about Israel and Bible prophecy, something about the whole world turning against Israel at the very end of days. Randolph Faust had recently mentioned Israel and a prophesied attack by hordes of enemies. Did the... vision...have something to do with that? The other visions that he saw—the immortal, winged warriors... the sarcophagus...Michael. Was it all part of a common chord?

Was Morticai the man to tell? Or Randolph Faust? Was Faust the one to whom he should report the vision?

*Neither would appreciate being awakened to hear him talk about a...vision...*of a plot being hatched against Israel. Although, what he had seen was there, in front of him. It was real. And it was like some sort of closed-circuit television capture of plans to...change the world—or at least to alter it profoundly.

Tyce grabbed his phone and searched for Randolph Faust's San Marcos, Texas, number.

No... It would be better to wait until the morning. As he set it back down, the phone chimed.

A text. He read it aloud: "Zechariah 12:1–3."

The message was signed "Miykael."

The Scripture! That was the passage he had been trying to remember!

He sat on the edge of the bed near the nightstand and pulled open the drawer. There! A Gideon Bible. He quickly thumbed through the pages until he found the book of his search.

He looked again at the phone for the message. It wasn't there.

"Zechariah," he said aloud, remembering, then, the chapter and verses. "Zechariah 12:1–3." He continued to flip pages, then read the result of his search silently.

> *The burden of the word of the LORD for Israel, saith the LORD, which stretcheth forth the heavens, and layeth the foundation of the earth, and formeth the spirit of man within him. Behold, I will make Jerusalem a cup of trembling unto all the people round about, when they shall be in the siege both against Judah and against Jerusalem.*
>
> *And in that day will I make Jerusalem a burdensome stone for all people: all that burden themselves with it shall be cut in pieces, though all the people of the earth be gathered together against it.*

SLEEP HAD COME QUICKLY—HAD, before he felt it coming, overtaken his anxious cerebral meanderings on what he saw in the vision-state, or whatever the sights and sounds were that had insinuated themselves within his brain the night before. One thing played over and over in that besieged mind—the text message and the name signed beneath, appearing then disappearing. He suspected what it meant but wasn't sure.

Essie walked from her own bedroom at 5:01, proving

she did indeed arise early. Tyce greeted her from the small sofa in the suite's living room.

"Good morning," he said, causing her to look startled when his words disrupted her concentration on her movement toward the small kitchen.

"Oh! Good morning. I didn't expect you to be awake at this hour," she said, managing even at the early hour to smile brightly in his direction.

"I didn't expect me to be awake at this hour either," he said, standing to walk the few feet to where she had stopped.

"What's up with you?"

"What do you mean?" she asked.

"What's up with your being just as beautiful at five a.m. as you are at five p.m.? Maybe even prettier…"

He hugged her lightly. "No, that's not possible. One can only be so beautiful, and you've reached that level, no matter what time of day or night."

She giggled and punched him gently on the chest.

"You are…how do you say? You are *corny* with your charm this morning."

"Yeah, well. I might be, but you're still gorgeous to the max."

"I will make coffee," Essie said, going to the kitchen counter to begin the task.

Tyce reseated himself on the sofa in front of the low table and began working with his phone. He glanced again at her and caught her studying him. She looked away and focused on the coffeemaker when she realized he was looking back at her.

"What time do you think your father will get up?"

"He is probably awakening about now," she said, manipulating the filter apparatus on the machine. "Why?"

"I have to tell him about what...about something that took place last night. Actually it was probably just after midnight," Tyce said, stopping his work to look at her while he talked.

"Essie, I had another of the—whatever they are...a vision is all I can think to call them."

"The winged creatures doing battle?" she asked with raised eyebrows.

"No. This was more down to earth. Do you think I'm going crazy?"

"Well, you do say that you think I'm beautiful, so, yes. You probably are going crazy." Her tone was meant to show the foolishness of his question.

"*That* is my one point of absolute sanity," he said, putting the phone on the table, standing, then joining her in the kitchen.

She said, in a more serious tone, "I don't mean to tease about these *visions*. What happened? What did you see?"

"It was a scene as clear and as real as you and me standing here, Essie," Tyce said. "There were these Russians, both civilians and military men. They were with several Arabic-looking guys. They were in the full Arab garb, headdress—all of that."

"What is this about?"

Morticai Kant spoke from the living room. "You had another of the episodes?"

"Yes, and it involved Israel. I didn't want to wake you up, but probably should have," Tyce said walking nearer the Israeli, who sat and began putting on his socks and shoes while listening as Tyce explained the whole matter.

"These Russians wearing the business suits, standing

in the big room. Did you hear any names?" Kant asked, looking up from tying the second shoelace.

"No. But in the first scene, where the Russians talked with the Arabs, I remember the name. This one guy called the man who seemed to be in charge 'Comrad Kaskakov'."

The Israeli squinted in concentration. "This Kaskakov, do you remember about his appearance?"

"He was taller than all the others. Had a full head of salt-and-pepper hair."

"Sounds like Ivan Kaskakov," Kant said, taking on a faraway sound. "They were planning to destroy Mecca... with a nuclear ordnance?"

"Yes. The plan is to satisfy the sect of Islamists— whichever they are—by getting rid of what they consider a blasphemous place of worship of Allah. But the real objective is to get Israel blamed for the destruction."

Kant said nothing. Tyce saw in the Israeli's eyes that the man's thoughts were racing.

"Thank you for sharing this, Tyce."

"So you don't think I'm completely nuts?"

"No, no—you aren't...nuts," he answered almost in a whisper.

"I'M TOLD that the project is being switched to Tel Aviv," Eldridge Stanton said, while Tyce and Essie walked toward the Lincoln Memorial.

"Yes. We'll fly out of Reagan around seven this evening," the journalist said into the cellphone.

"Good, good," Stanton said. "Do you know the scope of the project? What is expected of you in writing the piece?"

"I haven't gotten a look at the artifact yet. Just the sarcophagus. They tell me I'll be given a look at what's in the sarcophagus once it's safely secured in Tel Aviv," Tyce said, seeing the huge, seated figure of Lincoln in the distance.

"Where are you now?"

"We're just doing some sightseeing this morning while Kant has his meeting in the White House."

"We?"

"Essie and myself—Morticai Kant's daughter."

"What about security? Isn't it a bit brave of you to be walking around in DC, considering the attempt on your life?" Stanton's tone projected concern.

"We have at least two of Kant's security men babysitting."

"Must be a profoundly important artifact," Stanton said.

"Must be," Tyce agreed, stopping with Essie in front of the massive Lincoln statue. "That, and lots more, methinks," he added in his best Shakespearean attempt.

"Oh? What else is involved?"

"I'd have to kill you if I told you."

"Well, okay, Mr. Bond. I'll wait to hear all about it through my own channels."

"I'll call you from Tel Aviv when we arrive."

When the call was concluded, they looked into the bronze image of Abraham Lincoln's face, which appeared to gaze downward at them.

"Our Israeli secret service guys are pretty good. Not a sign of them," Tyce said, scanning their surroundings.

"They are here, I assure," Essie said. "They appear and disappear as if they are magicians."

"Sounds like you've had lots of experience with them."

"Morticai has them somewhere within my vicinity at all times," she said with resignation.

"The abduction thing?" Tyce said, continuing to try to see the Israeli security agents.

"There have been attempts, so I am never without my guardian angels."

Tyce looked back to the Lincoln figure with increasing concentration into the recesses of the eyes. His senses began to darken, as if he was losing consciousness. The next instant, he stood transfixed. He appeared to be in a gargantuan cave opening—a void within which pulsed a force that drew him ever deeper into its darkness.

A point of light expanded from somewhere within the blackness, spreading until he stood within its ambience. The scene was familiar, one as clear as when he had stood in the very same oval room on several occasions during his journalistic career. Two men stood in front of the ornately carved desk. He heard as clearly as he saw the president of the United States, who spoke to the slightly shorter, much older man.

"There will never be peace with the present government," the president was saying. "No matter what we do here, they will always cling to their Jewishness as reason to murder Palestinians. The operation must be of sufficient force to produce the crisis that's needed."

The older man placed the fingertips of his right hand on the presidential desk and leaned slightly forward as he braced his aging body to shift his standing position. His voice was stronger than a man of his apparent age would indicate.

"The crisis will be quite sufficient," he said in English, with a distinctive, European accent. "Although we don't know the precise timing, it will be more than is needed to bring all to the table of peace—even the most obstinate Jew."

"Then what we are doing here will all have been worth the effort," the president said. "Kant will doubtless report to the leadership in Jerusalem that there is little hope of this nation providing for Iron Dome—or for much of anything else, if they don't agree to our terms in the next round of talks."

The old man moved toward one of the two sofas at the center of the Oval Office, assisted by the president, who cradled his elbow and helped him be seated.

"The whole world is about to turn against them," the man said. "They will have no choice but to agree to whatever terms are offered."

Essie's pulling at his arm caused Tyce to return in his thoughts to the Lincoln Memorial.

"Tyce! Are you okay?!" She continued to shake his arm vigorously, looking upward into his face to determine his state of awareness.

"Are you okay?" Her tone was more gentle, less frantic, seeing that his eyes were no longer glazed, his expression less stuporous.

"Yes...yes. I'm okay, I think," he said putting his fingertips to his head and massaging his temples. "It...it was another vision, Essie. I was there. It was the president, in the Oval Office..."

CHAPTER 5

Morticai Kant spoke to be heard above the engines of the Gulfstream. "This man—the old man with the president…did you recognize him?"

"No. I don't remember seeing him before," Tyce said.

He sat across from Kant, whose chair the Israeli had unlocked from its forward-facing position then swiveled 180 degrees to face the journalist.

He had gone over the vision several times, but Kant wasn't satisfied.

"It was the old man, as you say, not the president who said the crisis will be 'sufficient' to cause Israel to acquiesce to whatever demands are made of us? It was *not* the president who made that statement?"

"The president only said that the 'operation must be of sufficient force' to produce the needed crisis."

Kant frowned in concentration a few seconds before speaking. "And this 'crisis' is supposed to be sufficient to cause Israel to give in to the demands of whatsoever nature the United States demands."

"The old guy didn't say the United States. He said

'this nation'—meaning America, I suppose," Tyce said after a few seconds of thought. "He said that 'the whole world is about to turn against them'—meaning Israel, I took it. He said that they will have 'no choice but to accept whatever terms are offered'."

Essie, seated beside Tyce, leaned into the conversation to be heard. "Tell him about the text message."

"I forgot to tell you. Last night, after seeing the scene with the Russians and the Arabs, I was trying to remember a prophecy...from the Old Testament, about Israel and the end of days, that Israel will be hated by all other nations. About that time, a text message came into my phone. It said 'Zechariah 12:1–3'."

Kant took only a moment of reflection to remember. "'The Lord...will make Jerusalem a cup of trembling, a burdensome stone—'"

"—Yes, that's it! I looked it up," Tyce said.

"Tell him its sender," Essie said.

"It was signed 'Michael,'" he said.

"This 'Michael' again," Kant said, surprise in his voice.

"Yeah, but it was spelled *M-i-y-k-a-e-l.*"

Kant's surprise was even more pronounced. He looked at Essie, whose knowing expression was evident. "Hebrew. It's the Hebrew for Michael—the archangel," he said.

"Since you said you don't think I'm nuts, what do you think this is all about?"

Kant thought on Tyce's question. "You aren't nuts," the Israeli said. "But what it might be all about is a crazy notion."

Both looked at Kant with increased curiosity.

"There is another prophecy," he continued. "But, of course, I don't hold to legend and folklore, whether of the past or for the future."

Tyce was surprised. The old man was an agnostic?

"But…there is supposedly a foretold matter by the Hebrew prophet Daniel." The Israeli searched his memory, the thought coming, causing his eyes to brighten. "The prophecy says that in the latter days, the archangel, Michael, will stand up for Daniel's people."

"That's Israel, right?" Tyce said.

"Yes—the Hebrew children."

"'He will…stand up.' What, exactly does that mean?" Tyce asked.

"It means that Michael will come to Israel's defense," the Israeli said.

~

"THERE IS A SURPRISE FOR YOU," Essie said, putting her arm through the crook in Tyce's arm when they walked up from the ramp after landing in Tel Aviv.

"I don't know how many more surprises I can take," Tyce said with a chuckle, walking more quickly to keep up with her pace.

"You will like this one, I think," she said, preceding him through the door to the private lounge.

Morticai Kant and his security entourage were already engaged in conversation after departing the plane while Tyce and Essie remained behind to gather their on-board items.

The Israeli turned toward them when they approached.

"See who is here!" Kant put a hand on an older man whom Tyce had been unable to see clearly until Kant presented him.

"Dr. Faust!"

Tyce moved to shake Randolph Faust's hand, then give him a brief hug.

"How long has it been?" Tyce asked, genuinely pleased to see the old archeologist.

"More than two years, I think," Faust said.

"You look younger now than in Jerusalem those years ago," Tyce said, honest in his assessment.

"The Lord is good," Faust said, enjoying the compliment.

"Dr. Faust has agreed to join us in…this…mission," Kant said.

"Let us move to more hospitable arrangements," the Israeli said, prompting the six security men, led by Ehud Begin, to exit the door leading to the parking ramp and the vehicles awaiting them.

The two dark-gray sedans, followed by a large van carrying some of the security men, drove from the aircraft parking ramp and minutes later moved along a three-lane highway toward the hotel.

"The Euphrates artifact is a matter I couldn't resist," Faust said, answering Tyce's question about the reason for his coming to Israel.

"That, and there are things you and I have to look into together," he said, reaching across Essie to pat the journalist's left knee, while the car whisked them toward downtown Tel Aviv.

Essie listened from her seat between them, while her father sat in the front seat beside the security man who drove the car.

"Did you tell our young friend why he was chosen by the Mossad to undertake this mission?"

Kant half turned to be heard above the road noises. "No, no, I haven't had a chance to tell him, Morty," the archeologist said.

"How much do you know about your getting asked into the project?" Faust said, looking at Tyce.

"Really, not much more than what Essie told me. That you had recommended me for the job to her father."

"And when did you first have these visions? When did they start occurring?" Faust asked.

"The night of the accident. At least, I guess it was a vision—that winged thing in my windshield." Tyce shifted restlessly, the remembrance stirring him to recall more. "But the first really strange one was when in a hotel in DC. I was looking out a window and I was suddenly in a scene of a couple of these winged creatures. They were fighting with swords, supernatural swords, like I told you when we talked before."

"What makes you say they were supernatural?"

"Because they would strike and wound the creatures, but in the next second, the wound would heal, and it was as if there had been no injury." Tyce reflected for several seconds before speaking in a tone of incredulity. "I guess it was more like the creatures were supernatural, rather than their swords. They were immortal, I guess."

"Then you had the visions involving the plot against Israel?" Faust probed.

"Oh, Morticai told you about those," Tyce said, surprised. "Yes. It was like I was standing in the room with them—the guys I saw and heard. Only, they couldn't see me. They were plotting an attack in the first…vision. I still can't say that word—*vision*—without feeling weird, Dr. Faust. But that's the only word that can express the experience."

"It's a good word, a biblical word—and, it was a vision, I have no doubt," the archeologist said.

"The second time I was in a place I sensed was the

Kremlin. Three men were discussing how the energy supplying Europe was at stake for Russia. That was what I took from...that meeting."

"Strange," Faust said to himself.

"And, then the text message came on my phone while I was trying to think of that Zechariah Scripture about Israel becoming—what was it, Morticai?"

"A cup of trembling and a burdensome stone," Kant said from the front seat.

"Yeah, that Israel would become a cup of trembling and burdensome stone to all nations of the world at the end of days," Tyce said.

"Yes, Zechariah 12:1–3," Faust said.

"That message appeared on my phone just at the time I was searching for the verse in my mind. It was signed 'Michael'—'M-i-y-k a-'e-l. Morticai said that's the Hebrew spelling of the name of Michael the archangel."

Faust said nothing, his thoughts obviously analyzing Tyce's revelation.

"Then there was the...vision...of the president and this old man in the Oval Office," went on.

"Yes, Morticai told me," Faust said, his voice inflecting puzzlement.

"What do you think it means, Dr. Faust?" Essie asked, seeing the archeologist in deep concentration.

"I don't know, Essie," he said quietly. "But I'm sure we will soon be shown."

MORTICAI KANT'S brow was more wrinkled than usual, his serious expression presaging his words.

"The Islamic State wild asses are advancing toward Jordan," he said, after walking from the room where he had been talking with someone in Jerusalem. "The prime minister will not allow this to go much farther."

Several of Kant's men came from the room, carrying large and small bags.

"I must meet with the government in Jerusalem. We must leave immediately," he said, turning to his daughter. "Your things are still in their cases?"

She said nothing, her facial expression not the one of willingness to comply he was used to seeing.

"Something wrong, sweetheart?" he said, touching Essie's arm.

"Is it necessary that I accompany you, Abba?"

The father's instinct picked up on her nuance of meaning. He glanced at Tyce Greyson, then at Essie. "No —no. You may stay for now if you wish."

"There are others who can assist," she offered, her words as much an assurance to herself as to her father.

"Yes…Luha will be there to help," he said, speaking of one of his closest administrative assistants in his Jerusalem office.

Essie turned to Tyce. "I am interested in the sarcophagus and would like to learn more, if you will allow me to join you in your examination of the artifact," she said, trying to sound professional with her request.

Tyce was hopeful the reason for her staying by his side was much more personal.

"TOMORROW WILL BE a career-culminating event for me, Tyce."

Randolph Faust sipped on the demitasse cup of herbal tea Essie had moments before handed him. Finally, they were together in a private setting where they could discuss things. The old archeologist professor had much to say, and the journalist student, Tyce Greyson, was all ears.

Kant had seen to it that Faust and Greyson, along with Essie, Ehud Begin, and two other security men, were quartered in the safest possible government housing available for the days they would spend exploring the project dealing with the Euphrates artifact. The next day would bring them to an up-close inspection of what had been dug up in 2003, then was sequestered out of sight and mind of most until the science for examining the contents had progressed to the level it had now reached.

Faust and Greyson relaxed in big, leather recliners in an inner sanctum of one of the massive, concrete-and-steel Israeli government buildings. Both were anxious to explore the strangeness of what had brought them together.

"To begin," Faust said, setting the small cup on the stand beside the recliner, "the things that transpired in Patmos, they are key in trying to grasp things happening to you, Tyce."

The journalist leaned forward in the chair, giving full attention to Faust's words.

"Especially the vivid visions of the prophetic matters, the years when you had the hellish dreams of the destruction of Damascus and the vanishings."

"This is all part of things going on now?" Tyce asked, surprised at Faust's assessment.

"This was—and is—a spiritual battle. This is Ephesians, chapter 6, on steroids."

"What's the connection?" The journalist's curiosity overcame the surprise revelation, and his words cut the air with laser crispness.

"The spiritual battle...the struggle against the 'principalities and powers in the high places' mentioned in Ephesians 6...goes to the very heart of what is transpiring at present. They—the visions—revolve around the nation of Israel—or, I should say, the rebirth of that nation."

"Yes. I'm somewhat familiar with the end-times prophecies as they relate to Israel. But...but what do these things have to do with the visions I'm having now?"

"I don't know exactly, Tyce," Faust said, a distant look in his eyes while thinking on the question. "That's what we have to find out. I think looking at this sarcophagus, looking at the project and all it entails, has something to do with the answers to all of this."

"Why do you think so?"

The archeologist took time to sip the tea again before answering.

"Have you read or heard the prophecy in the book of Joel?" Faust asked, setting the empty cup again in its saucer on the table.

"I don't know. What is it?"

"Joel 2, verse 28, says: 'And it shall come to pass afterward, that I will pour out my spirit upon all flesh; and your sons and your daughters shall prophesy, your old men shall dream dreams, your young men shall see visions.'"

Tyce let the verse ramble in his thoughts before speaking. "When, and who is this prophecy talking about?" He didn't remember the verse.

"It's a prophecy about God sending dreams and visions to the people of Israel. The Jews. Some believe it is for the era that will be the Millennium, the thousand-year reign of Jesus Christ. Others believe it's for the Jews

—God's chosen people—during the time of Tribulation...Daniel's seventieth week. Still others, like me, believe it's a prophecy for the last days, and will become more pronounced the closer we get to the return of Christ."

"You are saying this applies to you and me—we're part of this prophecy? I'm not a Jew...well, not in the purest sense. My dad's grandfather was Jewish. But, other than that, there's no Jewish blood I know of."

"And, I have a Jewish grandmother, and no other tie genetically to the Hebrews," Faust said.

"But that qualifies us to have these...dreams and visions?" Tyce asked, another question coming to mind. "I guess you're the old man between the two of us. Have you had any dreams?"

"That's what I wanted to talk to you about, Tyce. I believe that having those Jewish ties for both of us does 'qualify us', as you put it, for fitting within that prophecy." Faust sat forward in the recliner to make his points with fingertip-to-fingertip gesticulations while he talked.

"First, we know about your...strange visions, even dreams...going back to your childhood, and now the visions of these flying, winged creatures above Jerusalem. The inexplicable appearance of this stranger you call Michael—who apparently uses the Hebrew spelling of his name. Then, the visions of the plot against Israel...the Oval Office vision."

Faust paused to more intensely prepare to make his points.

"Second, I've had *dreams* of the Temple Mount in Jerusalem...of Moriah, dreams that I remember vividly, unlike normal dreams that fade within hours or days at most. These are about the children, the white-haired, blue-eyed children seeming to float in some sort of clear, viscous liquid above the Temple Mount…the children strange, smoke-like beings told me were Nephals—Nephilim—the products of hybrid genetic intervention—"

"—I remember your saying those beings informed you that the children were the products of both human DNA," Tyce interrupted, the memories flooding back of the old archeologist telling him the surreal events of that time that seemed now part of a strange dream.

"Yes. Human DNA was extracted and mixed somehow with demonic, supernatural genetic material to create the Nephilim children. It was the same sort of things that happened in the Genesis six account, when the sons of God, the fallen angels, took human women and the Nephilim, the giants of legend and folklore, were born upon earth. Only today, the creation of these 'transhumans', as science would have it, is done not through sexual intercourse, but through laboratory experimentation and manipulation."

Both men sat in silence, letting the facts Faust had laid out sink in.

"These are the dreams I was given those years ago," Faust said. "Then, I more recently vividly saw in dreams the things you went through…your visions…while in your serpent bite-induced coma."

"When did you have these dreams?"

"It was, I'm told, on the very night you had the accident on the road in Maryland."

"And you contacted me after that?" Tyce asked. "You were prompted in the dreams to contact me?"

"Yes. The voice of the Lord? I don't know. Maybe of one of His Heaven-sent representatives—an angel. I just don't know. The voice said I was to contact you, that you were to have a special purpose in—the way it was put— you are to serve a special purpose in these final things."

An hour later, with Randolph Faust retired for the night, Tyce walked onto the veranda overlooking the city. He marveled silently at the magnificence of the night sky, despite the lights of Tel Aviv. The city's illumination did nothing to dim the brilliant points of the stars against the blue-black, velvet canopy of space. He drew the crisp, evening air into his lungs, cerebrally patting himself on the back for having given up cigarettes more than five years ago. His devotion to a healthier lifestyle was paying off, and he had a right to be proud.

"What are your thoughts?" Essie's voice startled him. He turned slightly to take her arm and pull her gently to himself when she reached to touch him. She moved compliantly to his side and rested her face against his arm. He put the arm around her, to warm her against the chill of the night air.

"Thanks for staying rather than going to Jerusalem," he said. "I know that would have been an exciting time… to be with the prime minister and all those intrigues." He tightened his warming embrace around her shoulders.

"Learning about the sarcophagus will be exciting, too," she said, laying her face against him, while they both overlooked the lights of the city and the spectacular night sky.

"Oh, yeah. Getting to look at a four-thousand-year-old dead guy can be exciting, no doubt about it."

"I think it's quite exciting. Just not knowing what is in the burial chamber is intriguing, don't you think?" She continued when he said nothing. "Have they said what is in the sarcophagus?"

"They haven't told me. Your father must know. Hasn't he said something about the contents?"

"My father is Maglan, the most secretive of IDF clandestine services. He has told me nothing much of the project."

"Then, it must be very closely held, the contents of that artifact."

"He tells me very little about any of his work," she said with what Tyce perceived as a slight sigh of resignation.

"Oh? He holds you close, it seems to me. He takes you with him when he travels."

"He is paranoid about the attempts to take me. He says I'm his number-one associate, but he really is determined to never have an attempt like in the past. He just wants to make sure I'm secure and keeps me with him except in his most secretive meetings in matters involving Maglan."

"He let you stay while he went to his Jerusalem meetings," Tyce said.

"But he left his top three security men to guard me," she said.

"Oh? I thought they were looking after yours truly. Boy, was I having delusions of grandeur?"

Essie laughed, hugging and patting him. "You certainly come under my umbrella."

An uncomfortable moment passed between them before Tyce spoke again. "There's been rumors for a lot of years among the news community…that the sarcophagus dug up from the ancient Euphrates riverbed back in 2003 is the burial vault of Gilgamesh the earliest ruler of that region. He—so the story goes—was among the first to rule the region some centuries after the biblical Flood, Noah's Flood."

"And do you think that is possible?" Essie asked,

looking up at Tyce while he stared into the Tel Aviv night.

"Anything is possible, I guess," he said. "They've kept this thing so hidden from view that there's no knowing what they've made of it. I don't know why they are just now bringing it out for show and tell, even if to just a few people. Guess we'll find out something tomorrow."

"Tyce." Essie's voice was a whisper, and he could tell a question involving something important to her was on the way. "Was…Marial…beautiful?"

"Very," he said, without looking down at her.

"I know you loved her very much."

"Yes…I did," he said quietly.

"Do you think you…might ever…" She let the thought die.

"Might I what?" Tyce asked, looking into her eyes just before she looked away. "Ask me anything. Don't be shy."

"Do you think you could ever love someone again like you loved Marial?" She asked her question with more resolve in her voice.

He turned to look at her, into the lovely face, whose eyes reflected the brilliant, star-specked night sky. He kissed her deeply, and their lingering moment of passionate embrace gave her the answer she had prayed for without the need for words.

"RANDY!"

Harnak al Mufi, smiling broadly, thrust his hand out to take that of Randolph Faust. The men embraced and Faust turned to introduce Tyce Greyson.

"Ah, yes. I have met Mr. Greyson," the Egyptian said, taking Tyce's offered hand.

"And it is so good to see you once more, Essie," he said, hugging her warmly.

"Mr. Greyson and I met while at the institute in Bethesda," al Mufi said, turning to lead the three new arrivals deeper into the building.

"This laboratory is not unlike the previous you visited," he said, addressing the journalist. "However, on this occasion you will find we can be much more forthcoming regarding the Euphrates artifact and the project."

"I hope that means I'll get to see what's in the sarcophagus," Tyce said.

"Absolutely. We will see all momentarily," the Egyptian said, standing to one side to allow the three to pass through the large door. He walked to a table near one wall of the semi-darkened room, pressed a button on a table, and spoke into an intercom microphone. "Please—may we have some assistance in LC66?"

He pushed another button and the wall slid apart, revealing a large room even darker than the one before. "We must keep the lighting as subdued as possible, as you know, Dr. Faust. To prevent deterioration is always of the essence."

"How have the contents held up?" Faust said, while they approached the huge, golden sarcophagus sitting atop a three-foot-high platform of what looked to be made of solid concrete.

"We have not seen any apparent deterioration."

"Is this thing made of solid gold?" Tyce asked, amazed at the size and polished brilliance of the massive burial chamber.

"It is gold overlaid upon a composite structure of wood, indigenous asphalt, and other material. We are not certain of its precise makeup," al Mufi said.

"It's beautiful in its own way," Essie said, moving

closer to see the ornate engraving along the edge of the top nearest them.

"Yes. There was much care involved by the ancients in preparing this chamber," al Mufi said, bidding with his hand for the three lab-coated men who had just entered the room to step forward. Two of the men moved to each end of the sarcophagus and the third stood at the center. They lifted together, having to strain to move the lid until it rested against the back wall.

A dark-gray covering lay across the open vault, and the Egyptian moved in to remove it from right to left.

"Behold Gilgamesh!"

Al Mufi's exclamation seemed appropriately spoken as the contents were unveiled. Only Essie's slight gasp of amazement broke the silent astonishment of the three who were for the first time seeing the figure lying face-up in the sarcophagus.

The mummy was a smudged gray color in its overall appearance. Occasional dark, greenish tints of various gradations covered the surface. The head, considerably more than twice the size of a man's, bore distinctive facial characteristics, the large, slightly curved nose ending at a sharp point just above the definitive mouth formed by the tightly pressed-together lips.

The thick, swept-back hair was clearly discernable, despite the substance covering its surface. The hair streamed over part of the upper-left ear. The giant looked as if he were merely asleep.

Tyce thought how he had never seen such a mummy. Its state of near-perfect preservation most likely could be credited to the substance used rather than use of bandages like on mummies of Egypt.

"How long does the being measure?" Randolph Faust

asked, moving close to the figure's head and looking it over carefully.

"Just over four meters," al Mufi said.

"More than twelve feet?"

Tyce stepped to beside Faust, looking into the vault and following the legs to the end, where the mummified feet looked to be more than twice the length of ordinary, human, male feet.

"The substance covering the mummy—how thick is it?"

"About three centimeters, no more," al Mufi said in answer to Faust's question.

"You mean there are no bandages? There's a substance of some sort."

"It is a substance found from ancient times," al Mufi said. "The best way it can be described is that it is an asphalt-like material."

"It's the slime of the plain of Shinar referred to in Genesis chapter eleven, Tyce," Randolph Faust said, bending near the gigantic corpse's face. "It's the substance that was used to build the ziggurat—the Tower of Babel."

"Then, it is true—giants existed in ancient days," Essie said quietly, as if speaking to herself while trying to take in the immensity of the being before them.

Faust held a large, square-shaped magnifying glass by its handle, going over the left side of the face and neck. "This one is much larger than the biblical description of Goliath," he said. "He was just over nine feet tall. This fellow was more than twelve."

"Are you sure it's not some kind of a created figure of a man?" Tyce asked al Mufi, who looked at the giant with a magnifying glass similar to that used by Faust.

"It's no fake," Faust said, putting the glass to within

two inches of the figure's tightly shut eyelids. "They've proven that by numerous lab tests."

"That is correct," al Mufi said. "There have been many thorough genetic tests done."

"What kinds of tests?" Tyce asked, moving closer to look at the immense fingers of the giant's hands clasped across the abdominal area.

"Cellular tests...DNA. We have technology today that has never been available before to study the genetic makeup. It has proven most provocative in the case of this being."

Tyce considered the Egyptian's answer for several seconds, his reporter's mind going into hyperdrive.

"You, Randy—you, too have called this thing a 'being'. You haven't once referred to it as a man. Why not?"

Both men looked at each other, taking their magnifying glasses away from examining the artifact. They straightened and turned to look at Tyce, then glanced at each other again.

"That's very observant," Faust said. "You want to tell him, Dr. al Mufi?"

Harnak al Mufi's facial expression took on a look of concentration while he thought how best to explain. "You are familiar with DNA?" he said to Tyce.

"Yes, basically," Tyce said. "They are able to get precise genetic identification on rapists and do IDs on bodies through DNA testing."

"Forensics are now moving at fantastic speed," the Egyptian scientist said, nodding agreement. "Until this moment in time, we thought there was no living or dead being with any DNA that could be found that could not be identified and thoroughly defined."

His face twisted into a frown of consternation. "But, with our large friend, here, it is a stopping point."

"What do you mean?" Tyce said, when al Mufi paused longer than his curiosity could stand.

"It means that we cannot identify this particular DNA," al Mufi said. "There is none to which to compare it. The genetic material taken from this being is not purely human."

"What do you mean 'purely'?"

"Part of the DNA is human, but the other we cannot identify. It is totally new to us."

"What does all that mean?" Essie's question caused the Egyptian to turn to face her, his face again in a frowning expression of concentration.

"Although we have only begun to explore, this…finding…does seem to give some credence to the contention of some within the scientific community that humanity was somehow placed here by extraterrestrials. Although, like I said, we have only begun to investigate."

Tyce looked at Randolph Faust, who returned his questioning regard.

"We will have to discuss this matter, Tyce. For now, let's just think on it for a bit."

"You can believe I will be thinking on it," the reporter said, moving close to the sarcophagus again to look more closely at the sleeping giant. "This will be a fascinating writing project," he then said quietly to himself as Essie moved to his side.

"Do you think this might mean there is some truth to things they have been saying regarding ancient astronauts?" she asked, feeling somewhat reluctant to get as close as Tyce, who used the magnifying glass he had borrowed from Faust a minute earlier. "You know that they came and seeded the earth with human populations?"

"It has something to do with something…*ancient.* I'm

certain about that." Tyce straightened from his close inspection of the being's face, while continuing to intensely peer at the massive head. "I sense it's not from some other planet, though."

"Genesis, chapter 6," Faust said, moving to stand beside them. "Is that what you're thinking, Tyce?"

Tyce said nothing, turning to again look closely at the greenish-hued corpse's face.

"What about Genesis 6?" Essie looked toward Faust for understanding.

"That's where we read that the sons of God had sexual relations with the daughters of men," Faust said. "There were giants born of those unions. Mankind gets some of the legends of the ancient gods from those days before the Great Flood of Noah's time—you know, Zeus, Hercules...all of those gods and demigods."

Essie considered Faust's words. "Then, you are saying this...giant—" she gestured toward the sarcophagus, "—is such a creature, the result of those sexual unions?"

Tyce turned from his examination of the being to face Randolph Faust. "Is that what you think, Randy?" he said, his tone tinged with skepticism.

"Well, it is a real, once-living being. It isn't a fake of any sort. It's over twelve feet in height—probably six, seven hundred pounds at a minimum. Do you have a better explanation?"

Tyce grinned, seeing the professor's questioning of the student in Faust's stern gaze. "No, sir, I certainly don't."

"THE CAR IS WAITING." Essie's call to Tyce from the adjacent room broke his concentration on the being before him only slightly.

"Yes, yes. Be there in a second," the journalist said, gazing intensely at the face that seemed not at rest, but in troubled sleep.

The dark-greenish preservative material added to the look of tension projecting from the wrinkled brow above the clinched eyes. Although frozen in death, the ancient being seemed to emit secrets of life beyond life while Tyce was unable to resist being drawn ever deeper into the giant's state of repose.

Momentarily, Tyce found himself immersed within darkness, from which burst a single point of light that grew to illuminate a scene before his astonished senses. He stood in his mesmerized state upon a vast, sand-packed plain. There materialized at the plain's center a rounded, tapering ziggurat. To its outermost walls were attached road-like ramps that spiraled around its surface to the structure's top. Atop the ziggurat was a figure of a man. His hands were lifted to the heavens, his arms fully extended.

In the next instant, the ziggurat began changing, transitioning into a large, modern building. Tyce recognized the familiar structure as the United Nations building. The figure became larger in his view until it was as if he was standing in front of the man-being, staring at his upturned face.

It was the giant! The being in the sarcophagus!

The creature stood atop the UN building. It was alive and looking upward into the sun, its eyes solid, white orbs.

The gigantic face then lowered to look directly at

Tyce Greyson, the being's eyes turning into glistening pools of black, fathomless intelligence.

The creature's massive arms and hands lowered to point directly at him, and he felt a mighty suction drawing him toward the massive building—toward the gargantuan man-beast.

He knew he should—but could not—resist. He must not be drawn to it; he must break free of the painful, immensely powerful tug.

Suddenly, a burst of brilliant light blinded him, obscuring all but the gigantic, winged creature, whose piercing, all-encompassing gaze broke the spell of the man-being's magnetic strength.

The winged creature's very aura seemed to engulf him in warm assurance. It gently placed him again upon the sand-strewn plain. The UN structure changed again into the ancient ziggurat, which diminished in size until it vanished completely.

"Tyce!" Essie's voice repeated his name as she tugged at his arms and looked into his eyes. "Tyce!"

He realized that he again stood in the room with the sarcophagus, Essie trying to pull him back from the things he had just witnessed.

"Tyce—are you okay?"

"Yes," he said, "I think so." He blinked, feeling his strength and consciousness return. "Another of the… trips…into la-la land," he said through the haze of returning awareness, knowing she wanted an explanation. "Wow!" he said, before pulling Essie to himself for assurance that he was again in the presence of the one who meant the most to him.

CHAPTER 6

Tyce pulled slowly on the steaming first cup of coffee of the morning. He had slept well—probably, he considered, the result of the fatigue he felt following the vision he had been a part of the evening before.

The giant man-being still stood at the center of his remembrance while he watched the news footage on the television screen. A network correspondent narrated while the view from above presented the smoldering complex.

A knock at his room's door drew his attention from the screen.

"You are watching it," Essie said, having opened the door and peeked in. "We were successful, thanks to you," she added with delight in her voice.

"Successful at what? What did I do?" Tyce stood to meet her, and they embraced.

"Haven't you seen what's going on?" She gestured toward the screen.

"I just took my first sip of coffee," he said. "Just turned on the TV."

"The complex of buildings that are burning. Those are the result of you telling Morticai about what you witnessed in your vision."

"How did they know where—who—to attack? I didn't give them any details."

"They are Maglan," she said. "They have ways of finding out. Those who were at the center of the plotting have been, as Morticai put it, decapitated."

"Well, that's fitting, considering the method these murderers use to terrorize the world."

Tyce watched while the helicopter shots of the burning complex of buildings below filled the screen. His eyes widened and his mouth gaped when the scene changed to a room full of milling men and women, with an Israeli spokesman stepping toward a battery of microphones.

Among the people in the crowded room stood the tall, familiar young man, looking not at the proceedings in the room, but into the camera. His eyes seemed to pierce to the core of Tyce Greyson's cognitive process.

"What's wrong? What do you see?" Essie said, seeing the stupefied look on his face.

"It's him," Tyce said.

"Who?"

"It's Michael."

Essie looked intensively at the crowd, trying to see the object of Tyce's amazed attention.

"He's the tallest. There—the guy in the navy suit," he said, pointing at the screen.

"I see no such individual," Essie said, earnestly searching the crowd.

The screen changed to a close-up of the microphones as the Israeli spokesman stepped in front of the centermost mic. He spoke in accented English, wasting no time in getting to the purpose of the hastily arranged briefing.

"Today, the Israeli Defense Force has interdicted a plot to attack Mecca and Medina. This was to be an action that would place blame on Israel for the destruction of Islam's most revered sites. The Saudi government is aware of the true plotters who intended to destroy these sites and was aware of and approved of the IDF's action to prevent those attacks."

The dumbfounded journalist continued to search among the people gathered in the room of the press briefing when the cameras showed a wide shot of the milling newsmen and women.

"He's not there. Can you see him?" Tyce spoke without looking at Essie. "He's not there, now."

"The Lord works in mysterious ways," Randolph Faust said after knocking lightly on the door, then entering Tyce's room. "We are in strange times, my friend." He walked to stand and watch the screen.

The Israeli spokesman said, in answer to a question from a reporter, "We have no confirmation that any perpetrators other than a group of radical Islamist terrorists were at the center of the plot."

"Well, I guess it's okay to lie just a little bit when you're dealing with the world press and other Israel-haters," Essie said lightly.

"He didn't lie," Tyce said. "He said that it hasn't been 'confirmed' that any other group was involved. He didn't say that no one other than the Islamist terrorists were involved."

"Just amazing!" Faust said, watching the screen change again to the image of the smoldering carnage the

IDF jet fighter-bombers had inflicted less than an hour earlier.

"I guess that was the real reason Morticai left so suddenly for Jerusalem," Essie said.

"It wasn't because the ISIS forces were moving toward Jordan?"

She thought on Tyce's question a moment before conjecturing. "Perhaps, but I believe this was his primary reason for the hurried trip. This matter was more pressing, I imagine."

"There's been nothing on any news I can find on the Internet about the Islamic State trying to move into Jordan," Faust said. "Morticai's reason for the hasty trip must've been this preemptive strike against the plotters."

"Probably, they determined this plot was very close to being put into action," Essie put in.

"If the Russians are so serious in this plot to implicate Israel, using nukes to take out Mecca and Medina, things are at the point that they can't be controlled, even by the preemptive planning by the likes of Israel's intelligence services."

"That's probably very accurate, Tyce," Faust said. "And that's exactly why I believe you and I are experiencing the prophetic implementation of Joel 2:28—old men dreaming dreams, and young men having visions."

"What do you mean?" Essie asked.

"I mean that because of interference by the powers and principalities in high places, the struggle not against flesh and blood, but against those supernatural influences that are ratcheting up their nefarious evil, the Lord is unleashing—in equal and opposite reaction—His own supernatural intervention."

They turned their eyes toward the screen again when it projected the president of the United States walking quickly to the podium that displayed the presidential seal.

The president waited for the rustle of the reporters and the camera clicking to subside before beginning to speak, looking first to the right teleprompter, then to the left while he spoke.

"The actions by Israel today are considered by most within the international community as being somewhat too harsh in the collateral damage done by the Israeli Air Force. A number of innocents, civilians, were killed and injured. However, the sparing of the holy places of Mecca and Medina, which were to be targets of these rogue agents of loosely knitted insurgents, served to at least avert a wider conflict, in the opinion of this government. We, therefore, because of the more immediate presence of Israeli military assets, gave permission, in concert with permission by the international community and by the government of Saudi Arabia...for Israel to debilitate the center of the plot to strike Mecca and Medina."

"'Loosely knitted insurgents.' Now, that," Essie said, "is every bit most definitely a lie."

"You think the United States had little to do with the decision to hit the plotters?" Randolph Faust asked.

"Absolutely," Essie answered. "The Israeli government hasn't trusted this American president with anything of importance for many months. For almost the full eight years, really. Why should we trust them? They consistently take the side of our enemies. They spit in our faces at every opportunity."

"I don't have to be convinced," Tyce said. "The... whatever I'm having...the vision I had when I witnessed the president and the old guy talking in the Oval Office is proven true by what we just saw."

"You still have the American people," Faust said, looking into Essie's eyes. "A majority of our people still support Israel. Many millions feel a strong kinship. And this presidency will be ended within a short time. There's always hope for a friendlier administration," he said.

"And that's why the pretense will continue," Essie said. "We will continue to pretend that this president isn't doing all within his power to bring us under the drive toward establishing the desired Islamist Khalifa."

Tyce watched the beautiful face in its—to him—unseen-before expression. This was a woman of depth of understanding in matters of geopolitics. Her father had chosen well his assistant; he hadn't just brought her on board for reasons involving nepotism.

"Tyce, you are wanted on the phone," Ehud Begin called from the doorway. "Jerusalem is calling. Mr. Kant."

Moments later, Tyce picked up the receiver, standing over the end table. He seated himself on the sofa while answering.

"Tyce Greyson here."

"Ah, Tyce! How are things in Tel Aviv?" Morticai's voice had an upbeat intonation.

"Everything here seems good."

"And my daughter?"

"Essie's fine. We were just talking."

"Wonderful! Wonderful!" Kant said. "Did you hear about the strike?"

"How could I not?" Tyce said. "That's the big news."

"This is a direct result of your...intelligence." The Israeli emphasized the last word.

"Is that what you're calling it? My brain glitches are bouts of 'intelligence'," Tyce said with a chuckle.

"All I know, or care about, is that information we

gathered from your 'intelligence' helped us complete this most-important mission."

"Then, I accept your word 'intelligence' as the operative one."

"Good! Good! And now a new assignment," Kant said. "We need you to accompany the artifact back to its place of origin. The Iraqi government wants it returned. However, the scientific team will be allowed to accompany the sarcophagus to Babylon."

"To Babylon? Not Baghdad?"

"To Babylon. That is where the museum has been built to house the artifact, and where all scientific matters—experimentation and so forth—are to be conducted. You will produce your writing project from very near the spot the artifact was extracted. It is the cradle of civilization, after all, you know?"

"I've never been to Babylon," Tyce said. "Sounds exciting."

"You will have very nice quarters, the Israeli said. "The Iraqi government people are quite interested, for purposes of tourism, that the publicity be handled exactly right…and by professionals."

"And what about the other part of my assignment? The part you're really interested in?"

"We don't discuss these matters by phone, secure though it is."

"Okay," Tyce said. "But there is something you need to know."

"Oh? And what is that?"

"I had another vision."

"About the artifact—the mummy—you mean?"

Tyce was surprised at Kant's words.

"How did you know? I haven't had time to tell anyone except Essie. Have you talked with her?"

"We have our ways, my young friend. We are Maglan."

~

"I AM NOT COMING to Jerusalem. I am going with him."

Essie's voice cut the air in near anger. She listened to what was being said on the other end of the line.

Tyce stood in the partially opened door to her bedroom, seeing her with the phone pressed against her ear.

"Then, assign someone to accompany me. I know you are sending Ehud and a couple of others—"

She was interrupted by the voice on the other end, before responding.

"Morticai. I am going to Iraq with him, and there's no talking me out of it. It will be okay. I will be protected."

Tyce opened the door a bit wider and placed the suitcase he was holding against the partially opened door.

"We are about to leave for the airport. We will stay in close contact while I'm there. I must go." She listened while cutting her eyes at Tyce, whom she now realized was in the room. She said something in Hebrew, then listened more before again speaking. "Yes, Abba. Yes, Abba, I will. I love you, Papa. I have to go."

"Are we about ready?" asked Essie, fiddling with her earring. She glanced at Tyce, then moved quickly to the open suitcase on the bed.

"You're really going with us?" he asked, walking to the bed, watching her hurriedly tuck some items of clothing in the bag.

"Yes," she said, buckling the straps across the packed clothing.

"Essie, I heard. Morticai doesn't want you to go."

"I'm not going to have trouble with you, too," she said in an irritated but calm tone. "I am going, so you might as well accept it."

"I understand his concern," Tyce said. "It won't be like we are in America or Israel. We will be in enemy territory, with ISIS or who knows who all over the place."

"Then I'll carry my Walther with me at all times," Essie said matter of factly, pinching her other earring in place and shutting the suitcase.

Tyce laughed, putting his hands on her shoulders and gently twisting her to face him. "You are really a work, you know it, Essie Jorba, or Essie Kant, or whatever your name is." Her expression had dissolved into gentle affirmation. He pressed his lips against hers, and she submitted unreservedly to his embrace, their lingering kiss sealing their determination that nothing, not even the head of Maglan, could ever separate them again.

LESS THAN TWO HOURS LATER, the Gulfstream 5 climbed out of Tel Aviv for the brief flight to Baghdad. The cloudless, bright sky hinted that the trip would be without turbulence—of the weather kind. However, trouble of the other sort always was possible when traversing air space in the region, and Morticai Kant had done all within his power to see to it that the G5 would have a clear air pathway into the much-troubled environs of Iraq.

A single Mirage fighter shadowed the Gulfstream not far off the bird's right wing. Tyce Greyson watched the powerful machine stay just above the G5, without so much as a wing dipping slightly, the bright blue Star of

David dominating the surface of the fighter's vertical stabilizer.

"He will have to break off relatively soon," Randolph Faust said from his seat across the narrow isle. "An Israeli jet fighter isn't welcome in Iraqi air space."

"Yes, but Morticai will have arranged for someone to pick up the escort," Essie said, admiring the beautiful Israeli fighter out the porthole to her right.

"There must be some working relationship between the IDF and the Iraqis, then," Tyce said.

"Oh, yes. Since the time of Saddam's overthrow, they have found common ground for…cooperation," Essie said. "The relationship is not particularly friendly as in the case of Israeli-American relations. But there has been a very dependable working relationship between the IDF and the new Iraqi defense force. The ISIS matter has as of late caused worry, though. There is fear that some within Iraq's newest regime will defect to ISIS and eventually erode security that has been developed."

"Let's hope that doesn't happen while we're there," Tyce quipped, watching the Israeli fighter's swept-back wing tilt upward and the bird turn right, leaving its position of guardianship. On cue, another fighter momentarily took its place in the position the Mirage had occupied. It displayed the symbol and colors of the Iraqi Air Force.

"We have a new escort," Tyce said, then turned to Essie. "Who's flying our plane?"

He considered how he hadn't seen the crew, the cockpit door being closed and the aircraft's engines already running and ready to move toward the end of the runway when they had hurriedly come aboard and the cabin door had been shut. "Are they IDF, civilian, or what?"

"I really don't know," Essie said. "I suppose Morticai assigned pilots from one of his agencies of responsibility."

"Whoever they are, they seem to know their business," Randolph Faust put in, lightly. "As long as they give us a landing to walk away from, they get my vote."

"Well, I hope they know their stuff," Tyce said, eyeing what looked like a black thunderhead a number of miles in the distance. "It looks like some dark skies are building to the right. Looks like we might be heading into some rough going."

The G5 closed in quickly on the towering thunderhead, causing the archeologist to conjecture, "He's not trying to climb above it, so it must not be anything much to worry about."

"Our new escort seems to be missing," Tyce said, ducking slightly to peer upward through the top of the porthole.

"Thunderstorms the size of that one are rare in this part of the world. That looks more like the kind we get in the spring in south Texas," Faust said.

"I guess the Iraqi pilot took another route or something," Tyce said, still looking for the missing escort.

"He is just separating from our immediate vicinity," Ehud Begin said from the seat behind. "There must be considerable space between us and him to avoid collision in case of turbulence."

"Of course," Tyce said. "Makes sense…"

Suddenly they were within the boiling storm, the Gulfstream encountering the buffeting winds. The jet hit pockets that slammed it violently into deep troughs. The wings of the small aircraft disappeared into the swirling clouds and reappeared as it tilted spastically in the storm's powerful throes.

Tyce concentrated, straining to see, just beyond the wingtip, a black, swirling mass from which ejected brilliant shards of lightning that thrust wickedly at the aircraft. It materialized, then, into an enormous, winged manifestation of black, outlined and energized by a sparking arc of lightning. This was a creature of immense size, its white-hot eyes blazing, its gigantic wings spread as it swung—with clinched, fist-like talons —a huge sword of radiant effulgence toward the wing just outside the porthole.

Tyce was dumbstruck, unable to take his mesmerized gaze from the sight before him.

The Gulfstream's right wing dipped instantly, taking the cabin in a severe roll to the right. The plane continued to roll until it was inverted, then shook violently when it nosed over and began a plunge toward earth.

The jet spiraled out of control, the G-forces tightening his neck and his body while the plane twisted ever downward toward the Middle Eastern desert. The craft would hit the earth at any moment. Tyce clinched his eyelids shut, readying to absorb the inevitable impact.

"Tyce!"

The voice caused him to open his eyes, his reeling mind returning to full realization that someone was calling his name.

"Tyce!" Essie pulled at his left arm, trying to bring him back from his transfixed state.

"What's wrong?" she asked, continuing to tug at him.

He looked around the cabin, seeing that all eyes were upon him while he tried to get his bearings.

"Where were you that time?" Essie said, reaching to touch his cheek.

"We were about to crash, weren't we?" The stuporous glaze was still in his eyes as Essie looked into them.

"No," she said. "We weren't. It did get a little rough for a few minutes, but we went through it just fine."

"Another vision?" Randolph Faust said, standing over Essie to look past her at Tyce.

"I guess so...the plane was spiraling out of control, after this gigantic thing with massive wings struck the airplane with a weapon, a sword or something."

"The battle rages on," Faust said, using his thumbs to pull Tyce's bottom eyelids downward to examine him, seeing that his pupils were slightly dilated.

THE GULFSTREAM SAT DOWN GENTLY onto the Baghdad runway. Essie intertwined her slender fingers with Tyce's.

"So, this is the place Hussein ruled with a fist of terror," Tyce said, squeezing her hand gently.

"Now it is ISIS that will rule it with an even more horrible terror, if they have their way," Essie said.

"I'm amazed that hasn't already happened," Tyce said. "They've come as close as ten miles but haven't managed to come farther for more than a year. I'm amazed, because this president refuses to commit to opposing them, except with air strikes, even after all these months of ISIS constantly trying to advance. The limited US and coalition ground forces now in place have helped, I guess. Surrounding Iraqi forces aren't capable of stopping them, according to all reports I've gotten," Tyce concluded.

"It's a spiritual battle, and the resistance is spiritual," Randolph Faust said from across the aisle. "The Lord is in control. It's all winding down—or maybe that should be winding *up*, for the grand climax of the age."

"Bible prophecy," Essie said with resignation in her voice. "Jesus is coming…"

Faust ignored her mild tone of sarcasm. "He is coming, Essie. The signals are everywhere."

"So is ISIS," she retorted. "He had better hurry."

A minute later, they gathered their carry-on items from the storage bins above the seats. Essie, moving forward after Begin and his contingent of security men had departed, followed by Tyce and the others, shuffled to the front of the plane. Tyce, seeing the cockpit cabin door ajar, tugged on Essie's sleeve.

"Hold it. I want to tell these guys 'thanks'."

Tyce nudged the door open a few inches and peered in. The man in the left seat removed his earphones and turned to look at the passenger who stood at the door, and whose eyes widened in amazement.

"Michael" was the only word uttered in a barely audible tone.

The blond man in the captain's seat smiled brightly, his eyes meeting Tyce's in a moment of unspoken interaction.

"Tyce," Essie said, trying to look past him to see the reason for his apparent paralysis.

"It's Michael," he said, confusion showing on his face.

She looked at both men who had piloted the G5. "Who?"

Tyce looked again at the pilot in the left seat, who nodded in greeting. His hair was dark brown. It wasn't Michael.

∼

THE GLORY of the days of Nebuchadnezzar certainly were long gone. Tyce scanned the region ahead while he sat beside Essie, the van sent by the Antiquities Research Center bumping along a road badly in need of repaving. The undulant ripples in the brownish, sandy terrain showed no signs he could perceive as having millennia ago hosted the wonder of the world known as the Hanging Gardens of Babylon.

"I thought Saddam Hussein had been rebuilding Babylon," Tyce said.

"Desert Storm pretty much stopped all of that," Randolph Faust said from one of the rows of back seats in the rear of the van. "He had a factory that manufactured bricks to restore the old Babylonian area. It was a natural construction project. He was making the bricks out of all this sand, also using some of the asphalt material bubbling up naturally. He had his name stamped on one side of each brick and that of Nebuchadnezzar stamped on the other. Either Nebuchadnezzar's name… or Saladin's…I don't know which."

"There is much unfinished construction in the distance," the driver, a burnoosed Arab said, said in near-perfect English. "There is much to be done, but the project continues."

Tyce Greyson couldn't shake the man from his mind. The one who called himself Michael was becoming a fixture in his thoughts every waking moment—and even in his non-awake moments. Michael—Miyka'el, as written in the message that night—haunted him, invaded his senses at every turn. Even contemplating the strange mission—that of involving himself in the doings concerning the not-so-jolly-green-giant in the sarcophagus—couldn't suppress the intrusion.

"There certainly is no sign that they had gardens

around this place," Essie said. "There's nothing green to be seen."

"The big guy in the sarcophagus—remember? He's green...well, greenish," Tyce joked.

"Nebuchadnezzar apparently made the Hanging Gardens for his favorite bride, who was a mountain girl," the archeologist said from behind them. "It must have been quite a project to build the walls and keep greenery growing out here."

"Maybe the ecology was different," Essie said. "There was the Euphrates. Maybe it meandered a little closer... made it easy to water the vegetation."

"This is the roughest fifty-eight miles I've traveled—on roads that are supposed to be of modern vintage," Tyce said.

"There is a rough section that you have not yet endured," the driver said, glancing at Tyce in the rearview mirror with a glint of amusement reflecting in his dark eyes. "We have yet to go through the Valley of Death," he said, again with amusement in his tone.

"Boy howdy, I'm looking forward to that," the journalist retorted, turning to Essie. "Aren't you glad you came along for this exciting ride?"

She said nothing, but gave a look of resignation, seeing in every direction she looked the forbidding landscape of the area called, in Bible times, Shinar.

A billowing cloud of dust boiled in an ever-ascending plume behind the van, the sandstorms of the region making it impossible to keep the deteriorating road a clear path of travel toward Babylon.

"The guys behind us must be enjoying our dust," Tyce quipped, craning his neck to glance through the van's rear door window panels.

"We take the shortcut here," the driver said, turning

the van onto a narrow, sand-dirt road. "This is the Valley of Death I told you about. It is a little rough, but it cuts off about ten kilometers."

The dust plume grew even thicker than when they had been on the asphalt, totally obscuring the small van trailing them. Ahead lay high cliffs seemingly cut in their center by the little road that looked as if it dropped out of sight ahead.

"We will be going a steep grade, but don't fear. I've driven it many times," the driver said, gripping the steering wheel more firmly and clenching his jaws in anticipation of the coming descent into the valley.

Tyce put his arm around Essie when the van started to shake violently because of the severely pocked road-way. "Hold on, this should be an adventure," he said.

The road narrowed in the distance as it led into a ravine, where the reddish-brown cliff walls, Tyce estimated, towered at least two hundred feet above. The bright sky that spanned the narrow slit between the cliff tops of the gorge had turned a darkening grey.

"We are going to endure haboob," the Arab said from behind the wheel, ducking his head to cut his eyes upward to see the sky between the cliff ridges.

"A major dust storm," Faust translated. "But it looks to be a lightning storm—rare in these locales," he said.

"Very bad...very bad," the driver said, again ducking to see the clouds above the narrow space between bordering cliffs that constituted the valley's high walls.

"Why? Why is it so bad?" Essie asked.

"Much rain can cause much trouble in these narrow places," the driver said, wrestling with the steering wheel to keep the van under control while he negotiated the cratered valley floor.

Their surroundings grew increasingly darker as they

proceeded farther into the gorge. The Arab switched on the vehicle's headlights, while the brilliant lightning danced in wicked, intricately connected shards throughout the blackened sky above.

Essie moved closer to Tyce, welcoming the security provided by his surrounding arms while the van bounced roughly. The driver wrestled with the wheel, struggling to maintain control as they negotiated the primitive, cratered road.

The gorge appeared to come to a point several kilometers in the distance, perspective giving the illusion that the high walls met to form a barrier. A sense of *déjà vu* caused ripples of chills to traverse Tyce's spine. The sensation was the same as when he had stood on the balcony of his apartment before the vision came upon him—and the same as when the vision came upon him on the flight from Tel Aviv.

The looming storm evoked the sensation that it was beyond natural. Another vision—was he going into yet another brain paralysis, or whatever the experience involved? No. He sensed the closely surrounding presence of the others in the van, felt every tension movement of Essie, who clung to him as she, too, experienced the buffeting of the pocked road—the apprehension over the swiftly approaching storm that boiled in the ever-nearing distance.

The Arab ducked slightly to gather in the full scope of the storm, the likes of which he had never experienced. Each flash of lightning brightly exaggerated the look of fear on his face while he wrestled the steering wheel, no longer able to concentrate on the deeply scarred roadway.

Without warning, the narrow path ended, a large, black object moving to block the road.

"This isn't good!" Randolph Faust's words were punctuated by the driver's scream of fear. He shouted something in Arabic, causing Tyce to quickly scan their surroundings while the driver brought the van to an abrupt stop in front of what Tyce now recognized as a military vehicle painted with desert camouflage.

The Israeli security team of three was already out of the following van, machine guns pointing in the direction of the military vehicle, which seemed driverless—without anyone around it. In a matter of seconds, armed men—some dressed in military fatigues, others in Arab clothing and headdress—surrounded both vans and closed in.

Ehud Begin and his two companion security men had no choice but to hand their weaponry over to the men, who chattered at them in Arabic, demanding they drop their weapons. The ambush was thorough, and the circle of militants closed around them, pointing their weapons at their victims.

One of the men, dressed in light-colored, desert-camo military fatigues, shouted something in Arabic to the others.

"What did he say?" Tyce said, holding Essie tightly.

"He said to not shoot until they take the girl. She is not to be harmed."

Tyce's senses darkened. This would be his final moment. They would take her only if he was no longer able to breathe...no longer able to fight.

The sky suddenly opened up, lightning illuminating the surrounding terrorist band. Their faces were masks of fear as the streaks of lightning began crashing against the huge stones—against the cliff walls not twenty feet on either side of the roadway.

Their eyes were all turned upward, their mouths

agape. They began to scream while the brightness of the wicked lightning caused their faces to shine with an intense glow. The clouds were now at ground level and seemed alive with electricity as they mingled with the gathered humanity on the roadway.

"Praise God!" Randolph Faust's words were the only sound to be heard other than the crashing thunder and fragmenting of rock along the cliff walls, the would-be captors at first dumfounded and mute.

They scattered in every direction, some dropping weapons while they fled. The man obviously in charge ran for the vehicle that blocked the road, his eyes upward, terrified at the sights he apparently saw.

Now they were alone on the roadway, but the clouds, out of which slashed powerful streaks of lightning to strike all around them boiled in increased opaque thickness.

"Let's move!" Ehud Begin commanded, picking up from the ground several of the dropped weapons the terrified militants left behind.

"'Praise God' sounds right to me," Tyce Greyson whispered while he held to Essie as they entered the van.

CHAPTER 7

"The Iraqi authorities have given the van driver a thorough going over," Randolph Faust said, walking from the room adjacent to the one in which Tyce and Essie stood looking at artifacts behind glass. "He obviously had to tip them that we would be traveling through that gorge."

"So, what do you think? Was that an act of God, you think?" Tyce's tone wasn't jocular; rather, it was genuinely inquisitive.

"Let me throw it back to you," Faust said in a lighter tone. "Do you think it was an act of the Almighty?"

"I must admit that it was something most unusual," Essie said. "It started as seeming to be more from the evil one than from God."

"Now you see, sort of, what I've been living with for months now," Tyce said.

"We are all alive and well, and it's because of direct intervention, I'm convinced," the archeologist said, putting a hand on Essie's elbow and beginning to direct them toward the doorway he had just walked through.

"They are ready for us. I think you will find all of it quite fascinating," Faust said, standing aside while Tyce and Essie walked through the doorway.

The room was illuminated only by the bright screen, in front of which stood a tousled-haired man in a white lab coat. He held a long pointer in his right hand while he stood to the left side of the screen and pointed to a graphic projecting from it.

"You see here that the DNA from our friend is not as we thought...not from one human source, but from two distinctively separate DNA donors—that is, from two sources. There is the human." He pointed to one of the graphics. "Then, there is this source." He tapped the pointer's end on the other graphic image.

"We have just, within recent days, because of great advances, been able to get a profile—to make at least some sense of it."

The other lab-coated men and women sitting in folding chairs facing the screen mumbled to each other as they studied the information their colleague divulged.

"This means, of course, that some specie beyond earth actually interbred with a human to produce our friend," the scientist said. "He wasn't simply a man who grew to such size because of other factors, such as a different ecological factor or factors as we previously had postulated. He is the combination of two distinct species."

The scientist again pointed to the screen. "This is to say that this being, rather than having evolved, is a result of direct interbreeding of two totally different species. We can easily determine the human factor or DNA. We have no idea of the other. We presume it to be extraterrestrial."

"Interdimensional," Randolph Faust whispered out of

the right side of his mouth to Tyce who sat beside him. "This guy is a Nephilim."

"What did he say?" Essie asked Tyce from her position on his right.

"He said the creature in the sarcophagus is partly from interdimensional, not extraterrestrial, DNA," Tyce whispered in her direction.

"There are other factors," the scientist with the pointer said, turning to the lectern to address his gathered colleagues. "Within this DNA combination there seems to be life that has never extinguished. That is, the...being...is dead, but at least part of his genetic composition is still alive. This, as you realize, opens some interesting possibilities for the cloning project, the experimentation to proceed."

Again, there was rustling and whispering among the white-smocked audience.

"This will be the thrust of our work here in trying to understand exactly what this all means."

The screen filled with an image of the open sarcophagus, filmed from high above. The dark form of the huge man-figure lay in repose, its hands folded across its abdomen.

"It is the consensus that this was the one known as Gilgamesh—probably one and the same as the biblical ruler known as Nimrod, of Tower of Babel infamy," the scientist said, bringing increased rumbling from those in attendance.

One of the scientists stood, and the man at the lectern acknowledged her desire to say something. She spoke with a German accent. "How can this being have such a living component if he has been deceased for—how many? Four, five thousand years? We know of no such precedent occurrence. Are we to believe that this suggests that extraterrestrial life has unheard-of longevity in our understanding of biology? Or are we to believe the DNA that is from extraterrestrial sources has an immortal property?"

"Answers to that factor are part of the study we must pursue, certainly," the speaker answered. "Tissue yet alive after the death of the organism defies physical law. Yet, this foreign DNA, this tissue, is alive—very much so."

"It's angelic DNA," Faust again whispered toward Tyce.

～

"YOUR FATHER IS ANGRY," Ehud Begin said, holding the phone toward Essie. "He wants to speak with you."

She took the phone apprehensively as Tyce watched her brush her auburn hair aside and repetitiously cut her pretty eyes toward the ceiling before speaking. "Yes, Morticai," she said softly.

"Daughter. I should have not let you go to Baghdad," he said. "It was inexcusably stupid and a breach of security. I should fire myself."

Essie shut her eyes tightly and bit her lower lip as she listened to his rant. "Yes, I understand your worry." She listened to more of her father's raving before trying to break in with calming reason. "Now, Papa, all is well. We are here and I am safe. We are all quite secure."

She listened a bit more before speaking again. "Ehud did a magnificent job, as did the others. Yes, they are questioning the driver. They suspect he somehow tipped the…thugs."

She said "goodbye" a few minutes later, turning to Tyce after handing the phone to Begin. "He is one angry

Jew," she said, returning Tyce's embrace when he moved to take her hand. "He is sending more security, since I won't return to Jerusalem while you are still here."

"He loves you, Essie," Tyce said. "You're his daughter. And that was a very close call we had yesterday."

She stood with her face turned against his chest as they held each other. "Why were they intent on taking me hostage?"

This woman, as knowledgeable as any operative within the Israeli security services in such matters, was asking the obvious of him. The thought of her not really expecting an answer, although crossing his mind, never-theless—to his own surprise—resulted in the answer spilling from his lips...more to remind himself than to inform Essie.

"For leverage in dealing with the Israeli government," he said. "They treat women like the lowest form of humanity—think of them as being lower than their... camels. But they know that the rest of us, especially your father in this case, will protect women, we value women."

"Do you think we are worth such consideration?" she said, her face still pressed against his chest.

"Not really. But we do at least prize you above our camels," he said, evoking laughter from her while she looked into his deadpan expression. "In your case, they would have great leverage, you being the daughter of a top Israeli clandestine service official," Tyce said, more serious.

"They do not know Morticai," she said. "Israel is top priority no matter what. It is a divine calling with him."

"He didn't seem to be religious...that's the impression I got."

"Israel *is* his religion. He believes in the nation's

divine destiny, even though he believes in an existential God."

"Oh? How so?"

"He believes that Jehovah—and he does believe in that sense of the Old Testament God—He believes that Jehovah set all things in motion with Israel as the prototype nation. Then God left it up to the Jews to take it from there."

"Interesting. And you? What do you believe?"

"I'm beginning to think that Jehovah isn't so existential."

Tyce said nothing. Essie took the side of her face from against him and looked into his eyes. "And you? What is your belief?"

Tyce studied the question for several seconds. "I'm still not sure about Randolph's version of God. But it's impossible for me to deny supernatural goings-on in my life."

"Were you raised Christian?"

"Yes. Mom and Dad are Christians. They raised my sister and me under teachings of a fundamentalist, evangelical-type church structure."

"But you don't call yourself a Christian?"

A knock at the door to the small room of the antiquities complex drew their attention. Randolph Faust opened it slightly and stuck his head in the opening. "Excuse me. Am I interrupting you two?"

"No—come in, Randy," Tyce called.

The archeologist came the rest of the way into the room, excitement in his voice while he moved toward them, his steps seeming to have a more youthful spring in them. "This thing is far beyond anything I expected," he said. "They think they've found the fountain of youth, but they are about to open Pandora's box. The prophetic implications are mind-boggling. I just don't know what this thing portends at this point."

"They actually believe this creature is probably Nimrod? Do you think that's possible?" Tyce's question brought an excited response.

"Not only possible, but I believe the corpse is exactly that—the mummy of Nimrod."

Tyce chuckled, both Faust and Essie looking at him, puzzled.

"Nimrod is a name given to the stupid among us. That's always been my take on that name," Tyce said by way of explanation for his amusement.

"That comes from the Bugs Bunny cartoon character," Faust said. "It's a twentieth-century term that comes from Bugs calling Elmer Fudd a 'Nimrod'. It was in a cartoon that Fudd was dressed as a hunter, and Bugs was mocking him. He was calling him a 'poor, little Nimrod', or 'hunter'. Nimrod, you remember, was called a 'mighty hunter' in Genesis."

"Well, that certainly didn't look like any cartoon character in that sarcophagus," Essie said. "It's about the creepiest thing I've ever seen."

"There's nothing amusing about this guy, I assure," the archeologist said. "He is, according to the Bible, the son of Cush, grandson of Ham, and great grandson of Noah. Orientalists, Assyriologists, and mythographers have long tried to make links between Nimrod and historically attested figures in Mesopotamia. Berossus in the third century BC stated that the first king after the Flood was Euechoios of Chaldea. He identified him with Nimrod. Sumerologists…scholars of more recent times have connected accounts of a number of names in ancient times to the one called Nimrod."

Tyce saw that the archeologist was enjoying again having students to inform.

"Nimrod, so the myth goes, saw a black cloth with a crown in the air. He commanded Sasan the weaver to make a crown like the one he saw, with jewels added. Nimrod, it is said, was the first king to wear a crown. People, therefore, from then forward, said that a crown came down from heaven to old Nimrod. Nimrod is linked in Greek mythology to the legendary King Ninus, said to have founded Nineveh. He is often in ancient references said to be a giant."

"Really?" Essie said, eyebrows raised.

"Yes," Faust continued. "For example, in the Hungarian legend of the 'Enchanted Stag', or as the 'White Stag', or 'Silver Stag', he is often described as Nimrod the giant."

"Yeah, but that's just mythology, only legend," Tyce said.

"Ah...but mythology often documents true events throughout history by repeated stories, even cave-wall paintings and so forth. For example, there are such paintings and stories of a great flood and a great boat that carried survivors in many, many cultures throughout history. And, likewise, there are ziggurats throughout the world, some in the form of pyramids, that attest to the veracity of the tower God's Word says Nimrod had built on the plain of Shinar. Many cultures also call him a giant. Even in literature, we see Nimrod's existence as a giant reflected. In the *Divine Comedy*, Dante Alighieri depicts Nimrod among the other giants in his inferno."

Thoughts of his most recent vision traversed Tyce's memory. "What do you think that...episode...I had with the giant, whoever he is, meant to what's going on in this whole thing, Randy?"

The archeologist didn't hesitate in his answer, looking first at Essie then at Tyce when he spoke. "This...part-man, part offspring of the fallen ones, the angels that rebelled, was the first king on earth following the Flood of Noah's time. He wanted to throw off the shackles of heaven...the restraints of the Creator."

Faust's demeanor became intensive. "There is a passage in the Bible, in the book of Psalms, directly linked to this whole matter, I'm convinced, Tyce. It links that first attempt at a world order ruled by man, totally apart from any influence from God, to a future such attempt that will be made by man to tell God to go fly a kite."

Faust took only moments to recall the portion of the second chapter of the Psalms he sought to recollect.

"The Scripture says, 'Why do the heathen rage, and the people imagine a vain thing? The kings of the earth set themselves, and the rulers take counsel together, against the Lord, and against his anointed, saying, Let us break their bands asunder, and cast away their cords from us. He that sitteth in the heavens shall laugh. The Lord shall have them in derision. Then shall he speak unto them in his wrath, and vex them in his sore displeasure. Yet have I set my king upon my holy hill of Zion. I will declare the decree: the Lord hath said unto me, Thou art my Son; this day have I begotten thee. Ask of me, and I shall give thee the heathen for thine inheritance, and the uttermost parts of the earth for thy possession. Thou shalt break them with a rod of iron; thou shalt dash them in pieces like a potter's vessel. Be wise now therefore, O ye kings: be instructed, ye judges of the earth. Serve the Lord with fear, and rejoice with trembling. Kiss the Son, lest he be angry, and ye perish from the way, when his wrath is kindled but a little. Blessed are all they that put their trust in him.'"

Tyce reflected on the archeologist's words, then said, "You're saying that this is a prophecy for a future attempt at one world order. The being—Nimrod—standing on top of the ziggurat I saw, then the ziggurat changing into the UN building, represents that all this is tied to an attempt to construct a global government?"

"I couldn't have said it better," Faust said, patting Tyce on the shoulder. "You get an A."

~

ALL-ENCOMPASSING blackness and cold engulfed him. Tyce Greyson, this time, was ready for whatever came. It was another trip to the land of vision the otherworldly powers assigned him to go to whenever they chose. He didn't know where he had just been, or where it was leading, just that he was here, now, and the darkness would, he knew, soon burst into light and into scenes he was to see and hear.

A pinpoint of light, as always, first pierced the center of the blackness and seemed to shoot directly into his consciousness. The scene before him then burst into totality, filled with a number of lab-coated men surrounding a large computer monitor screen, upon which all eyes were locked.

"Dr. Gravelan," one of the men to the left side of the screen pointed to something in the information displayed. "See, here. This is what must be comprehended if the serum is to stabilize, thus attain transferability from the material taken from the subject to the human DNA for the results we must obtain."

"Very well," a short, balding man standing directly in front of the screen said.

Tyce's eyes widened in astonishment while looking upon the scene before him. A dark, shadow-like figure in the shape of a man emerged from the scientist who had first spoken. The being entered the scientist who had answered, taking on the man's shape, then disappeared.

Moments later, the scientist whom the shadow figure had just possessed spoke, while continuing to study the screen.

"Yes, I see now; it is all very clear. Unless there is a complete restructuring at the subatomic level, nothing changes. But, here and here," the scientist touched the screen with an index finger, "we restructure, and the transferability is achieved."

Another of the men, after studying the screen for several moments, spoke.

"When will the human subjects be prepared for the injections?"

"Each must be individually genetically made compatible, their genetics reengineered according to the precise directive for each. The slightest variance from the exact model tailored for their DNA profile will cause mutation that will prove calamitous. Probably death would be inevitable within hours," the scientist who hosted the shadow figure said.

"And they agree to that risk?" the questioner continued.

"How could they not? This is an offer of ultimate opportunity. It presents possibilities that those who seek the power and authority of leadership have always coveted."

"And, what of the individuality factor—the soul that

is the individual? There is an inalterable effect, I understand," the questioning scientist said.

"This is a matter each fully understands and accepts," the scientist whose body the shadow being had entered said. "To assume the responsibility, they will be called upon to carry out, they will have to attain…extradimensional…abilities."

"What is the timeline for the total conversion? When will the transformation be complete?" another of the scientists asked.

"We must proceed judiciously," the scientist directly in front of the screen said. "The time factor for complete conversion is not clear at this point. There has not been any similar attempt. However, the conversion should be complete within a maximum of two months, I should think."

"Then, the procedure will progress much more rapidly, once we have established parameters and protocols within our methodologies, and so forth," he added. The scientist who seemed to be in charge concluded, "It will then be possible to initiate entire populations within, say, a matter of weeks."

He spoke, then, while running his fingers over the controls as the screen changed accordingly. He said, as if to himself, then, "All will then be in place for the one chosen to be Earthlord."

Tyce's senses began changing while the scene before him suddenly filled with many people within an immense science laboratory, all wearing the familiar white smocks. Dark, shadow-figures, like the one that had entered the scientist, intermingled with the humans. He gawked, astonished at seeing the smoke-like beings enter and exit their human hosts, while the people in the lab coats went about various duties within the laboratory.

His surroundings faded quickly to total blackness, before the now-familiar, brilliant point of light burst from somewhere in the center of the ambient vision encapsulation in which he stood.

When his environment changed from quickly growing brighter surroundings to a scene he could see clearly, it became obvious that the same, small scientist that was the leader of the group—the one the shadow being had entered—stood, speaking to a small group of men dressed in business attire. The rumpled scientist spoke in good, but broken, English, while the others sat in rapt attention to his every word.

"So, this is the essence of our work, thanks to your beneficence and largess. Now, I will be pleased to answer any questions."

Immediately, a man Tyce recognized as the German who had helped inculcate him during his initial introduction to the being in the sarcophagus stood from his chair and blurted his question. "So, you have determined that the giant being is offspring of extraterrestrial visitors to earth at some point, probably at the time of the first settlers in Mesopotamia?" he asked.

"Yes," the scientist answered. "We have proven our postulate in that regard beyond any doubt, I think. The studies prove the creature is from the human element and another element not of this sphere."

The German continued, "So, what are the next experiments to be done on the mummy? Are there any commercial applications to be extracted from this creature's…contributions to science, do you anticipate?"

"Our—that is, the scientific community chosen by the Brussels Commission to investigate—our conclusions satisfy that earth was once visited, and that many of the wonders of the world at that time were directly built, or directed in being constructed, by these...visitors."

The German pressed, "And, these were—that is, the offspring—were giants?"

"They were giants, in many cases, both physically and intellectually. We have concluded, for example, that the Great Pyramid of Giza was constructed by such giant entities, perhaps even by the visitors who themselves sired those like the one who lies in the golden sarcophagus—"

"—Yes, yes," the questioner interrupted. "All of the scientific findings on behalf of history is understood and are duly noted as quite fascinating, even amazing. But we have investors who expect much more than to fatten history books or scientific journals."

There were rumblings of muffled laughter, with the British man Tyce recognized from days earlier saying, "Hear, hear," with amused agreement in his voice.

"We are aware of the financial exigencies that hold sway over this project," the scientist said, nonplused in his retort to the German. "We have concluded that, for at least a number of months, it will be wise to proceed slowly in trying to find the application that might be made to the improvement to the human genome—to the gene pool—so that great physical and intellectual advantage can be developed."

"You mean, so you can find ways to create growth hormones, or whatever?" an American among the group of men stood and asked.

"Well, 'hormones' perhaps is not the correct term, but yes...we believe we can substantially improve the human biological future with the work we are doing."

"Then, the improvement of the human race is the

whole, the entire, purpose involved, here," the American followed up.

"That is accurate. That is the primary thrust of the effort. What could there be beyond that? This is why we were asked to proceed. Naturally, there should follow great financial benefits from improving one's children, in helping to create a healthier, heartier breed of people…greater longevity, and so forth, I should think."

Tyce watched the agreement on the seated men's faces—faces whose features began to dissolve as his senses again gathered the reality of his own surroundings.

He stumbled as he tried to move his legs for the first time since the vision began…how long ago? He looked at his watch. It was 2:18. Was that a.m., p.m.? When?

He stood, still trying to regain equilibrium, in the middle of the large room he had been assigned while at the Babylon facility. He shuffled to the window and pulled the curtain to see the darkness of the early morning sky. It was 2:18 in the morning. It had been just under three hours since he last looked at his watch before falling asleep.

RANDOLPH FAUST WAS UP and doing things, as old men do. Sleep had come fitfully to him for most of his nights since he was in his late sixties, his mind a constantly moving stream of cogitation between the spiritual and the ephemeral. He sat at the little desk, pecking at the keyboard of his laptop when the knock on his door disrupted his online reading of Daniel, chapter 2.

Tyce Greyson pushed the door open and looked in when he heard the archeologist bidding him to enter.

"I'm glad you're up," he said, hurrying to the old man's side. "I've waited for more than an hour, hoping you would get up at the time you said is your usual."

"What's wrong, Tyce? You're pale. You okay?"

"Another vision, Randy. It's about the artifact—the jolly green giant in that sarcophagus."

Tyce described the scenes he had witnessed—the dark, smoke-like beings moving in and out of the scientists, their working on things phenomenally different from what they claimed, different from the DNA experiments to improve the health and longevity of earth's human population.

"They are working to develop a serum of some sort—one that will, as I take it, change the psychological makeup of the person injected. No, it's much more than that, I think. They want to change the *soul*, as the guy who apparently was the head of the scientists said. He said a couple of 'subjects' had volunteered to be the first to receive this serum made from the genetic material taken from this Nimrod being, combined with normal DNA, or genetic material from humans."

Faust said nothing, weighing carefully Tyce's excited description of the scenes he had just witnessed.

"Then, the vision changed to this same scientist talking to a group of men in coats and ties—suits, you know? They were some of the same guys we met with back in DC. I recognized the one, the German, and the English guy."

Tyce paused to collect his memory of the scene.

"What was he—the scientist—saying to them?" Randolph asked.

"He was explaining the project," Tyce said. "But he was telling them that it was totally intended to find new, beneficial ways to improve the makeup of human beings.

You know—to improve health, longevity by tampering with the genetics, I guess. He didn't say anything about the serum, or the beings that were, as I gathered, giving the scientists all this supernatural wisdom or whatever."

An afterthought punctuated his memory. "And I just remembered—he told the scientists something else he didn't tell these guys. He told the scientists that all would soon be in preparation for the one chosen to be Earthlord."

Both men remained silent, each reflecting on the strange matters. Faust reached for the heavily worn Bible to the right of his computer monitor. "Here's what we are right smack in the middle of," he said, flipping pages quickly, then stopping to read aloud. "For we wrestle not against flesh and blood, but against principalities, against powers, against the rulers of the darkness of this world, against spiritual wickedness in high places."

The archeologist looked up from his reading, concentration etched in his expression.

"Yeah. I can see where those verses have relevance, here," Tyce said. "But how do you deal with this…supernaturalism…or whatever it is?"

Faust didn't answer but continued to read. "Wherefore take unto you the whole armour of God, that ye may be able to withstand in the evil day, and having done all, to stand… Stand therefore, having your loins girt about with truth, and having on the breastplate of righteousness… And your feet shod with the preparation of the gospel of peace… Above all, taking the shield of faith, wherewith ye shall be able to quench all the fiery darts of the wicked. And take the helmet of salvation, and the sword of the Spirit, which is the word of God… Praying always with all prayer and supplication in the

Spirit, and watching thereunto with all perseverance and supplication for all saints."

The journalist stood, looking at the open Bible, then at Faust. His questioning expression then came out in words sounding perplexed. "Okay. So, what does that mean? We are up against some spiritual forces. That's plain to me. But, what about the rest you read? Is that how we're supposed to combat this 'supernatural warfare'?"

"It means, my young friend, that we are at a time when we must rely on the God of heaven to prepare all who are here on this fallen sphere at this moment in history for Satan's last stand."

CHAPTER 8

S he came to him, their lips meeting. Essie's fragrant warmth and firm though softly feminine body against his produced in Tyce the sense that theirs was a union already consummated.

They hadn't coupled in the sexual togetherness he had longed for during the nights spent in a bedroom one door away—being a healthy male who had fallen totally for this stunning girl. He had been far too respectful of her as a woman of self-discipline and intellect to succumb to the raw lustiness that ruled in these times.

But they had become as one in the deepest part of their humanness—their embrace of each other. Each managed to remain just outside the bounds of the sexual union both had yearned to know. Each moved away from the tipping-point instant each time the urge within welled. The urge was becoming, for Tyce, almost impossible to resist. So, it was with both regret and with welcome that his phone's chime separated them.

"There's no number," he mused to himself, while Essie looked over his shoulder at the iPhone screen.

"Good morning, Tyce," the strong, baritone voice said in greeting.

Tyce was stunned, unable to return the expected response.

"It is I, Michael," the voice continued. "I am sent to again thank you for undertaking the mission you have accepted. This will be a most crucial time for Israel. Always carry the knowledge that you are not alone. Soon you will enter a season of seeming trouble out of which there is no safe pathway. It is then you will be shown the way of escape. You shall never be without remedy."

"—Michael," Tyce tried to interrupt. "What is this all about? Who are you, Michael?"

The line had the silence of disconnection.

"It was Michael? The same guy?" Essie's words broke Tyce's almost hypnotic state while he looked at the phone that continued.

"Yes, it was him," he said in a dazed response.

Less than an hour later, Tyce and Essie joined Randolph Faust while he emerged from a meeting with several of his archeologist colleagues. Harnak al Mufi led the way down the narrow hallway. Tyce pulled on Faust's shirtsleeve, leaning to speak in low volume near the old man's left ear.

"Michael again," he said, excitement in his voice despite trying to keep it at a whisper.

"Michael has spoken to you again?"

"I got a call on my cell. He said that I will soon have a season of trouble. It will look like there's no way out. But I am supposed to know that I'm not alone. He said a way will be provided."

Faust let the thought traverse his mind for a few seconds. He stopped to look at Tyce, while all others but

Essie, who stood beside Tyce, moved farther down the hallway.

"And, what happened then?" he said.

"Nothing. I tried to talk with him, but the line was disconnected."

The three of them again began moving slowly toward their destination.

"We will have to talk on this once your interview for your writing project is out of the way," the archeologist said.

Moments later, they entered a large room Tyce recognized as the one he had seen in the episode the night before. A chill of eerie realization ran down his spine. He was about to begin something he both looked forward to and dreaded. When he saw the small gathering of lab-coated men near the center of the room, his premonition came to life. The short man who turned to give a quick, tight smile and offer his hand, upon Harnak al Mufi's introduction, was the man he felt as if he had already met. It was the scientist he'd seen in the vision, the one the shadow being had possessed.

"Dr. Rudolf Gravelan, Mr. Tyce Greyson," al Mufi said with a smile, while the men reached for each other's right hands.

"Mr. Greyson is writing the articles introducing the world to the fabulous find and the marvelous things going on here at Antiquities," the Egyptian said with a bright tone.

"I am pleased to meet you, Mr. Greyson," the scientist said, then looked past him to Essie. "And, you must be Essie, Morticai's daughter," he added, smiling broadly and taking Essie's hand, holding it lightly, and patting the top of her hand with the tips of his fingers.

"Nice to meet you, Dr. Gravelan," she said, a quick smile crossing her lips.

After several other introductions, Gravelan lightly gripped Tyce's elbow and pulled him aside.

"Our interview was scheduled for this morning, Mr. Greyson, I realize. Something has developed that requires that I leave for Europe as soon as possible, however. I am sorry that I must ask that you speak to several of our other scientists on the project, if you don't mind terribly."

Gravelan had poked one of Tyce's pet peeves in its most sensitive places—an interviewee trying to weasel out of a promised interview—and something within his combative spirit caused him to blurt the words.

"I'm terribly disappointed, of course, Dr. Gravelan. I had specifically wanted to ask you about the Earthlord. I'm most interested—fascinated, really—with your serum, the DNA combination of the two distinct species, and the results you anticipate with regard to the infusion of the first two volunteer subjects. I understand you expect the result to be complete within two months."

Tyce watched for the scientist's reaction. Gravelan stiffened and stood more erect, almost reaching Tyce's own height. He heard a guttural groan that seemed to come from somewhere within the man's throat. Gravelan's eyes widened, then resumed a normal look that turned into a transfixed stare at Tyce.

Tyce had no idea why he had blurted the information that he knew Gravelan wouldn't expect him to know. It came from an unconscious thought about the scene he had witnessed. But there it was, and the scientist was visibly shaken by its bluntness.

Gravelan spoke after several seconds of obvious reflection on the journalist's unexpected remarks. "Perhaps I can delay my departure for a time longer," the still somewhat flustered scientist said, almost whispering the words. He looked around them sheepishly, as if to learn whether others had heard the exchange. "Let us move to another room so as to conduct the interview in a quieter setting," he said, again lightly gripping Tyce's elbow and moving with him toward a door several feet away.

Tyce winked at Essie just before he and Gravelan entered the small room just off the large laboratory. He would give the reluctant scientist with a dark side a grilling worthy of the esoteric information he harbored.

"Your series of articles for this project, as I understand, consists of informing the world of our findings," the scientist said, after they were seated across a small table from each other.

"Yes," Tyce said. "That's my understanding, too. However, I sense there are two, distinct projects going on in this lab." He was getting right to the point he knew troubled Gravelan.

"And what would those be?" the scientist said, coyly.

"What I thought would be the *only* information collected from the project—that is the *main* information —was that this big guy in the sarcophagus is a combination of human DNA and that from some alien civilization—of extraterrestrial origin."

"Yes, that is our finding. And what other…information…do you believe is forthcoming?"

"Oh, do you plan to announce the other?"

"What other, Mr. Greyson?" Gravelan's countenance had metamorphosed. His skin had changed from a reddish, hypertensive hue to pallor, as if most of the blood had been drained from his face. The demeanor had shifted from almost nervous to calm that bordered on drowsiness. The voice, too, was different. It was deeper, more measured—almost sinister in quality.

"What I mentioned a few minutes ago," Tyce said, reaching into the briefcase he carried to retrieve the microcassette recorder. "I'm particularly interested in the serum you want to produce for, apparently, injecting the entire world with, eventually."

"Where did you get any such information?" Gravelan's words came with a tone of incredulity.

"I'm sorry, Dr. Gravelan, but I'm the reporter, not the interviewee. Suffice it to say that I know such an outcome is sought through the experimentation on this giant being."

"And…what else have you heard that might be part of our little project?" Now the scientist's tone was mocking.

"That the injections somehow will change the very soul of the individual. That someone—or something—called Earthlord will come from this genetics manipulation."

Gravelan's expression changed from amusement to somberness. His voice became as hard as his look.

"If you write that, Mr. Greyson, you will make our entire work here the laughingstock of all of the scientific community. It will greatly damage the wonderful work our people have in fact accomplished. And it will do your journalistic integrity no good to write such things and be later proven wrong."

"Then you are denying that what I have just laid out has any truth?"

"I am denying it completely—emphatically," Gravelan said with a quick nod of his head, while glaring at Tyce.

Tyce started to say more, to tell about the shadow beings he had seen entering and exiting Gravelan and the others during the vision. He thought better of it, and instead thumbed the small recorder and spoke into it.

"Dr. Rudolf Gravelan flatly denies that any other outcomes are being worked toward than that of proving the giant man-creature in the sarcophagus from the Euphrates Riverbed is the genetic offspring of two distinctive species—one human, the other, apparently, extraterrestrial."

When he had finished, Tyce looked back at Gravelan with resolve as tough as that exhibited by the scientist's demeanor. "I hope I've accurately reflected your answer to the allegations about the possible secondary purpose of the project, Dr. Gravelan. I wouldn't take any pleasure in uncovering secrets that lead to malfeasance of any sort."

The scientist paused purposefully before responding.

"Do not worry, Mr. Greyson. I personally guarantee that you will not report—that is, not find—such allegation to be true or such *malfeasance* to be the case."

He needed this key man's cooperation, at least to some extent, in order to write the series of articles. Tyce decided to take on a less confrontational persona. "I just want the truth of the matters involved in this project, Dr. Gravelan. This is one of the great finds of history, as I understand it. Any facts I can put into the information we release are crucial to successfully informing the world."

Gravelan stared at Tyce for several seconds, his own stern countenance then changing to a more accommodating one. "Yes. That's all any of us want, Mr. Greyson. I will see to it that you receive all you need to complete your mission on behalf of the project."

"Thank you," Tyce said.

"Now, I must be on my way to Brussels. I will direct

the others in the project to cooperate fully with your interview needs," the scientist said, arising from the chair and reaching to shake Tyce's hand.

MORTICAI KANT HAD FOLLOWED up on his promise to send additional security agents. Tyce counted at least ten new faces, each seeming to surround them while trying not to be overly conspicuous with their cocoon of protection.

Essie was irritated at the intrusiveness her father had perpetrated.

"This is all so unnecessary," she grumbled, walking quickly beside Tyce while they moved from the van to the building looming less than a hundred feet in the distance.

"I guess next he'll have them stationed just outside the shower curtain as I bathe," she said, bringing a grin to Tyce's lips.

"Well, I'm sure they wouldn't mind that assignment," he teased.

"It's not funny. You would think I was a child, the way he treats—"

"—You are his child," Tyce broke in. "Don't you understand? Your dad loves you so much. And, we already know there have been...attempts."

"Yes, I know that's true—but a dozen?"

"The way Ehud explained it is that most were sent to protect the sarcophagus while they might have to move it, in case this ISIS movement threatens Baghdad in a serious way," he said, opening the door to the building and letting her precede him through the opening.

"Twelve Israelis—as much as my father thinks of their capabilities—would not stop those murderers."

"Samson slew a thousand," Tyce said.

"Well, that's the story anyway," she said. "However, we have fifty thousand up there. But Morticai's intention is good, I'll concede that."

"I wonder what this meeting is about," Tyce said while they, along with three Israeli security men, walked the hallway leading toward a set of double doors. One of the men opened one of the doors when they arrived. Randolph Faust met Tyce and Essie when they entered.

"There's concern that the forces amassed north of Baghdad are preparing for some sort of attack. They want to move the project," the archeologist said, walking with them to the center of the big room. They were seated facing a podium with several microphones affixed to its top.

"Essie and I were just talking about something like that. Where do they want to move it?" Tyce said, settling into the chair between Faust and Essie.

"Rumor has it they want to take the sarcophagus to somewhere in Europe, possibly Brussels," Faust said, watching the several men mount the platform on which the podium sat.

The room began filling with men and women, some in white lab coats, many in uniforms, and others in civilian business attire.

"Makes sense," Tyce said to Faust.

"Dr. Gravelan said he was leaving for Brussels when our meeting was over."

Faust and Greyson turned their attention to the podium when the meeting was called to order.

〜

TYCE GREYSON SAT, leaning over the laptop, while typing furiously on the keyboard. He was a fast writer, and the information he had accumulated rampaged through his mind to a point in the center of his brain where it coalesced into orderly presentation.

Despite Rudolf Gravelan's warning, he would put forth in the initial report on the Euphrates find the most esoteric possibilities of the project. He would put his ponderings to paper for the magazine article as hints of what might be in the offing.

Such a diluted offering was about all he could do. He had no hard evidence. So, the piece would have to be tempered with the words "sources say...".

If he revealed that the "sources" were his dreams and visions, he would be branded a lunatic, just as Gravelan had implied.

A knock at the door to his bedroom snatched his attention from the writing. Essie stepped through the doorway when he opened the door.

He didn't at first hear her words, seeing her, resplendent in her nearly all-white blouse and slacks, her face so pretty beneath her auburn hair, its radiance highlighted by the sunlight sifting through the half-shuttered blinds near the doorway.

"I'm sorry, Essie?" he said, looking into the green eyes that caused the emotions of his growing love for her to churn. "What did you say?"

"I said, they've decided to move the artifact to Europe today. They will be leaving within two hours."

"How do you know?" he said, finally able to center on what she said rather than how she looked.

"Morticai said so a few moments ago," she said, her voice breaking into a stifled sob, a single tear beginning to run down her cheek. She wiped it away with a slender index finger.

"I can't go with you this time," she said, regaining control. "Papa has set his jaw. He will not allow me to accompany you."

She went to Tyce and embraced him. He said nothing in return, thinking on how to console her.

She spoke first. "Morticai says your…mission…the *true* mission…will have you coming back to Tel Aviv and to Jerusalem very soon." She looked up at him, tears now spilling from her eyes.

"I'm afraid that's the only thing that will be on my mind, sweetheart," he said, touching her cheeks to try to wipe away her hurting. "I'll have to tell your Papa that his decision is going to have a very adverse effect on me completing my mission. I'll be able to think only about his beautiful daughter."

They came together in a lingering kiss that affirmed theirs was a bond that would not be broken by distance or time.

HE WATCHED the jet lift off the runway and climb quickly. He followed it, shielding his eyes from the noonday sun until the plane became a speck of black against the blue sky.

The farewell had been tearful for Essie. Although he, too, felt the tug of emotion about their being apart, he did the manly thing. He was strong for her, assuring her that he would be with her by the time another week had passed. Saying so made him feel better, too, and he reminded himself of his own reassurance of their reunion while turning to walk to the van where Ehud

Begin was waiting to drive them back to the Euphrates project headquarters.

"The sarcophagus will arrive in Belgium within the hour," Begin said.

"They haven't wasted any time moving the project," Tyce said, looking across the runways at a number of military vehicles moving together toward the north. "There's a lot of military activity—more than I've noticed since we've been here," he added while Ehud drove them south of the airport and toward the soon-to-be former project headquarters.

"ISIS is on the move," Begin said, a hint of disrespect for that army in the sound of his words. "I guess they just aren't so sure Baghdad can be secured. If there's anything the Iraqi Army will defend, it's Bagdad."

"I don't know what ISIS could want with this desolation," Tyce mused. "I don't think they're interested in artifacts."

"This is just a steppingstone for their real objective, like all of Islam," Begin said.

"Israel?" Tyce studied the Israeli's expression upon offering the question.

"Jerusalem," the driver said. "We will welcome them with open arms," Ehud said, turning to grin at his passenger.

CHAPTER 9

Tyce Greyson adjusted the lamp that sat slightly off-center on the desk behind the laptop. He forced his eyes to focus on the small font. Unsatisfied with the effort, he punched at the keyboard to make the type larger.

"Miyka'el—Hebrew for 'Michael'. Heaven's most powerful archangel."

Tyce's mind wend to the moment he had last seen the mysterious man with the penetrating gaze that he had last encountered in the captain's seat of the plane. Then, he had suddenly no longer been there, replaced by a dark-haired man—apparently the actual pilot of the aircraft.

It just wasn't possible. Despite all the strange things that had gone on in his life—the strange things still going on—it just wasn't possible. This man he felt he almost knew had appeared at the most unexpected times. He just couldn't be...couldn't be the being Randolph Faust had conjectured.

Miyka'el. The Hebrew spelling of 'Michael'. The greatest of heaven's archangels…

To what purpose? Why choose him, Tyce Greyson, to carry out…to carry out what? A mission from the Almighty?

Memories flooded back. His trip to Patmos…the Jewish rabbi who told him those years ago at the Temple Mount in Jerusalem that Israel was the key to the end of days.

The reptile that clung to his hand while he explored the cave at Patmos—the cave that might have been the very one in which John, the writer of Revelation, the Apocalypse, wrote his world-rending prophecies.

The terrible visions that followed him…

But the visions were all coma-induced. None of it was real—except for the reptile bite, the injection that brought on the coma.

Was all this now not real—rather, just a continuation of the results of injected venom those years ago?

But the sarcophagus—the giant within. The frightening reality burned at the core of his every waking moment. Their plans involving the creature…staggering beyond comprehension…

Thoughts of his own apparently heaven-directed part in what it all involved caromed through his weary brain while he lay back against the pillow.

Blackness of the Iraqi night engulfed him when he snapped off the bedside lamp. Momentarily, much-needed sleep did the same.

Sleep came to an end as quickly as it had fallen. Crashing sounds against the door to the room brought him to a sitting-up position. Suddenly, he found himself surrounded by a number of people pointing weapons at him. One of the weapon-wielding men shouted at him in broken English.

He put his hands behind his head as ordered, while a couple of the intruders roughly frisked him, then jerked him to his feet from the bed. They forced his hands behind his back and handcuffed him before moving him toward the open door. He felt as if he would faint, so sudden was the attack and so quickly did they rush him to an awaiting vehicle.

There was no one to help him, no one to stop the abductors from carrying out their assault. Where were the Israelis? The forces of the Iraqi army? He could see no signs of anyone who might come to his aid. There was only the darkness of the Babylonian night and the creaking and jarring movement of the rattling military transport.

His thoughts reeled with fear of who the kidnappers were. They spoke Arabic. They were dressed in ragtag khaki fatigues. Most wore headdress.

The fact that he could see them was a question that made the fear grow. Most abductors would blindfold their captive—unless they didn't intend to release their victim. Did it mean they intended to kill him?

But, if so, why take him captive? Why not just do it on the spot?

A hand grabbed his hair in the back and pulled his head backward. Another shoved a wet, wadded-up cloth into his face. A choking, caustic odor made him realize the action was meant to rob him of consciousness.

His vision was too hazy to make out his surroundings when he emerged from the blackout caused by the chloroform-soaked cloth. His burning eyes finally focused on a grinning face two feet in front of him, as the burnoosed, bearded man looked into his eyes to check for consciousness.

The man turned and said something in Arabic, a smirk in his voice.

When the man moved from in front of him, he saw a camera on a tripod facing him. A group of his captors huddled to the right of the camera before breaking up their meeting. One of the men stepped behind the camera.

Two others came in his direction. He sat on a stool-like chair, his hands clasped behind his back and his knees and ankles tied, making him unable to move more than an inch or two. His mouth was gagged by a rolled cloth.

The realization hit him in senses-blinding recognition. The memory of the atrocities he had seen on film. The execution of the reporter beheaded; the murder by burning of the Jordanian pilot. He was about to become an executed victim for the pleasure and propaganda of ISIS…

The man behind the camera moved into place and started the camera whirring.

He felt a hand grab his hair and pull his head back so that his face was toward the ceiling. He felt the cold steel against the left side of his neck…

He began to scream, his throat not seeming to respond to the attempted protest against his coming decapitation.

The door to his right suddenly exploded, as if a grenade had pulverized it. Tyce's mind snapped to attention.

"Tyce!"

Ehud Begin's shouted words forced his addled brain into full focus.

The Israeli stood with semi-automatic pistol at the ready, looking around the room.

"Ehud," Tyce said. "Thank God, it's you."

❧

"It wasn't like a dream. It was as real as you sitting talking to me now."

Tyce stood from the chair across from that of Randolph Faust. He paced to the window and lifted the blind to peer between the slats.

"You've certainly had enough of the…strange experiences…to know dream from reality, I should think," the archeologist said, watching Tyce return to the chair and seat himself.

"Was it a warning? A vision or something giving a heads-up about somebody wanting to take me out of these crazy things going on?"

He looked at Faust for an answer he didn't really expect to get. He spoke again before Faust could respond.

"And how *did* I get drawn into this—this whatever it is that's going on?"

Tyce stood again and paced slowly back and forth in front of his chair, then went to look at the laptop screen a few feet away on the small desk.

He turned to again look at Faust. "I still don't know how I was brought into this…into Kant's Israeli orbit."

"I guess it's time we can tell him, Randy."

Both men were startled at Morticai Kant's words. The stocky Israeli moved quickly through the door he had just opened and walked to where the men stood, facing him.

"We just flew in," he said, sitting then putting a briefcase beside the chair. "I have some last-minute things to complete before we can move everything necessary to the project."

"I just spoke with my daughter, Tyce. She said to take care of you." He looked up at the younger man. "I see that Ehud has done just that."

"You know about my...my dream or whatever?" Tyce sat across from the Maglan chief and studied his face.

"Yes, Ehud told me all about it. Said you were in quite a state when he burst into the room."

"It was as real as anything I've experienced," Tyce said. "When you have a cold, steel blade pressed against your throat, and somebody in a terrorist headdress is about to film your beheading...that's not something you can easily chalk up to some imagined or dreamed situation."

"And that is why we must get to the heart of the matter, to the reason you were brought into my 'orbit', as you put it."

The silence following Kant's words was broken by the archeologist. "I guess I should begin with the explanation, Tyce."

Faust paused to look at Kant, who nodded his approval.

"I had a high temperature. A high fever. I had a case of pneumonia, was the consensus of the several of my doctor friends who looked at me." Faust paced slowly around the other two men while he explained.

"It was a dream which, like yours last evening, was real to me. I could not differentiate between reality versus the experience. It was the same evening that you had the accident in which you were given your first view of the sarcophagus."

Faust stopped pacing and seemed to concentrate on

memory of that night. "I was in a desert area...somewhere in the area that must have been Iraq. I saw a golden object. It was a golden sarcophagus, I now know."

Faust again frowned in concentration while recalling the fever-driven experience. "You were in that dream... so was Morticai. You, Tyce, turned into Morticai before my eyes."

The archeologist seated himself across from Tyce and leaned forward, his elbows on his knees. "I knew, somehow I knew, I must call Morticai. It was something I was compelled to do—"

"—And he did," Kant interrupted. "He finally got in touch with me as we were in the process of routing a contingent of ISIL murderers in the Jordanian Valley. The golden sarcophagus was the key. When he told me his dream, the vision of the golden object he saw confirmed in my mind that this was something...something, maybe, from Jehovah. I was, as now, deeply involved in the project that has at its center the sarcophagus and its contents."

The thought flashed that this wasn't a man who was easily moved by anything proposed as supernatural. Tyce saw on the Israeli's face an expression of total acceptance of Faust's vision.

Faust said, "I told Morticai that not only he, but you, were central to that vision."

"I've come to understand that our friend, Tyce, has the ear of the Almighty," the Maglan chief said. "I knew nothing of you, my young friend. But Randy told me about your experiences in that cave on Patmos...of the many things you have gone through since."

"I told him all about your recurring visions," Faust said. "How you have a sixth sense of some sort. I believe it is from the Lord."

"Then," he continued, "I learned, when you called me, that you had the view of the sarcophagus. About your encounter with the winged creature as your vehicle left the highway."

Kant interrupted. "He told me about your extrasensory perception, or whatever it is. That your reporter's curiosity drives you to explore anomalous things. That you have been shown to have the ability to—I don't know how else to put it—to Remotely View things. Our scientists are convinced these things, this extrasensory perception...the ability of Remote Viewing, is a reality. A scientific fact."

Faust said, "I would say, Tyce, that your ability is a God-given gift for these times so near the end of the age. The ESP is something my spirit within tells me might come from the other side, not from the heavenly side."

Morticai Kant roared with laughter. "So, our Remote Viewing is of the devil."

"The Bible warns of dabbling in the occult, Morticai," Faust said. "The books of Deuteronomy, Leviticus, and others forewarn of such activity."

"Then, why is it not a terrible thing when our young friend here engages in the same?" Kant's question was put with good humor.

"Joel 2:28 tells us that, in the end of days, young men will have visions and old men will dream dreams," Faust said. "I believe in my spirit that both Tyce and myself have been placed, for whatever reasons, within those who are assigned by Heaven to prophesy as we near the time of Christ's return."

"Ah! But why do I, a Jew who is accused of putting Christ to death, embrace both of you? It all smacks of something too strange to figure."

"Indeed," Faust agreed. "God works in mysterious ways, His miracles to perform."

"Well, all I know is that our young man has done great service to my beloved nation with his Remote Viewing ability."

The Maglan chief gripped Tyce on both shoulders as they stood face to face. "And this is why you have been brought into my orbit," he said with a hearty laugh.

≈

ESSIE RAN TOWARD HIM, her arms outstretched. Despite her tears of joy, she was more stunning in her beauty now than when they had said their goodbyes.

She sobbed into Tyce's chest while embracing him tightly. He held her just as close, catching the familiar scent that was the perfect essence of femininity.

"Abba was right," she said while they held hands, walking toward the terminal building. "Our having to be apart for a time makes seeing you again even more wonderful."

"Maybe so," Tyce said, "but the time in between, I could do without." He said, stopping then to pull her to himself. She said nothing before their lips met and lingered in a kiss that sealed the joy of the reunion.

≈

THE CONTRAPTION WAS UNWIELDY. When the man in the lab coat placed it on his head, Tyce instinctively tried to shift in a way to more easily accept the placement.

"Hold still," the scientist said gently. "The Stimulator will settle in the correct place momentarily."

"The Stimulator? That's what this thing is called?"

The scientist said nothing, continuing to adjust the device against Tyce's head. Finally, he spoke.

"Yes, Mr. Greyson. It is called the Stimulator, because it uses certain electrical impulses to...*stimulate*...thought process. It enhances the ability of the cognitive process. More than that, it stimulates the subconscious abilities within the human brain."

Tyce digested the man's words for a few seconds then said, "This thing has been fully tested, I take it?"

"You aren't the first, if that is what you are asking," the man said making the final, gentle twist of the instrument then stepping back to look over its disposition on the head.

Tyce again let the man's words make their way through his thought process.

"And were there...are there any side effects?"

"There have been none thus far," the scientist said, walking to and sitting down before the control cabinet a few feet away.

"How many have you...tested...this thing on?"

"You needn't worry," the Israeli scientist said, touching glass control plates on the console in front of him. "The Stimulator is perfectly safe. There will be no side effects."

Tyce glanced around at the strange confines of the small enclosure in which they had placed him. The scientist closed the door that fit its frame snugly like a sealed, airtight compartment door of a ship.

Tyce, now sitting in semi-darkness, illuminated only by a series of lights embedded in the enclosure's walls, heard the voice of the scientist through the device's headphone. "When the Stimulator is activated, you will sense only a moment of slight dizziness. You should then

begin extrasensory perception when I induce an electronic stimulation."

"Okay," was Tyce's only response; he was a bit antsy
about what he could expect in the next minutes.

"Here we go," the man sitting at the control board
said, while manipulating the board's circuitry.

There were at first no noticeable effects, while Tyce
stared into the darkened environment. Would the experience be like the many he had been subjected to over the
years since the snake bite at Patmos? Since the accident
on the highway in Maryland? Would there be the brilliant point of light that then bursts spectacularly into a
full-blown vision?

His thinking ability darkened and began undulating,
seeming to ride a wave of emotion. Still, there was no
vision-like image or thought that manifested—only
memories of most recent times spent with Essie, of his
talking with Randolph Faust and Morticai Kant.

"Prepare for a slight electrical infusion," the accented
voice of the Israeli at the control board said into his ear
through the Stimulator device. "You should sense somewhat of an elevated imagination. Do you sense a change?"

"Only a kind of coming and going, like a fever when
you close your eyes," Tyce responded.

"Good, good. That is exactly the sensation you should
have at this point. I will now increase the infusion of
stimulation," the Israeli said.

Tyce's mind suddenly seemed to explode with
thoughts of every sort—a cacophony of thoughts that
produced confusion. The tumbling together of thought
grew more problematic while the scientist turned a
rheostat to increase the electrical stimulation.

At the crescendo of the massive brainstorm, when he

was at the point of tearing the device from his head, the cerebral scene smoothed to a serene landscape. His mind transported him over a lush green and multi-colored field toward a body of water reflecting a dark, purple mountain. A slightly chilling breeze wafted over his body, and he landed softly, gently, in front of the lake.

The figure of a man was walking toward him—traversing the smooth water that reflected the brilliant blue sky above. The man stood on the water's surface, looking into his very soul, it seemed.

"Tyce Greyson. You are selected for this moment to perform tasks on behalf of the chosen. The evil human stimulation will not assist in your mission. It will only hinder the purposes for which you are called."

It was Michael! His voice penetrated to the core of Tyce's brain in euphoric clarity. He stood upon the water, making Tyce Greyson understand his commission from on high.

The man, his eyes like sparkling waters, blue beyond any blue he had seen, spoke with deep, echoing reverberation into his very spirit. Bursts of inspiration that piqued his perception in every corner of his exponentially enhanced cerebral capacity seemed to fill his mind and spill over to run downward through his body.

Otherworldly things that couldn't be contained through the filling process seemed to move outward from his bodily presence and coalesce somehow, somewhere he couldn't determine.

He wanted to ask questions, to probe the—the all-inclusiveness of what the euphoria entailed. To know heaven's reasons for what he knew was directly from that realm.

Yet it all was there. It was now within him to know. The knowledge from on high had, he somehow knew, collected somewhere without, then flowed inward and pooled within himself. For whatever purposes, Tyce Greyson had been infused with knowledge withheld from mankind—from the human creation—to this point in time, space, and dimensional existence.

Just as quickly as the electronically induced infusion had begun, it was over. The sensation left him drained, emptied of emotion and thought.

Recovery over the next minutes brought increasing intensity to his effort to remember what his time under the influence of the Stimulator had meant. Try as he might, he couldn't recall even a moment. But the absolute understanding that something beyond human experience had taken place burned at his brain's core.

"How do you feel?" The scientist looked at Tyce, lifting his eyelids to keep them open. "It will take a few minutes to completely awaken," the Israeli said in a comforting tone.

Still, Tyce couldn't speak, couldn't fully form thoughts to verbalize the things he wanted to say —to ask.

Within minutes, his thinking had cleared, and he sipped on the unsweetened tea he had been handed by a lab assistant.

"Now," the Israeli said, putting his hand on Tyce's shoulder. "What do you remember of the...experience?"

"I can't remember anything," Tyce said, "except that whatever was going on it was like something...something beyond reality...from a supernatural source. I don't know how else to describe it. I just know there's something there. There's something I'm supposed to know, or do, and it's the most important thing that can be imagined."

Puzzled, Tyce looked up at the man, who continued

to examine his subject's eyes. "This is not an unusual response for those who have undergone the experience of the Stimulator," the man said, patting Tyce's shoulder and moving away to examine the control-board monitor.

"The amnesia should be temporary," he continued. "The memories, at least in part, should return. Come see what the technology has gathered from your venture into the sphere of the Stimulator." The scientist beckoned for Tyce to join him while he looked into the monitor screen and adjusted a few glass-plate controls. The scenes displayed upon the monitor changed as he did so.

"These images were recorded directly from your brain's experience," he said. "See how your thoughts were taking you across a lush, green landscape, toward a lake. A beautiful scene, don't you agree?"

"Yes. Quite beautiful," Tyce agreed, seeing the image on the screen he still didn't recall. "This is what I saw in this...this experience?"

"Yes. The Stimulator has reached the capacity to actually photograph, through the subject undergoing the experience, cerebral, cognitive experience. You seemed to stop here and stand in front of this lake. This is somewhat problematic at this point. You don't move from here. There are no images recorded by the Stimulator, even though you were under full infusion."

"What does it mean?" Tyce stared at the monitor screen, straining to remember anything of the experience.

"It's hard to know," the scientist said. "We've never had brain activity become frozen while under Stimulator process. But the data here shows your mind is fully functioning—that your imaginative brain processes are normal in every respect as you stand before the lake scene. Perhaps the memory will return of your experience at that moment."

～

"MAGLAN IS the only clandestine service in the world with the Stimulator."

Morticai Kant walked to the big window to his left and pried the blinds apart with his fingertips, peering into the Brussels' early morning. "That is, our version is the most advanced for Remote Viewing purposes," he said, releasing the blinds and turning back to face Tyce Greyson and Randolph Faust.

"How do you know others aren't as advanced?" Tyce's reporter's mind forced him to question the Maglan chief.

"Remote Viewing, for one thing, gives us the advantage…and the vantage!" Kant said with a growling laugh. "That's why we are called a 'clandestine service'. We have ways of knowing what others have in this regard."

"Not even the US has it?"

Kant's face contorted in an expression of consideration of Tyce's question, before answering.

"A…*different*…version of our technology. America's hasn't reached our capability."

"I thought you and the American government would share such technologies," Tyce said.

"It is not the same America as years ago, my friend," Kant said, again peering between the window blinds.

"The so-called deep state is indeed a matter of great concern. Our investment is in the preservation of Israel. Our very existence depends upon remaining vigilant. There are many things we don't share with anyone—

especially not the American clandestine operations…or intelligence services if you prefer."

Kant again released the blinds and walked to take a chair facing Greyson and Faust.

"We can no longer trust the black-ops people in American government, or in any other government. The covert entities are like governments in general. For whatever reason, the Jewish state is on their hit lists…or so it seems."

"Zechariah 12," Randolph Faust said.

Kant and Greyson looked at the archeologist, questioning puzzlement crossing their faces.

"Bible prophecy coming to pass," Faust continued. "We have reached the end of the Age of Grace. The time of the end is near."

"Ah! Your prophecy again," Kant said with mock exasperation. "I say it is jealousy that Israel is at the forefront of advancing technology. The rest of the world cannot catch up. They are angry about that. That, and, for some reason that is beyond all sanity, they take Israel's enemies' part in every case."

"For whatever reason, it is the fulfillment of Bible prophecy," Faust said.

"What's the prophecy?" Tyce said.

Faust turned to Tyce after taking a moment to consider the reporter's question and recall the passage he long ago memorized. "The prophecy is about Israel at the time just before Christ's return. It's from the prophet Zechariah. From chapter 12, verses 1 through 3.

"'The burden of the word of the Lord for Israel, saith the Lord, which stretcheth forth the heavens, and layeth the foundation of the earth, and formeth the spirit of man within him. Behold, I will make Jerusalem a cup of trembling unto all the people round about, when they shall be in the siege both against Judah and against Jerusalem. And in that day will I make Jerusalem a burdensome stone for all people: all that burden themselves with it shall be cut in pieces, though all the people of the earth be gathered together against it.'"

Tyce's expression brightened with enlightenment. "Yes! The Scripture given me in the text message! The one signed with the name of Michael...in Hebrew," he said. "That night following the vision I saw while standing in front of the bathroom mirror."

MORTICAI KANT LOOKED toward the ceiling and frowned a frown of recognition. "Ah, yes! I had almost forgotten that one," he said, shaking his head and smiling.

"I was under the impression you didn't hold with prophecy," Tyce said.

"We learned in school and inculcation programs much about and from the prophets," Kant said. "We memorized many such...prophecies. But I suppose that one didn't take very well in the memorizing process."

"At any rate, this is where we are...where your nation is...in the timeline of history," Faust said. "Just considering how every vote with the exception of America goes against you in the UN is fulfillment enough of the prophecy."

"If this election in America ends the way we fear it will, we will lose the US as a friend, too. This is one more reason we will not trust the full scope of our technological advances to those within America's covert operations."

"I don't see how any of this applies to me," Tyce said. "You tried your Stimulator on me. It apparently had no effect...none that did much good. What did you hope my interaction with the device would produce?"

"We are a bit disappointed that your...unusual abilities...weren't brought to the surface with the experiment," Kant said. "But our people say there might be delayed reaction, that the memory of your experience under the influence of the instrument might yet emerge."

"The device...the Stimulator...is a thing I can't condone. It opens the mind to the powers and principalities, to wickedness in high places," Randolph Faust said sternly. "I believe it opens the mind to dark, evil spiritual forces. I don't see how the Lord will bless such experimentation."

Tyce Greyson suddenly vaulted from the chair. He pounded a fist against the palm of his hand. The explosion of movement caused his partners in the conversation to jerk in surprise.

"That's it! That's what I saw...what I heard!" He looked at the men, a broad smile of recall crossing his face. "What you said, Randy. That's it!"

Neither man said anything while Tyce spun and again pounded his fist against his other hand. "Randy, you said it's evil—the Stimulator device."

"Yes? I said the Lord couldn't approve of such an opening to the evil spirit world."

"That's it! That's what Michael told me."

"Michael? The man you have seen so many times?"

"Yes, Randy. Michael told me while I stood there at that lake. He was standing on the surface of the water. He said I was 'selected for this moment' to 'perform tasks on behalf of the chosen'." He said, 'the evil, human stimulation' wouldn't help me in my mission, it would 'only hinder' the 'purposes' I'm called for."

It all flooded back. The deep things of the heavenly

realm that the man of his visions had spoken to him. Not the details, but assurance that he would fully understand in time. God's directives were on their way. They would be made known at the right moments.

"I am to indeed work for you...for Israel, sir," Tyce said, the euphoria experienced during the time standing before the man at the lake reemerging to fill his core being while he looked into Morticai Kant's startled countenance.

CHAPTER 10

November 2016

Rain fell from the heavy clouds above Brussels and pooled along Avenue de Stalingrad while Tyce sat next to Essie in the SUV.

"The election results are just unbelievable," Randall Faust said from the other side of Essie. "Who would have thought he could beat her?"

"Yeah. Well, I for one am not going to spend a lot of time thinking about it. Just will accept it as a gift from the political gods," Tyce said.

"From the only *God* there is, Tyce," the archeologist corrected in solemn inflection. "There's just no way most anyone thought it would turn out this way."

"Was it really that big of an upset?" Essie directed the question at Faust.

"You bet it was. Trump is a total outsider. He's his own man. The ramifications of this election...well, they could be staggering."

"Why? What will make the difference? Why will the

new administration be different from the Obama administration?"

"The social issues, alone, will make all the difference," Faust said. "The new people in power will champion cultural issues more in line with traditional values held by Americans. Israel will be beneficiary of the new administration's way of doing business."

"The current one certainly hasn't taken our side," Essie said.

Thunder over the city followed the flashes of lightning that illuminated the hulking buildings just ahead.

"I'll find a basement parking entrance," Ehud Begin said from behind the steering wheel. He searched the lightning-brightened side streets, trying to recall the most direct entrance to the building nearest the area they sought.

"What do you think your father has in mind, wanting me to meet him here?" Tyce had lost sleep, struggling to come up with answers to troubling questions. One... Why did the enigmatic man he knew only as Michael tell him that the Israeli technology—the Remote Viewing technology—would only inhibit, not assist, his ability to engage...engage in what? Two...Exactly what was he expected to do in the use of his strange ability? Three... Why was he, of all people, chosen to...to what? To somehow help Israel...help Israel do what? Four...What did all of it have to do with the giant mummy being and the serum project his ESP, or whatever it was, had revealed in a vision, the revelation about the Earthlord?

"Morticai is a man of deep thoughts nobody can fully mine," Essie said. "That's why he is head of Maglan. But he is deeply convinced that there are those even in the supposedly friendly American places of covert operations who want to see Israel diminished, or even removed. He is going to use any and all at his disposal to prevent those from being successful."

Begin swung the big vehicle to the right and onto a down ramp into the subterranean parking expanse.

"Your father's one love he would die for, besides you, Essie, is his beloved Israel," Randolph Faust said while Begin searched for and found a parking place. "That's why he always seems totally absorbed with what's directly in front of him. He knows that Israel can't afford any mistakes in understanding the nation's enemies...or even its supposed *friends* within American covert operations."

"Papa was always exactly that way," Essie said, "even before becoming head of Maglan. Always it was his *duty* he was devoted to while an officer in the IDF. Mother understood and supported him totally."

"Well, I'm sure that's why he was made Maglan chief," Faust said while exiting the vehicle as Tyce held the door open for Essie on the other side. "Your mother is some kind of strong, wonderful woman."

Faust continued the conversation while they followed Begin farther into the immense parking chamber. "Your father has told me that a new American president was absolutely essential in order to relations to improve. He didn't have much hope for that happening. But he said if the miracle...as he called it...*did* happen, and someone who truly was friend to Israel became president, there would be major...internecine conflict...as he put it."

"Of what sort?" Tyce held the door open for both Essie and the archeologist to pass through, following Begin, who was already ahead of them performing security duties.

"America's clandestine services...NSA, CIA, even the DOD and State Department...all are loaded with entrenched operatives who are globalists. Their loyalty is to those in this very building, to the internationalists who want nationalism…national borders done away with."

"And within Washington, DC, itself there are bureaucratic enclaves devoted not to American interests but to internationalist interests," Faust said.

Several minutes later, Morticai Kant hugged and kissed his daughter before taking the offered hands of the journalist and the archeologist. "Welcome to Brussels," he said, waving his hand in the direction of several chairs. "We have much to accomplish. The American election has…has electrified us all!"

TYCE'S brain was still reeling from the things Kant had revealed, had told him during the hour following his coming to the European Union annex. The Maglan chief had immediately led him to a helicopter pad atop the building, from where just the two men and Ehud Begin were whisked to another location—one that, Kant had told him, was 100 percent secure from snooping devices.

The Israeli had informed him that not even Essie could come along to the building, a one-story, blockhouse structure some miles from downtown Brussels. To bring her into the secretive matters would be to endanger her life. Tyce had agreed wholeheartedly with her father's decision to let her stay back with their mutual friend, Randolph Faust. There she would be protected by more than fifty IDF covert operatives.

"The internationalists are Israel's number-one enemy," the Maglan chief had said. He then had proceeded to lay out the plans for the destruction of the

Jewish state Maglan had learned of. "America, I'm sorry to report," he had told Tyce, "is at the epicenter of this cabal's determination to shake up geopolitics. Israel is the place they intend to start this great shaking."

Now Kant preceded Tyce into a room the journalist recognized as similar to that of the Remote Viewing facility. The chamber with the sealable door sat in the big room's corner.

"This facility is significantly more...proficient...than the one you previously experienced, Tyce," the Maglan chief said. He walked to its portal and looked around its interior.

"I don't think it will work, sir," Tyce said.

"What?"

"I said I don't think the Remote Viewing apparatus will work with me," the journalist repeated.

"Oh? Why not?" Kant's question was tinged with skepticism about Tyce's motive in declaring such a conclusion.

Tyce stood at the portal to the chamber looking into its semi-darkened interior, then turned back to Kant.

"Remember that I told you that the one called Michael told me the device would inhibit my being able to...look into these...viewing matters."

"Then why accompany me here?" Kant asked, more with curiosity in his tone than irritation.

"Because I want to help, and this is the center of your Remote Viewing efforts. I figured that this would be the logical place to try to do whatever I can to help."

Kant peered at Tyce, his head slightly cocked, one eye squinting in concentration. "Tell me again—this Michael. What, exactly, did he say to you?"

"He said the Stimulus device won't help me to...to accomplish the things for Israel you want. The device would only inhibit me being able to… see…what you want me to see."

The Maglan chief stood mute for a moment, his fingertips tapping against a bookcase. "And what do you think, Tyce Greyson? What do you think Michael's advice will net us in our Remote Viewing efforts?"

"I have no idea, sir. This whole thing is beyond my understanding. This strange guy, Michael, has appeared to me from the time I told you about him, just before I met you the first time in DC. He suddenly was in the room and left just as abruptly. I didn't see him come in the room or leave."

"Oh yes," Kant said. "The one you said announced our arrival that day. You thought he was part of my contingent."

"Yes. That's the guy."

Kant said nothing for several seconds. He then let his gaze into Tyce's eyes linger until he turned to answer the chiming phone he retrieved from a coat pocket.

"Very well," he said into the phone, nodding his head while listening to the voice in the receiver. "Yes. This is quite possible. We must make the attempt to view proceedings."

The Maglan chief snapped his fingers while still listening to the voice on the other end of the cell transmission. One of the men walked beside Kant to retrieve a note he handed the operative. The man hurried into the Stimulator chamber and sat at the control board, beginning to manipulate the glass control plates. Another man nudged Tyce to sit in the chair and began adjusting the Stimulator apparatus around Tyce's head.

"What's going on?" His question solicited no response as both of the operatives continued to do their work.

The board lit up with lights of varying brightness and colors.

Finally, Kant stepped into the chamber. "That was Brugland at EU headquarters," he said, "A meeting has started there. It was not announced—a surreptitious, unplanned meeting. There is something up we must learn about," Kant went to stand near the man operating the control board. "Make sure your coordinates are precise," he said to the man who continued to manipulate the board. Kant looked to the operative just finishing up placing the Stimulator device on Tyce's head and ears.

"Yes, sir," the operator said, looking again at the piece of paper on which Kant had scribbled the numbers.

"We are counting on you, Tyce," the Maglan chief said, patting Tyce's shoulder. "Just relax and let the Stimulator work."

The men left the chamber and shut the portal hatch. Tyce glanced around his surroundings, the flashing lights from the control board seeming to increase the undulant sensations within his cognitive process.

Within seconds, he sensed that he stood before the crystal blue lake as in his previous introduction to the device's effects. Again, the figure of a man approached, walking atop the lake's surface.

"Michael!"

Tyce's own words startled him, while the familiar man stood before him. "Tyce, the device isn't necessary," Michael said calmly, softly. "Remove it. It only inhibits your mission."

Tyce did as he was instructed. When he had removed the device completely, he found himself suddenly surrounded on all sides by brilliant light that seemed to pulse with life of its own. Yet the light wasn't harsh; it wasn't so bright as to make him squint.

The profusion of light that cocooned him parted, and a large hand reached through the light veil to grasp his arm. The hand was one of effulgence, its skin possessed of inner light from which emanated power and strength. Yet its grip was gentle while it tugged him through the opening of the light that had engulfed him.

The door to the chamber popped open, the control-board operator rushing in, followed by Morticai Kant.

Tyce heard in echoing voices as if they were far distant. Somehow, he saw in his mind's eye the men as they entered the empty chamber.

"He's gone!"

The operator's words brought about stunned looks on the faces of the several men who now stood looking at the chair in which, moments before, Tyce Greyson had sat.

BRIGHTENED surroundings obscured his vision as he sensed his feet contact a solid surface. So stunning had been his circumstance that he had neither time nor ability to make sense of moving from the Stimulator chamber to this now-coming-into-focus environment.

A number of men sat around a coffin-shaped conference table. Some wore business suits and ties; others wore military uniforms.

Although Tyce stood near the table, they didn't appear to notice. He walked behind the men in their chairs nearest him. No one was aware of his presence.

He recognized four of the men as US senators. Two were members of both major political parties. One man in conversation he recognized as a top Pentagon general.

A door at one end of the room opened, and two men

in business suits hurried through to take their places. Tyce instantly saw that they were the executive heads of two of the major broadcast networks.

"Sorry we're late," one of the men said, taking his seat at the center of the table. "A bit of a traffic jam."

The voices echoed in his ears, as if they were being transmitted, not like he was physically in the presence of those speaking.

"We need to get right to it," the man in a business suit at the table's end farthest from the door said with a slight accent.

"While we were all totally surprised at these developments, we, as you know, were and are fully prepared, contingency-wise."

Tyce no longer feared detection. He decided he would test just how far he could intrude without being noticed by the cabal. He moved forward and touched the back of one of the high-backed conference chairs in which no one was sitting.

He couldn't feel the hard, leather surface. He watched his right hand melt into the chair's back. His hand had passed through it!

Tyce was even more emboldened now and determined to see how far he could take this newfound capability. He walked forward, his body passing through the chair. He stood, then, within the center of the table, having passed through without being noticed. He listened to the conversation from his unique vantage.

"This means that the project's timeline will be thrown off," the man at the end of the table said. "We cannot let this take place. We'll put into effect, here in this country, the alternate plan for now. Hopefully, with you being totally on board—" the man nodded at the two broadcast executives "—we can soon remove this…intruder…from office and get on with Project Earthlord."

The words echoed within Tyce's hyper-enhanced understanding. "Earthlord" reverberated in his senses and harkened his memory to the earlier time when he, himself, had used the term to shock the man who headed the sarcophagus project into talking to him rather than shuffling him off to the man's underlings.

"The extract is still some time from perfection," the man at the end of the table continued. "This…election… has further complicated the process of producing the serum. I can't overemphasize the necessity of keeping US resources in this project under absolute lock and key. This new administration must not be allowed to restrict the use of these…assets…in any way whatsoever.

"All of the intelligence operatives—those at the top— are in complete agreement. We can't allow a trend back toward nationalism for the United States. We cannot achieve our goal, apart from an all-out effort to neutralize this election. This man the foolish people have brought to this office must go. If we can't prevent inauguration, then we must use every means we have to remove him at the earliest possible moment."

"And how far do we go with carrying that out?" All eyes turned to the uniformed Army general several chairs down from the end of the table.

There was silence as Tyce looked to each face from his position at the center of the tabletop.

The man at the table end answered after a few more seconds. "By whatsoever means necessary," he said, his eyes narrowing in a look of determination.

"And what about Treasury? What about the Secret Service?" The US senator directly across from the general had an expression as sternly etched as that of the man to whom he had asked the question.

Again, there was silence for a few seconds before he answered. "As I said, *ALL* of our collective are on board. At least those in control—those at the top."

Assassination! They were proposing that *assassination,* if necessary, was on the table!

"Gentlemen, we will meet again upon conclusions reached in the Higher Council. Be prepared to implement things directed when we next meet."

Tyce watched the meeting's attendants stand from their chairs. To his astonishment, a dark cloud shaped like a human form emerged from each man and dissipated into thin air.

CHAPTER 11

"This defies physics!"

The man in the white lab coat was in near-hysterics while touching Tyce Greyson's temples and looking into his eyes.

"There has never been such a thing," he said to nobody in particular. "No physical being can just... disappear then reappear."

"What about the cloaking technologies?" the Maglan chief asked calmly while watching the frantic scientist examine Tyce from head to foot.

"But that is with the aid of technology. That happens with years of painstaking experimentation at the molecular, even atomic, level. This...is just phenomenal. There's never been anything like it!"

"Tyce," Morticai Kant interrupted the man's ongoing exasperation. "What, exactly, happened?"

"I had the device...the Stimulator...placed as it should be. I started seeing a...Remote Viewing, I guess you call it. Then the man, Michael, he walked toward me on the surface of that same lake." Tyce paused to remember the encounter.

"Yes? Then what happened?" the Maglan chief put in.

"He told me…again…that the device, the Stimulator, would just inhibit my mission. He instructed me to take it off. When I did, I was suddenly shrouded by this light, engulfing me."

Again, he paused, still awed by the experience.

"Yes, yes. And what happened then?" Kant said with urgency in his words.

"Then this huge hand," Tyce continued. "It was glowing with light. It grasped my arm and hand and led me along. I felt it tugging, and then I was suddenly in a room. I knew instinctively that it was a room somewhere in a government building or something."

"And this room—you don't know where it might have been located…in government, or whatever?"

"No. It had this huge, coffin-shaped conference table, with high-backed chairs all along its sides and at the ends." When he paused to collect his thoughts, the Israeli prompted him.

"And people? Were there people in this room—at that table?"

"Yes, sir. I recognized two United States senators and a few generals in uniform. I didn't know two of them. One, I think, was one of the Joint Chiefs of Staff."

"And, what happened next?"

"I…I was undetected. They didn't know I was there. And…when—"

He stopped his explanation in midsentence, seeming paralyzed by remembering the experience.

The Maglan chief intervened, "—and what then? What happened?"

"I touched the back of one of the empty chairs. My

hand sliced right through the chair." Tyce looked at the men with a quizzical expression. "It just went right through that chair."

"What then?" Kant said impatiently.

"Then I...I don't know why...I just walked through the chair and through that massive table. Then I stood at the center, my feet and bottom half on the floor and the top part of my body on top of the table. I was watching each of the men in conversation. They had no idea I was there."

All was silent in the room as the men glanced nervously at each other for a few seconds.

"What were they discussing, Tyce?" Kant pressed for more details. "Can you tell us about their conversation?"

"Yes. They were discussing the election. The US presidential election. They were talking about how they wouldn't let it stand."

"The election? And do you remember who was leading this conversation?" Kant asked.

"I don't know who he was," Tyce said. "But he appeared to be in charge. The others all seemed to...to look to him for their directions."

"And what did he...direct them to do?"

"He said the election can't stand. He said the people were foolish for electing the new president and that the election must be...neutralized. Yes. He used the word 'neutralized'."

Kant glanced at the men listening to Tyce recounting the experience.

"And what did he say about this thing that must be done—this neutralization?" Kant said.

"He said that it must be done by any means necessary. A general...not the chief of staff, but another uniformed man, asked, 'What about the secret service?'."

"And then what was the response?" Kant probed.

"The man at the end of the table...the one in charge, apparently, said that all of the people at the top of the...I guess the appropriate agencies in government...were *on board* with doing whatever must be done."

Tyce looked to each man surrounding him before continuing. "The man said one thing more before they adjourned. He said they should be ready to do what was necessary when they next came together. That first the 'Higher Council' must meet to decide what that action will be."

"Higher Council?" the Israeli chief stroked his chin in thought.

Tyce spoke before Kant could talk.

"And...here's something I can't understand. As each man stood to be dismissed from the meeting...it's almost too strange to talk about. You'll think I'm nuts—"

"Look Tyce," Kant said. "If we don't think already that you are nuts after telling of these things so far, we aren't likely to ever think of you in that way. After all, you disappeared and reappeared, defying all the laws of physics, as our scientist friend here says."

"I guess you're right," Tyce went on. "So I'll just say it: When these men got up from their chairs to leave, dark, gray human-like forms—like clouds with arms, legs, and heads—emerged from each of the men. One of these... things...came out of each person."

"What happened then?" Kant pushed further.

"They just disappeared. Just dissipated into thin air and were gone."

～

TYCE STOOD when he saw Essie coming toward him. She approached hurriedly, her auburn hair elegantly resting in a tightly wrapped way that exquisitely framed her face.

"Sorry to keep you waiting," she said when she reached to embrace him. "Morticai had me doing some last-second things."

"Our orders are on the way, according to your instructions," he said. "They should be here shortly."

"Good. We're expected at the preview at eight."

She was seated across from Tyce while they dined. His desirous thoughts, generated by his dinner companion's loveliness, left abruptly when her words brought him back to business at hand.

"You know, Papa is quite impressed with your calmness in all of this," Essie said before sipping the wine the waiter had just poured.

"Yeah, well, I'll probably have nightmares tonight," Tyce said.

"I guess that's about as far as we should go with this subject," Essie said, sitting back to let the waiter arrange the plate in front of her.

"Yes. Your father cautioned us to say nothing while we're not in a secure setting."

"That's just standard operating procedure for Maglan. But this is a serious matter. I haven't seen greater security than what is around these matters."

"I guess we're getting too far into the…matters," Tyce said with a chuckle. "On another matter, when can we get some alone time?" His question brought a softened expression that initiated a spark of piqued warmth from somewhere at the center of Essie's emotion.

She was silent for a moment, then said, almost shyly, "I don't know, maybe…"

"I love you, Essie Jorba, or Kant, or whatever your name is," he said, interrupting her hesitating search for an answer to his question.

Then they were silent, letting the meaning of Tyce's question traverse their thoughts. Each felt the growing passion of the moment roll through their emotions. Essie looked away, unable to maintain the intensity of the unspoken contact, but finally, she spoke, her eyes returning to his. "Tyce—I love you so much." A streamlet of a tear ran from one corner of her left eye, and she dabbed at it with the napkin she took from her lap.

The balance of dinner time would be spent in near silence, unspoken thoughts of the unnamed time of being alone together in intimacy serving to heighten their desire.

～

AN HOUR AND A HALF LATER, the Israeli Maglan chief was agitated. He paced the room while his daughter and Tyce entered the small room.

"Tyce, are there more details of the…the viewing you experienced?"

Kant tugged the journalist by the arm to a chair and was, himself, seated in a chair directly in front of him. "We need details, if you can provide them."

"Why? What's wrong?"

Kant ignored the journalist's curiosity. "Let me know if you heard anything else about their plans to…neutralize…the American election. It is very important. Do you remember anything else, other than what you've told us?"

Tyce looked cerebrally into the question as he stared at the space on the floor between them. He shook his head after several seconds of trying to recall his time spent among the men around the conference table. "No…no, I can't think of anything I haven't told you."

"And what are your thoughts on what you heard?" Kant pressed. "What do you think the leader of this group meant by saying that all were on board…that they were for taking whatever steps necessary to…to neutralize the results of the election?"

"Assassination. That was the thing that popped into my mind at that time. I thought they were talking about assassination, if necessary—especially since they brought up the question of the Secret Service. When he was asked about the Secret Service, that's when he said *all* were on board, whatever it takes."

Kant mentally digested the words before speaking. "And this…Higher Council. What do you think this means?"

"I keep coming back to those dark, cloud-like figures that emerged…that exited the people at the table. That's what comes to mind when you ask that question."

"What are your thoughts in that regard, Tyce?" the Maglan chief continued.

"That Higher Council…it's some sort of otherworldly influence. From somewhere other than here."

There was silence for a moment as both men let Greyson's words run through their thoughts. Finally, Kant spoke. "So, it is your…theory…that these cloud-like figures somehow possessed these men at the table—"

"—possessed, occupied, entered, and exited," Tyce interrupted. "I don't know. All I know is what I saw. At the end, when the guy adjourned the meetings, these things came out of each of the people and just, just dissipated into…nothingness."

Again, silence hovered over the conversation for a

few seconds before the Israeli spoke. "You think these men at the table...US senators, the generals, and the rest are somehow the underlings of this...this Higher Council?"

Tyce let the question carom within his mind before answering. "All I know is what I saw and heard," he said. "The guy at the head of the table said, 'We will meet again upon conclusions reached in the Higher Council. Be prepared to implement things directed when we next meet.'"

"Then the dark, human-like forms left the peoples' bodies?"

"Yes. They just seeped from the people like smoke, but in human-like shape. Then they just...*poof*," Tyce gesticulated to emphasize his description. "They just vanished, like smoke in the air."

The Maglan chief leaned forward, his expression one of total concentration when he asked the question. "And what do you make of your...seeing—experiencing—all of this, without the assistance of our Stimulator technology?"

"It's Michael. It's the only answer I have. Michael took me to that room...to be in the midst of that meeting. I believe, like Randy says, the whole thing is supernatural."

"From God, you mean?"

"From the heavenly dimension. That's the only explanation about any of this...this crazy vision stuff that's been part of my life now, ever since that snake bite on Patmos."

The Israeli's expression of concentration dissolved to a look of raised eyebrows and wrinkled forehead. "Well, heaven, hell, or high water...Israel will be defended."

Randolph Faust's voice interrupted Kant when the

archeologist entered the room and heard the Israeli's words. "And that's exactly what is happening," he said, coming to the men where they sat. "Michael is standing to defend Israel…"

Tyce and Kant turned their attention to Faust, who stood over them.

He said, "It's Daniel chapter 12, verse 1. 'And at that time shall Michael stand up, the great prince which standeth for the children of thy people: and there shall be a time of trouble, such as never was since there was a nation even to that same time: and at that time thy people shall be delivered, every one that shall be found written in the book.'"

ENERGY in the room was seismic. The scientists were abuzz, while the politicians from the various nations sat chatting with only slightly less expectation indicated through their volume of conversation.

Essie leaned close to Tyce, whispering into his ear just loudly enough to be heard.

"Why do you suppose there is so much interest tonight? Is it all just over the mummy in the sarcophagus, do you think?"

"I guess we're about to find out," Tyce replied, glancing at the men and women in conversations throughout the auditorium.

Moments later, the lights began dimming and conversations died while spotlights lit the raised stage platform. A man wearing a navy-blue suit approached a series of microphones at the center of the stage. He carried pages of paper, which he set atop a small dais.

A spotlight illuminated his face while TV cameras

and clicking camera shutters of the gathered newspeople captured his image.

Tyce's eyes widened as the man's features became clearly visible. He leaned to whisper to Essie, "It's that guy! The one I saw in the viewing facility."

"What guy?" she asked, seeing the man spread the papers as he prepared to speak.

"The one at the head of that conference table. It's him, no doubt about it," Tyce said, his mind filling with memories of the meeting.

Another figure approached the dais quickly. It was Rudolf Gravelan. Tyce straightened in his chair, while the scientist stepped in front of the man who had headed the conference during his vision.

Gravelan adjusted one of the microphones attached to the small podium.

"Ladies and gentlemen, we are honored to have with us Tuerelo Gavachee, of Vatican Council."

Gravelan stepped aside and waved his right hand toward the dais, inviting the taller man to step forward. The auditorium erupted in applause. When the clapping died, Gravelan spoke again.

"Counsel Gavachee will fill us in on the Vatican's ongoing interaction within Project Sarcophagus." Again, there was applause for twenty seconds before it died down to near silence.

Gravelan exited the stage and disappeared into the darkness. Gavachee looked around at those gathered in the barely lit auditorium anticipating his words.

"I bring you greetings from his Holiness, and from the council which I represent." He spoke in English, with only a hint of an Italian accent, Tyce thought, seeing the man move the papers in front of him on the podium.

"Of all relics of antiquity under Vatican auspices, the

golden sarcophagus and its contents are by far the most significant the Church has attained. The great scientific, biological, and—yes—*spiritual* blessings are enormous."

Gavachee paused and again scanned his audience, his expression one of determined confidence. "We shall use these fantastic blessings from on high for the betterment —dare I say—for the *salvation* of mankind!"

Tyce Greyson wondered while, for the next thirty minutes, the Vatican counsel waxed eloquent on plans for the great archeological "gift from on high". What part might it all play in their efforts to remove the newly elected president of the United States?

"AND DO YOU BELIEVE THIS...THIS Tuerelo Gavachee...to be the one who was in charge of the...the cabal you viewed?" Morticai Kant stood face to face with the American journalist while he posed the question, his face a hardened mask of intense concentration.

"Yes...it was the same guy, there's no doubt about it."

"Tell him about your thoughts," Essie put in while standing near Tyce and tugging gently on his shirtsleeve.

"What about your thoughts?" Kant said, his expression tightening even more.

"Well, I just remember his words. He said that all of the top intelligence operatives are in complete agreement. He said that they can't allow the US to continue to trend back toward nationalism. He said that they can't achieve their goal, apart from an all-out effort to neutralize the presidential election. He said the people were fools for electing him—the new president must be gotten rid of. He told them that if they can't prevent inauguration, then they'll have to use every means within their power to remove him as soon as possible."

Kant looked away in thought before returning to see Greyson's expression. "I see," Kant said. "What is the Vatican's part in all this? Is that your thought?"

"Yes, sir. That's exactly at the heart of my question. What's the Vatican's top counselor—or one of the top counselors—doing mixed up in all this?"

"You shouldn't be too surprised, Morticai," Randolph Faust said after hearing the back and forth. "You of Maglan are deeply involved in wanting to look into the evil being plotted against Israel."

Kant turned to see his friend, who had stood while listening just behind the Israeli.

"The Vatican has never been and is not now Israel's friend. Their entire religion is based upon their contention that the Catholic Church has taken the place of Israel in God's economy."

The archeologist waited for Kant's response, and when it was slow in coming, he continued. "All of heaven's blessings have been transferred to the Church, they believe. The pope, the so-called 'Vicar of Christ', now has the mantle of the first pope, who was Peter the Apostle and disciple of Christ, they contend. Israel is just a secular state to them, with no heavenly protection or divine, prophetic future."

"Yes. I've heard some of these things," Kant said. "The Vatican has a much different view of the Jewish people…of Israel…than the people of the…the Protestants."

"Many of the mainline Protestant denominations… those of the Reform sort…still hold to much of the Catholic dogma regarding the Jews and the modern nation of Israel. Many who emerged from the Protestant

Revolution under, of course, Luther, hold to the same dogma in terms of prophecy as the Vatican."

Tyce said, moving closer to Faust, "So is it this religious or prophetic anti-Semitism or whatever that is driving this...this intervention by the Vatican? Is this what this globalist demand to get rid of the man the people elected all about?"

"The plan doesn't originate from the Vatican, Tyce. It is from the mind of the first rebel against God's design for mankind. It's Luciferian—from the old serpent, the devil."

"But why does one of the world's major religions want the American election overturned, or...neutralized?" Essie said. "What do they hope to gain?"

"Yeah? And what is the Vatican doing mixed up in this mummy thing? What's the great importance in this to the Catholic Church?"

Tyce's words caused Randolph Faust to place a hand on his shoulder and smile brightly while explaining. "My boy, you've hit on what I believe is at the very heart of the sarcophagus project. Bible prophecy is what it's all about. Globalism is to be the driver of religious fervor as things wrap up for Christ's return."

"Religion? How so?" Essie said.

"And how can this sarcophagus project benefit the Vatican?" The Israeli Maglan chief said, following up on his daughter's question.

"I don't know," Faust said. "All I'm sure of is that by having one of the Vatican's top people from their council involved, we can be sure it's a power play of some sort."

"The men around that table...all of them were Americans," Tyce said. "I recognized even the top television network heads. But this guy...this Tuerelo Gavachee... from Rome—he was running the show."

"So will the ultimate head of such a cabal, Tyce—a much larger and much more evil cabal."

Tyce listened intently, trying to get Faust's meaning. The archeologist, seeing Tyce's puzzlement and that of Kant and his daughter, explained further. "The one who will ultimately head the final global order just before Christ's Second Advent will be a Roman. The 'Beast' of Revelation chapter 13...the Antichrist."

"This guy I saw at the head of that table is the Antichrist?" Tyce's question came with both amusement and surprise.

"No... no," Faust said with a chuckle. "But the fact is that 'Beast', as the book of Revelation calls him, will indeed come from where the Vatican is located. Rome seems to be at the center of that future fuhrer's power base."

"Where do you get that, Dr. Faust? Is that in Scripture? I've not heard that in the reading of the Torah."

Essie's question brought a response from her father.

"They get it from our prophet, Daniel, sweetheart," Kant said.

"Your father is right, Essie," the Israeli said. "From Daniel chapter 9, verses 26 and 27. He will come out of the people who would destroy the city and the sanctuary."

"And that is a future time we haven't yet reached. The city—Jerusalem—and the sanctuary—the Temple atop Moriah—were destroyed by the Romans in AD 70," Faust said, looking to Essie. "They were the Romans... the Roman army under General Titus, sent to put down the Jewish rebellion by his father, the Roman Emperor Vespasian. But, that one, the Antichrist, who will come out of that people, the Romans, is yet to appear. He will be from the people who made up the main part of that Roman army in AD 70."

Kant said in a roaring voice that left little doubt about his own thoughts. "Well, I don't know about some *Antichrist*, but these human minions of the devil—if there is a devil—are going to feel the full wrath of the IDF and of the forces of our American friends."

CHAPTER 12

Little news of progress had been divulged by the Project Sarcophagus scientists. About all that had been told was that it was promising. The DNA was definitely of nonhuman origin and was, somehow, living after thousands of years and could replicate under certain laboratory conditions. The extracts that could be obtained might therefore, the scientists agreed, offer greatly enhanced chances for human longevity.

Tyce Greyson let the thoughts of the things learned in the briefings about the project ruminate. He considered how he might present the notes he had taken and had recorded—the ones for the magazine articles he was expected to write. All this was part of his undercover activity for Maglan, yet deeply of interest to his journalistic mind if they were telling the truth...if they had in fact found DNA that couldn't die. The prospects were spectacular beyond anything previously discovered. Was the supposed *life* discovered within the golden sarcophagus of extraterrestrial origin, or was the finding from, as Randolph Faust believed, of a source far more profound?

"I'm surprised that Morticai gave me permission to come with you to Washington," Essie said, her arm resting, wrapped around his, on the armrest between them. "But I'm very pleased he did."

"Yes," Tyce said clasping his hand over her left hand. "But he didn't trust me to keep you safe. We have Ehud and our two other friends back a couple of seats."

"Yes. Papa is very careful with me. Too careful."

"No. I don't trust me to keep you safe either," Tyce said, squeezing her hand gently.

"I'm safe with you," she said, coming to his defense.

"Oh, no—you might not be safe with me," he said with a mischievous tone.

"Well, I think I want to be in danger…if the *danger* is from your intentions," she teased back. Silence hovered between them for a lingering moment before she spoke.

"Why does Abba want you to go to the inauguration?"

"It wasn't his idea. It was mine."

"Oh?… Why?"

"I'm a reporter. This is history-making. Besides, something within prompted me—as did Randolph. Something's up in all this. I've got to be part of it."

"Why did Dr. Faust want you to attend?"

"Of course, his thinking is always about Bible prophecy. I really don't know all the whys and wherefores. But it's this guy, Michael, that keeps popping up. Randolph is convinced he's Michael the archangel."

"What does that have to do with you attending the inauguration, though?"

"It's just a sense…a feeling…that both of us have. Randy believes it's something heaven wants done…"

Tyce paused, then said with a chuckle, "Boy! That's

quite some ego, isn't it? God wants *me*, of all people, to do something in Washington, DC."

"Oh, I don't think that's so out of the question," Essie said, laying her cheek against his shoulder again.

"Thanks for the vote of confidence, Ess, I need all the validation I can get, because I haven't got the slightest idea of what I'll be doing in DC."

Essie let his words pass through her thoughts, then said, "I don't know about an archangel...this Michael. But something beyond the normal is in all of this. That Scripture Dr. Faust quoted. Do you think it has meaning for the things happening?"

"You mean the verse about Michael standing for Daniel's people?"

"Yes. Do you think this prophecy, or whatever it is, is at the center of all this plotting against the president you witnessed?"

They listened to the captain's announcement that they would be landing at Reagan International in ten minutes, then Tyce said, "I don't know, Ess, but if this Michael is who Randy believes he is, it's a sure thing he's at the center of what's going on."

WASHINGTON, DC was abuzz. But the buzz was droning in a severely tempered hum.

Talk was not of excitement of a new president about to take the oath of office, but of the systemic shock of the wrong candidate getting elected.

Media, from news to entertainment, suffered just below their surface in an undertow of depression. Reporters and pundits had watched their influence on and access to government at the executive level slip away during the reporting of an election-night electoral landslide.

The candidate and the party more than 90 percent of mainstream media disdained were chosen by middle America over the woman they all thought was a shoo-in. The depression was visceral, and the dark mood of his colleagues was more than apparent to Tyce Greyson after settling in the hotel, then mixing with them in the lounge.

"It's sad," one young reporter said while sitting next to him in the crowded booth. She dabbed at the corners of her eyes with a tissue, speaking to be heard above the music and chatter. "Something went terribly wrong," she said to those in her party at the long table. "She should be president, not that…Cretan."

Tyce smiled beneath his somber façade. Although not of a right wing or even conservative political bent in his self-assessment, he was far removed from the ideological left. He silently enjoyed the girl's lament, knowing that her ilk had for decades ruled in the liberal "swamp", as the winning candidate had termed Washington.

Tyce stood and held out his hand to Essie, who had to maneuver carefully between men and women standing near the booth waiting for people to leave so they could be seated.

"Is it always like this during inaugurations of American presidents?" she asked, following him as he directed her into the space on the long bench of the booth he had saved for her.

He laughed and said into her ear to be heard above the noise, "This is a subdued crowd. Most of these people aren't a partying mood."

"Oh?"

"Their candidate lost."

Tyce sipped from his drink, letting his eyes scan the crowd while he looked over the rim of the glass. Men and women chatted to each other, the clanking bar noises and many voices drowning out specific conversation.

He suddenly felt frozen in place, his eyes widening.

"What's wrong?" Essie's words made him blink in a return to his immediate surroundings.

"It's him!"

"Who?" She gripped his arm, looking to see the object of Tyce's still-searching eyes.

"He was right there, just beyond that crowd," he said, pointing in the direction he wanted her to look. "Do you see him? He's the tall, blond guy in the dark blue suit."

Tyce slid from the seat, keeping his gaze in the direction of the crowd and the man who stood just beyond, looking in his direction.

"I…I don't see a blond man," Essie said, straining to look between the people who milled about.

Tyce said nothing but left the table and moved quickly through the crowded bar, causing people to look at him with irritation while he bumped against them. He turned to excuse himself to a woman he had bumped, then looked, trying again to find the object of his search.

It was Michael. Michael had been staring at him from across the expanse—from between the milling conversation groups. But search the room as he might, the man he knew as Michael was no longer there.

He threaded his way toward the room's large, open doorway, his only thought of getting to the elusive Michael. Looking in all directions after he left the restaurant's main room, the object of his search was nowhere to be seen. When he walked away from the restaurant diners who had stepped from the elevators and were moving toward the big, main dining area, the thought struck. Maybe Michael had gone onto one of the elevators.

He looked to the lights atop the elevator doors that displayed the cars ascending or descending. While he watched, the door in front of him slid apart. The interior was pulsing with purple-hued illumination; the car was empty.

Without thinking, he stepped in. Before he could turn to face the door, it slid shut and the car began a swift ascent. Tyce had the strange sense that he was being drawn by a non-sentient force—not at all the same sense as a normal elevator power source.

The carriage moved smoothly, without lurches or mechanical sounds normally associated with elevator movement. The lights above the doors indicated he was nearing the building's top floor. Just as smoothly and silently as the elevator had taken him upward, it came to an almost imperceptible stop. The light above the elevator door before it slid open read "20".

The area outside the elevator seemed to pulse in the same purple hue of light that had enveloped him inside the carriage. He stepped carefully from between the sliding doors, craning to look at his surroundings. He saw across the small, room-like space a large door that looked to be of mostly glass. Beyond the door, he saw the blackness of the Washington, DC, night sky.

Before he could touch the big, double doors of glass, they swung slowly open. The crisp evening air wafted about him, engendering a chill that gave him a slight shiver. He walked onto the area that was obviously a rooftop, open-air space for observation of the city below.

Tyce looked left, then right, and noticed out of the

corner of his eye that the glass doors were closing. When he looked back toward the city's skyline, his eyes met those of a tall man several feet away.

"Michael?" Tyce's voice questioned his own eyes.

Yes! It was the man he had come to know as Michael.

"Tyce. It is I, Michael. I am pleased that you have come. Let us move a bit farther toward the city lights." The voice of the man sounded deeper, more mature than his apparent age would indicate.

Michael gripped Tyce's arm and urged him to come with him near the area designed for viewing the Washington skyline.

"Look and see the city, Tyce," Michael said. "It is a most profound sight of earthly import." Tyce glanced at the man's profile while they moved forward. His face seemed illumined from a source within him rather than from the lights shining from the city.

He motioned toward the city with a wave of his hand. Tyce's senses heightened when, unable to do other than what the man commanded, he peered intensely at the scene before him.

"See the throne of earthly power, Tyce. Look deeply into that which exalts the creature and opposes the Creator. Witness that which requires judgment, Tyce Greyson."

The blackness surrounding the many illuminated structures of America's capital city began to change, turning from dark crimson and grew to an ever-intensifying red, until the entire city appeared to have a red-hot glow.

The Washington Monument thrusting upward looked to be a dagger blade that came fresh from a crucible of smelting. The Capitol building and all other government structures radiated a fiery-red aura while

Tyce stood transfixed before the irresistible horrific glow.

"What is this you witness this night?" Michael's question echoed cavernously within his senses. He couldn't answer, nor did he want to answer, so mesmerizing was the holocaust before his awe-struck observation.

"See the Holy One's touchstone of humanity." The scene before Tyce changed in a twisting, white-hot turning of time and space while he stood as if paralyzed.

"Behold the city of man's salvation." Michael's voice thundered within Tyce's ears. "Can you tell me the meaning, Tyce Greyson?"

Michael's question brought forth from within his paralyzed silence the thought that, more than anything, he wanted to know the answer.

Washington, DC, was no longer the city lying before him. The Mosque of Omar instantly marked the skyline as that of Jerusalem. The scene before him began to change. Jerusalem shrank at the center of the vision-scene while the surrounding Judean hills became more prominent.

The hills, themselves, morphed, then, becoming a glinting spectacle rather than an earthen promontory in the intense, Middle Eastern sun.

The sarcophagus…it was the sarcophagus!

CHAPTER 13

"And you say it seemed an actual meeting with this...this Michael? Not a dream or strictly a vision?"

Randolph Faust's frown of concentration intensified while he watched Tyce's change of expression to one of absolute certainty. "It was as real as you and I standing here," Tyce said. "I was on that roof with Michael, and we walked to the edge of the observation deck. That's when the vision came. Until then, it was very real... actual, moment-by-moment walking across that deck."

"Then it became a vision..."

"It changed from the DC skyline to a city that looked to be on fire, all the monuments burning...the whole town lit up with fire—"

Tyce's description was interrupted by Mordicai Kant's question. "—And the scene changed? It became Jerusalem?"

"Yes. The whole scene looked as if it was put into a slowly mixing, tumbling vat or something. It twisted and swirled until it settled into the scene that was

Jerusalem...the Mosque of Omar...all the landmarks. It was definitely Jerusalem."

"And what happened next?" The question by Faust brought a moment of silence and a look of deep thought to Tyce's face.

"I really don't know," he said. "I remember Michael asking me what it all means. He wanted me to explain it. No, it was more like he was wanting me to *consider* what it *might* be all about."

"Then what?"

Tyce looked at Faust, who posed the question, then to Kant and to Essie. "The next thing, I'm back at the table with Essie in the restaurant—"

"—He was just standing there," Essie interrupted. "I didn't see him approach. There were many diners all about. He was just standing there at the table suddenly, a blank stare on his face. I had to lead him to sit down. It was a minute or two before he seemed to become aware."

Morticai Kant wanted to get back to the meaning of Jerusalem being part of the vision. "And you remember not at all trying to answer this...this Michael's question as to what it all meant?"

"No," Tyce said, shaking his head, his eyes staring in a blank expression, as if looking into his own thoughts. "I don't remember anything—just, next, Essie tugging at my arm to get me to sit at the table."

"I wonder if one of our psychiatrists might pull from your memory what happened on that rooftop." Kant drummed his fingertips on the wooden arm of the chair in which he sat, his gaze toward the ceiling of the hotel suite's lounge area. He put his cellphone to his ear after dialing. "I know of such a doctor nearby," he said.

"He just presumes you are willing to be subjected to the Masada's probing," Essie said, rolling her eyes while

TERRY JAMES

she watched her father glance again at the ceiling while he awaited the rings to be answered.

"Dr. Leventhal can do it now," the Israeli said after a minute of conversation. "It is most important that we learn what is remembered from your meeting with this Michael."

Within the hour, Tyce was seated with his shirt sleeve pulled up, his right arm resting on a small table.

"This injection will help you to relax your thought processes," the Israeli psychiatrist said while he examined the arm just below the bicep for an appropriate vein.

"It won't knock me out, will it?" Tyce's words were stated with a slight tone of humor. But he wanted an answer.

"No. this will just help you feel relaxed…able to think more clearly as I take you into the hypnotic state."

"Is it sodium pentothal?"

"No…no. We are far advanced from those former injectable," Leventhal said, finding the vein he was looking for.

From the moment the cold liquid entered the vessel, Tyce's senses began darkening. If it was the drug relaxing him, it was a strange sort of relaxation, he thought, feeling his whole body seeming to tense up to the point of discomfort.

"Just relax," Leventhal said softly, soothingly.

But the descent was swift and deep, and he was tumbling, as if caught in a vortex that suctioned him toward some inner matrix from which he wouldn't escape—a matrix that was, he sensed, the very origin of life in his mother's womb.

But suddenly, powerfully, he burst from the suctioning force. He stood beside the man, Michael, who

212

now moved with him in tow, holding him by the arm while they seemed to glide on a cushion of air toward a black veil—a veil that they, together, pierced, then moved down corridors and through walls, coming finally to stand just inside a chamber with men sitting in a circle so that each could easily see all others.

They noticed neither Tyce nor Michael. Small spotlights beamed from the concave ceiling onto each of the men directly.

All else within the chamber was constituted of shadows that obscured the surroundings, at the center of which sat the men in business suits.

The voices were clear as each spoke. But the voices weren't like the voices of men. They were mechanized… droning. Each spoke in what sounded to be artificial speech. It was apparent that each was of a different nationality, with a different language. But each understood the others perfectly, Tyce surmised.

He heard the conversation of all involved in English, even though he didn't have the earpieces the men at the table wore. There was obviously computer-translation technology involved.

The men's synthesized conversation began to play clearly in his ears. A balding man spoke into a microphone that extended from the ceiling at the end of a thin, curved, gleaming rod of chrome. The instantaneous translation communications technology provided such a microphone to each of the men sitting in plush chairs in a circular configuration.

Tyce was understanding the words with no need of the technology, he noticed with great surprise. He and his companion stood unnoticed by those of the circle of ten.

"So, we are agreed," the man said, glancing at each of

his fellow members of the council. "The objective is to bring about biological controls through perceived need for a prophylactic against...against a worldwide pandemic."

A man in dark gray business attire seated across from the man who had just spoken answered. "We are assured that such a vaccination coming from the Earthlord Project can produce tracking methodologies that will guarantee controlling populations on a global basis."

"This assumes, of course, that nationalism is swept aside," another of the men said. "While we have been able to achieve this in many cases across the entire spectrum of sovereign national entities, we know of one that is the holdup to this plan."

The man who had spoken previously said, "Yes. It is the United States that has just thrown...how do you say it? A monkey wrench into the mechanism?"

Tyce studied the faces of each of the interlocutors of the cabal. Each man's expression showed agreement and nods that the assessment was correct.

Another spoke, "I am assured by our associates at the top tiers of the governmental controls...the intelligence services...the clandestine heads...are prepared to do whatsoever necessary to resolve...to dissolve this election result."

Yet another man joined in. "How is it proposed that this...pandemic...be initiated? And how can nationalism, especially that of the United States, be...disrupted? That is, disrupted to the point that the people will start thinking as international citizens...as citizens of the world, not of America? No other people have been permitted to live under such freedoms...with such luxuries, as the American people. Detaching them from such a lifestyle will be problematic."

The bald man immediately answered. "Fear is the primary instrumentality to be used," he said. "Fear of death from a microbic enemy. With it we shall divide and conquer. Divide through fear of each other. We must keep them apart…destroy their individuality by quarantine and distancing. By taking away their individuality as much as possible. Removing family members from each other through fear of being too close. Causing gatherings, such as church meetings, sports, and other venues to be closed to audiences, to congregations. That is the answer to tearing apart nationalism."

The man's eyes seemed ablaze with excitement while he continued. "Then, when fear has wrought its maximum results of dividing them one from the other, the solution will be presented that will promise a return to some degree of normalcy. The solution will be the vaccine allowing them to again interact in a new normalcy."

"Ah…then the Earthlord serum will be mandated to prevent further virus spread," another of the men said with newly attained, excited realization.

"Exactly," the bald man said. "Then the serum will be induced containing the new trackable module that interfaces with satellite and computer breakthroughs."

"But what of those who refuse the…the vaccine?"

"Then it will be up to governments to pressure, through all means necessary, all who run commerce and governmental services to keep anyone who will not comply from buying, selling…from social interaction of any kind."

Yet another of those in the circular cabal spoke into the curved microphone just inches from his mouth. "The Earthlord serum possesses properties that work within the very genetic structure…the DNA…in effecting compliance. Such biological engineering will almost certainly overcome the American will to resist our new order."

Tyce watched while excitement seemed to travel in a wavelike motion that moved upon each face and posture around the circle.

The bald man spoke again. "This president has been unreachable for some reason," he said. "He possesses an impenetrable defense. The resistance, we surmise, comes from our perpetual nemesis."

"What is the battle plan, then?" another said. "What can be done to, as you say, dissolve, the results of the American election?"

"The process of neutralizing him has begun. He calls the new environment he has entered the 'swamp'. He has no idea of the alligators that await his entry into the DC waters."

Low-level laughter growled from those whose expressions indicated understanding.

"These are those of which Daniel was given knowledge," Michael's word disrupted Tyce's concentration on the conversation. "These plot great resistance to the Most High. From this circle emerges power and authority from wickedness in high places of earthly rebellion."

Michael's words resounded cavernously within Tyce's mind while the taller man looked into his eyes, his lips unmoving. Michael's eyes…they were…they were the eyes…the eyes of the creature of light that night on the rain-blinded interstate. The night his car had flown into the darkness when the semi's brake lights had suddenly caused him to whip the wheel to the right. The eyes of the creature of excruciatingly brilliant light that had glared at him through the windshield…

"HE'S RESPONDING."

The voice of a female, somewhere in the distance, as if in an echo chamber. At first it increased in volume and clarity, before fading to become almost inaudible.

"Yes. This is finally it I think."

The male voice seemed, too, as if an echo chamber. But the words soon took on the tone of normal conversation.

"Mr. Greyson…"

The scene was at first as if looking from a 737 at thirty-five thousand feet—squares of farmland somewhere over middle America. But the colors weren't like those of farmland. All patches of land were of shades of gray.

Tyce's thoughts moved erratically within a dark, cerebral soup. Finally, a face took the place of the squares that looked to be land below. A female face peered directly into his quickly focusing eyes.

"Mr. Grayson?"

The question was offered as if he should affirm his identity. He tried but couldn't answer.

"Tyce…Tyce Grayson." The male face from whence the voice came replaced the female face and voice. "Tyce. Are you back with us?"

The doctor pulled Tyce's eyelids up with his thumbs. He took an instrument from the nurse and shined a beam of light into one eye, then the other.

"What…?" Tyce tried to question the man's actions. But the thought still wouldn't come in ways that made sense.

"You're in a hospital," the doctor said, continuing to examine Grayson's eyes. "Looks like you're finally back."

Tyce struggled to understand, his eyes finally able to see the squares again when the man's face moved away from being directly above him. His vision and understanding cleared simultaneously. The squares...they were ceiling tiles.

"I'm in...in a hospital?"

The face again appeared directly above his own face. "Yes. You are in St. Anthony's in Baltimore," the doctor said while again examining his eyes.

"What...What happened? Why?"

"You had an accident. You have been in a lengthy...in a state of sleep for quite some time."

He tried to straighten out, tried to raise from the pillow, the bed. His efforts were futile. There was no strength within him. He felt paralyzed. Yet he could feel sensations. He could feel his feet move, his hands, his fingers. He wasn't paralyzed.

"You will just have to lie back and be patient, Tyce," the doctor said in a soothing tone. "You've been in this condition for a long time. It will take a long time to get back to normal."

"How...how long have I been like this?"

"Several years, I'm afraid."

"Years?"

The words stunned his sensibility. They didn't register. He squinted to try to see the doctor's mouth...to make sure he had heard the words right.

"Years? I've been here for...years?"

"No. You've not been here all that time. You've been in other facilities for...comatose patients."

"Comatose?" Again, his senses darkened as he delved into the doctor's revelation.

"You've been in several different facilities while we tried to bring you back to consciousness. This hospital was the last step in the process," the doctor said matter-of-factly while turning to his nurse to issue instructions.

He turned back to Tyce while examining and working on his neck area.

"What accident? What happened?"

"You had an auto accident. You were in a rainstorm, as I think they said. You ran off the road and into a ditch."

Tyce let the words sink in before framing his question. "And when was that?"

"It was a number of years ago. I don't know the details...the exact year."

"And I've been...in a...in a coma ever since?"

"Yes. But you've had the very best therapy since the accident. We've been able to keep your body from atrophying to a large extent. We believe the extraordinary care you've received will help you to walk and move about relatively normally—that is, with a great deal of rehabilitation, the right medicines, and specialized stimulation with the help of some new technologies."

"But what about...Essie? What about Randolph Faust? Morticai Kant?"

The doctor stopped working on the patient and began trying to answer the questions that would inevitably be forthcoming. "I've heard one of those names. But the others are new to us."

The doctor turned to the nurse.

"Mr. Faust has visited. Do you know the other names?"

He turned back to Tyce. "What were the names again?"

"Essie Jorba...Morticai Kant," Tyce said.

"No. I haven't heard those names," the nurse said. "But Mr. Faust—Dr. Faust. He's been here several times."

"Where is he? Is he here now?" Tyce's excited demeanor made the doctor push gently on his shoulder to keep him from trying to rise.

"I doubt it," the doctor said. "But we will see that he visits soon, Tyce. You just relax for now. It's important that you come back into normal activity at a very slow, steady pace."

"When can I see Dr. Faust?" Tyce's question had a tone of urgency, and the doctor nodded to his nurse, who reached to twist a device on the IV tube attached to the patient's arm.

"Your visits will have to wait awhile longer, Tyce. You need to rest and come back slowly."

Sleep, they wanted him to sleep. He had been asleep for years, he thought, as his senses darkened. *I've been asleep for years and they want me to...to sleep...*

CHAPTER 14

Fourteen days later

"Your mobility is remarkable."

The doctor watched Tyce move in the manner directed: He stepped, raising his knees high, stepped to one side then to the other.

"Truly remarkable," the doctor said again.

"Need you to do these exercises every day. We can't allow for the possibility of relapse. Even when you'd rather just sit and write, or whatever, remember that the exercise physiology is all important. That, along with the pharmacy regimen and lots of rest—and of course, the diet we will give you. All of these will help you see continued improvement."

Tyce mopped his face with the towel he retrieved from the back of a bench.

"I'll do it, Doc. I promise. But I need to get on with things…get into the years I've lost."

"Dr. Krestbaum says the years you spent in a coma are as clear in your memory as if you had lived them. He hasn't had to use any sort of drug therapy or hypnotic therapy to help you remember the things you say were as real to you as if it was actual life."

Tyce considered the man's words while seating himself on the bench and mopping again at the perspiration on his face. "It is just as if everything that happened was as real as you and I are talking here, now. And it's as if it all just happened yesterday. I've got to get into those remembrances. Gotta find the people I knew in that time in a coma as well as I know you."

"And where will you start? That seems like a monumental task."

"Dr. Randolph Faust. He's the one person who was in my...my otherworldly life. He's invited me to his home near San Marcos."

"What do you mean, he was with you in your 'otherworldly' life? You mean the strangely real existence you experienced during the comatose condition?"

"Things...strange things that neither of us can understand are at play in this whole matter. Things from the moment I flew off the highway that night. Dr. Faust said when we talked by phone just last night that there are things that have surrounded his own life over these... missing years. At least, missing years from the standpoint of my own life."

"It's good that you have such a friend to...help you recover—come back to life, so to speak," the doctor said, walking with Tyce to the door of the rehab facility.

"That's a good way to put it. Yeah. It's like coming back from the dead, I suppose. Only, it's as if I've never been away, at least not in my own thinking."

"We will want you back here within a month to do further evaluation," the doctor said, holding the door open for his patient to pass through the doorway.

∾

IT WAS AN ALTOGETHER different world from the DC, Maryland, expanse of concrete and bulky buildings of like construction —the monotonous urban, governmental architecture that filled every square mile.

Looking out the window of the Ford Ranger that whisked him along the freeway leading to San Marcos after leaving San Antonio International, the mesquite trees that dotted the rolling landscape offered welcome relief from city living. He had not been to south Texas, although he once barely missed the chance to see the Alamo in 1996. He had come down with a respiratory illness and couldn't make the trip with his fifth-grade class.

"Dr. Faust is looking forward to your visit." The Hispanic driver glanced over at Tyce, a smiling friendliness in his words. "We'll be glad to have you with us."

"Thanks. I'm looking forward to time with all of you. It certainly is different territory than I'm used to. Lots of rattlesnakes?"

"Pardon?" the driver looked puzzled before his expression melted into understanding.

"Oh…yes. There are plenty of the rattlesnake. But no worry…they stay well away from people. Except at rattlesnake roundup time."

"Rattlesnake roundup?"

"Yes…for cooking…for chili, and other eating…"

"Well, better to bite them, than for them to bite you, I guess."

Ramon Gutierrez laughed. Nodding, he said, "Yes! Yes! It is true!"

Tyce wasn't without employing his most intensive observation powers when he moved from the truck. The snake wrapped around his hand while had had been in the Patmos cave was never far from his thinking. The scattered scrub brush, which included small groupings of cactus, might easily hide one of the reptiles.

Randolph Faust met him with an effusive greeting when he reached the porch. "Tyce! So the dead has revived!"

Tyce returned the old professor's embrace and was led into the house, Faust urging him to be first through the door.

Questions poured from his old friend from the moment he entered. They were the first of many that would be asked over the ensuing days.

Tyce spent the week telling Faust intricate details of his life in the coma. The first among things that spilled from his memory involved the girl who traversed his mind every waking moment.

"Essie!" Faust had exclaimed at Tyce's first mention of her. "Essie was part of that...that unconscious state?"

"I'm telling you, Dr. Faust, it wasn't like a dream or some other state of existence. It was real life. We were all but engaged to be married."

"And her father? Did you meet her father?"

"Morticai Kant," Tyce had told him the first time he revealed the reality of his comatose remembrances. The revelation had stunned Faust into silence.

"I was working for Israel...their clandestine services," Tyce had said, seeing the wary expression on Faust's face.

"Tyce. The Lord of heaven is in this...this most profound matter. We must explore everything...all you remember."

"And that is at the center of this...this coma...vision,

or whatever it was," Tyce had told Faust in their first conversation since his coming to San Marcos.

"The Lord's being in it?" Faust had said.

Tyce responded, "Michael. He's at the center of the whole vision."

Perfectly remembered facts surrounding the strange man's part in the time he had spent in coma spilled from his memory. The first meeting at the Reagan Airport. Michael being on TV in Israel at the news conference when he only minutes earlier had been in the US. Michael's interventions at the exact moments they were needed. The discussions between Morticai Kant, Faust, and himself about the one called Michael…about what it meant in terms of biblical prophecy that Faust had, during Tyce's coma-vision, laid out for him to understand.

Most stunning were the visions within the comatose state the one called Michael led him through. The final vision before he came out had been when they had stood near the ten men in the room as they plotted a *coup d'état* against the newly elected president of the United States.

Both men stood now, looking across the sprawling landscape of the land in south Texas that Randolph Faust called home. The late afternoon sun cast shadows, creating from the hilly terrain valleys of stark browns against the sandy soil that shone with a golden hue in the fading, reflected light.

"What does the creature in the sarcophagus mean?" Tyce said, turning his head from the scene before them to look into his old friend's eyes.

"Indeed," Faust said, remembering the time before Tyce's accident on the highway into Baltimore. "The giant wasn't part of my…my vision. But the golden burial chamber, the sarcophagus, was definitely a part of my experience."

"And you saw it somewhere in the desert, then—"

"—Yes. It was at first in a place like Qumran," Faust interrupted. "Somewhere in an area that looked like the south end of the Dead Sea."

"And then the scene changed—" Tyce started to question when Faust finished the thought.

"—The scene changed to DC. I heard a voice call my name. I turned to see and there was no one there. I turned back to begin climbing the promontory. I looked and the surroundings had changed. The sarcophagus glinted in the sky. It was atop the Washington Monument. I again heard the voice and I turned again to see who called my name. It was you, Tyce. But as you approached me, you changed into my old friend, Morticai Kant. Then I looked for the sarcophagus again, and it rested in the middle of a gigantic Star of David."

Both were silent, trying to make sense of things of their visions—both apart and together—that drew and held them within the mystery, at the center of which were the man Michael and the gigantic man-figure that Tyce described.

"The Lord is in it," Faust said. "He will direct our path." He put his hand upon his companion's shoulder as they began walking back toward the house.

WHILE THE 737 landing gear thumped to the open position, the jet shuddered slightly as it slowed and descended toward the Reagan runway.

"I've told Morticai the entire story," Randolph Faust said. "He is totally receptive to exploring...looking into what it all means. There is no need for you to be apprehensive about meeting him."

"But it will be like I know him, and he doesn't know me at all. Don't you think that will freak him out?"

"This guy has been involved in things you and I can't even imagine being a part of, Tyce. Nothing freaks him out. He is, as you know, the chief of Maglan, probably the most clandestine of all covert operations on the planet."

"Well, it freaks me out," Tyce said, to no one in particular.

The tires bumped smoothly on the runway, and moments later, the thrust reversers brought the craft to taxiing speed.

"It's all so eerie, Randy. A life I've already lived, yet am just now about to begin..."

Faust patted his companion's knee and spoke above the whine of the engines as the 737 moved toward the concourse receptacle for deplaning. "It is something we've not determined, Tyce. God has determined it. Therefore, it will all work together for good, if we, as I heard a preacher say, just obey Him, no matter what, and leave all the consequences to Him."

Just over an hour later, they moved through a large doorway that led into a government office suite. A security guard walked in front, finally opening a door and standing aside to allow Tyce and Randolph Faust to pass through the opening to the private office.

"They're here, sir," the uniformed man said into a handheld device.

"Thanks. We will be out in a second," the voice replied loudly enough to be heard by all three men.

"Thank you, gentlemen," the security officer said. "Please be seated, if you wish."

The man quickly exited through the doorway they had moments before entered.

"I always pictured a secretive operations office to be…more…more *secretive,*" Tyce said, looking around the room. Photos of other government office buildings hung at various places around the walls. A photo of the president hung by itself on one wall.

"I guess the really secret places are somewhere else in the building," Faust said with a laugh.

When the door against one wall near the president's portrait opened, a man in a dark suit, followed by a shorter, balding man with a full beard, smiled and offered his hand. "Glad you both could make it," he said.

The older man, rather than offer his hand to Faust, grabbed him in a vigorous hug.

"My friend, Randolph," he said enthusiastically.

Morticai Kant glanced at Tyce, then offered his hand. "And this is the young man you told me about…Tyce… Tyce Greyson, I believe."

The man really didn't know him. This agent of Maglan whose daughter he loved deeply…he really didn't know him. The thought ran strangely while he took the hand. "Yes, sir. Tyce Greyson."

The other, younger, man shook Tyce's hand. "Clint, Clint Wayne," he said, smiling and urging Tyce toward a nearby chair.

"We are secure here, Tyce. We must assure absolute integrity in safeguarding our conversations," Wayne said, after being seated on a sofa across from his guests. "The matters we have to discuss are critical. Has Dr. Faust given you a briefing?"

"Only that it involves matters that have been going on…since my accident. That there are…people who want to remove the president, who have been trying to… since the election."

Clint Wayne glanced quickly into the eyes of the other two men, then again into those of Greyson. "That's the nutshell of it," he said. "But the details—the attempted killing of this presidency by a thousand cuts is something that must be grasped."

Wayne continued. "You are in a unique position, Tyce. Coming out of a coma that kept you from knowing what has gone on during these past four years. You can approach the whole matter without prejudices and biases from the constant bombardment of news. And it is that news—the so-called mainstream news entities— that has been as much a part of this…this attempted *coup d'état* as those in any of the…opposition …forces."

Wayne looked to Kant, who sat to his right. "I want Morticai to fill you in about Israel's part in all this. I'm with a very exclusive group within collective intelligence agencies. We have formed to battle the internecine enemy operatives. The 'deep state', as it has come to be termed. Morticai is in the same branch of our group in Israel. He is also chief of Maglan, the most covert clandestine service within the IDF."

"He knows," Randolph said with profound assertiveness in his tone. There was silence before Kant spoke up.

"And this is what you intimated by phone when we spoke last evening?"

"He knows more than you can imagine, Morticai, Clint. He has told me things that are…are truly astonishing." Again, there was silence, each letting the gravity of Faust's words soak in.

Finally, the Israeli said, "And that is why I arranged this meeting, Tyce. If what I have been told by my friend Randolph is factual, the implications are staggering."

"And that's understatement," Clint Wayne said. "We believe that once we learn things you say you...experienced...during your comatose state, you can be of immense help in this...this fight for the future of the nation and the world."

"Everything I experienced, as you call it, I remember vividly," Tyce said. "As a matter of fact, it's all like it was part of me living in real time."

"That's what we want to know," Kant said. "Everything you lived during that time."

He then looked deeply into Greyson's eyes, his own steel blue eyes narrowing in an expression of the seriousness contained within the statement he was about to make. "Tyce, you must understand that we cannot take any chances in taking into our confidence someone who might...somehow...betray our cause. The stakes are too high. We believe that civilization... Western civilization...might hinge on maintaining security."

Tyce's thoughts ran quickly. *They've brought me into this dangerous position, and now they're threatening to kill me if I'm in any way out of line.*

"I understand," he said.

"Good," Kant said, sitting forward with his elbows on his knees and leaning toward the younger man. "So, I must ask you to prove that you have...knowledge you claim to have. Can you give me something that will help us know that we can trust you before we entrust you with the most intricate details of our operations?"

Tyce let the question ruminate in his reeling thoughts. "Your daughter, Essie. She and I were in love. That is, when I was in the comatose state, we became very close. We would soon have been married...that is, I was going to ask her soon."

Kant's expression changed to one of amazement, before coming again to a frown of concentration.

"Essie Jorba, not Essie Kant," Tyce went on. "That puzzled me, so I asked her early on…when our relationship was just starting. I asked her if she had been married. She said no. I asked why her last name wasn't Kant. She said that it was a family name. Her mother's maiden name, I think. She said that you, because you were Maglan chief, you were afraid that if certain people knew she was your daughter, they would kidnap her…be able to compromise your position. So she took the other family name of Jorba."

Morticai looked to Clint Wayne. "He is correct. I am most cautious when it comes to my Essie."

"I know the name of one of your closest aids," Tyce said. "You assigned him to accompany Essie and me to a number of places we traveled. He drove the trips in DC and other places."

"And what was his name?" Kant said.

"Ehud Begin."

Kant said nothing, but smiled, thinking of his faithful assistant.

"And he is the great nephew of Menachem Begin," Tyce added.

"He is indeed," Kant said, his expression turning more serious in preparation for his next question. "And the sarcophagus. I'm told your…vision…included a sarcophagus. There was great detail you…divulged to Randolph about this object. What did you think you came to understand about the object?"

"Again, just like the whole…experience…of the vision if that's what we want to call it. It was all as real as you, I —all of us—sitting here talking right now," Tyce said hesitatingly.

"Tell us all about it," Clint Wayne put in. "We want all the details you can provide."

"I will. But first, Mr. Kant...Morticai—I have to know about Essie. I can't think of anything else until I know. Is she still...unmarried?"

Kant glanced at each of the other two men, his expression relaxing to one of mild amusement, of understanding.

"Tyce, Essie hasn't had time for romance. She has been busy in her father's work of saving Israel, and the world."

Kant and the others chuckled, Kant's countenance becoming serious again. "We will see that you...meet... my daughter at earliest opportunity, young man. I promise."

Tyce said nothing, the release of emotion he managed to keep hidden flooding his thoughts.

"Now. Any and all details you can give about the experience with the sarcophagus...is essential," Kant said.

"I first saw it right after the accident...or what I thought was right after it," Tyce said. "Coming out of the wreck was, during that comatose time, within fifteen minutes or so, I was told by EMT or the guy who helped me out of the car."

"And when did you see it next? We are really looking for details of what you know about what might be involved in this object being in this country, according to the vision," Kant said.

"You, Essie, Dr. Faust, and others were part of viewing the contents of the burial chamber. When I finally got to see it, it was a corpse—a mummy. It was of a man, at least twelve feet in length. It was covered in a greenish substance that we were told is from the area of

Mesopotamia…the biblical land of Shinar, the place where Nimrod was reported to have built the Tower of Babel."

"And what did you learn further about this…this mummy?"

"That they were able to extract DNA. The scientists said part of the DNA was human. The other part they couldn't identify. They said it had a strange component to it."

"And what was that?" Kant asked.

"They said it was still alive. They didn't know why or how it could possibly be, but it was still living."

There was silence while Kant and Wayne glanced nervously at each other.

"And did you find out more about this…this being in the sarcophagus?" Clint Wayne sat forward after asking the question, carefully watching Tyce's face.

"Yes," Tyce said. "But it was a vision within a vision. I guess that's the way you would put it. I saw in a strange vision…while I was in the coma…a group of men… scientists, I think They were talking about the creature in the sarcophagus. They said they would develop a serum from its DNA. They said the serum would create supernatural traits within people inoculated by the it. They'd be given extradimensional powers. I don't understand it all. But they said they eventually would use it to inoculate the whole world. This would give them…give the powers that be…control, would make people soulless zombies, as I take it. That would be the ultimate results."

"And you told Randolph that two people in particular were being prepared?" Kant said, prompting Tyce to remember.

"Yes, there were two, they said, who would be the first to take the serum. They were being prepared for leadership in some sort of a coming world order, as I took it."

"It's in Bible prophecy," Randolph Faust said energetically. "I believe these are the first and second beasts of Revelation chapter 13 being prepared for their Antichrist and False Prophet roles."

Again, the men fell silent, Kant and Wayne obviously assessing things they had learned. Finally, Wayne spoke.

"Tyce, you have told us things no one could know but a very few people within our circles. Your revelations are on the mark in every case. Therefore, I must insist that you dedicate your knowledge...your clairvoyant abilities...to ensuring that your nation stays secure. We will look now at ways your special abilities can best be used to help in that security process."

CHAPTER 15

There was no choice offered in Clint Wayne's words. He, Tyce Greyson, was now an asset of the United States Defense Department—the most covert part of the clandestine intelligence branch.

The dichotomy pulled at his sensibility. On the one hand, it was an honor to be considered as having abilities that could serve his nation in some spectacular way, as Wayne intimated. On the other hand, it was an involuntary loss of freedom—freedom that he'd most likely never get back. And now, his aged friend, Randolph Faust, was equally destined to be locked within the covert operations of both America and of Israel.

Yet, the part Tyce would play was so strategic, so confined in scope, that only Clint Wayne, Morticai Kant, and a few very elite operatives could be made privy to the extent of his activity.

All of it was secondary to what was truly on his mind at the moment. All he could think about was Essie. How would she react to him? How could their relationship ever be the same as...as when in that comatose world that seemed as real as the one he moved through now?

"I will arrange a meeting that will be most conducive to a favorable outcome," Morticai Kant had told him upon the adjournment of the meeting.

Tyce had thought Essie's father sounded like he was acting in a diplomatic mission for the Israeli prime minister—something he did on a regular basis.

"Please don't tell her about my comatose experiences," Tyce had said. "If I'm to be so lucky as to have her give me a notice, even slightly, let it be on that basis. I don't want her given a heads-up on any of what I experienced," he had told her father.

Now, while he splashed on cologne and gave himself a last second look in the hotel room's bathroom mirror, he wondered why he had made the request to her father. He needed to have every advantage in meeting her in this, the strangest of circumstances.

Perhaps her knowing might lead to a more significant interaction upon their first meeting. Maybe it would bring them together where they left off...

No. Not possible, he thought while slipping into the blazer, then adjusting the tie in the mirror.

Whatever happened, this was the best tack.

His sensation both amused and alarmed him. He hadn't felt this nervous about meeting someone of the opposite sex since his first date in junior high.

The cellphone rang, and Tyce quickly searched the room to see where he had left it. Finally, he picked it up from beneath a shirt in a chair at the end of the bed.

"Mr. Greyson...Tyce Greyson?" the voice of Essie Jorba said on the other end when he answered.

Tyce wanted to blurt her name, shout his greetings

with enthusiasm. But he caught himself, instead answering, calmly, "Yes. I'm Tyce."

"I'm Essie Jorba," the voice said with a slight Israeli accent, the sweet voice that was part of his life, real or imagined.

"Essie—I'm so glad to hear from you," was all Tyce could think to say in response.

"My father, Morticai, thought we should...speak with each other. I understand you will be working within his...our...service to the Israeli and American governments."

"Yes. I've been enlisted, I guess you could say."

"Papa...Morticai...tells me you were in a coma that lasted quite some time."

"Five years to be exact. From 2015 until this year. I've been...awake...about a month."

"They say it is a miracle...a miraculous recovery," Essie said.

"It's all so strange," Tyce said after a pause of several seconds. "I still can't believe...that it was a...a dream existence or whatever the psychiatrists and psychologists say it was."

Again there was silent for a long moment.

"My father tells me that I was a part of that...time you spent in the coma," she said hesitatingly, sounding unsure as to whether she should breach the matter.

"Essie, you were at the very center of it," he said without hesitation, pleased that her father had betrayed his request not to mention the coma and her part, pleased that she had therefore broken the ice so early in their becoming reacquainted.

She said, after an uncomfortable pause, "Do you think it's okay for us to meet—I mean at this time so soon after your...the episode you suffered?"

"I thought we are going to meet this evening," he said.

"Tyce...would you mind if we don't? At least not for now?"

Her tone was one of gentle persuasion. She seemed not to want to break the potential relationship before it had started. Or maybe it was just his wishful imagination.

"Yeah, I guess so," he said, his own tone neutral to not betray his disappointment. "Sure...it's fine."

∾

"This is Shiva Rabine," Morticai said, gesturing toward the woman who reached her right hand to take Tyce's.

"She is our key instructor in the area of psychoenergetic perception," Kant said. "This is the area we think you will be of highest value in. Your...talents...seem suited, as do that of few people we've analyzed, according to our experts."

"Psychoenergetic perception?" Greyson's question was directed at the female in a white smock, her gaze taking in his query while standing at the center of the covert ops laboratory.

"It's defined as the acquisition and description by mental means of information booked from ordinary perception by distance, shielding, or time," she said clinically. "You might have heard of it referred to as 'Remote Viewing.'"

"I've more than heard of it," Tyce said. "While in my... other existence...I was involved in technology, a device, meant to make Remote Viewing possible...to most anyone, I guess."

Shiva Rabine looked suspiciously at him before speaking. "What was this device?"

"They called it a Stimulator."

"Who are *they*?"

"The members of Morticai Kant's covert operations group—at least the group that was there in my comatose experience."

"Another proof of his… enhanced sensory perception," Morticai Kant said, interrupting their conversation. "How could he know about the Stimulator device, other than through an extrasensory experience?"

"This is one of our most strictly kept secret matters," Rabine said. "What was your…experience with this device?"

"I wore the device. It sent me into some sort of mind trip. But I didn't need it. It inhibited me. I was told to take it off."

"Who told you this?"

"A man called *Michael*."

"This Michael again…a tall, blond man who pops in and out of your…your vision," the Maglan chief said.

"Who is…Michael?" Rabin turned from hearing Kant's words to asking for Tyce's further explanation.

"It was all while I was in the coma," Tyce said. "How can I know? He was a figment of the imagination," he said almost flippantly.

"The Stimulator is not a…figment, Mr. Greyson—Tyce. It is one of the most advanced cognitive technologies in existence. Nobody knows about it."

"I don't know who Michael was in this…this vision state. We can only guess."

"And who do you…guess…he is?" Rabin's tone took on a hint of impatience.

"Dr. Faust believes Michael is the archangel of Daniel's prophecy. Michael the archangel," Kant said.

"What makes him think it's that literary figure?" Her question was laced with skeptical sarcasm.

"Daniel said that, in the last days, Michael will stand up for Daniel's people...for the Jews...will supernaturally defend Israel," Tyce said. "With all that was going on...in the coma...the prophecy and the angel, Michael seemed to fit."

"Morticai," Shiva Rabine said, turning to the Maglan chief, "you can't believe this Michael led him to knowledge of our most covert business."

"All I know, Shiva, is that he knows—about the Stimulator, and about so much more."

"Well, we'll see just how much you can find out for us with...with your super-sensitive ability to Remote View," she said, nudging him toward the door that led deeper into the lab facility.

SHIVA RABINE, dressed in a hip-length, white lab coat, held the manual in her hands while Tyce sat at the opposite end of the table. She read slowly from the pages.

> Remote Viewing theory postulates a nonmaterial "Matrix" in which any and all information about any person, place, or thing may be obtained through the agency of a hypothesized "signal line". The viewer psychically perceives and decodes this signal line and objectifies the information so obtained.
>
> A Remote Viewing session consists of both the interaction of a Remote Viewer with the signal line, and the interaction between the viewer and the monitor. The monitor and viewer are generally seated at opposite ends of a table. The viewer has a pen and plenty of paper in front of him. The monitor observes the viewer, and determines when the viewer is ready

to begin when the viewer places his pen on the left side of the paper in preparation to record the coordinate. The monitor then reads the coordinate, the viewer writes it, and the session proceeds from that point according to theory and methodology.

Ravine looked up from her reading from the manual. "Do you understand, Mr. Greyson?"

"So far," he said. "I've read through the get-acquainted section."

"Yes…well, we're going to go through it until it becomes second-nature. This is the best way," she said clinically. "Let us continue."

She nodded toward the pen and paper, not bothering to instruct him to pick the pen from the table, which he nonetheless did.

"You said during your session about your…experiences…that there was always a pinpoint of light to begin one of the visions?" The woman seated herself at the other end of the table while she questioned.

"Yes. Everything is…was…totally black or dark gray as I stood unable to move. I was surrounded by almost total darkness."

"And then what happened?" she said, fidgeting with an electronic device while she spoke.

"Then there would appear this point of light. Very small at first. Then it seemed to explode and instantly fill the entire…*vista.* That's the only way I can describe it."

"And the…vision…just took shape. Just unscrolled, like a video?" she said.

"It was more like I was a visceral part," said Tyce. "I was within the scene, not just looking at it like it was a TV screen or big theater screen."

Rabine silently mulled over her student's words for

several seconds before offering in a tone of understanding.

"You are describing, I think, the very ability that will
make you an effective sensory preceptor for Remote
Viewing. The pinpoint of light 'exploding,' as you put it,
from the blackness seems to confirm your natural gift to
pull from Matrix information—not only of the present,
but from the past and possibly even the future…we shall
see."

"Matrix? Exactly what does that mean?"

Shiva Rabine again opened the manual and read.

*The Matrix has been described as a huge, non-material,
highly structured, mentally accessible "framework" of information containing all data pertaining to everything in both
the physical and non-physical universe. In the same vein as
Jung's Cosmic Unconsciousness, the Matrix is open to and
comprises all conscious entities as well as information
relating to everything else living or nonliving by accepted
human definition."*

"And this is a gift?"

"Most definitely. If true, I believe you will be one of
only three people of my knowledge who possess such a
gift."

"Must've been the snake bite," Tyce said to himself,
barely above a whisper.

"What? Snake bite?" the woman said.

"Oh…nothing," Tyce answered with a subdued laugh.

She let it drop, going directly into the Remote
Viewing session process.

*From the Matrix, the Signal is accessed. The Signal is like a
carrier wave received by a radio receiver. The signal line is*

hypothesized as a train of signals emanating from the Matrix.
It is then perceived by the Remote Viewer, which transports
the information obtained through the Remote Viewing
process.

"Can't I just get in it and drive it…without having to learn what makes it run?"

Rabine looked up from her manual, a look of puzzlement on her face. "What?"

"Never mind," he said. "Look. It sounds so complicated. Do I really have to know exactly how it works?"

"We require anyone who is authorized to be part of Remote Viewing to learn as much about the process as possible. It facilitates the actual moving of information through the wave."

"The wave?"

"Yes." She again read from the manual:

A disturbance or variation that transfers itself and energy
progressively from point to point in a medium or in space in
such a way that each particle or element influences the adja-
cent ones and that may be in the form of an elastic deforma-
tion or of a variation of level or pressure, of electric or
magnetic intensity, of electric potential, or of temperature.

She watched his expression of cluelessness, and her own countenance softened into a brief smile.

"Very well. We will dispense as much as possible with the technical details. Bottom line is that we must evoke, or call up, from the signal line that comes from the coordinates within the Matrix."

"Oh. I'm glad you cleared that up for me," he said lightly.

"From this point, your own sensory perception is

vital. The evoking calls up the signal line, causing it to impinge on the autonomic nervous system and unconsciousness. This is preparation for transmittal through the viewer and on to objectification. In other words, your own intracerebral cognition evokes or calls from the signal line the exact coordinate where resides the desired objective to be viewed."

Tyce let her explanation move through his thoughts. "It was easier in the...coma world," he said. "I just stood there, and things happened. I never tried for them to happen."

"Well, Mr. Greyson, this is reality, not your *coma world.* It will soon become second nature."

"ESSIE IS JUST wary of relationships...of *new* relationships," Morticai Kant had said when the first session of learning the Remote Viewing was completed. "She had an interest in a man about a year ago. It turned out he lied to her. Told her that he was single...had never been married and had no children. She was starting to come under his charm rather heavily, I think. She then found out that he had been married twice and had four children, two by each of the wives. He was still married to the current wife and she was about to have another child. Her experience has rather soured her in the matter of romantic involvement. I'm sorry, Tyce."

Rather than dishearten him, the revelation gave him a degree of hope—hope that he could map out a plan of how to win her heart again.

Her voice was the same. It was Essie's voice on the phone. But was it her? Was she the same girl of those years ago? Surely fate, or heaven, or whatever or whomever had not led him through that reality of their love to now dismiss their ever having been together only to perpetrate some cruel, ethereal hoax.

As sleep tugged him from consciousness, the thought encouraged him. They would meet tomorrow in the course of doing business for the American-Maglan Remote Viewing project. He would have his answers then.

TYCE AWOKE, at first not able to determine his surroundings. Was it another vision like in the coma state? His eyesight quickly cleared, and the awareness came into focus. It was the government-provided hotel room somewhere near the laboratory for Remote Viewing.

The realization hit. He had, for the first time in—as long as he could remember—not had a dream or vision during sleep. He felt refreshed once the things around him became clear. What had caused the peaceful sleep? Was it just the getting farther from the coma world in which he had been embroiled for years? Was it the concentration during the Remote Viewing session that relieved his brain in some way?

He made his way to the bathroom and before exiting began making coffee in the corner nearest the bathroom door.

Momentarily he heard the familiar chime…the smartphone on the nightstand between the beds.

"Clint Wayne here, Tyce."

"Good morning," Tyce answered while seating himself on one of the beds.

"I'll get right to it," Wayne said without returning the

greeting. "There has arisen a...a crisis. It requires our immediate attention. It will require *your* input."

Tyce let the man's ominous words and tone run through his thinking before answering. "Me? I just got started on learning..."

"Don't say it," Wayne said emphatically. "Our line is not secure. We will have our people there within fifteen minutes. Please be ready. It is vital that we move quickly."

Tyce sat in the rear seat of the sedan while it moved down Pennsylvania Avenue. "Where we going?" he questioned, seeing they were headed toward the most prominently considered address in the United States.

"Sorry, can't say. You will know shortly," the man riding next to the driver said.

Tyce didn't have to guess. He knew their destination was most likely the White House.

Two men in suits, like the driver and the other agent, met the three when they had reached a set of elevators. The White House hadn't changed significantly since his visit as a reporter during the Obama administration—at least not that he could determine, while he looked up and down the large hallway. The off whites and pastels for contrast, the darks and lights of the checkered-patterned hardwood or composite flooring were the same, so far as he remembered.

The agents said nothing while they moved down the elevator shaft with Tyce at their center. The conveyance bumped to a stop after what Tyce perceived to be two floors beneath entry level.

"This way," one of the men invited. The two who had driven him from the hotel went in one direction and Tyce and the other two men went down a hallway in a different direction.

One of the men inserted a card in a slot against one wall when they stopped at a door marked OPS 3. Several men and women in business attire milled about, bending over a table that had an illuminated, glass-covered top of a square configuration.

"Tyce. Welcome to the White House," Clint Wayne said, offering his hand, then leading Tyce by his elbow to the area where the activity was centered.

He introduced the people, who smiled, shook hands, then returned their concentration to the lighted tabletop.

"Tyce, I am pleased to inform you that you now have Clearance Level 3—else you wouldn't be here with us, I can assure."

"What did I do to deserve it?" Greyson continued with Wayne's attempt at humorous introduction to the bowels of the White House.

"Let's just say that you've had the anal exam without even knowing it."

"I hope I'm found worthy, then," Tyce said.

"Actually, Tyce, we moved your…exam, your vetting, along at warp speed. Normally you wouldn't be allowed at this level for at least a month."

"Oh? And how did I achieve this…privilege?"

"It's your history with the information you've provided. It is among the strangest of stories to be verified in the history of covert ops."

"You believe me, then, about this stranger…about Michael?"

"No. We haven't a clue about…Michael. It's the matter of the sarcophagus. The mummy inside. The story of the serum you said they plan to produce," Clint Wayne said, again taking Tyce by the arm and leading him to a door. He opened it and ushered Tyce through.

The office was spacious, well-appointed—with leather furniture, a large oak desk and shelves of books around three of the walls. He noticed several brass-framed photos of children and of a woman atop the desk. He surmised it was Wayne's office and these were pictures of his family.

Once both were seated, Wayne spoke. "As I told you, a crisis has developed. We believe that you are the one to help…lessen…the severity of that crisis."

"Why me?"

"It is your…unusual ability to…see things that others can't. We have people who do the Remote Viewing. But yours is something beyond the normal. Your history is one of extrasensory capabilities…beyond any we have come across."

Tyce studied Wayne's face. This was a man not given to supernaturalism or believing in even Remote Viewing as a factual matter. At least he seemed to be one who doubted such things, despite the fact of his bringing himself into US covert operations to be involved in Remote Viewing.

"So, you really do hold that Remote Viewing and that sort of psychic activity has merit? Excuse me, Mr. Wayne…Clint…but I've sensed that you view such things as a figment of the imaginations of those who wish such things really existed."

Clint Wayne stared at his partner in conversation for several seconds before his own frown melted into a smile.

"You are very perceptive in many ways, my friend. I'm a very recent convert to…believing in these psychic matters. It is you, actually, who have convinced me of the validity of Remote Viewing and other things like it."

"What about me convinced you?"

"Your detailed account of those you perceived; that they are determined to use this...this mummy being, whatever it is, in their plans to bring this nation into a changed world order, a one world order...a *new* world order."

"Why does that convince you that I really did experience what I've described?"

"Again, it's the details. Plus, we have...ways to know such a project is indeed underway."

Tyce said nothing, allowing Wayne to form the thoughts that his expression told him was on its way.

"You have provided the details our...other sources of investigation into the sarcophagus project can't provide. Our capabilities can't get behind the façade of it being only an antiquities preservation and archeological and anthropological project. We believe you've already gotten behind the scene...for some reason we can't determine. That is, we can't figure out why you have been...allowed—chosen, provided the ability, however you want to say it—to see, to experience these things. We are people of rationality, of literalism. But when we are hit in the face with supernaturalism or anything else that will move the needle forward in protecting this country, we will cast aside our prejudices. And what about Morticai Kant, Israel, the Massad...Maglan?"

"This president is devoted to preserving Israel as strongly as he is devoted to keeping this nation free and vital," Wayne said, his tone one of absolute certitude.

"And you? What office do you hold in this government?"

"A true reporter's mind," Wayne said, leaning back in the executive desk chair from his elbows-on-desk position and putting his clasped hands together behind his head. "I can tell you because you are now part of us. We are not an official part of this administration. Yet we are at the most covert center of this presidency."

Tyce studied Wayne's facial expression, seeing in it his expecting a reaction. "Okay...who are *we* who are part of this...intimate, covert, group?"

"We are those who have watched this nation being... *diminished*...for the past couple of decades, at least. There has been, and continues to be, an assault against this republic that requires...*special* action," Clint Wayne said, again pausing to await reaction from the journalist.

"Okay, I'll bite. What kind of action?"

"Such action in the past, such *proper* action, would have been through constitutional, governmental instrumentalities. The Constitution itself, the Congress...the Supreme Court. But these have been rendered...ineffective at best and have been totally corrupted at worst."

"So—this intimate, covert, group is a militia? A vigilante organization?"

"We are a group consisting of patriots from every level of society. We have enlisted to protect and preserve this great republic, to uphold the Constitution. We are in this capacity because those elected to do so have become corrupted by a combination of the money powers elite, the lobbyist organizations, and even foreign, globalist entities who want to bring America down so their international order can be established."

Tyce said nothing, letting Wayne continue.

"America is the apex nation of the world...of history, as a matter of fact. We—America—are the holdup to the globalist master wannabes' desire to establish the one-world platform for governing. The United States must be brought down...must have its sovereignty, its autonomy, stripped. That's what they've been in the process of doing: tearing down every facet of what makes this nation the America the founding fathers intended."

Clint Wayne stood and paced as he talked, in professorial fashion.

"It started with education. They managed to completely turn education from America as founded to we are the bad guys. They have managed to make Marxist-Leninism appear to be some sort of socialist utopian thing to pursue. Our universities are filled with these purveyors of lies about what truly is at the heart of *the collective,* as they frame it. Now we are seeing the revolution spirit develop. It is ramping up and threatening to foment civil unrest that borders on war."

Tyce watched the man pace and lecture, interrupting him when Wayne paused for his next thought. "How does your nongovernmental group interact...how do you act against the globalists, or whatever they are?"

"We have many within the military, both active and retired, many at just below Joint Chiefs of Staff level, who see things...this attempt to destroy America as founded...exactly as we do."

"Again, who is this "we"?" said Greyson.

"Those of us who are civilians consist of many from government, the professional class...doctors, lawyers, engineers...from every walk of life. We have people you would recognize from clergy, and others. Many from the intelligence services, CIA, NSA, FBI...many of the clandestine services. They don't like—nor do they carry out their duties—the way their top leadership does in undermining this president at every turn. The leaks, the lies. They recognize the danger. They are vowed to fight against the forces within our government who want to take down this president and what he's tried to do to turn this ship right-side up again."

"I've been briefed on the things that have been going on during those years while I was in the coma," Tyce said. "The Russian collusion...all the things that were designed to bring the president down, to remove him with impeachment and all the rest."

"And don't forget the news media. They are directly at the heart of the globalist intentions. The so-called *fourth estate* are complicit in every aspect of this attempted *coup d'état*. The entertainment media, likewise."

"And Israel's part? What about Morticai Kant? The Maglan part, how do these fit in?"

"This gets again to why you are...enlisted...to join in this effort, Tyce. The things you have divulged are so compelling, so directly related to everything we are involved with here, that there's no doubt it is all, some-how, foreordained that you be brought into our effort."

"My knowing things that were going on while I was in that comatose state—this convinced you?"

"Yes. Dr. Faust and his close friendship with Morti-cai...we learned from Kant, through Faust, about these things you know."

Wayne again seated himself behind the desk. "Your eerie—I don't know how else to put it—your eerie ability to see things in those visions, then, Faust's own dreams or visions or whatever they are...it just all became so compelling that we needed to bring you into our orbit."

"And, the president, is he aware?"

"Absolutely. Else we wouldn't be sitting in the White House caverns as we are."

"And others? The Secret Service, the Cabinet?"

"Some do know, others don't. We've been highly selective in bringing people into our group."

"You mentioned the Joint Chiefs of Staff...that officers in the military just below that level are included. But now the chiefs themselves?"

"There is one among them we trust. The rest are sold out to the globalist establishment. And you use the word 'officers'. But not all from the military are officers. We have some of the most dedicated and powerful operatives who have joined us from the enlisted among the special forces—Berets, SEALs, others."

"And I take it that Israel—the prime minister, others in high places—are part of your…group?"

"In your briefing on what has been going on while you were in the comatose state, I'm sure you learned of the assaults that have been constantly launched against the prime minister. Even assassination plots that have been foiled…"

"Yes…it all makes sense," Tyce said. "He has been suffering much of the same attempts to bring him down as has the president."

"And this is why I have been authorized to give you a full accounting of all of this. You will be expected to use your…gifts and talents…to assist in preventing the globalists from bringing in their one-world regime."

"China and Russia? They'll never go along with a one-world scheme."

"No, but the globalist powers are so influential, especially in matters of finance and economy, and of movement of assets such as oil production and other vital things, that the pressures they can exert on China and Russia are immense. China is dependent upon the rest of the world to buy and sell their products, and Russia is dependent on petroleum just to stay afloat. They can, at the very least, be *governed*. That is, they can be kept within boundaries, so far as their opposition to a one-world plan…at least from the perspective of the globalist elites who want to rule."

The things Wayne had explained all came together in the realization that he, Tyce Greyson, wasn't here on a frivolous whim. His involvement was deadly serious in the minds of those determined to stop the war against liberty, against human freedom. The evil that had for decades been underway—the assaults against this presidency offering stark testimony of that attack—must be battled against at all costs.

Wayne sat forward, his hands clasped tightly on the desktop. His words were wrapped in an intonation that left no room for equivocation. "We must get inside their thinking, their planning, in order to have a chance to win this war, Tyce. We are counting on your…special gifts…to help us do just that."

He continued. "The crisis we face is imposing—has grave implications, that is. I can't inform you at the moment due to a meeting I've got to attend. We will get into the details when you begin tomorrow."

CHAPTER 16

"Tyce?"

The questioning female voice snatched his attention from the laptop screen. His eyes met those of the voice's owner. They were the marvelously green eyes of Essie Jorba.

He straightened and stood quickly, the shock of her sudden appearance and call to him leaving him unable to speak.

Essie stretched her arm to offer her hand. "I'm Essie Jorba," she said, smiling while he responded.

"Dr. Faust said it would be okay if I dropped in to say hi," she said, removing her hand from his grip while he stared at her, still stunned at being suddenly and unexpectedly in her presence.

"I…I'm so pleased that we can talk," he said hesitatingly. "I've just been working on a magazine piece," he said, not knowing what else to say.

"Oh. I hope I didn't disturb your train of thought," Essie said.

"I-I'm so glad you…are here."

"I thought you might be off put with me, after my rudeness to you on the phone," she said, her smile fading to an expression of apology.

"No...no. Absolutely not. I thought nothing of it," he lied, remembering how her begging out of the date they had arranged had ruined his night and set in motion fears they would never be together again.

Essie said nothing, her own thoughts examining the man standing awkwardly in front of her who, her father had said, had been so close to her in a world other than that of reality. He appeared to be normal in every way, even though he seemed unable to express his thoughts. *Could he really be a highly rated journalist?* was the thought etched upon her face—the beautiful face Tyce knew so well and could at this moment do no more than hold fast in his stupefied gaze.

"Well, that's good that you forgive the way things were handled," she said after several seconds of their staring at each other.

"Do you think we might make a new start at..." She let the question trail off, her tone saying the relationship was already more than she had anticipated.

"Oh, yes—I mean, that's what I want. To start again." His clumsy way of answering both warmed and amused Essie. She gracefully moved to react in a way that would put them both more at ease.

She touched his arm with slender fingers while she spoke, the touch he knew so well. "I would like that."

The suddenness of their meeting and the intense feelings generated danced through his thoughts for the hundredth time since that previous evening. He had fought to keep from reaching to hold her, to pull her to himself. But he had to let her go, had to be satisfied for that moment only with their at last making a start on...

on what? On recovering what was love already made in the reaches of time and space—by something, someone, somewhere?

⁓

"How was the...the reunion?" Randolph Faust patted Tyce's knee when the old archeologist slid into the back seat.

"She was even more beautiful than before, Randy," Tyce said. "It was like we had never been separated by... by being in two different universes. At least that's how it was for me."

"When I told her you were working on something in the hotel coffee shop, she asked right away if I thought if it would be okay if she went there to meet you. Morticai and I were meeting in their suite. I told her you sometimes like to have a little conversational chatter going on —a reporter's unique ability to concentrate on putting down a story while amidst the action. She seemed more than glad to hear your name, Tyce. She was, I would say, quite excited."

"Really? You think so?"

"Absolutely. She immediately asked if it would be okay if she interrupted you."

"Well. It is the greatest favor you've ever done for anyone," Tyce said. "It was as if our relationship reignited instantly. At least it was that way for me. I can't get her off my mind."

"And when will you see her again?"

"We'll go to a restaurant somewhere in DC tonight at seven, someplace she has picked out. But she said she will be at the White House ops meeting this morning, unless her father has other plans."

"I can guarantee that she will be there. Morticai knows this is important, to the both of you, but as importantly, to the playing out of what it all portends. There are things afoot that he knows he must not get in the way of."

"What's it all about, Randy?" Tyce's voice was inward turned while he watched the DC landscape pass outside the car window.

"We will find out. It will all become clear. Heaven is involved, and heaven never leaves anything in which it is involved unresolved."

Activity in Ops 3 was more dynamic than during Tyce's previous visit. The same people surrounded the illuminated glass tabletop. No one looked up as he and Randolph Faust entered the room.

Their escorts, the same two men as before, led the way to another door, inserted the card key, and held the door open while Greyson and Faust entered through the doorway.

Morticai Kant and Clint Wayne looked up from the corner where they were huddled.

"Welcome," the American said, standing to greet the men. Morticai followed suit, before he spoke.

"Essie will be here momentarily," he said, addressing Tyce. "She very much enjoyed meeting you," he said with a smile. "She said it was like you had been friends many years," he said with a wry grin that expressed the background knowledge of the younger man's history.

"I felt the same," Tyce said. "Your daughter…is…very special." He was unable to bring himself to tell about the deep feelings he truly felt for Essie.

"Indeed, she is," Kant said, patting Tyce's arm, then guiding him to a sofa that faced Wayne's desk.

When all were seated, the American looked at Faust

then at Tyce. "We want to get you involved as quickly and as deeply as possible into our mission," Wayne said. "We must find out, learn what is involved in the…evil… we face, Tyce. We are hopeful that your special abilities —your gift—will help us get inside this absolute treachery that this nation—and the world—faces."

"On behalf of the prime minister and the people of Israel, I join Clint in saying how vital it is to learn the extent of this…this threat," Kant said, a frown of concentration upon his face. "We say, to you, thanks for your willingness to help."

The door to the inner office opened and one of the escorts that had accompanied Tyce and Faust held it open, allowing Essie to pass through.

Tyce, without thinking, stood quickly to his feet and reached to take her hand. The older men glanced at each other with looks of understanding.

"I'm sorry to be late," Essie said, her eyes studying Tyce, who stood awkwardly, holding her hand. She gently broke his grip.

"Welcome, daughter," Morticai said, bidding her to be seated on the sofa beside the journalist.

"We were about to begin with Tyce's help in dealing with developments with China," Clint Wayne said, addressing Essie. "We believe he can help us discover the answers we need to…to battle against this action we believe is being perpetrated. You got here just in time. I was just about to begin explaining what's involved."

The American operative stood and paced as he talked. "The Viewing Cauldron, as we call it, the group you see looking into the device, is a technology we have had a very short time. Those people are monitoring something very critical going on around the world at the moment—the movement of a pathogen that is deliberately being spread. How it works is unimportant. That is, understanding how the technology follows this spread is not key to what we will be doing here—what Tyce will be asked to do. Suffice it to say that this...technology... allows us to follow what is happening in regard to the pathogen spread."

Wayne paused to sip from the cup of coffee he lifted from the corner of the desk, before continuing. "We know this...this microbe, for lack of a better definition, originated in a province of China. It comes from an area known by our intelligence services to have laboratories that produce pathogens—possibly, we think, for weaponized germ instrumentalities...germ warfare, if you will."

He again sipped the coffee before continuing. "This is something that must be analyzed. Why have the leadership in Beijing decided to do this? Why have they chosen, at this time, to unleash this virus?"

"At first we thought it—this pathogen—had accidentally escaped," Kant put in. "However, we are certain now that it has been deliberately unleashed."

"With China's aggression in the South China Sea and all the other things that are showing up on our intelligence, we know something is up—something profoundly important to the safety of our nations, of the world," the American operative said. "Their objective, it is obvious, is to infect the world with this...this virus."

"The intrigues go much deeper, we believe, Tyce. Much, much deeper," Kant said. "We believe it is tied to esoteric matters that you are somehow a part of."

"I had no...no experience in that...coma world...with China," Tyce said, glancing at Essie sitting to his right. "None at all. And I remember vividly every detail of that time. How can I help in this effort to find out about all involved in this virus from China?"

"It's the sarcophagus, Tyce," Randolph Faust said. "That's why I've been brought in to this…this effort. Why else do you think they would ask a person of my age into this meeting?" Faust's words were offered light-heartedly.

"We are not part of government, Tyce, as we've said. We work with our own group of…of patriots—with the full support and even the commission of the president. We include in this group dedicated to preserving America, defending this president, and seeing to his personal security many among those who believe that the Almighty has…blessed…this group, at this time, for His own purposes."

Wayne placed the empty cup on the desk and turned to face Tyce and Essie on the sofa.

"The people supposed to be serving the president," he said, "those in the intelligence services, are instead engaged in an attempted coup. They are devoted to globalism and to who knows what else. They can't be trusted to do what is best for this nation. That's where our group has stepped in. We are looking to cleanse the executive bureaucracy, particularly the intelligence services that are so entrenched. These who are globalist in their ambitions—they, we think, are in collusion with the Chinese communist regime in some way. We must learn their designs, if this is the case."

"And the sarcophagus?" Tyce questioned. "It has something to do with this…this pathogen?"

"We are convinced it has profound importance in the spiritual realm…the realm of the overall scheme of history playing out," Wayne said.

"In the sense of Bible prophecy yet to be fulfilled," the

archeologist jumped in, "I'm not necessarily in favor of… of this Remote Viewing. I have my deep reservations about using such things to do God's work. It seems to me to be akin to divination…practices forbidden by God's Word, like in the Old Testament book of Deuteronomy. But I have no doubt that you and I have been brought together, Tyce, in order to perform some end-times-related activity of the Lord's choosing. He has us here, at this particular time in history, for His own reasons…just as He has us all here. We must not let the Lord of Heaven down."

"Indeed," Mortacai Kant said, with a tinge of humor in his agreement.

~

ESSIE HAD STOOD beside him when they had all arisen from their seats to adjourn the White House Ops 3 meeting. She had held to his arm and leaned close to him while they listened to Clint Wayne explain where Tyce Greyson's part in the mission would begin.

Tyce had to fight to listen carefully, while feeling the warmth of the girl he loved against him—the girl who didn't really know him, but clung close as she also listened.

"You will be given coordinates to a specific place," Wayne said. "We suspect there is routine, though very closely held, secret conversations taking place within an office complex here in Washington. We believe it involves top people in government who…who are working to bring this president down. They have been trying to do so through all of the Russian collusion hoax, the phony impeachment, all the other lies they have employed to try to bring about their *coup d'état* ambition.

We have our…people…watching for unusual traffic entering these coordinates, these offices. We have our people reporting, people who secretly work for us… secretaries who keep appointment schedules and so forth."

Wayne had taken on an even more serious expression. "As you now see, Tyce, we are bringing you into our most intimate operations. This is why your own life will be very closely monitored from this point forward. We have no choice. It means giving up some personal liberties…for all of us."

He had nodded agreement, while with Essie holding his arm and leaning against him, he listened to the operative divulge the mission's initial steps.

"Specifically, we believe these intelligence people, both in American clandestine services and in Israel's such services, are in direct talks with those who are about to perpetrate… What? We don't yet know. But it involves, we think, a pathogen, a virus, that's designed to carry out some plan to bring about a world pandemic. A pathogen of the sort whose virulence hasn't affected the entire world since, we believe, the Spanish Flu in 1917–1918. Since we are talking about the same cabal of people we have found complicit in the other attempts at a coup, we believe this to be yet another such effort to destroy this presidency and make America vulnerable to their globalist designs."

Essie had said softly near Tyce's ear, when Wayne's explanation was finished, "Do you suppose we may still have our dinner together this evening? You will have such a full rest of the day."

He was quick to respond, "Oh, no. You aren't going to get away with calling it off again."

He could see she was very pleased with his answer.

~

"I THINK you need much more inculcation. But based upon your...sensory abilities, perhaps we will be on safe grounds speeding the process," Shiva Rabine walked in front of him, plopping her armload of papers down on one end of the long table. "What is your feeling? Do you think you can access the Matrix? Detect the signal line and trip into the Liman, as we've practiced?"

"I guess we'll find out," he said, seeing on the scientist's face her disapproval of his glib answer.

"Then be seated and let's get started," she instructed, sitting in a chair at one end while he was seated at the opposite end.

"Remember what you learned," she said. "Concentrate, now," she said. "You should receive through the very narrow aperture we learned to access a large energy...a gestalt of information proceeding from the Matrix. Do you yet sense this access?"

Tyce shook his head. "No, not yet."

"As the aperture widens, the flow of information proceeding along the signal line should increase. Be patient and keep focused on our purpose."

She continued, "Begin writing your viewing results as you receive signals. You must avoid analytic overlay. There is always the tendency to project the Remote Viewer's own biases upon that being perceived. In other words, the tendency is to want to make the outcome in line with your own ideas of how things should be, rather than view them—that is, accept them—as they actually are.

Shiva Rabine watched while he did as he had learned and practiced during a number of previous sessions. "The ideogram will manifest through the impingement of the signal on the autonomic nervous system," she said, "and it is subsequently transmitted through the system to the arm and hand muscle, then transferred to the pen and onto the paper."

Tyce sensed his mind undulating slowly, with wave-like movements that began to stabilize and lock into place a scene. Human figures moved, at first out of focus, but slowly tightening into clear definition.

He heard the woman's voice as she continued to instruct in a soft, even tone. "The system has now integrated into and integrative biological and metaphysical image. You will view the target with increasing clarity."

Tyce's sensation was one of disembodiment. He was here, in this room, among these people, yet he had no awareness of his own body. He must concentrate, focus on the subjects—their activities. The writing—the recording of the viewing—was automatically being transferred onto the paper...

His hearing, as well as his vision, was greatly enhanced—so much so that he had to fight cerebrally to control the volume and brightness of the visual reality of which he was now an integral part.

He realized, then. The scene before him was the same as the cabal he had seen while in the comatose state. The same men. The chrome projections that curved downward from the ceiling in front of each man. The men seated around the circular table. Ten men, each speaking different languages—or many speaking different languages.

But all understood each other. He understood them as they conducted the meeting.

The remembrances flooded back in a gush. These were the men who told of plans to bring upon the earth a pandemic that would induce great fear upon the populations of the world.

His mind went into hyper speed, remembering precisely when he had stood beside the one called Michael in that moment while he had been in the coma. He recalled the exact words of one of the group's members: "Fear is the primary instrumentality to be used. Fear of death from a microbic enemy. With it we shall divide and conquer. Divide through fear of each other. We must keep them apart…destroy their individuality by quarantine and distancing. By taking away their individuality as much as possible. Removing family members from each other through fear of being too close. Causing gatherings, such as church meetings, sports and other venues to be closed to audiences, to congregations. That is the answer to tearing apart nationalism."

It was that declaration that bounced within his thought processes. When the sudden memory storm passed, his thoughts snapped to the voice commanding the attention of the other nine seated around the table. The same man spoke who, during the comatose experience, had uttered the words he had just recalled.

"Our shutdown of the US economy, as you know, was carried out as called for by the blueprint. America's election year was targeted, and the effects were immediate. The people reacted as expected. Fear of contracting the virus was immensely generated, and the masses accepted the lockdowns almost without exception. The pandemic propagation that has permeated all areas of the world has opened the pathway to inducing the vaccine on a global scale."

The spotlights beaming from the ceiling above the

men around the table illuminated the pleased expressions on each face, while the speaker continued.

"The revolutionary spirit has been unleashed. Soon the rage throughout major cities will be in full fury. Change in the chief nation in opposition to the Blueprint will be moving swiftly as the revolution explodes. Storming the bastille is just months away!"

Again, the man paused to look at the faces of those around the table before continuing.

"All has worked masterfully to bring America into the order. The pathogen has been introduced at precisely the right time to combine with the efforts of those entrenched within government and media."

The man paused, his tone changing from pleased to somber.

"These efforts should have already brought this administration to an end. We have worked with all at the highest levels to change the outcome of the election. Despite all these things in combination, this man remains in the most powerful office on the planet, so far as government is concerned."

The speaker leaned forward, his mouth coming within two inches of the curved microphone projecting from the ceiling.

"Despite all these efforts, and in spite of our massaging the polls to convince the people that this president hasn't a chance of being reelected, the internal polls tell us that it will be an electoral landslide in the direction other than the way we wish things to go."

He paused and turned to look in the direction of another of the interlocutors several seats to his left.

"Marcell, please introduce the next step in Operation Earthlord."

The man addressed by the speaker straightened in the high-backed chair and leaned forward until his mouth was near the microphone. His black hair slicked back in a defined style framed his pale face as he began to speak.

"Thank you, Gunther. We have come to a most crucial point in time. As you indicated, despite the best efforts of all concerned, even that of those within this administration's Cabinet, we are moving farther from our objective, which is, of course, to remove this man and reestablish the way we were moving things before this intruder disrupted plans."

He paused to look around the table before moving to within inches of his microphone and beginning to speak once more. All around the table showed facial expressions that indicated rapt interest in what was about to be divulged.

"In our previous meeting, we concluded that this must be accomplished at all cost. We agreed that the key ingredients and the key people are all in place to do what is necessary. The time has come to institute that last-resort option."

All the men nodded silently in agreement with the man's words. Tyce's thoughts went to the meeting when he had stood beside the one called Michael. He knew what was coming next.

"We will take executive action through the only means we think is foolproof, that is guaranteed to succeed. Our executioner has been chosen. He will perform the deed and be instantly executed himself by one of his colleagues. Of course, the executioner has no suspicion whatsoever that he will be immediately eliminated. He believes he will be taken into custody, then released surreptitiously. His family and he, he believes, will then be established in a secret location with wealth that will provide for the rest of their lives."

"And what about the executioner's executioner?" a man across from the speaker interrupted.

"He will simply be seen as having tried to protect the president—although too late to be successful."

"Does anyone within Treasury know of this, besides the executioner himself and the man who will eliminate him?" Another man posed the question, and the speaker addressed it after a momentary pause.

The Secret Service—the one group that can get close enough to assassinate the president. It is already in their... blueprint, Tyce thought as he viewed the cabal who seemed collectively pleased with the plot.

"No. We have not attempted to...to meld the Secret Service director or his people at that level into our Blueprint. They are the most untouchable of all the executive services. Great efforts have gone into compromising the agents who are chosen for the...mission."

"And do they know that they are both chosen for that mission, as a team, or whatever?" another of the round-table asked.

"Yes. The agent who will immediately fire upon the assassin is supposed to—the assassin thinks—immediately take him into custody. But, of course, the assassin's part will be finished."

The same man asked, "And what about the other agent? What will be his fate?"

"He will be a hero, of course, even though he will be a bit late in saving the president's life. He will receive a promotion, no doubt," the speaker said, bringing muffled laughter from the group.

"Who knows the names?" another put in.

"Only we, here, will know the names of the agents.

The High Council will control the operation in the tightest of grips."

The speaker passed sheets of paper around the table so that each man received a page. "These are their names," he said.

Tyce's Remote Viewing perception, he found, gave immediate access to a position above one of the recipients. He read the names typed in boldface black ink: Jeremy Flagstone and Jonas Braddock.

"And when is this...mission...to be completed?" another of the meeting said.

"It will take place during the interloper's movement toward the helicopter, when he stops to address the press as he usually does. At that time, Jonas Braddock will quickly fire at less than a meter. Jeremy Flagstone will then immediately kill Braddock. We have not yet determined the best time to accomplish the matter. That will be determined on a very tight timeline on the day it takes place."

"Thank you, Marcell," the original speaker said, leaning toward the microphone. "Now, to address a most important matter in regard to the sarcophagus," he said, looking around at the group while shuffling papers in front of him on the table.

"The next stage of the Blueprint for Earthlord is now prepared for implementation. I am pleased to announce that the locater element that will be integrated with the vaccine has proven 100 percent successful. Third-stage experimentation is proving to be somewhat more problematic. Testing done in Africa and some in China have produced only a 60 percent success rate."

The speaker looked to one of the interlocutors directly across from his own position at the table's edge. The man had his right hand raised for attention.

MICHAEL

"Yes, Rashman, you have a question?"

The man let his eyes move toward each of the others around the big table before speaking in an Indian dialect, which instantaneously was converted to other languages so all could understand.

"Will this...injectable...be a permanent, one-time vaccination? Or must there be subsequent inoculations in order to keep—to assure—that the subjects remain under control?"

"This is part of the 40 percent that continues to keep us from achieving complete success, as I understand," the moderator said. "The...vaccinations have yet to come up to the point of assuring permanence with regard to compliance. We have tested, using thousands of subjects. Still there continues to be a large number who are not fully brought to compliance. Some within that test group are brought to full compliance, but the effects soon wear off."

Another spoke, "And when might we anticipate 100 percent success?"

The moderator paused to think on the question before leaning with his mouth near the microphone.

"The viable DNA seems to die within some subjects sometimes immediately; in others, it lives for as long as several days before becoming inert. The scientists tell us that the cause or causes of this disparity seem impossible to determine."

Tyce's senses began to darken, the scene before him fading to shades of gray, then to black. His mind was suddenly again staring at Shiva Rabine's face at the other end of the table.

CHAPTER 17

"Does it really work? A person can actually go in their mind to another place? It's not just a hypnotic state or something like that?"

Essie Jorba studied Tyce Greyson's expression while she asked the question. Her lovely countenance, however, took his thoughts in a direction other than that of the Remote Viewing experience of three hours earlier.

"The viewing I'm doing right now is far more interesting," he said, watching her nose wrinkle in amusement over his lame attempt at flirting.

"Well, then...your experience this afternoon must certainly not have been very interesting," she said happily.

They sat in a favorite restaurant from Tyce's days as correspondent for a cable TV network. He fiddled with the cellphone in his left hand while punching numbers with his right index finger.

"What are you doing?" Essie had watched him dealing with the device for the past several minutes during their conversation.

"Trying to find a piece I wrote right after the session today," he said. "I don't want to have to do it again, and it looks like I might have to," he said. Then his expression changed, his eyes locking on the small screen.

"Thank God," he said, scrolling through the document. "It's all here."

He put the phone aside and looked at Essie from across the table. "Sorry. I just couldn't relax until I found that piece. Deadline is eight in the morning."

"Does it have to do with your session today?"

"Yes, it's a report of things I experienced."

"And what did you experience? Or is it a secret?"

"You have the clearance...probably above mine," he said, taking in the full scope of her beauty for the first time since they had sat down. He thought to himself what a fool he was for putting the business of writing before her, the woman he hadn't been able to dismiss from his thoughts since awakening from the coma.

"To be honest, I don't know what my level of clearance is," Essie said before sipping from the long-stemmed wine glass. "Morticai takes care of all that. I can go anywhere, into any meeting he has...except the Maglan Council meetings. Does that give me...clearance...to know about your session today?"

Tyce had a delayed response to her speaking. Finally, he said softly, "I have nothing at all to hide from you."

"Actually, Tyce...I'm more interested in what my father told me about...about your—and my—time...in the life you described while you were in what you call your coma world."

Tyce could tell she wanted to know how she fit in to that strange time that was still as real to him as his life of the last minutes since they had sat down together.

"Were we...close? Were we engaged? Papa said something about engagement."

"No. We weren't officially engaged," he said, unable to bring to the surface the best tact to enter the conversation she wanted. "But I was on the brink of asking you," he said.

"And do you think I was...ready...to say 'yes'?"

"We were...we loved each other," he said. You wouldn't have said 'no', I'm fairly confident."

Again, there was silence between them, each thinking of the strangeness of their dinner meeting. To Tyce, it was as if they had never been separated in time, distance, or whatever the spatial divide. To Essie, it was an odd sensation that she didn't know him, yet felt deeply a sense of being as close to him as to her own father.

"And in your life before the coma—you were married?"

"Yes. Marial."

"You loved her very much," Essie said, affirming that she knew he had loved her.

Tyce felt the sense of *déjà vu* overtake his thought process. He said before he thought, "Essie...that's the very question you asked...in my experience of the coma."

When looked a bit embarrassed, Tyce moved quickly to assuage any misperception of his finding displeasure in her question. He reached to place his hand on top of hers across the small table. "I didn't mean anything by that except that it touches me that it was so much like that...time. It was a special moment for me, and it is as clear in my mind as when you asked the question."

She smiled briefly; she was trying to understand.

"The next question you asked was even more touching," Tyce said.

Essie said softly, cocking her head slightly, "Do you think you could ever love someone like that again?"

THE MOMENT HAD DOMINATED Tyce's every thought when the evening ended. He had drifted into sleep with the lingering remembrance of the passionate kiss he and Essie shared.

Was it that comatose time of their embrace? Was it the time at their first meeting...the time last night at dinner he stood to come to her and kiss her after offering his hand to help her from her chair?

Both embraces—their kissing—had been real, not imagined. The memory of both made that night's sleep the best he could remember.

Now, next morning, he awaited the arrival of those who would debrief him on his Remote Viewing of the previous day. Clint Wayne had been exercised to the extreme upon talking with him on the phone after reading the report Tyce had prepared. It was extensively detailed and had the OPS 3 agent in a state that was frenetic as he entered the office.

"This is spectacular!" Wayne removed his suit coat after plopping the sheath of papers onto his desk. He was seated and immediately reached for the button on the phone.

"Get everyone together," he said into the speaker, then turned to look at the journalist.

"You say in your report that this is the High Commission you believe the group of American plotters mentioned—that is, in the coma vision you saw involving that group of generals, senators, media, and so forth? This High Commission, you say, is the top echelon of global principals that the American group of plotters was talking about?"

"Yes," Tyce replied. "The cabal in the Remote Viewing session was the same as the group of global 'principals', as you call them. They were all the same men I saw then."

The OPS 3 agent looked at the pages for a few seconds before speaking again.

"These details are just stunning. I haven't dealt with Remote Viewing to any great extent, but certainly I haven't seen this level of detail from any such session."

"All was recorded while in the session," Tyce said. "I had no idea of what my hand was writing. I was amazed to see the results of that…automatic writing… myself."

"But you remember these things as you saw them? I mean, what you've reported and after reading your own report, you fully remember all of the details of the session?"

"Yes. The details are fully remembered, and exact. Like I said, they amazed even me—the specifics in that report."

Wayne shuffled through the pages, stopping at one in particular and holding it while he scanned it. "And you've never heard these names of these agents, these Secret Service agents who this group…this High Commission…say will carry out an assassination attempt?"

"No," Tyce said, turning to see the door to Wayne's office open and several people begin entering.

Clint Wayne said nothing, standing from behind his desk while the others walked into his office. "Please find a seat," he said, addressing them. "We have lots to do this morning."

Tyce looked around the group while they retrieved folding chairs from against one wall. He recognized none of them—eight men and four women, he quickly counted.

Once settled, they gave their attention to Wayne, who stood beside Tyce, his hand on the journalist's shoulder.

"This, ladies and gentlemen, is the guy we've been buzzing about. Tyce Greyson, a talented journalist who we'll call our most secret weapon." Wayne patted Tyce's shoulder and urged him to be seated in a nearby armchair.

"Tyce, these are OPS 3 agents," Wayne said. "We call ourselves CUES —stands for Covert United Endgame Strategists. We just use the letter Q for brevity's sake."

Wayne continued speaking to Tyce. "Each person here is a volunteer. We all come from various intelligence agencies. There are others from the government, civilian entities, and the military. We, as you're already aware, are devoted to saving this presidency. Thereby, we are dedicated to preserving this nation, its founding principles, and its citizens' right to life, liberty, and the pursuit of happiness—exactly what the founding fathers intended."

Wayne scanned the room, hesitating before continuing.

"Ladies and gentlemen, our secret weapon here has many things to report. His reconnaissance has made possible our interdiction into the most dangerous assassination plot yet encountered. I think you will be most encouraged by what you are about to hear."

"THE PRESIDENT WAS MADE aware of the assassination plot less than an hour ago."

Clint Wayne spoke after putting the phone down

following the two-minute conversation. He looked at the three men who sat in his office.

"The agents haven't yet been nabbed. The Secret Service director, in conjunction with a number of the people who were in our meeting, Tyce, want to follow their movement a bit...track their off-duty movement and put eavesdropping devices in just the right places. Meantime, neither of them will be allowed to get near the president or vice president. There are various excuses being used to assign them to different duties... on temporary duty assignment, they are being told."

"We have been cautious," Morticai Kant said from directly in front of the Ops 3 agent's desk. "This... international cabal—the High Commission, as Tyce has informed us—has induced this violent activity that has sprung up in America. The 'revolution', as they call it. They no doubt have something equally as dastardly planned for Israel...for the prime minister and our other leadership. We can be assured of this because Bibi is of the same mindset in maintaining sovereignty and autonomy for Israel. It is obvious now that the globalist principals will stop at nothing in order to bring the United States into their Blueprint for changed world order."

"So you have some operatives in mind?" Wayne asked. "Do you suspect a plot?"

"We have no one in particular we are considering. It is very difficult because of the nature of vetting our security. All are proven warriors dedicated to the prime minister's own ideology, so far as it is possible to tell. We are, however, keeping track of several upon which some suspicion rests."

"Do you suppose our secret weapon here might be

utilized to help you determine the fealty of these people you suspect?"

Tyce shuffled uneasily in his chair to the right of Randolph Faust when the other men looked at him and smiled at him mischievously.

"That was my next question. Do you think we might borrow him for such an intrigue?" The Maglan chief looked at Tyce, his own face twisted in an expression of ominously feigned inquiry.

He turned then to Randolph Faust. "What do you think, Randy? Is our young friend ready to do battle on behalf of the biblically prophetic people of Israel, do you think?"

"We wrestle not against flesh and blood," Faust said, sizing up the journalist to his right. "But against principalities and powers, against the darkness and wickedness in high places. He knows...Michael...personally. One apparently lesser angel once slew eighty thousand in one night on behalf of Israel. Michael is the mightiest of all of heaven's angels. There's no telling what Tyce can do with Michael at his side."

His companions emitted a collective, but muffled, laugh. Tyce's only reaction was a subdued smile.

CHAPTER 18

"We are told more details about that pathogen released from a Chinese laboratory. A virus of some sort. It is unclear exactly where it came from or how it was released. Our intelligence tells us it is highly transmissible...very contagious."

Morticai Kant spoke to Tyce Greyson, Essie, and Randolph Faust after talking with someone in Tel Aviv.

"The virus has already spread to Italy and parts of Europe, as well as Asia. The prime minister has ordered that all of Israel be temporarily locked down. We will have to undergo medical checks upon landing."

TWO HOURS after touching down in Tel Aviv, Tyce, Essie, her father, and Randolph Faust moved down a corridor after having received medical clearance. The big, metal door opened when they approached it and a pleasant-looking Israeli met them.

"Director, it is good that you are with us again," the tall, young Mossad agent said, welcoming the party. "We have learned much," he said, issuing the four arrivals farther into the recesses of the IDF operations center.

"Oh? And what is the latest?" Morticai's question was put in his usual, blunt fashion. His younger underling spoke with excitement in explanation.

"We know that the virus moved first from Wuhan, China, from a lab there, and it was transported by human agents to Milan, Italy."

"And how was this intelligence gathered?" the Maglan chief asked.

"Through Gideon-Surveillance Ops since the cyber-implementation. It has worked phenomenally."

Once seated in Kant's office, Morticai turned to Tyce. "Refresh our memory about what you remember from the cabalists when you were in the comatose state. It is my understanding that it was the same group of...inter-nationalists...that you recognized in the Remote Viewing session."

Tyce searched his memory. So much had taken place. Surprisingly, the remembrance rolled clearly through his thoughts when he concentrated on the moments in the coma when he had stood with Michael, listening to the men plot their evil.

"Yes...the same group. I remember the men, ten of them, each speaking a different language, but able to understand each other through some sort of translation technology."

He paused to remember as exactly as possible how the session had unfolded.

"The man who seemed to be head of the group—later I heard his name as 'Gunther'—he said, 'So we are agreed. The objective is to bring about biological controls through perceived need for a prophylactic against a worldwide pandemic.' Another guy answered from directly across from Gunther. He said, 'We are assured that such a vaccination coming from the Earth-lord Project can produce tracking methodologies that will guarantee controlling of populations on a global basis.'"

All in the room considered Tyce's words. Finally, the Maglan chief spoke. "What else do you remember? Can you give more details?"

"I remember vividly," Tyce said. "It's almost like I have verbatim recall. I wonder what that's all about?"

"The Lord's hand is in it, Tyce. That's the answer," Randolph Faust said.

"Well, we will take the information, regardless of the source," Kant said. "Tell us all you remember," he said.

"I remember another guy in the group. He said, 'How is it proposed that this pandemic be initiated? And how can nationalism, especially that of the United States be disrupted? That is, disrupted to the point that the people will start thinking as international citizens, as citizens of the world, not of America. No other people have been permitted to live under such freedoms with such luxuries, as the American people. Detaching them from such lifestyle will be problematic.'"

Tyce stopped to think a minute, then continued. "Gunther, the one called Gunther, he gave the answer to the man's question. He said, 'Fear is the primary instrumentality to be used. Fear of death from a microbic enemy. With it we shall divide and conquer. Divide through fear of each other. We must keep them apart... destroy their individuality by quarantine and distancing. By taking away their individuality as much as possible.

Removing family members from each other through fear of being too close. Causing gatherings, such as church meetings, sports and other venues to be closed to audiences, to congregations. That is the answer to tearing apart nationalism.'"

Tyce paused to collect his remembrance of the coma-induced vision while he stood with Michael before the group around the circular table. "Then he said, 'When fear has wrought its maximum results of dividing them one from the other, the solution will be presented that will promise a return to some degree of normalcy. The solution will be the vaccine allowing them to again interact in a new normalcy.'"

After a moment's pause, Tyce continued. "Another man said, 'The Earthlord serum will be mandated to prevent further virus spread.' Gunther, apparently the head of the group, then said, 'Exactly. Then the serum will be induced containing the new trackable module that interfaces with satellite and computer breakthroughs.'"

When Tyce had finished, Randolph Faust said, "There is more to this vision, I remember you telling me."

"Yes. I remember it all exactly," the journalist said with a quizzical lilt in his words. "Another man said, 'But what of those who refuse the vaccine?' The one called Gunther then said, 'Then it will be up to governments to pressure, through all means necessary, all who run commerce and governmental services to keep anyone who will not comply from buying, selling. From social interaction of any kind.' Another man said, 'The Earthlord serum possesses properties that work within the very genetic structured, the DNA…in effecting compliance. Such biological engineering will almost certainly overcome the American will to resist our new order.'"

Tyce again gathered his recollections of that vision. "Gunther then said, 'This president has been unreachable for some reason. He possesses an impenetrable defense. The resistance, we surmise, comes from our perpetual nemesis.' Another asked, 'What is the battle plan?' He then asked, 'What can be done to dissolve the results of the American election?' Gunther said, then, 'The process of neutralizing him has begun. He calls the new environment he has entered the "swamp". He has no idea of the alligators that await his entering the DC waters.'"

Faust broke in when Tyce finished. "And you told me what your friend Michael said, at that time."

"Yes," Tyce said, recalling the words of the man who had set him before the vision. "Michael said, 'These are those of which Daniel was given knowledge. These plot great resistance to the Most High. From this circle emerges power and authority from wickedness in high places of earthly rebellion.'"

Randolph Faust leaned forward in the chair. "Morticai, I believe what this is all about is a globalist group…a 'cabal', as you call it. These represent, I'm convinced, a group being driven by…spiritual entities…to prepare for what happens following this dispensation."

"More of your prophecy talk," the Israeli said lightly. "We are looking at the *Left Behind* fiction being played out. Is that it?"

"You've been told enough about my views over these past few years to know what I believe comes next," Faust said. "You know what I mean by the term 'dispensation'."

"*I* don't know," Essie said emphatically from her position next to Tyce on the small sofa.

"You care to tell her, Papa…or shall I?" Faust's words and tone were equal to his friend's in their intended jab at the Israeli Maglan chief.

Kant grimaced, then broke into a smile that said he was only faking that the jab had hurt. "The *Left Behind novel* series were written from the viewpoint...the belief...that there is coming a worldwide disappearance. Millions over the world will simply vanish. The event they believe their Bible teaches is called the 'Rapture.'"

"Oh, yes," Essie broke in. "I've heard of those books. I have friends who have read those."

"Well, our dear friend here believes this...Rapture... is not fiction but will soon come to pass."

"This dispensation is called the Church Age or Age of Grace," the archeologist said, looking toward Essie. "When the Rapture occurs, this dispensation will end, and the next will begin."

"And he believes this will issue in a changed world order," Essie's father said to her.

"And that's what this group Tyce has seen and has told us about involves," Faust said. "I believe they are a group who want to bring in the last tyrant, the last great dictator of human history—the Antichrist."

The Israeli sat forward, concentrating to frame his question. "And, Tyce, you spoke of the time in your coma about an American meeting, one where those attending spoke of this High Commission. Can you tell again about that?"

"It was your group, Maglan, that had me put on the Stimulator, as it was called. Only, Michael met in the... the vision...and he told me the device would only inhibit me from carrying out what needed to be done. To see what that group of American operatives were up to."

"And do we have such a device as this...Stimulator, Abba?" Essie's question and tone said she was surprised that she had been left out of the loop concerning what her father had divulged as a reality when Tyce had first met Shiva Rabine for familiarization with Remote Viewing.

"Experimental, daughter. The fact is, it does exist. Tell us, young man. About that meeting."

"They were a group of men. Some were dressed in business clothes; some were in uniform. Well, only two were in military uniforms. They were discussing a project involving the sarcophagus."

Tyce let his eyes gaze at the floor while he recalled the strange meeting.

"One, the guy at the head of the long conference table, said, 'This means that the project's timeline will be thrown off.' He said, 'We cannot let this take place. We will put into effect, here in this country, the alternate plan for now.'"

Tyce paused to recollect further, then said, "The guy in charge looked at the two men who entered late...the men I recognized as television executives. He said, 'Hopefully, with your being totally on board, we can soon remove this intruder from office and get on with Project Earthlord.'"

Tyce stopped again and the memory came to him in vivid detail. "Then they turned to what I believe was the seminal moment of the plot to assassinate the president. The head guy, at the end of the conference table, said, 'The extract is still some time from perfection.' He said, 'This election has further complicated the process of producing the serum. I can't overemphasize the necessity of keeping US resources in this project under absolute lock and key. This new administration must not be allowed to restrict the use of these assets in any way whatsoever.' He said, 'All of the intelligence operatives—those at the top—are in complete agreement. We cannot allow a trend back toward nationalism for the United

States. We cannot achieve our goal, apart from an all-out effort to neutralize this election. This man the foolish people have brought to this office must go. If we can't prevent inauguration, then we must use every means within our collective to remove him at the earliest possible moment.'"

The journalist remembered the words that had troubled him during the coma-induced vision. "Then they got down to the assassination plot itself, I think. One of the men in military uniform, a general, asked, 'And how far do we go with carrying that out?' The head guy said, then, 'By whatsoever means necessary.' One I recognized as a senator then said, 'And what about the Treasury? What about the Secret Service?'" Tyce sensed absolute recall, as if an inner-cerebral prompter scrolled the remembered words. "The head guy said, 'As I said...*ALL* of our collective are on board. At least those in control... those at the top.'"

Tyce looked into the eyes of each who surrounded him. "That's when I knew it was to be an assassination plot that would form at some point. The man at the head of the table said, 'We will meet again upon conclusions reached in the Higher Council. Be prepared to implement things directed when we next meet.'"

"Your...gift...is most useful for our purposes, young man," the Maglan chief said. "I suppose I can see where one could believe that it is heaven sent."

"Morticai, I more than *suppose*, as you suggest. This is certainly something that has been given for just this time so near the end of the age," Faust said. "The Remote Viewing part...I'm not so certain. It seems in every respect to go against the word of God, to my way of thinking."

"The way in which he can recall in great detail...it is

beyond the natural, don't you think?" Essie directed her question at her father.

"Agreed, daughter. There is something going on that is inexplicable to be sure."

"It just seems to start rolling in my thoughts," Tyce said. "I guess it's like that automatic writing in the Remote Viewing, only it's inner-cranial. "Automatic talking," I guess would be the way to describe it. After it starts, the remembrance goes until it plays out to the end."

"What would happen, do you think, if he wore that Stimulator thing?" Essie's question was put to no one in particular.

"All I know is that Michael, in my vision, had me remove it before I left the Maglan viewing chamber," Tyce said. "He said it would only inhibit my ability to... view...the scene I eventually saw and just described to you."

Faust cleared his throat and the others turned to look at him as he spoke up. "I have no doubt the Lord has you here at this moment to assist in whatever is about to play out...to bring in the end of these prophetic matters," he said. He shifted in his chair, in obvious concentration. "I've been thinking on it, and my thoughts have changed a bit. Tyce was told by this...Michael...not to wear the Stimulator. Obviously, he went on to see and hear what he saw and heard. It was all heaven's doing. I now believe that this...Remote Viewing...wasn't really needed, either. Heaven was directing that automatic writing, just like God is directing the 'automatic speaking' scrolling through his mind."

Randolph Faust's assessment brought silence before the Maglan chief spoke. "If this is the end, Israel will survive even if it means all-out nuclear exchanges."

The archeologist smiled, seeing in his friend's demeanor and hearing in his adamant declaration the reason he was chosen to head Israel's fiercest covert IDF entity.

"Indeed, Israel will survive," Faust said in an upbeat tone. "That's God-guaranteed."

CHAPTER 19

"The president and prime minister are on the line as we speak," Morticai Kant said, looking to Tyce Greyson, then to his daughter. "They've both been given all of the intelligence you have provided, Tyce. We await their decision as to what to do next."

"What do you think, Papa? Will they put him in danger?" Essie's question was issued with intense concern.

"Whatever their conclusions and directives, why should we worry about him?" Kant's tone was light-hearted. "If the God of heaven...the Creator of the universe...has Tyce on the payroll, as Randolph believes, what harm can possibly come to him?"

"Not funny, Morticai," she said with irritation. "We both know what kind of predicaments are possible with Maglan."

"Well, I can't absolutely guarantee a result as Yahweh in heaven can do. But I can certainly guarantee that no matter what, he will get the best protection available on this planet."

Essie rolled her eyes and nodded negatively at her father's glib attempt at making the situation seem less foreboding.

"Do you have any idea what they're talking about...I mean regarding my involvement?"

"Yes," the Maglan chief said bluntly, saying nothing more, leaving the journalist's question hanging in the air.

"He is like that, Tyce. He is Maglan and knows *everything*. The rest of us must just wait and play the guessing game."

"It's a terrible job," Kant said. "But someone has to do it."

Again, his daughter rolled her eyes and nodded negatively.

"You will both have your answers shortly," Kant said. "At least you will know the things I'm allowed to divulge."

The door of Kant's office opened, and a man leaned inside. "Sir, they would like for you to come to the phone," he said.

When Kant left the office, Essie moved to sit on the sofa beside Tyce. She reached to take his left hand in both of hers. Tyce felt the cool flesh of her slender fingers while she held his hand. Her affectionate moment tested his resolve to refrain from embracing her. It was the only touch he longed to experience for the rest of his life.

"Promise me, Tyce. If you don't want to do what they ask, no matter what it is, promise that you will say no to them."

He studied her expression. "I can't think of anything they would ask of me that would be...would be overly dangerous."

"You don't know my father. Morticai can plan things you wouldn't believe."

"Has he ever placed you in danger?" Tyce's question made her assess his reason for asking.

"No," she said. "If anything, he protects me much to excess. But you are not his daughter."

"Do you think he has no thought about putting others—other than his daughter—in danger? He doesn't seem like that kind of guy to me."

"It's Israel," she said, still holding his hand, her expression becoming a bit harder. "There is no one he would spare—not even me—if Israel could be kept from danger of destruction by using them."

Tyce put his right hand on top of both of hers. "Essie —I...I have such a special...feeling for you. It's no different than in my other world."

She let her eyes dart quickly from his intense gaze. Her demeanor became shy as she spoke. "I...I sense that...that I've known you forever, Tyce," she said softly. "I've never felt this way about anyone."

When she lowered her face, Tyce put his index finger beneath her chin and raised her face to look into her eyes. "I love you, Essie," he said quietly.

She said nothing but smiled and looked away. He lifted her chin and face back into his direct gaze. "And I'm not sorry to say so so soon after meeting you again."

While passion ascended, their lips met. It was, in the deepest reaches of Tyce's inner being, as if they had never been apart.

～

CLINT WAYNE WAS on a secure line from Washington, DC. His voice boomed over the speaker while Tyce,

Morticai Kant, Randolph Faust, Essie and seven Maglan operatives listened.

"As you know, Morticai, the president and the prime minister have agreed that this…plot…must be explored to the fullest before we preempt their plans. With the ongoing coup attempts by those formerly at the top of the intelligence agencies…some still in those positions… we must determine the exact nature and makeup of this sedition. The forced collapse of economic conditions with the release of this pathogen has to be part of the calculus in our countering these traitors."

"The president and prime minister agree that our… secret weapon…should be brought into that effort," Kant said.

"Yes. Is Tyce there with you?"

"Yes, sir. I'm here," Tyce said.

"Tyce, we will have coordinates for you shortly that will make your Remote Viewing of the two Secret Service agents possible. They've been surveilled for several days. They've been meeting…separately…with a number of people of interest within the covert-ops sector."

The Maglan chief turned toward Tyce. "This covert sector includes some Israeli operatives we suspect."

"Yes. We know almost certainly that this plot to assassinate includes both the president and the prime minister," Wayne said from DC. "We need to know their exact plans. You are to find this out for us so we can learn how deep this plot to bring down the American president and the Israeli prime minister goes."

His sense of noble purpose should, he knew, rise to the surface of his patriotism. It didn't for some reason, as his thought was that it was a much larger task than his likes could successfully undertake.

"Are you up to the challenge?" Wayne asked.

"Guess so," Tyce said, without really meaning it. "I guess we'll see."

"There's someone here that wants to talk with you, Tyce," Wayne said. There were noises of movement coming from the speakers.

"Tyce," a familiar voice said. "This is the president. We're counting on you to help us get to the bottom of this disgrace to our nation. I know you will do a great job. We have every confidence in you."

He was still numbed from the brief conversation with the president. The helicopter ride from the IDF headquarters to the concrete blockhouse building miles westward lasted less than fifteen minutes, and he watched while the chopper hovered above the flat roof before its tail rotor swung to the left and descended. The bird tapped down lightly on the building's top and he, Morticai Kant, and three Maglan agents scrambled from the chopper and into a nearby door leading to the building's interior.

"I've been here," Tyce said, once inside.

"No. I don't think so," Kant said. "I hold clearances of all who come here. You haven't been here."

"But I've been here, Morticai," Tyce held firm. "I remember this building from the time of the coma…"

Kant looked warily at the younger man while they followed the agents through an elevator door. When the elevator bumped to a stop, Kant took Tyce's arm and nudged him through the opening and into the large room full of people milling about.

"Tell me, then," Kant said, pausing near the center of the room. "Where did you go in this building in order to do the Remote Viewing you told us about—when you wore the Stimulator?"

"This way," Tyce said, taking the Maglan chief by his arm and walking him toward a set of double doors against one wall. "I went through these doors."

Once through the opening, he nudged Kant toward another door down a small hallway. "This is the room I remember," he said. "It has a sealed chamber…like the doors on ships. They seal to make them watertight. It's like those doors on ships."

Kant said nothing but walked ahead and through another opening without doors.

"This is it," Tyce said, looking at the sealed door he had just described—had described a number of times in recounting the visions.

The Maglan chief, Tyce could see, was in somewhat of a stunned state of incredulousness. Kant ducked to enter the door to the chamber and Tyce followed. The journalist looked around, experiencing the strange sensation of unbelievability himself.

"This is the room," he said. He stood behind a chair and held its back. "I sat in this chair while they put the Stimulator on my head."

"Okay. I believe you. It's just all so incredible," Kant said, glancing at several uniformed men who joined them in the chamber. "We want you to wear the Stimulator again. Will your friend Michael mind, do you think?"

Tyce grinned, seeing in the Israeli's expression that he could do little more than try to be funny at this moment he didn't understand. Tyce, himself, didn't understand what this was all about—where it was going. There was no Michael to guide him, to discourage him from wearing the device.

"Since I don't see Michael around here, I guess it will

be okay to use the device," he said, returning the Maglan chief's attempt at ironic humor.

"Then, let us get started. Time is of the essence."

Kant turned to one of the agents standing by. "Do you have the coordinates, Mahl?"

"Yes, sir," the taller man said, lifting a clipboard so Kant could see he had what was needed to proceed with the viewing.

"Good. Let's get him into the device," Kant said, turning to leave through the doorway along with all but one of the agents.

Once seated, the man adjusted the stimulator on the journalist's head.

"You will have a sensation…an increase in wave-like movements. It's much like how one feels when one has a fever. Your thoughts move in wave-like undulations," the man said in an Israeli accent, finishing the adjustments.

"Yes. I've been here before," Tyce said.

"Oh? When was that? I've been here since beginning the technologies implementation…"

Tyce said nothing but just smiled, looking at the many blinking lights and switches on the control board in front of him. Moments later, the man sat at the end of the table that fronted the control board. "I will give you the coordinates of the meeting we are attempting to access," he said.

"This meeting is the one in which they are meeting now?"

"Yes, but if it had been one earlier, we could still access it," the operative answered.

"You can go backward and forward in time?"

The journalist's question, incredulous in tone, caused the Remote Viewing facilitator's own tone to rise in his excitement about the technology.

"We have found that it is not a matter of actual slippage in time that is experienced, but the Stimulator acts like a recorder when the RV, in some cases, can pull the past...the recording...from the Matrix.

"How does one do that? How can you...simply think in order to pull a scene from the past?"

"We are not sure," the Israeli said from his position sitting at the other end of the console table. "We are just satisfied that it is a side benefit we have learned can be accessed from the Remote Viewing process."

"This...ability to go back and forth in time—how long has it been part of the Remote Viewing process?"

"It is very new," the Israeli operative said. "Within the last month or two."

Tyce remembered Randolph Faust's words about biblically forbidden things. About Scripture that dealt with delving into things of a dark spiritual nature.

"What other things have you learned that you didn't anticipate?"

"You ask about going back in time. But with regard to your question of going forward, I presume you mean to be able to look into future matters. This was something that we have found recently. There was one...transcendental sensitive who actually reported viewing a future event. The report proved credible...was validated. I can't go into detail. It is a classified matter of the highest order."

The Israeli did something on a console and came to adjust the Stimulator device, securing the strap at the chin area.

"They now tell me you've done this before," he said, pressing the earpiece against his ear while making the final adjustment and heading back toward the chair at the other end.

"Yeah, sort of," Tyce said lightly. "It was while I was in a coma."

He expected the operative to be surprised, but the man's tone was level and controlled. "Yes. They said you had some really strange visions during your...unconsciousness."

"It was as real as this world we are sitting in," Tyce said. "It was like it was total reality. I still remember it like it was a day I went through yesterday."

"They tell me that you had a friend while in the comatose state tell you not to use the Stimulator during that...session."

"That's right. A man called Michael. He told me the Stimulator would inhibit me from being able to see the things I needed to see in the vision...the Remote Viewing episode."

"And how do you feel about it all now? What is the purpose, do you think, of that comatose state, as juxtaposed against what we are doing at this moment in...*real* time?"

"Can't tell you," Tyce said in a light tone. "It's classified..."

"Touché," the Israeli said laughingly. "Then we shall proceed and soon know where this adventure will take us."

His thought was first of a coagulant, fog-like envelopment. Moving into the Remote View had been instantaneous, unlike the first or even subsequent sessions. He wondered if a much swift ascent...or descent...into the process was one of the benefits of the device. He wondered, too, if he would meet Michael again, be told to remove the device before proceeding.

But there was no movement across a beautiful countryside of green lushness like in the comatose experience. No shimmering lake reflecting the brilliant blue sky. Just a haze…a fog that now seemed to be clearing, dissipating, as the scene seemed to engulf him. Men dressed in coats and ties conversed in a small room. Tyce, like in previous sessions, was undetected, even as his thoughts moved into the very midst of the gathering.

It came into his intensifying thought processes. He wasn't in their midst bodily, like in the comatose sessions' visions. It was only his thought processes that invaded the group of men, who, he somehow understood, spoke in Hebrew. Yet he comprehended perfectly every nuance of their words.

"The thing must be done simultaneously," one of the men said while the others listened intently. "We must not allow for any time to elapse between the taking of the prime minister and of the president."

The others nodded while he continued. "Our colleagues in every Western government will, once this is accomplished, move upon the various militaries— whose top people also are in agreement—to put into effect martial law."

"And immediately upon instituting this, each in government that are not part of us will be taken into custody," another said.

"Yes. It will all take place inside of a couple of hours."

"So, we are certain that we have sufficient military compliance?" the same man as before said.

"We are absolutely certain that the militaries of both Israel and the United States are in full agreement—at least, those in position to command that troops carry out the arrests and incarcerations."

The plan was of a military coup! Tyce tried to get a look at each of the cabalists. He would need to give those in the debriefing faces to identify. He couldn't know their names. Unlike the vision of the American conspiracy group, he didn't recognize any of them.

"And when will this...this corrective action...take place?" another of the men said.

"We are not certain of the precise timing yet. We await the word of the High Commission."

"Mr. Lashan," the man who seemed to be the leader then turned to yet another of the group. "Do we have an approximate date?"

The man responded, "The timing depends upon the coordination between the Global Initiative for Transition with the people in Rome."

"This will have to take place before this American election?" the group's leader questioned the same man.

"Not at all. The...transition...the final transnationalization...can take place after the election, most likely—easier than before the election," the man replied. "The American electorate's decision will act as an exclamation point in convincing some of the stragglers among us in key positions. It will convince them that the transition is absolutely necessary."

Tyce watched the group seem to withdraw within their own thoughts, before another among them spoke. "You are convinced the American election will go in the direction other than what we have presented for these many months?"

The man called Lashan spoke. "We have done all within our power to produce a narrative against this man. All have failed. We believe that the so-called internal polls...those indicators...show a much different outcome than we have done our best to portray."

The leader again spoke. "Whatever is done or whenever it's done, it must be done. The time to bring all under globalist governance is at hand. These two stand in the way more so than any other."

Another said, "So it is the collective's thinking that the results of the pathogen's effects…that is, the fear of the pandemic among the populations, if presented properly, will be enough to cause acceptance of the…the transition?"

The apparent leader answered, "The global power brokers at the United Nations, World Economic Forum, the British royal family, the International Monetary Fund, and the Vatican have laid out for us why COVID must be kept front and center in the human psyche for the foreseeable future. They've all identified it as the key to launching a 'Great Reset' of the global economic and social order."

"The removal of these leaders of these powerful coalition nations, then, will facilitate the expansion of fear. It will make the populations more receptive to the serum—that is, to the vaccination?"

The cabal's head again answered the man. "Once sovereignty—that is, nationalism—is put down, or at least seriously curbed, yes. We are convinced—that is, the High Commission is convinced—that the populations will submit, eventually. America in particular, and to a less degree, Israel, are the main holdups to bringing down the borders, to being rid of nationalism, as it has been instrumental as an obstacle to the Blueprint."

The men within the gathering were silent for several seconds before the group's head said, "We were surprised at the ease with which the American populace reacted. There were, of course, a number, particularly among those who look at things through the lens of the Christian Bible, who questioned the controls we have worked to implement. It will be even a greater challenge to

achieve compliance from these same people. They—
many of them—consider the vaccine to equate to their
Bible's tale of accepting a mark of some mythological
Antichrist."

Another chimed in. "Then it is quite appropriate that
we—that is, the Commission—have termed the eventual
bringing of all people together through this fear of the
pathogen the Babel Synthesis."

There was laughter while the group's leader said,
"Yes, quite appropriate to keep it in biblical terms, I
think." He paused to take in the humor of the moment
before speaking again.

"Although the Christian universe is in rebellion
against our design for one world, we have the Vatican on
board for controlling much of Christendom. This pope
is a true friend of the United Nations...of this Blueprint
for one world."

The cabal's leader continued the lecture.

"This pope, In his latest *Fratelli Tutti*—"Brothers All"
—encyclical pushed for all nations to give power and
authority to the United Nations, which he says will lead
to a new world order. Globalism has already weakened
the power of nation states and their individuality
through the transnationalization of their respective
economic and financial sectors. The pope believes
strongly that the time is ripe to set global government in
concrete, to create a system of global governance that
can never be dismantled."

"But it is impossible because the UN has no teeth," a
man to the leader's left put in. "That is no serious way to
enforce."

"Yes. The pope himself has addressed this. He said
that nations need 'legal limits' to prevent them from
becoming too powerful individually.

"The only way to give the UN the teeth you mention, and that the pope thinks it needs in order to rule the world is to place clear legal limits on all individual nations—meaning stripping their sovereignty. This will prevent any one of them from acquiring too much power, which the pope says could result in cultural impositions or a restriction of the basic freedoms of weaker nations on the basis of ideological differences.

"But, again, this is impossible at present. This man, along with this prime minister and others, stands in the way," the man to the leader's left said.

Just as the one in charge started to speak again, the door to the room opened and a man hurried in to hand a piece of paper to the group's leader. His face contorted strangely while reading the note, his expression one of surprise. He began searching the room with his eyes.

The others became unsettled. One said, "What is wrong, Avi?"

"We are being watched," he said in a disbelieving tone. "We are being Remotely Viewed."

TYCE FELT as if he was being drawn backwards through a narrow tunnel, his senses darkening to near black before again seeing light. The illumination became more pronounced, and several seconds later, his senses were fully returned as he sat in front of the console.

"You report that your RV mission was discovered," the Israeli said. "What did you witness before losing the signal line transmission?"

"This guy came bursting into the room. He handed the head of the group a sheet of paper. The head guy then told the others that they were being Remotely Viewed."

"This means that—" The operative at the other end of the table stopped in midsentence and quickly exited the room.

Momentarily, Morticai Kant led several men into the Remote Viewing chamber.

"What happened?" Tyce stood after removing the Stimulator device from his head.

"One of two things," Kant said. "Either we have a traitor in our midst who reported your Remote Viewing mission, or…someone was Remotely Viewing you while you undertook your mission."

"You mean they could have been watching me, like I was watching that group?"

"Yes. This likely is what happened."

"Then they will know that we are onto their plans."

The Maglan chief let the thought run through his mind before speaking. "Yes. This could give them a defensive window…time to plan against our interferences in their plottings. This facility is now out of the question. We will have to—" he cut off his verbalized thought.

While the helicopter moved through the Tel Aviv night less than fifteen minutes later, Kant turned to the journalist.

"I couldn't say back there, but we can no longer use that facility for our Remote Viewing. It is compromised. They obviously have the coordinates and can break into our activities through their own Remote Viewing technologies at any time."

"Their…'Blueprint'…as they call it, is too dangerous to give them time to accomplish all they want to do. What can you do to preempt them?"

"We will have to bring them in and force their plot from them," Kant said. "You will have to help us determine exactly who is involved."

"But I don't know any names."

"You will have to point them out from your recollection of their appearances."

"I do remember a couple of names...first names, I think."

"Good...good. That will be in the RV automatic writing. That is where we will start."

CHAPTER 20

"The president and the prime minister have directed that we identify each within the American cabal and within the Israeli group," the voice on the speaker phone said. "It is essential that we do this as quickly as possible," Clint Wayne concluded from his White House basement office in DC.

"Tyce believes he can easily identify some of the conspirators in your American cabal," Morticai Kant said into the speaker phone. "But he will have more difficulty identifying those in the cabal here. We are providing a file of photographs of those within government and military here who might be in position to form effective assassination planning."

"That's a good start, Morticai," Wayne said. "Have him send his list of the American group he believes he can identify, and we will begin our preemption very soon."

"Yes. And we will take our conspirators here captive very soon also. We are already partway through the process of identification," the Israeli Maglan chief said.

"Excellent! Then let's try to get our plan of execution finished by Friday." With that, the American and Kant broke off their secure phone conversation.

Kant hurried down the long hallway, accompanied by two Maglan agents. When they burst through the doorway into the large room full of milling clandestine operatives, all attention turned to their chief.

"We have our directive, ladies and gentlemen," he said, standing in the midst of the fifteen operatives, all of whom gave him their rapt attention.

"The prime minister and the president have authorized that we proceed full bore with excision. Our mission is to cut this traitorous evil from among our ranks, both in Israel and in the US."

ESSIE WAS OBVIOUSLY CONCERNED when she sat next to Tyce. "The enemy knows that you are being used to assist Maglan…and to act as a weapon with your… unique abilities," she said. "I am afraid for you, Tyce."

She reached to take his right hand in both of her hands.

"If they will plot the assassination of two of the world's top leaders, they will not hesitate to do the same to anyone who stands in their way. They have used the Remote Viewing and know what a powerful deterrence that is to their plans. I am worried—"

"—It will be okay," Tyce interrupted. "Like in your case, I have the world's best security guarding me. I'm their secret weapon, you know," he said with a chuckle.

"You are not so…secret…any longer. They know who you are and what you are doing on behalf of the Mossad and for your own country," she said, continuing to hold his hand in hers.

"Randy claims I'm protected by the Almighty. If you have heaven's protection, you can't get much more secure," he said, again with lightness in his trying to set her at ease.

"I'm not so certain about that. I prefer to rely on common sense, even in addition to my father's elite protective soldiers around you."

"Well, regardless, the...secret...is out. They know who I am and what I'm doing to some extent. I can't hide from them, so we will have to rely on your father's protection service and Randy's heavenly guard, I guess."

She continued to look at him, her expression dissolving to one of reluctant agreement.

"I can't just turn it off," Tyce said. "I can't decide not to be a part of the effort to do what's necessary."

"Yes. I know," Essie replied. "It's just that now I've found you..." She let the thought die.

"Now that you've found me...what? You can't just say that and not finish."

"It's nothing, Tyce. Just nothing..."

"We've found each other, Ess. That means everything to me. Is that what you mean?"

She said nothing, but nodded affirmatively, lowering her eyes shyly.

"Then there's nothing else that matters to me. We have each other. All is as it should be. Fate, or destiny, or whatever will be with us, no matter what."

RANDOLPH FAUST SPOKE EARLY in the morning from Texas. "It's shaping up to be just right for Bible prophecy to play out. The minions, both human and demonic, are in a rage. Satan's globalist design is being temporarily thwarted, and the wicked in high places are enraged."

"Temporarily? What do you mean, temporarily?" Tyce's question from early evening in Tel Aviv betrayed the journalist's genuine puzzlement.

"This is all a *delaying* action, Tyce. The devil's plan for a new world order is going to come to be. Bible prophecy tells plainly that it will ultimately be the order on planet earth…with few exceptions."

"Then what am I doing over here? Wasting my time?"

"You are where the Lord has placed you, Tyce. You are part of this…this delaying action, this delaying tactic to hold back the luciferic evil that's coming."

There was silence on the line while the journalist digested his friend's words.

"This satanic regime…the regime of Antichrist…can't come into being until the Church has been taken off the earth."

"Oh, yes. The Rapture," Tyce said.

"Yes. When Christ removes all believers, God's judgment and wrath will begin—that is, after confirming the peace covenant."

"And that's what is happening now—the forming of that peace agreement?"

"Well, we believe that this current peace process might well produce the instrument that will become the peace treaty or agreement. That is, it might be the very peace agreement that the one who will become Antichrist will confirm or sign onto, bringing supposed peace to Israel and her enemy neighbors. The Bible calls it the 'agreement made with death and hell'. It will initiate the Tribulation, the last seven years of human history leading up to Christ's Second Advent."

TERRY JAMES

"So it's the rage of those who want to establish a global order along with this peace process that convinces you that we are...delaying...their, that is, the devil's plan?"

"But it's not just the rage by the globalist minions and the movement toward that prophetic peace deal. The world is filled with wickedness, like in Genesis chapter 6 when God had to destroy the earth's inhabitants with the Flood. It's also that there's a movement to synthesize all religions into one satanically driven amalgamation of religions, led by an absolute apostate for a pope within the Vatican. All these things and more make us know how near this generation must be to the Rapture and the Tribulation. These things convince us that we are at the very end of this dispensation...the dispensation of Grace...the Church Age," Faust said.

"Who is this 'we'—this 'us'—you mention?"

"Those who hold to the pre-Tribulation view of the Rapture, those who study Bible prophecy and hold that the Rapture will take place before God's judgment and wrath begin to fall on rebellious mankind."

Again, there was silence on the line while Tyce assessed his friend's words.

Faust continued. "Then there's the astonishing developments in world economy. This virus and other developments such as greed and mismanagement by money powers that be...the world's economy must have a reset. All of this adds to the belief that we are very near the time of Rapture."

"What do you mean by 'reset'?" Tyce's question came after several seconds of letting Faust's words traverse his thoughts.

"The reset is the necessary changes that will be made to reestablish global order, particularly economic order, following this worldwide economic disaster that's in the making. The Bible, as you and I have gone over a number of times, foretells that the Antichrist, the first beast of Revelation chapter 13, will institute a world-changing economic system. It will be the 666 numbering-and-mark system of buying and selling. It will be Satan's answer to resetting things to make his Antichrist system…his regime…work. People will call for a savior. They have rejected Christ as Savior, but they will worship the first beast, Antichrist, and see him as their savior, particularly their *economic* savior."

Tyce spoke after mulling over the old archeologist's words. "And that's what all of the electronic monetary transfer is about? The digital currency becoming so dominant across the world?"

Faust nodded agreement. "Daniel the prophet foretold that at the very end of human history knowledge will be greatly increased. People will 'run to and fro,' as the King James Version of the Bible puts it. We have seen an increase in knowledge that has led the world out of darkness and travel by horse to space travel. We have gone from candles and oil lamps to computers that can calculate at incredible speeds and illumination that lights the entire world with flips of switches. We have television that pulls moving images out of thin air. We have satellites that encircle the globe and bring instantaneous, moving images from every part of the world. Daniel's technology is here, now."

"Electronic Funds Transfer—is that what this… Antichrist…will use to construct that prophesied marks-and-numbering system?"

"You've got it, my young friend. Satellite and computer technologies now make it possible to make instant transaction all over the planet. It's all moving in geometric progression. And now there are tattooing processes that are compatible with digital computerization. The mark that John the Revelator wrote about is possible now. It just awaits the satanically brilliant 'man of sin', as he's called, Antichrist, who will basically enslave the world with his 666 system."

"The guys I saw in the vision and in the Remote Viewing session later, the ones that each spoke different languages and are called the High Commission, talked about bringing all people on earth under control of, as I take it, a global government of some sort. They talked about a vaccination that would accomplish this control."

Faust interrupted, "You told me about hearing that they said such a vaccination coming from the Earthlord Project can produce tracking methodologies that will guarantee controlling the global populations."

"Yeah. They said that being able to create such control depended upon nationalism being swept aside. They said that while they had been able to accomplish much of their goal of getting rid of nationalism among many nations, there was one major holdup—the United States. Particularly, it was one man, they said. The president had thrown a monkey wrench into their plans."

The old man was silent on the other end of the line for an uncomfortable period, causing the journalist to ask, "You there, Randy?"

"Yes...yes," he responded in a tone of deep thought. "This project Earthlord is something we must learn more about. It has significant prophetic meaning."

CLINT WAYNE MOVED to the long credenza behind the desk chair. He lifted a spiral-bound booklet and held it up for Morticai Kant to see on the screen he and Tyce Greyson viewed from Israel.

"This is a study done over the past week...since the pathogen began its work in earnest here in America. It is a compilation of facts and projected figures on what will happen if the virus can't be curtailed. More than 2.2 million people in the US could die, is the conclusion by the CDC's sources on this."

The American sat down in front of the camera that relayed the video transmission. He held the briefing booklet with both hands while he leafed through the pages with an index finger.

"The president is about to announce that business and mass contact between individuals must be curtailed heavily in order for the virus to be brought under control. As I said, they are warning that 2.2 million will likely die if something isn't done."

Kant spoke from the other end of the transmission, while Wayne looked at his monitor screen.

"What does that mean, Clint?" The Israeli nodded to someone to his right, giving a non-verbal order.

"Shut down? What does that mean?"

"It means this booming economy that the administration has built from the mess the president inherited will come to a screeching halt, unless we can find ways to continue in a relatively normal fashion," Wayne said.

"Your prime minister will shortly be informing you that Israel faces the same type of...curtailment. As a matter of fact, the virus has spread so quickly and with such virulence that some countries in Europe—Italy, for example—have practically curtailed all business activity that requires retail traffic. For example, the restaurants and so forth."

"What is being done to deal with the virus spread otherwise?"

Kant's words caused the American to thumb through the booklet again and stop on a specific page. "The president has just announced that all flights...all travel from China...have been suspended. As a matter of fact, most traffic coming in from Asia has been greatly reduced."

"Then it is definitely of Chinese origin?" Kant said.

"Best that can be figured. But it's not been absolutely proven at this point. We just don't know, as we've talked about before, whether it was accidentally released from one of their biological warfare labs, or if it was deliberately spread by flying it all over the world."

"Which do you suspect?" Kant said, his eyes narrowing in concentrating at Wayne's face staring back on the monitor.

"We're learning more and more about the operatives within our and other governments who are determined to use the pathogen to damage this president. They've tried everything they have. They've used the news media, in close alliance, to try to perform a *coup d'état* against this presidency. We believe that the next step in their effort is to destroy the economy of America and of the Western nations, in cahoots with the Chinese leadership. They know the president can't be beaten in this year's election with the kind of successes he's had economically. We're learning more and more about certain powers within the former administration who have serious economic ties to China. These are of the opposition party, but more than that, they are the nucleus of the traitorous cabal within the highest ranks of the intelligence community."

Kant interrupted. "Even now? There are those who

serve this administration still in position to do such things?"

"It's an almost insurmountable task to rid the federal bureaucracy of those who plot this sort of sedition, Morticai. They're entrenched, interwoven at every level. That's why we have the constant leaks that are mostly lies going from these traitors to the complicit news media, who regurgitates the lies to the American people. And now, because there are those financial ties to China at the very highest levels of the former administration, we believe the Chinese leadership has agreed to release the pathogen…this virus…so that the great economy will be destroyed, and this president will lose this upcoming election. Thus, so those who lost the last election in such a powerful sweep of the electoral college vote will regain power and can continue their nefarious dealings with the Chinese."

"Makes sense," Kant said. "They have tried everything, just as they have tried everything here against Bibi."

"But it goes much deeper, still, we believe, Morticai. We will be discussing these things when you come to DC."

SHIVA RABINE'S image peered at him from the monitor screen. Tyce listened intently while she explained in tone that expressed her anxiety.

"We still can't understand how it happened, but this is one of those inexplicable times in these Remote Viewing experiences. The session involving that meeting you call the High Commission is a very rare occurrence."

"How?" Tyce asked. "What happened?"

"Somehow, the image of the meeting of the people you viewed moved from the Matrix and into the signal line as future portrayal. That is, it was a meeting that was yet to be held," she said.

"You mean I viewed and reported on something in the future?"

"Well, it you might say that," Rabine said. "We've only had it happen a few times. Yours is the third time in our experience, to be exact."

"Telling the future? How is that possible? That defies all rationality," Tyce said skeptically.

"We don't understand it. It does indeed defy all logic...all reality. But yours is also the most unusual ability we've encountered. Your comatose condition... the world you lived in, as you explained to us, the people and things you came out of that condition knowing in the actual world—these are factors, we believe, that add to this ability to see into the future to some extent."

Tyce remained silent, letting the things she had said run through his thoughts.

"As I said, we don't understand why or how this has happened," Rabine said. "It's very strange...and disconcerting. But it is exciting at the same time. It's something we must explore to see how best to use your ability."

"That explains the question I have about what was said during that session involving the High Commission," Tyce said, as if to himself.

"What question?"

"One of the guys in the group said the American people had accepted the things—like the lockdowns— better than the ones who started the virus had suspected. I wondered why they said that. The effects of the virus and the shutdown order by the president hadn't yet been put in place."

Rabine considered Tyce's words, then spoke. "Well, we determined it was without question viewing that involved as yet nonoccurrence signal line materiality."

He could see on her face staring at him from the monitor that she saw in his own expression a complete lack of understanding. He spoke before she could further explain.

"Never mind, Shiva," he said. "It was a future meeting, not one of the past or present. That's a good enough explanation."

She relaxed from her strait-postured position. "Very well. Yes. That is basically what I was trying to convey."

"But the other sessions, the ones involving the American cabalists and the one involving those here in Israel, they were in the present time?"

"Yes. Those Remote Viewing sessions were in real time," she said.

Before he could speak again, she added, "We are working on how to trip the cognitron process within your brain, thus, to bring the ability to access the future from the Matrix onto the signal line in future training sessions."

ESSIE PURPOSELY SAT AS TIGHTLY against Tyce on the sofa as possible. The realization pleased him, while they both listened to her father talk to those gathered in the Maglan operations room. He spoke in English.

"We now have in custody the cabalists plotting the prime minister's death. Our good friend here," he said, pointing to Tyce, "made this possible through his efforts in the Remote Viewing process."

The Maglan chief picked a long pointer from a

tabletop and directed its tip toward a huge screen against one wall in a position so that all could see.

"The areas in red here, here, and here," he moved the pointer's tip about the screen, "are where the most infections reside."

He pressed a button on the remote device he held in his other hand. The screen came alive with graphics representing other nations. "These are the areas in Europe and parts of Asia that are most infected, as you see."

He turned to again face those gathered in the room. "Travel in and out of these have been mostly curtailed," he said. "The virus, which almost certainly is a product of laboratories in China, has caused the shutdown of most economies, certainly in the Western world, including our own country as well as America. Believe it or not, we of Maglan and those in CUE, who are, like us, charged with analyzing and organizing against the evil being perpetrated, conclude that this virus is a purposeful attack."

Morticai Kant paused to look at each face in the room before continuing in a serious tone. "We are convinced, as you know, that the entire matter is centered around the ones at the highest levels in the internationalist circles plotting to destroy us—that is, wanting to destroy Israel and the United States. Our nations represent the holdup more than any other of their opposition. We are democracies that control how others do business and conduct life more than any other nations. The dollar ties all of the world's economy together, of course. Israel holds the key to much development in medicine and technology for the rest of humanity. They must destroy these two democracies and their economic systems to bring the world into their desired globalist configuration."

Kant again turned toward the screen, without pointing to it, and said, "These are some of those at the very top of this effort to bring down the president of the United States, and, of course, our own leader."

Several faces of the men appeared on the screen while Kant clicked for each frame to be shown. Tyce recognized them as the members of the High Commission.

"These are outside of the jurisdictions of Maglan and CUE, but only because our leaders won't let us get at them," he said, invoking laughter from those agents scattered about the room.

"We can, and will, however, deal with the cabalists both within our own nation and America. And there are plenty of them…as you well know."

Again, he turned from half-facing the screen toward his audience.

"I was informed shortly before our meeting began that the would-be assassins within the United States Secret Service, two agents named by our friend Tyce, were taken into custody after being surveilled as to their plot and its timing."

Kant again observed each expression while he continued. "Some of you will accompany us to the United States tomorrow. There we will further plan, with the CUE, under White House orders, and in conjunction with Bibi, how to deal with that wicked force plotting to take down both of our leaders so their own evil can be inflicted on the world."

CHAPTER 21

Tyce felt the increasing compression against his back while the Gulfstream 6 lifted off the Tel Aviv runway and climbed quickly to cruising altitude.

Essie's left hand rested atop his on the armrest between them as the jet finally leveled off and roared smoothly toward its next stop in Paris. It would be the jumping-off point from Europe, on the way to Washington, their ultimate destination in this hastily planned trip.

"Morticai thinks you have provided the greatest possible service to both our country and yours," Essie said, gently running her fingertips over the top of Tyce's hand. "He says we will soon get to the bottom of much of the terrible things they've been doing."

"Well, all I've done is report, through the weird things associated with Remote Viewing, what I've seen."

"Do you think they can see us now?"

"Who? Oh, you mean the Remote Viewing on behalf of those who read that note about me being present at their meeting."

"Yes. Do you think their Remote Viewing can see us now, listen to us?"

"No. As I understand it, there have to be specific coordinates for the Remote Viewing session. There has to be a specific location this...technology...can lock onto. We're moving at five hundred miles an hour or more. I don't think it's possible."

Essie looked past Tyce to see through the porthole.

"It looks like we've moved over the water now," she said.

"Yes. We left Israel behind a few minutes ago." Tyce looked out the window to his left. "The Mediterranean is quite a sight today. Very beautiful. Not a cloud in the sky."

Their sightseeing out the window was interrupted by Morticai Kant, who stood above them in the aisle. "Tyce, I just received a communiqué from Randolph," he said. "He says he will meet us in Washington tomorrow morning. We will meet at the Israeli Embassy."

"Good! It will be great to see him. His energy is amazing," Tyce said.

"Indeed, it is. And I am rapidly approaching that age. I can understand the increasing difficulties with travel."

"Papa, you are ageless," Essie said, tugging his sleeve to urge him near her.

"You are a good child, sweetheart," he said bending to accept a kiss on the cheek from his daughter.

The military G6 lurched when its right wing tipped upward slightly in an abrupt change of direction. The movement made Kant hold tightly to the seat's armrest and the top of the seat in front of Essie's.

"Please buckle your seatbelts," the captain said over the intercom. "Chief Kant, please come forward."

The Maglan chief, using the seats on either side of the

aisle to brace because of the violent lurching, quickly moved up the walkway and stuck his head into the cockpit.

"Sir, we are being pursued," the captain said.

"Pursued? By whom?"

"Satellite control tells us it's an unknown aircraft of the fighter variety. They are closing very quickly."

"Our aircraft have the very top defensive capabilities," Kant said. "I presume these devices are all activated?"

"Yes, sir. We are now making evasive maneuvers."

"Can we overcome these pursuers?"

"We're sending out chaff to deflect their locking on to us," the officer in the right cockpit said while the pilot worked with the controls.

"Do your best. I will leave it with you," the Maglan chief said and quickly moved back to Essie's side.

"I've got to buckle in. We have military-type jets pursuing us. Make sure you've got your seatbelts fastened."

When Kant moved quickly to his seat, the G6 rolled hard to the right and began climbing.

The pilot watched the radar scope and stayed in contact with the satellite control center monitoring the flight.

"They've fired upon us," the officer in the right said. "We are being tracked by two missiles!"

The pilot took drastic maneuvering actions.

"Still tracking on us!" the man in the right seat yelled.

"They're almost upon us!" the copilot said while the man next to him desperately tried to defeat the oncoming instruments of death.

"Prepare for detonation!" the man's shouted words rang throughout the cabin over the intercom.

The interior of the cockpit and cabin became blindingly bright, causing momentary loss of vision for all on board. There was silence for a number of seconds except for the muffled roar of the engines revved to full power.

The pilot and copilot, when they could see again, watched the radar scope at the center of the console between him and the pilot. It looked normal, with nothing showing on the screen.

They heard through the headphones the voice of the controller from satellite command. "We don't under-stand…the aircraft—no longer in view. Nor are their attacking ordnance. All have just vanished."

Morticai Kant, ten minutes later, after entering the cockpit to be briefed on what had happened, returned to where Essie and Tyce sat.

"The pilots tell me that, just before that burst of brightness, they saw out their cockpit windows some-thing that looked like a gigantic bird—a bird of brilliant light. Next thing that happened, they heard from satellite control that the attacking aircraft had…had simply vanished."

THE MEMORY BURST as brilliantly as did the light somewhere over the Mediterranean. It was more than a memory. It was as if a laser burned without ceasing the vision of that comatose time.

Morticai Kant telling about the pilots seeing an immense "bird of light" that exploded in their flight pattern like lightning burned at the center of Tyce's brain. He looked out the G6 window to his left while the plane taxied toward the private terminal on the outskirts of Paris. They had arrived safely, having survived an attack by fighter jets of unknown origin.

But it wasn't survival, he considered. It was preempted action. The jet's air-to-air missiles never reached the Gulfstream. They, like the aircraft they were fired from, disappeared within the burst of light.

They had experienced something akin to what had happened the night his BMW flew off the freeway during that storm all those years ago—the accident that set into motion the strange movement toward some undetermined destination, on a journey that even now seemed to suction his life toward an unseen vacuum held in the hand of something or someone omnipotent.

"I've never seen Morticai so exercised," Essie said, while Tyce's thoughts played upon the screen of his mind, memories of the winged creature that filled his windshield that night on the Maryland freeway.

"It was an attack intended to end our trip," Tyce said. "He'll get to the bottom of it. His resources with Maglan are probably the best on the planet for finding things out when it comes to this kind of thing."

Essie shook her head in affirmation. "It is true. He has ways to find out...and to get things done."

"What do you think that was all about? The light and the disappearance of those aircraft?"

"Randy would say it was a miracle. Action from heaven," Tyce said.

"And you? What do you believe?" Essie's question went unanswered when one of the security agents stood beside her seat.

"We need to disembark as quickly as possible," he said, offering his hand to help her out of the seat. "We can take no chances in thinking that their attempts won't continue."

With the concourse deplaning tube attached to the jet, they moved quickly to the interior of the terminal.

The Maglan agents walked on either side of Tyce and Essie, striding quickly along the corridors until they reached a secure room prepared in advance by Maglan operations.

Morticai Kant was already on the secure phone. He glanced at Tyce and Essie, then turned to speak into the phone.

"There was no interference, then from your end? You did nothing to intercept those aircraft or destroy the missiles?"

He listened and nodded silently while the voice spoke.

"Very well," he said finally, then broke off the call.

"Get me Wayne in DC," he ordered to one of the agents, then he moved to sit in the chair beside his daughter and across from Tyce.

"The action that saved us was not done by any of our people," he said, looking at Tyce. "Whatever that blinding light was, it somehow caused the disintegration of those planes…and their ordnance. They watched on their satellite screens and saw those planes and the missiles, which had already been fired at us, just vanish."

"What about that bird the pilots reported?" Essie said. "That huge bird of light?"

"Our people saw no such creature on the radar or in any other way," her father said. "They have no plausible explanation."

"I believe I know what happened," Tyce said. "Rather, I think I know…*who*…did the deed."

"Who destroyed the fighters and the missiles, you mean?" the Maglan chief said in a perplexed tone.

"Sir, I believe those planes and missiles were destroyed by an angel," Tyce said with a tone of incredulity in his answer.

The Maglan chief sat in silence, his eyes narrowing while he thought on his next words. "The angel of the Daniel prophecy?" he finally said.

"According to Randy, the prophet Daniel said that Michael, the archangel, will protect Israel in the last days," Tyce said.

"But it was us...our plane...that was kept from destruction, not Israel," Kant said.

"You *are* Israel, Papa. Tyce is working on behalf of defending Israel, too," Essie said.

"The creature the guys in the cockpit described, it fit the description of that creature of light I saw the night of that storm when I had the wreck in Maryland," Tyce said.

"There must be some rational explanation," the Maglan chief said. "We will get to the bottom of the matter."

～

"WE CAN TAKE NO CHANCES, Morticai. We *will* take no chances. We will ask the French to accompany your plane to the mid Atlantic, and we will escort you the rest of the way to DC with our own fighters," Clint Wayne's image said from the monitor screen that sat in front of Morticai Kant.

"I've informed the president, and he has instructed the secretary of defense to provide whatever escort is needed. So give us a couple of hours to prepare."

"Yes. This is a good plan. I will await your word before we proceed."

"We have much to consider when you arrive," the American said. "We have the people under interrogation.

They are giving up significant things about this side of the traitorous scheming."

"Our people will soon achieve the same level against the plotting in Israel," Kant said.

Clint Wayne said, "We have brought in Dr. Randolph Faust, as you know. It was done so with the full agreement of the president and vice president. There is building consensus that we can't fully understand or address this whole matter without considering the spiritual implications that might be involved."

"Considering what just happened over the Mediterranean," the Israeli said, "that seems a logical supposition," Kant said, nodding agreement with his American counterpart.

~

"I'VE BEEN TOLD about your encounter over the Mediterranean. What an experience!"

Randolph Faust was first to grab Tyce's hand then pull him to himself in a hug of affection.

"Yes. Being shot at by jet fighters is an unforgettable experience," Tyce Greyson agreed.

"I'm not talking about the jet fighters," Faust said, with a good-natured lilt to his voice. "I'm talking about your encounter with the greatest of God's angels!"

"Well, I won't argue that, Randy. Nobody has a better explanation that I've heard," Tyce said, walking with the old archeologist farther into the Israeli embassy's interior.

"Oh, here's Ramon," Faust said, watching his traveling companion bring suitcases into the room. Ramon Gutierrez set the cases on the floor and, smiling, stuck his hand out to Tyce.

"No rattlesnakes in this room, is there?" he said laughingly, pumping Tyce's hand vigorously.

"I haven't seen any yet," Tyce returned. "But DC has been termed the 'swamp', so who knows? Better check under the beds!"

"Yes, yes," Faust's close friend said. "Snakes are everywhere in Washington these days."

While Ramon began unpacking the cases, Faust nudged Tyce toward chairs in one corner of the room assigned to the archeologist and his assistant for the several days ahead.

"How about you and Morticai's girl?"

"What?" Tyce said, hearing in Faust's words affectionate probing.

"How are you two getting along? I haven't had a chance to speak to Morticai about you two."

"I love her, Randy," Tyce said matter-of-factly.

The direct answer took his friend by surprise. "That's pretty straightforward, my young friend. I like that. And how does she feel about you?"

"That would be a good question for you to ask her," Tyce said, continuing his playful bluntness.

"Perhaps I will...perhaps I'll do just that," Faust said. "Now, this whole matter is just fascinating. Who would have ever thought that an old Bible thumper like yours truly would ever be brought, at the request of the president of the United States, into something like what's going on here?"

"Or a journalistic hack like yours truly," Tyce said.

"There is much afoot here, Tyce. Wickedness in the very highest places is at play. Do you think we are up to wrestling against these flesh-and-blood thugs, and at the same time, these otherworldly powers and principalities?"

With a slight chuckle, Tyce said, "Well, if we have heaven's greatest angel on our side, I guess we can give it a whirl."

The old archeologist nodded agreement with a laugh, then said, "It's more than coincidence that we end up here, in the Israeli embassy. If these are indeed the times they seem to be, and if your protector over the Mediterranean…and before that in your accident leading to the comatose state and all that experience, is Michael the archangel…we have entered some very interesting times."

Tyce took in Faust's words. Then, shaking his head negatively, he said, "Randy, I know it's all so strange. And I know all that's involved in what I've gone through makes no sense…logically or rationally speaking. But to *really* believe that all this involves an angel sent by God… I'm afraid I'm still a bit too…*secular*…to accept things like you see them."

Randolph Faust's cellphone sounded, and momentarily Ramon handed it to him. "It's a Mr. Cahn from here in the embassy," he said as Faust took the phone.

After greeting the caller, the old man said. "Very well. Tell Morticai that we will be there at 10 as instructed."

Ending the call, Faust looked at Tyce and smiled tightly. "Morticai wants us to meet him tomorrow morning at the White House. He said they will have someone escort us into the Oval Office."

Faust's smile broadened. "How about that? The Oval Office!"

∼

THE DRIVE from the embassy to 1600 Pennsylvania Avenue was spent with one thought in Tyce's mind. Would Essie be there?

He hadn't been able to be with her since arriving in DC. She had duties to perform as part of her father's contingency. They had agreed to get together at their very first opportunity.

They had been apart for more than thirty hours, he calculated. If not at the White House, they would get together immediately after the meeting...with whom, he didn't know. But they would be together immediately after meeting, whoever would be in the Oval Office.

Two Secret Service agents met them beneath the portico when the Israeli SUV delivered them to the White House grounds.

"Sir, here are your credentials," one of the men said, handing a plastic card first to Randolph Faust, then to Tyce. "Please keep this with you at all times to present when asked. You must return these to us when your meeting is completed. We will come to you at that time."

They followed the men down a long corridor, large paintings of presidents of the past staring down at them from the off-white walls.

Approaching the door that led to the outer rooms near the Oval Office, the agents stopped at a booth of dark oak, behind which worked several women and two men, who, Tyce surmised, were also Secret Service.

After having Faust and Greyson step up and present their credentials, the agent behind the booth said with a subdued smile while handing back the cards to each man, "Welcome to the White House, gentlemen. Please enjoy your visit."

Moving through the first door, they were greeted by other men in business suits—obviously more Secret

Service, Tyce thought, watching them from behind while they led them farther into the complex.

A number of administrative assistants worked busily, a few looking up to see the men as they passed by.

Finally, they came to a large double door. One of the agents turned the brass knob, walked into the Oval Office, and stood by the door while Tyce and Randolph Faust walked into the office.

Tyce's immediate impression was that it was very small, considering the immense importance it represented. The off-white walls with some portraits scattered about, and alcoves for leather-bound books and small objects representing historic people and events decorated the curves of the office.

"Please be seated. The president will be with you shortly," one of the agents said, gesturing toward sofas facing each other across from the front of the large, beautifully carved desk—the same desk, Tyce reckoned, that John F. Kennedy had brought to the Oval Office. All other presidents, he remembered, had kept the desk for their use. It was a sort of memorial to the slain president, he thought, while perusing the rest of the room with his eyes.

After the agents exited, Faust said almost in a whisper. "Ever think you would be here?"

"Almost was once," Tyce said in a whispering voice. "Well, that is I almost met a president in the oval. I've been here, but not with the president present."

"Oh?"

"During Barack Obama's first term. The meeting was called off because of some incident in the Middle East that required his presence elsewhere. I was writing for the *New York Post* —a contributor reporter, not a full-time guy."

"You had a personal interview schedule?"

"No," Tyce said, disappointment in his voice. "I was just part of several newspaper reporters. We were going to get his early impressions when he first came to the office as president, that sort of thing. Just a PR-type interview his people wanted to take advantage of."

The door they had entered opened and Morticai Kant, followed by Essie and two Israeli agents, were let into the room. Tyce stood and walked toward Essie, first shaking hands with her father.

"Well, here we all are!" The Maglan chief said enthusiastically, going quickly to Randolph and shaking his hand.

"What's this about, Morticai?" Faust said.

"I'm not sure. Clint wasn't very forthcoming as to all the details. I believe it's because he really doesn't know the details. Imagine, a man charged with knowing details, and even he is in the dark...somewhat, at least. That means this could be exciting," Kant said in a happy voice.

On the sofa directly across from Kant and Faust, Essie sat against Tyce, and leaned to say in a near whisper, "Have you ever been here?"

"Yes. I was telling Randy I was here, but the president at the time wasn't. Almost got to come here to meet a president, during Obama's first term."

"But you didn't? What happened?"

"The president had better things to do that day, I think. I should say, more important things."

"I think you are important," she said patting his forearm.

He started to respond when a door behind them opened and several men in suits followed the president into the Oval Office.

The president walked and stood, turning to the men who had followed him.

"Tell the governor we will accept his invitation. Make it for the seventh, if nothing otherwise comes up."

One of the men quickly turned and left through the same door they had entered.

"It's great to have you here," the president said, while all stood listening to him.

"Please, be seated." They did so after he sat in a rocking chair between the two sofas. The other men sat in armchairs around the room.

He rocked slightly while looking at each of his guests while speaking.

"JFK had the right idea with these rocking chairs," he said with a smile. "Too bad I rarely have time to use them." He turned to look at a man sitting to his right in an armchair.

"Lawrence, will you please bring the letter? And check to see about Clint. I need him in on this. He must have gotten delayed for some reason."

"Yes, sir," the man said and quickly left the office.

The chief executive turned again and addressed Kant. "Morticai, I'm so pleased to see you've brought Essie. She reminds me of one of my daughters. Thanks for coming, Essie."

He turned to Randolph Faust. "And you, Dr. Faust. It's really great having you here today. I've heard a lot about your help in all this craziness with our unhinged opposition."

"It's very good to be here, Mr. President. Thanks for inviting me."

"And you," the president said, turning back to look in the direction of Tyce and Essie. "Tyce…that's your name, isn't it? A very nice name. It's great to have you with us.

I'm well aware of the tremendous…gifts you have in some of the covert areas that are so important while we face these challenges."

"'Thank you, Mr. President. Thanks for inviting me."

The door opened and Clint Wayne strode to take a seat near the sofas.

"Clint, glad you could make it," the president said.

"I'm sorry, Mr. President. An operative reported some news from the Vatican to add to today's meeting."

"Oh? Something about the letter?"

"No, sir. Well, not directly."

"Well, maybe we can discuss it in a minute," the president said.

The man returned with a leather-covered note pad. The president opened it after the man gave it to him. He held up several sheets of paper for the others in the room to see.

"I have read this letter a number of times. It reflects my observations and instincts about some of the things going on. It's the source that most interests me."

The president looked at Randolph Faust. "Dr. Faust, I wanted you here because this is of a spiritual nature to a large extent. The letter is from a member of the clergy. It's from Carlo Maria Viganò. He is Archbishop of Ulpiana. He is former Apostolic Nuncio to the United States, according to his sign-off."

He paused to look at the several sheets of paper he held between thumbs and index fingers. "Like I said," he said, looking over the paper into the eyes of each of the people on the sofas, "this letter contains thinking I believe is most relevant to things being plotted against this administration…against this nation. I believe you will find it to have spiritual connotation. I'll just read

334

some portions to illustrate what I'm talking about. It's a long letter, so bear with me."

He again scanned the sheet before saying, "It just says, 'Dear Mister President, etc., etc.' then says 'A global plan called the Great Reset is underway. Its architect is a global élite that wants to subdue all of humanity, imposing coercive measures with which to drastically limit individual freedoms and those of entire populations. In several nations this plan has already been approved and financed; in others it is still in an early stage. Behind the world leaders who are the accomplices and executors of this infernal project, there are unscrupulous characters who finance the World Economic Forum and Event 201, promoting their agenda.

"'The purpose of the Great Reset is the imposition of a health dictatorship aiming at the imposition of liberticidal measures, hidden behind tempting promises of ensuring a universal income and cancelling individual debt. The price of these concessions from the International Monetary Fund will be the renunciation of private property and adherence to a program of vaccination against Covid-19 and Covid-21 promoted by Bill Gates with the collaboration of the main pharmaceutical groups. Beyond the enormous economic interests that motivate the promoters of the Great Reset, the imposition of the vaccination will be accompanied by the requirement of a health passport and a digital ID, with the consequent contact tracing of the population of the entire world. Those who do not accept these measures will be confined in detention camps or placed under house arrest, and all their assets will be confiscated.

"'Mr. President, I imagine that you are already aware that in some countries the Great Reset will be activated between the end of this year and the first trimester of 2021. For this purpose, further lockdowns are planned, which will be officially justified by a supposed second and third wave of the pandemic. You are well aware of the means that have been deployed to sow panic and legitimize draconian limitations on individual liberties, artfully provoking a worldwide economic crisis. In the intentions of its architects, this crisis will serve to make the recourse of nations to the Great Reset irreversible, thereby giving the final blow to a world whose existence and very memory they want to completely cancel. But this world, Mr. President, includes people, affections, institutions, faith, culture, traditions, and ideals: people and values that do not act like automatons, who do not obey like machines, because they are endowed with a soul and a heart, because they are tied together by a spiritual bond that draws its strength from above, from that God that our adversaries want to challenge, just as Lucifer did at the beginning of time with his *non serviam.*

"'Many people—as we well know—are annoyed by this reference to the clash between Good and Evil and the use of "apocalyptic" overtones, which according to them exasperates spirits and sharpens divisions. It is not surprising that the enemy is angered at being discovered just when he believes he has reached the citadel he seeks to conquer undisturbed. What is surprising, however, is that there is no one to sound the alarm. The reaction of the deep state to those who denounce its plan is broken and incoherent, but understandable. Just when the complicity of the mainstream media had succeeded in making the transition to the New World Order almost painless and unnoticed, all sorts of deceptions, scandals and crimes are coming to light.

"'Until a few months ago, it was easy to smear as

"conspiracy theorists" those who denounced these terrible plans, which we now see being carried out down to the smallest detail. No one, up until last February, would ever have thought that, in all of our cities, citizens would be arrested simply for wanting to walk down the street, to breathe, to want to keep their business open, to want to go to church on Sunday. Yet now it is happening all over the world, even in picture-postcard Italy that many Americans consider to be a small, enchanted country, with its ancient monuments, its churches, its charming cities, its characteristic villages. And while the politicians are barricaded inside their palaces promulgating decrees like Persian satraps, businesses are failing, shops are closing, and people are prevented from living, traveling, working, and praying. The disastrous psychological consequences of this operation are already being seen, beginning with the suicides of desperate entrepreneurs and of our children, segregated from friends and classmates, told to follow their classes while sitting at home alone in front of a computer.

"'In Sacred Scripture, Saint Paul speaks to us of "the one who opposes" the manifestation of the *mystery of iniquity*, the *kathèkon* (2 Thessalonians 2:6–7). In the religious sphere, this obstacle to evil is the Church, and in particular the papacy; in the political sphere, it is those who impede the establishment of the New World Order.

"'As is now clear, the one who occupies the Chair of Peter has betrayed his role from the very beginning in order to defend and promote the globalist ideology, supporting the agenda of the deep church, who chose him from its ranks.

"'Mr. President, you have clearly stated that you want to defend the nation—*One Nation under God*, fundamental liberties, and nonnegotiable values that are denied and fought against today. It is you, dear President, who are "the one who opposes" the deep state, the final assault of the children of darkness.

"'For this reason, it is necessary that all people of good will be persuaded of the epochal importance of the imminent election: not so much for the sake of this or that political program, but because of the general inspiration of your action that best embodies—in this particular historical context—that world, our world, which they want to cancel by means of the lockdown. Your adversary is also our adversary: it is the Enemy of the human race, He who is "a murderer from the beginning" (John 8:44).

"'Around you are gathered with faith and courage those who consider you the final garrison against the world dictatorship. The alternative is to vote for a person who is manipulated by the deep state, gravely compromised by scandals and corruption, who will do to the United States what Jorge Mario Bergoglio is doing to the Church, Prime Minister Conte to Italy, President Macron to France, Prime Minster Sanchez to Spain, and so on. The blackmailable nature of Joe Biden—just like that of the prelates of the Vatican's "magic circle"—will expose him to be used unscrupulously, allowing illegitimate powers to interfere in both domestic politics as well as international balances. It is obvious that those who manipulate him already have someone worse than him ready, with whom they will replace him as soon as the opportunity arises.

"'And yet, in the midst of this bleak picture, this apparently unstoppable advance of the "Invisible Enemy", an element of hope emerges. The adversary does not know how to love, and it does not understand that it is not enough to assure a universal income or to cancel mortgages in order to subjugate the masses and convince them to be branded like cattle. This people, which for too long has endured the abuses of a hateful and tyrannical power, is rediscovering that it has a soul; it is understanding that it is not willing to exchange its freedom for the homogenization and cancellation of its identity; it is beginning to understand the value of familial and social ties, of the bonds of faith and culture that unite honest people. This *Great Reset* is destined to fail because those who planned it do not understand that there are still people ready to take to the streets to defend their rights, to protect their loved ones, to give a future to their children and grandchildren. The leveling inhumanity of the globalist project will shatter miserably in the face of the firm and courageous opposition of the children of Light. The enemy has Satan on its side, He who only knows how to hate. But on our side, we have the Lord Almighty, the God of armies arrayed for battle, and the Most Holy Virgin, who will crush the head of the ancient Serpent. "If God is for us, who can be against us?" (Romans 8:31).

"'Mr. President, you are well aware that, in this crucial hour, the United States of America is considered the defending wall against which the war declared by the advocates of globalism has been unleashed. Place your trust in the Lord, strengthened by the words of the Apostle Paul: "I can do all things in Him who strengthens me," (Philippians 4:13). To be an instrument of Divine Providence is a great responsibility, for which you will certainly receive all the graces of state that you need, since they are being fervently implored for you by the many people who support you with their prayers.'"

The president looked at the others in the room before looking back to the sheet he held.

"He then just signs off by writing, 'With this heavenly hope and the assurance of my prayer for you, for the First Lady, and for your collaborators, with all my heart I send you my blessing. God bless the United States of America!'"

The president searched all eyes watching him from the sofa. His locked then on those of Randolph Faust. "Dr. Faust, this is a primary reason I've brought you into these matters. The Bishop's letter has intrigued me significantly. My question to you...do you think the Bishop's take on all of this is something to seriously consider?"

The president stopped to think on his own question, while all remained silent in the room. "His referring to me as 'Instrument of Divine Providence'—do you think there's any credence to that idea?"

The old archeologist shifted slightly on the sofa. He began slowly in answering, the words coming as if from someone other than himself. They were measured, almost lecturing in tone.

"Sir, we—every person—each of us is here, now, exactly where the God of heaven placed us for this prophetic hour in human history. I must tell you that it is only that God who could have put you in the most powerful position on earth. You are indeed where you sit by divine providence."

"You believe, then, that what we are doing here, in fighting this insanity that has been coming at us, is...a fulfillment of a prophecy?"

"A fulfillment of Bible prophecy, Mr. President. It is all fulfilling Bible prophecy," Faust said.

The president said, "So this election in a few days...it is divinely destined, one way or the other?"

Faust sat a bit forward, leaning toward the president

MICHAEL

at the end of the sofas. "Mr. President, it is foreordained, predestined, from God's perspective, because He is omniscient. He knows the end from the beginning. He knows every detail of how it will all come to fulfillment."

"And, you, as a…a man of God…a prophet. Can you know how it will all end up?"

Faust smiled and shook his head negatively. "No. First, I'm not a prophet in the Old Testament sense. I'm a student of Bible prophecy. I can't tell, for example, how this election will turn out—at least not as a Bible student who understands prophecy. I can tell, in a broad, general, sense, how things concerning the end of days will be fulfilled to some extent. That's because God's Word has given us enough foreknowledge through His Old and New Testament prophets in order to know direction in which things are headed, thus to where they will end."

"And what does your…your study of Bible prophecy tell you about the direction things are headed and where it all will end up?"

The president's question was offered with an expression of deep concentration etched on his tanned face.

"Daniel, the Old Testament prophet, recorded something the angel Gabriel gave him directly from the throne of God about what I believe are the very times we are experiencing right at this moment."

The president's rocking chair ceased its movement as he sat forward a bit, listening intently to Faust's words.

"Daniel was told by Gabriel things about a final world ruler that would terrorize the whole world, and particularly Daniel's people, Israel. The prophet was very troubled and wanted to know the end of all the things he had been told would happen. The angel told him, 'But thou, O Daniel, shut up the words, and seal the book,

341

even to the time of the end: many shall run to and fro, and knowledge shall be increased.'

"Mr. President, the things Daniel the prophet wanted to know about the end of it all...about the total fulfillment of prophecy...is happening right now. That book the angel mentioned to the old prophet has been opened."

The president sat back and continued rocking, his hands and elbows upon each of the padded armrests.

"This...man of terror—it's the Antichrist?"

"Yes, sir. It's this lawless man of sin, the Antichrist. We are witnessing the opening of that book and developments that are leading to the earth's final and most vicious dictator having the stage set for his totalitarian regime."

"Specifically, what are you seeing that leads you to believe this is happening?" the president said.

The old man thought for a second, his face seeming to brighten with the approach he decided to use in addressing the president's question.

"Sir, in all of American history as we understand matters of politics—and presidential politics in particular—have you ever heard or seen anything approaching the vicious, ongoing attacks...these attacks that have come at you...at your administration? They are often called 'unhinged', 'insane'. They have been unleashed, and since their unleashing, it has been unceasing. I'm a very old man, and I haven't ever seen anything like what has been going on these past four years."

The man in the rocking chair said nothing, but nodded agreement slightly.

"I know that most political observers—most who deal with the ins and outs of political infighting—view all of this as just things as usual. But never has one political party become so enraged, to the point of supporting causes and organizations that want to tear the country apart to get their way. Never has the entirety of the news conglomerate, the mainstream news media, been so against one man as they have been against you. This is well beyond politics as usual to anyone who knows our history."

Faust paused to change expression and say with increased concern in his voice, "Sir, this is not simply political or governmental, or whatever you want to call it going on. It is satanic rage we are living in."

The president said, "And this is where the bishop's letter comes in? Is he saying the same as you?"

Faust straightened on the sofa and sat back to reposition himself, amazed that the man in the rocking chair grasped things much more deeply than the old archeologist had realized.

"Mr. President, my own view of what the Bible has to say and how Catholic clergy usually look at things theologically and prophetically differs greatly. But this matter, according to this letter and the profound statements it makes and conclusions it draws, is in alignment with biblical foretellings for the end times."

When the president said nothing, but seemed to be awaiting further explanation, Faust continued.

"I am convinced, sir, that for the Antichrist's regime to be brought into place for world rule as prophesied, this nation, our country, must be brought down. American sovereignty stands in the way of Satan and his minions, both human and supernatural. You, sir, have not been chosen to stop this development of the so-called new world order. But you are in this high office to *delay* that Antichrist one-world government from achieving full power. And that is why there is such an insane rage against the nation…against you."

"Why just a delay? Why just a delaying action? Why isn't it to put an end to this drive to tear America apart?"

Randolph Faust seemed reticent to address the president's question. There was groundwork to be laid, and he was unsure if the present circumstance was the time and place to do so.

"Mr. President, Bible prophecy is built, like much of God's Word, upon layers of…information. The full explanation you seek would require some time for explanation. However, I believe that the Lord, Himself, has brought me to this moment, so I must tell you. And I'll be as brief as I can."

The president nodded. "I want to hear what you have for me," he said.

"Paul explained in second Thessalonians, the second chapter, that the complete evil Antichrist will one day bring to earth can't happen as long as evil is being restrained. Jesus Christ, through the Holy Spirit, indwells each believer—each person who accepts God's grace gift of salvation through His Son, Jesus Christ, who died for the sins of mankind. The Holy Spirit within each believer is restraining—keeping back—the evil that Satan and his Antichrist will one day inflict upon all people of earth."

Faust paused to give time for his words to be digested, then spoke again.

"We call the total of all such believers the Church. This is the Body of Christ, in symbolic terms. The Body of Christ consists of all believers in Christ. As long as the Holy Spirit is present in believers, Antichrist and his evil world order cannot come forth. You, Mr. President, are used by God at this moment. You are instrumental in holding back the onslaught of satanic evil. You are head of the most powerful government on earth, and you champion most causes embraced by the body of believers...by the Church, the symbolic Body of Jesus Christ."

He again paused to try to discern whether the president understood. The chief executive's expression gave the impression that he wanted to hear more.

"That is why all their efforts have failed, Mr. President. Everything they have tried against you, against this administration, to this point has failed. It is the restraining influence that indwells the Church that holds back the wicked one...the Antichrist."

When the old archeologist went silent, the president stopped rocking and turned to Clint Wayne.

"These are things we've heard from you and CUE from a different angle, Clint. Now we have it from a Bible prophecy perspective."

The president again turned to look at Tyce.

"Tyce, I understand you have had numerous encounters with angels...one in particular. Michael, isn't it?"

The president's question startled Tyce, who shifted uncomfortably, quickly searching his thoughts for an answer. "Yes, sir. But the experiences were all while I was in a coma following a car accident in Maryland."

"Tell us about it," the president said, beginning to rock again, his eyes fixed upon those of the journalist.

Tyce described what he had seen the night of the wreck and related the many times Michael had appeared in his life. The president seemed to pay undivided attention to him during the telling of the story. When the journalist had finished, the chief executive spoke.

"And you think this...*Michael*...is important to Tyce's ability to do the things he can do with the Remote

Viewing and so forth?" The president addressed his question to Randolph Faust.

"Mr. President, although this was, as you've heard, a matter involving his experience while he was in a comatose state, I believe it is nonetheless a very *real* experience, from heaven's perspective."

The old archeologist's words caused the president to cease rocking and sit forward just a bit to listen carefully.

"There is a prophecy, Mr. President, that says that in the end of days old men will dream dreams and young men will have visions. By this pronouncement, I and many others who study Bible prophecy believe that we are in these end times. We believe that God's Word was foretelling that visions such as those Tyce has experienced are fulfillment of this prophecy about dreams and visions."

"And you, Dr. Faust? I'm told by Morticai that you, yourself, have experienced these...visions?"

"Dreams, Mr. President. Yes, I'm a very old man, as you see," Faust said with a smile. "I have indeed dreamed dreams that I believe are fulfillment of this prophecy I mentioned."

When the president said nothing from his position in the rocking chair, the old archeologist felt compelled to speak further. "So, Mr. President, to answer your question. Yes, I do believe that it is this heaven-determined matter, his visions with the archangel and so forth, that gives Tyce the ability to look more deeply into the Remote Viewing things. Although, I must add, I am not comfortable in use of such...divining practices."

The president shifted in the chair, his eyebrows raising in a look of surprise. "Oh? What's wrong with it?"

"Sir, several books of the Bible, in the Old Testament,

forbids looking into divining of things yet future. Israel's King Saul, for example, was condemned for bringing the witch of Endor into his effort to see into the future. God forbids any efforts to do such, with the exception of God's Old Testament and New Testament prophets. Beyond those facts, I can only say that it seems to me that such things as Remote Viewing is much more than a technology. It has all the indications of having supernatural or spiritual...otherworldly, elements."

Kant, in a lighter tone, spoke up from his seat near Faust. "But we can't see why that technology, even if... spiritual...in nature, to some extent, can't be of some heavenly use. Why can't it be sent from the Almighty to be used in this critical time?"

CHAPTER 22

Words of the president of the United States still sounded in his thoughts while Tyce and Essie slid into the backseat of the car provided by the White House.

"Tyce, I'm personally assigning you the job of applying your...gift...to learning about this reset matter the Archbishop writes about," the president had said. "You will have all the authority, and assets, needed to go in whatever direction this takes you. We have got to know as much as possible about what this bunch of traitors to America has in mind. Their plans obviously are far advanced, according to your own previous...sessions of Remote Viewing. And now this letter. It sounds alarming to me."

Essie moved closer to Tyce and reached to touch his arm while pressing against his side. Her action broke his concentration on the president's parting words.

"What comes next?" Her words were quietly asked near his ear, while she nestled more closely against him.

"What do you think you can learn through these...sessions?"

"I don't know at this point, Ess. Randy says the Lord will see to it that the truth comes out. Wish I was so sure...that I had his kind of faith in being able to help."

"There is a strangeness," she said. "There's so much that can't be explained about this...this 'reset' matter."

"Yeah. Randy says it's all wrapped up in fulfillment of prophecy, that this letter from the archbishop presents an understanding of the one world order the globalists want to establish. That it is nothing more or less than preparation for the coming of Antichrist."

She didn't say anything for longer than was comfortable to Tyce, so he said, "What are you thinking?"

"Do you believe there's anything to that? To Dr. Faust's fears that this is somehow part of a plot from the devil? Something that is bringing about fulfillment of prophecy?"

"He thinks this mummy I saw in the visions, and particularly the involvement of...of Michael...are proof that God wants to use me to...expose, I guess, this High Council's Blueprint or plans, or whatever."

She again paused to think on his words before saying, "But that was in the coma. You haven't seen a mummy, or Michael in your real, actual life."

"But why, if there's nothing to it but a dreamlike vision, did I know you in that time of coma as well as I've got to know you since meeting you for real? It was all so absolutely real. It is still like...like a memory of real life, as you call it. It's as if I recall it all, just as if I had really lived it all."

They drove quickly through the late-morning DC traffic toward the Israeli embassy. When his phone rang,

TERRY JAMES

Tyce turned his attention from watching the Washington Monument whisk by to trying to locate the device. When he answered, Clint Wayne's voice was on the other end.

"Our operatives have located the coordinates for the sarcophagus. Can you come to Shiva's lab this evening?" The question was issued with firmness that left little doubt of what the CUE director wanted as an answer.

"Sure. I guess so," Tyce said.

"I've already directed your companions, your driver, to drop you by the lab. They will take Essie on to the embassy," Wayne said before breaking off the call.

Within twenty minutes, Tyce exited the car. He leaned back toward Essie. Their kiss was still burning at the center of his thoughts as a burly man dressed in a suit and tie met him and walked him into the building.

Shiva Rabine stood at one end of the long table when he entered the room and walked to the other end.

"It is good," she said in a slight Jewish accent, "that we do this now as opposed waiting until this evening. The mind must be fresh, not fatigued, to provide the best viewing, as you know."

No "Hi, how are you"? No "It's so good to see you"? Tyce thought with amused recognition that this Jewish scientist was all business, all the time.

"Yes. I would much rather do it now than when I'm tired," he said, taking his seat at the end of the table opposite his facilitator.

"It is essential that we move now, as well, because we have learned that the subjects are together in their most concentrated leadership configuration. We should be able to learn much about their project Earthlord."

"What do you suspect the meeting...their getting together at this time is all about?"

"Our operatives think they are about to move in

implementing their plans. They have convened with regard to learning details about this…virus and the serum their scientists have produced to create a vaccine. Let us get started."

Tyce went through the preparatory steps and was soon receiving the initial impressions, while his mind moved almost involuntarily down a dark corridor, a cerebral pathway. As his brain-journey continued, and accelerated, a bright point of light appeared ahead.

The light suddenly burst brilliantly in blinding whiteness. His Remote Vision cleared, then, his surroundings became what appeared to be a high-tech chamber where a number of people dressed in white hazard attire were sitting. He recognized the scene as similar to what he had experienced while in his comatose existence.

All people in the vast chamber were looking intently at the man who stood, unlike them, dressed in a long, white lab coat.

"The reason you must wear the haz suits is because you come from the outside environment. We, of course, have been in the laboratory setting for many months. Our environment is acclimated to us, and we to it."

While he talked, the huge wall behind him split and moved apart, exposing the object of their meeting. The sarcophagus glinted in the bright spotlights. The golden coffin was an image, Tyce determined, not the sarcophagus itself. They were being given a view on a gigantic screen.

"We have detected a beginning of some deterioration due to exposure. Still, the mummy's DNA remains intact. It is alive, and seems impervious to any change, no matter its exposure. It is a living cellular entity. It seems nothing can kill it."

There was muffled rumbling of conversation, while

his audience members glanced at each other, surprised at the revelation.

"Our experimental serum doses have proved successful to this point. We will next introduce the subjects to the vaccine, with the serum added. This means that within no more than a year we can begin distribution on a global scale. Once the pathogen has created sufficient fear in the populations, it will be within our power to bring most under some degree of control."

While the man in the lab coat continued to inform his audience, the scene before Tyce began to morph into a fog-like haze. He started to believe he was being pulled away from the Remote Viewing session for some unknown reason. Rather than being extracted from the session, however, the scene began to take on shape and form. It was a room of some sort, with several men who looked to be dressed in military-type fatigues.

One of them emerged from the group and looked directly at Tyce while he continued the Remote View. The man began to speak, his face contorted with a frown while he spoke.

"Greyson, we have something here that belongs to you," the man said, then turned toward the group of men who parted to allow Tyce to see the object they had shielded.

"I believe you recognize her," the man said with a darkly humorous tone. "She belongs to us, now."

Essie! It was Essie!

"Don't bother asking questions," the man said, turning again to face him. "We can't hear you. You are in a remote fog warp. You can see us and what is happening here, but we can't see you—but we know you are Remotely Viewing us."

Tyce's senses heightened, his heart racing. He was totally immersed in the Remote Viewing scene and couldn't do anything to get to Essie.

"Now...Tyce. This is what you are going to do. You are not to report that you have seen your pretty little friend. If you want to see her again, you will do exactly as we instruct."

Essie sat in a chair, seemingly unharmed, but in a drug-induced state. Her eyes were wide, as if not understanding her circumstance.

"Upon arriving at your room within the embassy, you will find instructions beneath a pillow on the bed. If you want to see...Essie...again, you will follow those instructions precisely. If you divulge these instructions to anyone...if anyone tries to intervene, we will have to... eliminate this sweet little thing. Now we don't want to do this, Mr. Greyson. We only want you. Show up, by yourself. This is the only chance that...Essie...can live. She is drugged and can't tell anyone about us, so we can let her go without danger to ourselves. You will just have to take our word on the promise to let her go back to her father. No harm will come to her if you comply. If you don't comply precisely, I will, well turn her over to the guys here. They all think she's very pretty."

The man grinned a facetious grin while the scene again became shrouded by fog. Tyce felt his senses being withdrawn from the viewing session and momentarily was fully conscious of being at the end of the long table across from Shiva Rabine.

"You're back. Let us see what you have learned," she said.

He looked quickly at the automatic writing on the sheet. It described only the group and the man in the lab coat, whose words he recorded.

"There's not very much here," she said upon retrieving the papers. "Sometimes it just doesn't work like other times," Shiva said, satisfied to try again at some point.

Tyce was visibly agitated, and she looked him over, studying his demeanor. "Are you okay? Is anything wrong?"

"No...no. I'm fine. It's just like you said. Sometimes it just doesn't work as well as at other times. I think that's all that is making me a little nervous or whatever."

"Then we'll try another time soon. Perhaps this evening?"

"Yes. Let's do it again this evening," he said, thinking only to get to the embassy in the shortest time possible.

His thoughts raged within his head, which ached sharply while he hurried through the Israeli embassy's main lobby area. He moved into the elevator, barely acknowledging a woman who smiled and said something of greeting. Less than two minutes later, he entered the room they had assigned for his stay in DC while working with Kant.

Why had no one said anything about Essie? No one seemed to know she was missing. Whoever had her was trained in covert kidnappings, he thought frantically. Where was she...how could he ever get her away from them? He wasn't trained in such operations. If he sought help...that just wasn't going to happen. They would follow up on their threats.

He rushed to the bed upon entering the room and jerked the pillow nearest him from its place. Not there! He snatched the other and saw a folder flatly tucked between the tightly made-up bed covers.

He sat on the edge of the bed and opened the file that

was banded by an elastic cord. Two sheets of paper… typed instructions.

He stood and paced, his total concentration on the words. He was to go to a bus station near a restaurant. He was to bring no one. If they saw anyone following or who even slightly looked to be like someone following him, the girl would die. They would ship her to him in garbage bags in small pieces.

He shut his eyes and turned his head toward the ceiling. "Dear God, please help me get her out of this…"

His phone chimed, and he answered, hearing Morticai's voice. "Tyce, I'm needing to talk with my daughter. Have you seen her in the past few minutes?"

Tyce let it move through his reeling mind how best to answer, without panic in his voice. He managed to settle down enough to say calmly, "No, sir. I haven't in about the past thirty minutes."

The lie came out in a believable way, so he continued. "But when I see her, I'll tell her you're looking for her. She's probably talking with someone in the embassy."

"Yes, I suppose she will be calling me."

The Maglan chief said, then, "Shiva tells me the session didn't go too well. You only got a minute or two of things they were talking about. But what you reported is most vital to our understanding. We will review what you got shortly."

"Yes, sir. Whenever you say."

SLIPPING from the embassy was relatively easy. No one expected him to leave. They knew he was aware of the dangers of being without security. They would never suspect he would slip them. The enemy was onto his covert actions against them—the Remote Viewing. The enemy knew that his special gift or whatever it was would have to be dealt with, so would be determined to do just that. This must be the whole reason for kidnapping Essie, for the threats.

The thoughts ran swiftly, his heart racing. He met the Uber he had summoned and gave the location of the restaurant given in the instructions.

While the taxi negotiated the congested DC streets, his mind was in hyperdrive. How could he hope to do anything to get Essie out of danger? They would likely just kill them both.

His device chimed and he answered. "Yes. This is Tyce Greyson," he said, hearing the deep male voice on the other end.

"Good. We see you are on your way as we stipulated. You are very wise...Tyce. When you get to the restaurant, you will see a black SUV near the front entrance. Go to it and you will be driven to the location we have determined."

"What about Essie?" he said. "How do I know she will be freed?"

"You have no choice but to trust us. She will be... permanently missing...if you don't do as told," the voice said.

"That's not good enough. Based on what I know of you, I can't trust you. You'll hold both of us if I come without some sort of verifiable action that will let me know that Essie will be let go and returned to her father."

The line was silent for several seconds before the voice said, "We considered your...intelligent analysis of your situation. And here is our plan to assure you. When you come to the restaurant front and see the black SUV, make a call to her father. Ask him if she is with him. Remain at a distance in the car you're riding in, near the SUV, and when you are assured she is with her father, we will take you...into custody."

"That makes no sense. I can simply refuse then to go with you," Tyce said. "You would never let her go to her father. You'll have both of us. I have to know you'll let her go."

The line went silent again for several seconds before the voice returned. "We have no need for the girl. Others might use her to cause the Israeli grief, but all we want is you, Tyce. You can call her father, make sure she is safe, and we will then...deal with you...make sure you come with us. If you try to run, drive away or whatever, we will have our weapons trained on you from many angles. We will completely riddle your innocent driver and everyone who might get in the way, if you don't then just get out of your vehicle and come to the SUV. Do you understand all this?"

Tyce was silent, assessing the things he had heard.

"Mr. Greyson...Tyce...do you understand?"

"Yes. I understand. So, you...your people will have Essie near the embassy and her father as we get near the restaurant?"

"That's correct. We will let her go at the embassy when we see you positioned in proximity to the SUV." With that, Tyce heard a click. The conversation was ended.

His thoughts raged in many directions. They would never work such a plan, would never carry through on their promise to let Essie go. Still...he had no choice but to do as they asked.

Ten minutes later, his Uber driver said, looking at

Tyce in the rearview mirror, "There. I see the black SUV. You want me to pull next to it?"

"No. let's pull to curb right here for a second."

"It will have to be for just a few seconds. I'll get a ticket."

"I'll take care of any ticket. Just pull over here."

The driver did as instructed, and Tyce dialed Kant's cell phone.

"You've reached Morticai Kant's phone," the voice said. Tyce recognized it as the voice of Ehud Begin.

"Ehud, it's Tyce Greyson. Can I speak with Mr. Kant?"

"Tyce! Where are you? We have searched the embassy for you."

"Never mind right now. Let me speak with Kant."

"I cannot," the Israeli said with excitement in his voice. "He is dealing with his daughter. She was just left in front of the embassy. She is in a drugged state. Morticai is working with a doctor to help her."

"Is she okay?"

"She seems to be. Just is under the influence of something. They seem to have her awake. Yes. They have put her in a chair, and she seems to be more alert," the Israeli said.

"Ehud, I'm at the Madison Restaurant in downtown DC. I'm about to be taken by some thugs...I think they are covert operatives. I had to come here and make myself available before they would let Essie go. I'll be in a black SUV. That's all I know."

"What is this?!"

The Uber driver shouted, his eyes wide with surprise and fright. Four men, armed with machine pistols pointed in the direction of the driver and the journalist, surrounded the car.

CHAPTER 23

They hustled Tyce, blindfolded, to somewhere ever deeper into the bowels of a building. Tyce kept a careful record in his head while there were several transfers to elevators that always went downward. The smells were of increasing dankness, the odor of wet basements whose walls would never be dry because of constant seepage.

Finally, they stopped moving him by holding his arm. They refused to let him remove the mask over his eyes even after he had been seated for what seemed like a half hour or longer without conversation.

He jumped, startled, when a man said, "Well, well, Mr. Greyson. It is good to have you finally visit us. You may remove the mask now."

The voice was the same as the one on the phone giving instructions. His eyes met those belonging to the man who spoke.

"We honored your agreement to meet with us. Your… friend…is with her father. She is unharmed. She was given a quite strong sedative—but not a dangerous one, to one so young, at least."

The man was small-framed and thin for having a voice of such deep tone. His appearance betrayed the authority with which he addressed his captive.

"You are a journalist," he said with a lighter tone, his thick eyebrows raising to make it known that his finding was an interesting matter. "Therefore, we know you must have already analyzed your...situation...several times by now from the time you were met by our people."

Tyce said nothing, but stared into the man's dark eyes, while he continued.

"You have no doubt thought that we simply want to eliminate you. I assure that you can relax. That is farthest thing from our intention. We want rather to... *enlist*...your services. Are you curious?"

"Enlist me?" Tyce said. "For what? How can I be of help to you? I don't even know who you are."

"Oh. Forgive me, Tyce. I am Jason Bonnet. And I represent the deep state you have heard so much about," the man said with a tight smile and a facetious, uplifted intonation. "But we are of a much, much larger organization...things you have no need to know of. But you have...Remotely Viewed parts of that larger entity, the High Commission, as they are known."

"Then you are part of American intelligence, but work for globalist interests?"

Tyce's blunt assessment made Bonnet's eyes widen just a bit before the tight smile returned.

"You really do have a grasp on things as they are developed. I'm most impressed. No wonder Maglan has such an invested interested in you and your...gifts and talents."

"What do you want with me? How could I be of any help to you?"

"Right to the heart of the matter, huh? That is very good, because we need to get on with things."

The man squinted, his face taking on a look of brow-wrinkled concern. "Tyce, you notice I didn't mention America, or the president, or anything other when I said I was not surprised why…*Maglan…*has such interest in your gifts and talents."

Tyce said nothing, but his expression convinced Jason Bonnet that he was intrigued with the question.

"Well, it is, in fact, *Israel,* not the United States or other national interests we are concerned with in having you help us." Bonnet shifted in the chair in front of Tyce, his expression one of searching for the exact words to explain.

"In the war we are fighting, Tyce, we are not so concerned with governments and so forth. Oh, we care that we have met roadblocks to our ultimate goals. This president is indeed a major roadblock. You, Tyce, have been a major roadblock, too, because you have assisted our enemy. Rather than outright *eliminate* you, we want to first…*enlist…*you so that we can use your gifts and talents to fight our enemy more effectively."

"Who is your enemy, if not America and its obstacles? What's Israel got to do with all this intrigue?"

"*Intrigue!*" Jason Bonnet's face lit up with a bright smile. "What a way to express it! You are indeed a journalist of the first order to wrap it all up in one, gigantic headline. Yes. It is the *intrigue* of all the ages!"

"Thanks for the shout-out. Now, what's all the intrigue all about? Why is Israel at the center of your 'efforts', as you call them?"

"We know all about you, Tyce. You have gone

through the most in-depth...dreams and visions...of most any human being in the history of man. Can you, with your journalistic perception, not figure this out?"

Tyce looked into the man's dark, almost black eyes, imagining a pool of liquid evil that must lurk at the core of his captor's thought processes.

"It's not about government. I suppose it's not about anything to do with the physical world, then?"

"Ah! You almost have it, my friend. Although the things of economy and all other matters of the human condition are most important to us, it is not the 'physical', as you put it, that interests us ultimately."

"Then it is...metaphysical...or *spiritual*?"

"We serve a much higher power than any president, prime minister, or potentate of the human sort," Bonnet said, his eyes seeming to become orbs of gleaming, solid ebony.

"I guess Randy was right," Tyce said to himself in almost a whisper.

"What did you say?" Bonnet said.

"I said Ephesians 6:12," Tyce said, glaring at the inquisitor.

The man's expression melted to a mask of non-expression. "So. You do know of this...war we are waging."

"Oh, yes. I'm well aware. Like you said, I've been in the middle of it, I guess, since that night in the storm."

It all suddenly congealed in his memory—in his spiritual and mental senses. He was captive of the principalities and powers of wickedness in high places.

"Then you know that *Israel* is at the center of this war."

"God's chosen," Tyce said firmly.

"Yes. Well, chosen for destruction, in our view," the

man offered with the tight smile returning. "And we believe you can help us with that destruction."

"How?"

"We believe you have some…otherworldly…capabilities that we can, through our friends in high places, tap into to find ways to eliminate the enemy's protective shields over that illegitimate Jewish abomination."

"You must know that I know what it's all about… Bible prophecy and all the rest. At least, I've been given a pretty good idea over these years…through these weird experiences. You must know why I will refuse to help you in this hellish 'Blueprint', as it's called."

The man glared at first, but broke into a feigned, friendly smile. "Oh, my friend. Yes. We thought you would be very noble about the whole matter. We didn't think you would cooperate, seeing as how you are… 'onto us', as your Dr. Faust would put it, no doubt."

"Then you know my answer."

"Well, I would like to try one more time, if you don't mind."

Bonnet nodded to two large men dressed in business suits who had stationed themselves in chairs in the room. They stood and came to Tyce, lifting him from the chair.

"Let us go down the hall," Bonnet said, preceding the men and Tyce through a doorway.

Momentarily they arrived at a door, which Bonnet unlocked. They soon stood before a theater-like scene, with plush chairs covered in velvet facing a large screen. The men holding Tyce on each arm sat him down in a seat just in front of the screen.

"Now, we will try to again see if we can plead successfully with you, get you to cooperate with us in our…Blueprint," Jason Bonnet said, sitting on the folding seat on the other side of the chair that separated them.

The lights dimmed, and the screen lit with a scene of several people in surgical gowns standing over an operating table. "We had to assure your cooperation, Tyce. This was our decision in how to accomplish that cooperation."

"What's this about? What are they doing?" Tyce watched the three figures moving about the person lying on the table, covered mostly by a sheet.

"Don't worry. It's all very sanitary, I assure. Very professionally done," Bonnet said alternately looking at the screen then over at the journalist.

"Actually, it is one of the most advanced availabilities we have for assuring cooperation. Very technologically on the cutting edge."

He looked at Tyce, who glanced from the screen to hear his tormentor.

"You ever see the old film—*The Manchurian Candidate?*"

Tyce said nothing but glanced at the screen.

"This...technology takes that used in that film and multiplies its effectiveness by many times. It assures the cooperation of either the person being...implanted. Or, in your case, the person being...well, I don't know the proper term. Being, perhaps, *persuaded*...to cooperate."

"What is this? Just tell me," Tyce said, his irritation on the rise.

"It's your girlfriend, Tyce. We were afraid you wouldn't want to...join us in using your...talents and gifts...against the Israeli enemy. We determined this was the best thing to help you decide otherwise."

"Essie?"

"Yes, Miss Jorba is the…patient…on the operating table."

"What are they doing to her?" Tyce felt his senses redden in both panic and anger.

"Just be calm, Tyce," the man said as the two men behind him each placed their hands on his shoulders.

"It's okay, gentlemen," Bonnet said, glancing behind at the men. "Mr. Greyson is going to decide to agree, I believe. He is a very intelligent man."

"What is it about? What are they doing to her?"

"They are placing—well, have placed—a device about the size of a BB. They have implanted it near the brain stem. It is perfectly okay there, and will never cause any harm, not even discomfort. No one will even know it is there. However, if we wish to…or need to…we have the device that will set off that little pellet-sized object. It will explode, killing her instantly."

Tyce said nothing. He would do nothing to give them satisfaction. He wanted at the moment to have the calmness of the Sean Connery version of Bond in the critical challenges he faced. But it wasn't an act. Essie's life was at stake.

The thoughts, including foolish ones, ran quickly while Jason Bonnet spoke again.

"Now, Tyce, we have no desire to harm this beautiful young lady. But it's up to you, my friend. As long as we can depend upon your cooperation, no harm will come to her."

"What do you want me to do?"

"We will soon inform you of our plans. Just be patient. When we are finished using your talent, we will give instructions on how to safely remove the…the BB… without setting off the explosive."

∼

In White House Basement Ops 3, Clint Wayne was livid. He paced several feet in front of the Maglan chief.

"How could he leave without your people knowing it? The Israeli embassy is one of the tightest buildings in DC."

"Yes. This should not have happened," Morticai Kant said in a much calmer voice. "The way my daughter was taken so easily while your men were watching her is also quite disturbing."

The Israeli's words in parrying Wayne's anger seemed to stun the American. He stopped pacing, seeming to pause to reassess his own thinking on what had happened from the previous evening to the moment.

Finally, he said, "Okay...okay. There's blame to go around. Let's just get this fiasco settled as quickly as possible." He paused several seconds, then added, "Morticai, why did they bring Essie and drop her off like that? They have been trying to take her from under your security blanket for...how long?"

Kant said nothing, watching Wayne's hand gesticulations display his frustration.

"Is she okay?" Wayne said. "Have they made sure there's nothing to worry about with her?"

The Maglan chief knew the question went much deeper than its surface meaning. The CUE head was thinking not just in terms of his daughter's health, but in terms of technological entities that might compromise integrity of security that might be attached to her upon her return.

"She is okay, and in all ways," he said, knowing Wayne would get the full meaning that answered all questions posed in the American's inquiry.

Wayne calmed, then, in a more subdued tone, said, "Why do you think they returned her safely? They could have used her as leverage against you."

"It is a much more convoluted plan than it seems. I have no doubt of this. No offense, my dear friend, but the only way Tyce Greyson could have gone missing from among my men is through his own decision to slip from their security web. It had to be a deliberate action on his part to get away without being seen."

"How's that?" The American's question was issued in a way that portrayed his genuine puzzlement.

"Again, no disrespect, Clint. But your men lost Essie. They took her while there must have been a temporary lapse in security. In the case of our ward...Tyce Greyson...he had to leave, deliberately slip from our... our web of security. This is how it is designed—tighter than a spider web."

"Okay, saying I agree, what's the bottom line? Again, why was Essie brought back safely, and Tyce was taken— or deliberately slipped away, or whatever?"

"I believe they lured him to come to them...to slip away from our security, which they knew they could not breach," the Maglan chief said.

"So you believe they made a deal that they would return your daughter if he would come to them?"

"Exactly. They waited until they knew your people, incapable of—perhaps I should say 'unaccustomed' to— providing the tightest security possible, would be watching my daughter or Tyce Greyson. It is my fault. It was a major breach on my part. I never should have allowed Essie out from under Maglan's watch, even for that brief time when she was meeting her friends in Washington. She talked me into letting her go with just your security keeping an eye. I kept an uncompromising detail on Tyce, because he is an essential element in our defense, yet let my own daughter be taken by a lax moment. Unforgivable!"

There was silence between them for a few moments before Clint Wayne spoke. "We both made our mistakes, now let's get on with getting Greyson back. Do you think they took him just to neutralize him as an asset against them?"

"No, it must be much greater in import than that," the Israeli said.

Jason Bonnet directed his attention to the large screen of the monitor. Tyce saw on it a colorful display that flashed with various points of light.

His captor said, "You are no doubt curious to know what this is about, Tyce. We are about to give you at least partial knowledge of things."

The scene on the screen changed rapidly. The points of multicolored lights thinned until only a few dotted the visual presented.

"These represent locations within Israel's territory," Bonnet said. "The lights indicate the secret-most placement of the IDF nuclear weapons facilities. The red light points are indicative of Israeli aircraft locations that are locked and loaded…ready to launch against enemies, in case there are no other options than to go nuclear."

The screen changed again, bringing up one pulsing light of red at the center of several lights that surrounded. Tyce could see that the background on the screen was an aerial view, consistent with satellite shots from space he had seen in Pentagon briefings.

"This is the central command for the IDF for nuclear-launch function. We have, as you see, precise geographical coordinates, thanks to our satellite reconnaissance."

Tyce watched while the satellite drew the image of the building top even nearer and the red light was removed from the image.

"You see, Tyce, we now have the ability—the *capability*—to look into the very brain of Israel's nuclear launch-command center. We can, with your assistance, pick the very brain of the Israeli Defense Force and their precise strategic-strike objectives in case their conventional forces are overwhelmed."

"What can I do?" Tyce said, still looking at the building's top. "I don't understand any of this computer planning."

"You have heard of their 'Samson Option'?"

"That's the IDF's all-out nuclear weapons used against an enemy when they think they're about to be defeated. That's what I've understood it to mean."

"Very good. Yes. They have strategic initiatives in place that will be implemented the moment an enemy comes at them…if they assess that the enemy attack can be successful. They will put into action their Samson Option. It is all-out launching of their nuclear arsenal."

Bonnet manipulated the computer-generated graphics of the coordinates, which appeared on the screen crisscrossing in bright yellow and red lines over the image of the building.

"We have special…devices…that we will use in conjunction with your special abilities. These devices are part of top-secret developments as of late. Our own Remote Viewers have used them with great success in a few cases."

"What kind of devices?"

"It is like the one we know you're familiar with,"

Bonnet said. "The Stimulator. It is like that instrument. But it is more refined…more sophisticated."

The understanding crawled inside him, like a parasite gnawing at him from within. They would never free him. He would do their bidding until he was no longer useful. They had him locked into a straitjacket of knowledge that if he didn't commit fully to their plans, they would explode the device in Essie's head.

MORTICAI KANT WAS TORN. Clint Wayne had presented the way the inner circle surrounding the president wanted to deal with trying to locate Tyce Greyson. The Maglan chief listened from the chair facing the American while he talked.

"She will suffer no harm, our people say, Morticai. They have a serum, much like that of sodium pentothal. It has been used without harming the recipients for years."

"I can't have my Essie subjected to treatment like a captured agent of some kind," Kant said.

"The serum would be injected, then our experts— really just hypnotists—will question her under its effects. This is the only way we can learn if she has somewhere in her subconscious memory things said while they had her under their control. If we can learn some of what she might have heard, even while under the drug, we might find out what they're up to."

Wayne's tone became more somber, while he looked into Kant's eyes.

"It involves Israel, Morticai. As you yourself have said, it must be something profound they are planning against your nation. They know Greyson has been working closely with you…with your people…in all this. They will stop at nothing to bring about their Blueprint. We know just how determined they are. It's been nonstop war against this president—against your prime minister—for four years."

The Israeli kneaded his forehead between index finger and thumb, his eyes shut tightly in an effort to quell the headache. Finally, he looked at the American and stood from the chair.

"Very well. I will talk with my daughter. Explain everything. If she is willing, we will let your people try their…hypnosis."

Essie had been crying, her face surrounding her eyes swollen. She pulled a tissue from the vanity in front of her as she sat in the small area off the embassy suite's lavatory.

Her father bent to kiss her cheek and hugged her. "My daughter," he said, seeing the beautiful eyes that were usually dark green now reddened from a night and a day of tears. "We think we might have a plan that can perhaps help locate Tyce."

She brightened, her eyes returning to the appearance her father wanted to see again.

"How? Have you heard anything from them?"

"No…no. But we think you might have the key to how we can locate him."

"Me? How can I help find him? I don't know anything about any of it," she said, dabbing her eyes with the tissue and trying to stifle her sobbing between words.

"The…experts among the American operatives… medical personnel…those who are experienced in getting information from individuals. They say that you might have in your subconscious mind information from the time you were...were held captive."

"But they injected me with something, and I remember nothing. I only remember awakening and being taken into the embassy."

"I know, I know. But they believe that even though you were drugged and unconscious most of the time, your subconscious mind might have retained...have recorded...things said that would tip off who they are... where they had you."

She hesitated before speaking, trying to assess what her father had told her.

"If you are willing, Essie, we can try seeing if we can learn where Tyce might be held."

"Yes! Can we do it now? Papa, do you think there's a chance we can do this?!"

CHAPTER 24

"Our Remote Viewers…our Seers, as we call them, have been blocked from peering into these specific coordinates. We don't know why. None of our Seers have been able to produce automatic writing when using our device. This specific area is the only such area that they are unable to penetrate. This, Tyce, is why you have been…chosen…to view where the others can't."

Tyce Greyson looked at the American covert operative. "Why do you think I can see things you want while the others have been unable?"

The Remote Viewing technician, with Jason Bonnet looking on, said, after hesitating and glancing nervously at Bonnet, "We have been informed by those who know that you…have extrasensory…gifts…that transcend the abilities of the others."

"Who told you this?" Tyce's tone was one of skepticism.

"Those who informed us are of—"

"—Enough!" Jason Bonnet interrupted. "You don't

need to know who informed us. Your job is to do as we ask. You know the consequences of not helping us."

"What am I looking for?" Tyce's question offered with more curious inflection brought Bonnet's answer in a less confrontational tone.

"You will know once you are in the viewing session. But what you are looking for, specifically, is certain... codes...the IDF have in place. These are set to put their attack plans into action."

The American operative hesitated to think on offering further explanation. "The best analogy is perhaps our own codes, when it comes time to launch all-out nuclear attack on our enemies. These are top secret, of course, and strict procedures are in place at every code level. All must be done in perfect order and timing to make the all-out launches happen."

"And this is the way...the only way...that you can get these codes?"

Bonnet looked with a grimace at his captive, at first irritated almost to the point of responding angrily at Tyce continuing the unnecessary questioning. His expression dissolved to one of willingness to answer.

"As we said, there is something we can't understand that is blocking our Remote Viewers. The security is so tight that we haven't been able to move a mole into their Samson security circle. We have been told that you have the...call it 'psychic'...ability that none of our operatives possess. This is why you sit where you do at this very moment. We believe you can pierce their Samson circle of security."

The American intelligence operative saw that his answer wasn't sufficient to inform his captive. He moved to make absolutely certain Greyson understood the seriousness of the mission they were assigning him. To betray their mission in even the slightest would bring the most severe consequences.

"Tyce, I'm informing you fully on this assignment, if you want to call it that, about the essential nature of carrying out our directive." He paused to look into the distance before locking his eyes again with those of the journalist.

"Your history is known intimately by clandestine authorities at the international level, that is, by those in the highest commands. You have been in the channels of...a paranormal...force, we will call it."

"We know about your time at Patmos those years ago. That you...experienced...the snake biting you and all that flowed from it. Then we have been told all that you experienced while in a comatose state following the accident. That this was far more than a brain glitch, but rather was actual paranormal foretelling—the accident, the sarcophagus...all that flowed from your... vision. This is why we know that you have the paranormal capability we can use to get into the Samson inner circle, to learn the codes and other operational matters."

Tyce took in all of Bonnet's words and tried to digest them before forming his question.

"And my job is to help you bring down Israel's ultimate defense?"

"Yes. For the cause of *peace*. Israel is the holdup to peace in the region—actually, the hold up to peace globally," Bonnet said. "Israel is an illegitimate occupier. The Middle East will never have a chance to settle as long as that usurper entity exists."

While his captor talked, Tyce heard in his mind's ear the voice of Randolph Faust. "Zechariah the prophet said that Israel will become a 'cup of trembling and a burdensome stone' to the whole world. The globalists will want to eliminate God's chosen people...His chosen nation."

The epiphany struck. The *paranormal* was in actuality *spiritual.* The battle he was smack in the middle of involved what he, previously, couldn't understand— rather, what he wouldn't believe. He had heard it over and over through the words of Randolph Faust. He had looked at Scripture over and over. He had not fully seen it as it truly was until now! The globalist forces...the forces of hell itself, intended to use him, his spiritual ability or whatever it was, to help destroy God's chosen people...His chosen nation.

The further thought came from somewhere out of the cerebral ether. The dark, shadow beings...the humanoid, dark, human-like beings that entered and exited the scientists and others during the visions of his comatose state. These must have informed them of his paranormality. Hell's forces at work!

"SHE IS DEEP IN THE TRANCE," the woman said, looking over at Morticai Kant.

Essie's eyes were alternately closed tightly and opened wide when each warm-up question about personal information was asked. She answered her name, date of birth, and her father's name.

"Is she okay?" Kant looked long at his daughter's face, concern etched across his brow in aged lines of worried concentration.

"She is fine. Her reactions are normal for the proce-dure. What is the primary question you wish to ask?"

"We must know if she can recall anything, anything at all, from the time she was drugged until they released her," her father said, standing nearby and looking past the doctor who gently questioned.

"What did those who captured you do or say, once they put you into a drug-induced state?"

The doctor and Essie's father watched closely while awaiting her response. She said nothing, her eyes remaining closed. After a series of follow-up questions with no response, the doctor turned to Kant, shaking her head negatively. "Her subconscious cannot process the information we're asking. They used something that blocked retention of anything she heard while under the drug."

"Can you bring her out now?"

"Yes. It will take a few moments. I'll give her an injection to neutralize the drug, then take my time lifting her from the hypnotic state."

The doctor prepared the syringe and started to inject Essie's arm, but her eyes opened wide and she spoke before the needle could enter her flesh.

"They have Tyce," she said. "They will use his paranormal ability to break into our most secret chamber."

Her father came and stood over her above the doctor, his eyes wide in astonishment over her words.

"Ask her where Tyce is right now," the Maglan chief said.

"And where is Tyce, Essie?" the doctor probed as ordered.

"They are preparing him to invade the Samson Program facility. They are forcing him…because of me… to give them the codes to the Samson launch platform."

"My God!" the Israeli chief turned ashen, while trying to form thoughts on the next question he wanted asked. "What do you have to do with it, my daughter?"

The hypnotist repeated the question.

"I am in danger," Essie said. "Tyce is threatened with harm to me…"

"Who—How do you know this?" her father said in a near panicked voice.

"Michael told me…"

Morticai Kant's senses darkened. He had to plop heavily in the chair next to the examination table.

After several minutes of further questioning with no response, the doctor said, "It's no use. There is nothing else that can be gleaned."

"Very well. Bring her out of it," Kant said. "But tell her nothing. I don't want her conscious mind to know what her subconscious has divulged."

Ten minutes later, Essie was fatigued, but felt no other effects. The time under the drug, the hypnotic probing and the coming out of the ordeal, all had gone smoothly. She sat up, her brain struggling to recover while coming out from under the drug's influence.

"What did you learn?" she said, still groggy.

The woman in the white lab coat shook her head and said solemnly, "We tried, but couldn't extract the information we wished for. Whatever you were given must have been designed to prevent subconscious retention of any sort."

"But we haven't given up, sweetheart," her father said, holding her by the arm and hand and leading her from the table to a comfortable chair nearby. "We are redoubling our efforts. It's just a matter of time when Maglan finds the pathway that will lead us to Tyce. Just relax and don't worry."

Once out of earshot of his daughter, Kant shut the door behind him.

"This involves much more than Israel," Clint Wayne said, moving ahead of the Maglan chief to a chair near his desk. "Our people have run down several things that point to this cabal at the highest echelons. They're on the verge of taking action to perform a military *coup d'état* against the president. At the same time, these globalist ringleaders will try to remove your prime minister. How they plan to take him out, we aren't sure."

"How have you obtained this intelligence?"

"Our mole in the CIA got it from a female agent. He seduced her, I guess is the way to put it," Wayne said. "At any rate, we followed up in a number of ways and found it to be not only credible, but beyond any doubt already put into action at its earliest stage."

"We have much the same intelligence coming in," Kant said. "And there is much more going on, especially with our Samson program."

The CUE operative said nothing, awaiting Kant's explanation.

"With all due respect, Clint. Your people are such a small unit immediately surrounding the president...very effective and extremely essential to the preservation of your country's Constitution and American liberty. But the greater constituency of intelligence services, CIA, NSA, and all the rest, are now in the orbit of the global order diabolists—the 'deep state', as it has now come to be known."

"What are you saying? That we haven't got a real handle on all this...this subterfuge?"

"Not at all, my friend. Just that your concerns might be somewhat myopic, at least from our perspective in Maglan."

The American again remained silent, by that silence indicating to the Maglan chief that his words required further explanation.

"Your hands are full, with limited resources, with

limited operational personnel. For example, we know that at least two of your joint chiefs of staff are totally in colleague with the so-called High Commission."

"We are aware that much of the Pentagon brass are disloyal to this president," Wayne said. "They want things to return in DC to the way they were before. We know that the vast portion of our intelligence community is doing all they can, as is the bulk of Washington bureaucracy, to bring the president down."

"And you have done a majestic job of keeping the wolves away, my good friend. Your CUE organization is at the heart of this battle," Kant said consolingly. "It's just that there is just so much of CUE to go around. We of Maglan have the capability to view things on a much wider scale, in a far greater scope. Thankfully, we have come together to cover all bases."

Again, there was a moment of silence, Kant's words seeming to have salved the American's upset over the direction of the conversation.

Finally, Clint Wayne spoke.

"What about this *Samson* program? I presume you're talking about the *Samson Option*…"

The Maglan chief shifted in his chair across from the American. He searched for the way to begin explanation.

"The program goes much more deeply than the understanding most have of its reaches. I'm only confiding in you, Clint, because we are at the most critical point perhaps in the history of Israel. You are our only true ally. That is, you of CUE are the only ones we of Israel can depend on, can rely on. The American establishment…the globalists among them—and that includes almost everyone these days, as you are aware—think of our country as being the holdup to peace in the Middle East…thus to global peace."

Kant paused to let his words sink in before continuing. "Our one saving grace is our nuclear force. No one other than we with the most intimate details of the operation knows the extent of our program exactly. Until this moment, we have been able to deflect any efforts to hack our cyber security and learn of our codes and other much more secret elements of Samson. But things have changed. The danger is at condition red."

"What's happened? Why weren't we told?"

"Because that's just how secretive we've had to be in all this. Clint, our very existence has depended upon maintaining absolute integrity in matters surrounding our only assurance that our millions of enemies can't overwhelm us with conventional forces. They know that we will invoke our Samson Option if faced with annihilation."

"So your…Samson program is in danger?"

"Yes. If the enemy—and that includes your intelligence services heads disloyal to your president—can disrupt our Samson defensive operations even for a brief time, we are vulnerable to overwhelming attack by the many Arab states. We have word that they are in on the attempts to take down our Samson operation."

"What's changed? Why is it now all coming to a head and you're facing this crisis now?"

"Clint, I don't know how to say it other than that it is…supernatural, the way we have learned of the crisis Israel faces at this moment."

"THIS DEVICE EXCEEDS the capability of the Israeli Stimulator, Tyce. They tell me it is quite the advancement in being able to Remotely View."

The technician placed the helmet of gleaming chrome over the journalist's head and rocked it back and forth to assure a proper fit. The device was confining, not like the Israeli device that was mostly made of straps rather than configured like a football helmet.

"You are among the first to use this," Bonnet said, observing the fitting. "This will greatly step up your paranormal energy, I'm told. We will expect great things from your extrasensory reconnaissance mission to the Samson facility."

Moments later, the technician sat at the end of the long table and manipulated several glass-plate squares on the console board in front of him.

Tyce heard a muted hum begin, while his head beneath the device increased in warmth and a vibration, so slight as to be barely perceptible, began.

The coordinates in Israel were introduced by the technician, and he sensed the experience of remote travel not unlike the times he had used the Stimulator.

When the technician manipulated other glass squares, Tyce's senses reddened, and colored shoots of light flashed within his heightened thought processes. Within seconds, his mind's eye moved his inner vision down a hallway, piercing a wall at its end.

Men and women in Israeli military uniforms comingled with people in lab coats, while busily interacting with myriad scopes and screens of varying sizes.

The device honed his senses in on one specific area within his concentration—the Israeli Samson codes. He saw them plainly, as the device had been programmed, he was told, specifically to automatically write the codes he saw. He had no choice. He couldn't have stopped if he had to in order to save his life. And...he thought while the device did the stealing of the code and his hand automatically recorded, it was Essie's life that was at stake. Any refusal or deliberate code fabrication would mean the tiny device near her brain stem would be ignited by the cabalists in DC.

His eyes fixed upon the codes, his hand moved swiftly, recording them. He had no way to control what his hand recorded. How could he do something… anything…to record something other than what his Remote View was forcing him to channel through the signal line back to the DC operatives?

His vista before the codes visual seemed to be fading. Was he being recalled by Jason Bonnet—to the agency somewhere deep in the DC building?

His mind, then, seemed alive with brilliant light and thunderous vibrations of sound he couldn't identify. Not music, really, but ponderous boomings that had rhythmic intonation that was somehow melodious.

Colors of every hue of the spectrum burst in small explosions—as if fireworks had been ignited inside his cranium. When the cerebral display faded, a human figure appeared in his Remote Viewing vista.

"Tyce Greyson."

The man's voice…familiar.

"I am sent to say you are not to be afraid. This thing you have been sent to do shall not be accomplished. You will remove now back to your point of origin. Let not your heart be troubled."

Tyce's mind was in hyper drive, while he saw in his Remote Viewing vista the man—a man who, after making the proclamation seemed to unfold, morphed into a birdlike creature, its massive wings expanding to many times the size of the man's human form.

The eyes! He had seen them before—piercing orbs seemingly of fire penetrating to his very soul.

TERRY JAMES

There seemed a vacuum, a suctioning, that drew him swiftly backward. In the next instant, he sat in the chair, the chrome-like helmet vibrating his astonished thoughts while Jason Bonnet and several agents stood beside him.

"Thank you, Tyce. You performed perfectly. We have the codes."

Bonnet turned and gave orders to the men and handed one of them pages with the codes from the automatic writing. They quickly left the room.

"We will have these codes confirmed, Tyce, although I'm sure you haven't tried to deceive us. I'm assured that it is quite impossible for you to do other than return the correct codes from the Samson nuclear system."

Tyce said nothing, his thoughts still reeling with the image of the winged creature...and the eyes that were so familiar. They were...the eyes of the creature on the storm-drenched road to Maryland that night so long ago. They were at the same time the eyes of the man... the man *Michael*.

Bonnet left him sitting for the moment. Tyce's senses started to fade, then pulse uncomfortably. His head throbbed—not in pain from headache-like throbbing, but as if his brain had a pulse at its center.

He heard it then, an inner voice. It was clear, unmistakable. Had the helmet damaged his brain? Was he now having a cerebral hemorrhage...a bursting aneurism?

"Tyce, look in your hand," the voice said.

He did as instructed. He hadn't felt it before. He opened his hand, and in his palm was a silvery, metallic ball affixed to the skin just below the flesh of his fingers...a BB-sized object.

"It is the explosive device, Tyce. It is no longer

implanted within Essie. You will know what to do when the time is right."

Tyce blinked, looking again at the small ball. The explosive device! No longer in Essie's scalp. No longer in position to explode her brain!

The covert operative returned with a sandwich and a salad on a paper plate. "Might as well have some lunch while we await results of your Viewing," he said in facetious tone. "We should have the codes programmed into our system any second. We have you to thank, Tyce. The Israelis will now be neutered. They will have to comply or be eliminated."

Just as Bonnet started to take a bite of the sandwich, the two men he had sent out earlier burst through the doorway.

"The codes are phony, sir! And they have something about them that has divulged our position here and the Blueprint for destroying Samson." The men were angry, glaring at Tyce as he sat beside their boss and refused to divert his own eyes from their affixed stares.

Jason Bonnet's complexion reddened, from the sensation of both anger and extreme anxiety. They had been discovered, and his failure would not be acceptable to those who would be expecting to have this portion of their Blueprint compromised.

Still, the covert operative reacted calmly. He pulled a part-metal, part-plastic object from its cradle in the monitor base just in front of him.

"I don't know how you pulled it off, Mr. Greyson. But I must give the devil his due. You managed to at least delay our timing in ridding the world of the Jewish problem." He smiled slightly, an obvious cover for his obviously building anger.

He stood and moved to stand between his two agents. He whispered something to them.

Suddenly Tyce knew what to do...he just knew exactly what to do.

He lifted a corner of the top slice of bread of the sandwich Bonnet had left sitting on its plate on the table. He poked the tiny, BB-like device deeply into the tuna fish and let the piece of bread return to its place.

Bonnet returned momentarily and sat, fidgeting with the device he had removed from the base of the monitor. "You know what we have here, Tyce?" He calmly posed the question then took a bite of the sandwich and began chewing.

"No," Tyce said, watching him. Would he bite down on the ball, the explosive, or would he swallow it?

"This is the device I will now use to blow your pretty little friend's head off," he said, smiling tightly in Tyce's direction. "This little red button here is the detonator. Actually it is linked to a satellite, which is directed back down to your pretty little friend's device. You, somehow, betrayed me. We will deal with you a bit later. But first, we will deal with...what's her name? Is it Essie? Yes. First we will deal with Essie."

He held the device so Tyce could watch as his thumb came down on the red button.

EPILOGUE

R andolph Faust hugged Tyce to himself. "We can thank our God for this," he said, his voice broken with emotion.

Tyce said nothing but returned the old man's affection by tightening his own arm-wrapped tug.

Essie's eyes filled with tears that spilled over her cheeks when Tyce then turned to her, embracing her and kissing her.

"We thought you were lost," Clint Wayne said, smiling at Tyce, who turned to take his hand.

"Thanks for not giving up," he said.

"Our agents were going to be too late, I was afraid," the CUE director said. "We moved as soon as those code coordinates you gave us pinpointed where they were holding you."

Tyce looked surprised, gave an understanding grin. "Well, it was meant to be, I guess. You were in time. Thanks again for not giving up."

"How did you get us the codes that betrayed their

place of operation?" Morticai Kant said. "That was a stroke of genius."

"I had nothing to do with it," Tyce said, looking at Faust.

"It was a bloody mess. That man's head was all over the room," Wayne said. "What happened? We were afraid that blood was yours."

"'It is appointed unto man once to die, and after that, the judgment,'" Randolph quipped, winking at Tyce.

"Apparently so," the journalist said.

"Well, we are grateful. To you...to Providence...to whomever," Kant said. "Samson is secure and ready for battle."

"This president is very grateful, Tyce," Wayne said. "We don't know where, or how far this ongoing deep-state coup attempt will take us. And this globalist Blueprint is something we are trying to get our brains around. Very troubling. But he is grateful, as are we at CUE, for all you've done."

"You must explain further, my young friend, how did you accomplish this...this victory?"

Tyce hesitated before answering Morticai Kant's question.

"It wasn't me, sir. It was Michael."

A LOOK AT: JACOB'S TROUBLE 666

BY TERRY JAMES

Paradoxically, Jacob's horrific circumstances dynamically unfold through a compelling love story of many dimensions. Jacob Zen ambitiously climbs toward a top position within the US government, only to have his plans explode into chaos. He reacts through computer technology with INterface, human-kind's ultimately evolved beast-state government of absolute control. Drug-induced flashbacks plunge him into that past time when there was yet hope--while life with Karen promised a future filled with great hope and expectation.

When Jacob's life flies apart in one terrifying instant, events viciously sweep him toward a savage era beyond comprehension or endurance. He struggles mightily through his nightmarish world while powerful forces push and pull at him as he tries desperately to find Karen, the love of his life, who has been taken from him by the monstrous dictatorship. Yet other forces even more powerful influence his every thought, his every action, and propel him unerringly through the vortex of history toward some seemingly predetermined destination.

A novel for those who want a fascinating look into the dawning millennium and beyond. A deeply intertwined mystery of international intrigue, clandestine geopolitical manipulations and murderous betrayals.

AVAILABLE NOW

ABOUT TERRY JAMES

Terry James is author, general editor, and co-author of numerous books on Bible prophecy, hundreds of thousands of which have been sold worldwide. James is a frequent lecturer on the study of end time phenomena, and interviews often with national and international media on topics involving world issues and events as they might relate to Bible prophecy.

He has appeared in major documentaries and media forums, in all media formats, in America, Europe, and Asia.

He appeared in the History Channel series, The Nostradamus Effect.

He is an active member of the PreTrib Research Center Study Group, a prophecy research think-tank founded by Dr. Tim LaHaye, the co-author of the multi-million selling "Left Behind" series of novels. He is a regular participant in the annual Tulsa mid-America prophecy conference, where he speaks, and holds a Question and Answer series of sessions on current world events as they might relate to Bible prophecy.

Terry James has been blind since 1993 due to a degenerative retinal disease (retinitis pigmentosa). He uses the Jobs Accessible Word System (JAWS) –which is voice synthesis—to write and conduct business over the Internet.

His former profession was in public relations, advertising, marketing, and publicity and promotion.

He received his education from Arkansas Polytechnic Institute, Memphis Academy of Arts, and University of Arkansas at Little Rock.

He served in both corporate and government positions for 25 years, before becoming a full-time writer.

James also served in the United States Air Force from October 1966 through October 1970.) He served at Randolph AFB, Texas, in the T-38 section, a mission dedicated to training pilots in high-performance jet fighter-trainers.

Terry James and his wife, Margaret, live near Little Rock, Arkansas.

Made in the USA
Las Vegas, NV
12 December 2023

82611772R00223